PiNT OF CONTENTION

SUSANNAH NIX

Haver Street Press

This book is a work of fiction. Names, characters, places, incidents, tirades, opinions, exaggerations, prevarications, and dubious facts either are the products of the author's imagination or are used fictitiously. Any resemblance to actual events or persons—living, dead, or otherwise—is entirely coincidental.

PINT OF CONTENTION. Copyright © 2022 by Susannah Nix

All rights reserved. No part of this book may be reproduced in any form or by any electronic or mechanical means without written permission from the author.

FIRST EDITION: September 2022

ISBN: 978-1-950087-25-9

Haver Street Press | 448 W. 19th St., Suite 407 | Houston, TX 77008

Edited by Julia Ganis, www.juliaedits.com

Ebook & Print Cover Design by Cover Ever After

*For every woman who's been called a bitch (or worse)
for being strong and capable.*

PROLOGUE
THREE YEARS AGO

"Ryan! What a nice surprise. Does George know you're coming?"

I smiled at my stepfather's new wife, Heather. New being a relative term, given they'd been married more than sixteen years now. "He's the one who asked me to stop by. He didn't tell you?"

Heather flicked an unconcerned hand as she stepped back to admit me into the house. "Of course not. You know how he is."

I did know. I probably knew George King almost as well as anyone could claim to know the man who ran King's Creamery and therefore pretty much the entire town of Crowder. I'd known him since I was six years old, when my mother had become his second wife. Going from a rented double-wide in a trailer park to a sprawling mansion situated on forty acres of rolling Hill Country land with a pond, fishing pier, horse barn, greenhouse, gazebo, and swimming pool had been a life-changing event for both me and my mom.

I leaned in to kiss Heather's cheek as I edged past her into the house where I'd spent most of my formative years. Although Heather was a slight-framed woman, my bulky six-foot-five-inch frame filled most of the doorway, forcing me to sidle in sideways and suck in my gut to avoid crowding her against the wall.

"You should come round for dinner sometime." Heather's smile was bright and well practiced. "It's a shame we don't get to see more of you."

"That'd be great," I replied with a smile as practiced as hers, doubting that dinner invitation would be coming anytime soon. Heather and I got along fine, but neither of us had much desire to spend more time together. I'd been in college when my mother died and Heather replaced her as the lady of George King's house a mere six months later. We put on a good show of familial affection, but a show was as far as our relationship extended.

"He's in his office, as always," Heather said. "You can go on through."

As I strolled across the handwoven Mexican rug covering the terra cotta tiled entryway, I gazed around me at my old childhood home. The massive ranch-style villa, which had been custom built and decorated to suit George's particular tastes long before he'd married my mother, had hardly changed at all since the day I'd first set foot in it.

Based on the look of the place, George had wanted to be sure his visitors wouldn't have any doubt they were in Texas. The rough-hewn wood furniture, cowhide upholstery, and black-and-white prints of bluebonnets, longhorn cattle, and oil derricks adorning the stucco walls all paid homage to the Lone Star State that George King was aggressively proud to be from. The only substantive change that had been made to the interior of the house was who lived in it with him these days.

On my way to George's office, I paused in the doorway of the family room to greet George and Heather's two kids. Twelve-year-old Riley clambered to her feet and bounded over to give me an enthusiastic hug. Her teenage brother Cody, who was now too mature and cool for such childish displays of affection, kept his seat on the couch as he offered me a more sedate greeting.

"Want to watch *Steven Universe* with us?" Riley asked as she gave my hand a hopeful tug toward the TV.

"Wish I could, squirt, but I need to talk to your dad." However indifferent I might be to Heather, my fondness for her children was genuine. I liked kids in general, but I also knew too well what it was like to grow up with George King as a father figure, so I'd gone out of my way to offer them brotherly affection despite our lack of a blood relationship.

"Maybe Ryan'll stay for ice cream after your dad's through with him," Heather said as she slipped into the room to join Cody on the couch.

"Sure I will," I promised when Riley's face lit up like sunshine at the suggestion. "Save me some S'more Than a Feeling, okay?"

Leaving them to their TV watching, I made my way down the long hallway lined with vintage concert posters that led to George's office. The man was such a music aficionado that he'd given all eight of his children by his three different wives middle names inspired by his favorite Texas-born musicians. Riley and Cody bore the middle names Maines and Lyle, respectively, after Natalie Maines and Lyle Lovett. My two half-brothers, the sons my mother had given George, were Tanner Townes King and Wyatt Earle King after Townes Van Zandt and Steve Earle. The offspring of George's first marriage had been given middle names inspired by Willie Nelson, Waylon Jennings, Kris Kristofferson, and Janis Joplin.

As a stepchild, both my mundane middle name (John, after my maternal grandfather) and last name (McCafferty, my mother's maiden name) set me apart from the rest of the King clan. Privately, I'd always considered it a blessing not to be burdened by the King name, which conferred too much notoriety in our small town for my comfort.

My knock on the closed door to George's office was answered with a terse "Come in," so I did. It wasn't a room I'd spent much time in. When I lived here, George's private sanctum had been strictly off-limits to us kids without an invitation. Such invitations were generally reserved for serious, unpleasant conversations like the delivering of punishments or bad news, so it was with an uneasy feeling that I strode into the wood-paneled room now. Even though I was too old for punishments these days, bad news was something you never outgrew.

"Thanks for stopping by, Ryan." George rose from his high-backed leather chair to offer a handshake across his desk. As usual, his receding gray hair was pulled into a thin ponytail, and he wore his traditional work attire of Levi's with a short-sleeved button-down. He owned a million similar shirts in a whole host of ugly patterns. Today's was turquoise and covered with birds. "Have a seat."

Dutifully, I lowered my weight into the leather wingback facing the large wooden desk.

"You want a drink?" George offered as he carried his half-empty whiskey glass to the bar cart in the corner of the room. When I declined, he reached for a bottle of bourbon to top off his own glass. "How've you been?"

"Good. I've been good." My gaze wandered idly to the enormous rack of antlers mounted behind the desk in a not-so-subtle display of intimidation. "Same as always. You?"

He waved off my polite inquiry with an impatient grunt and set a fresh glass of bourbon on the edge of the desk in front of me. "In case you change your mind."

Hmm. I couldn't imagine that boded well for the conversation ahead. "You said you wanted to talk to me about something?"

"I did." George's chair let out a squeak as he leaned back and took a sip of bourbon before he focused his sharp grayish-blue eyes on me. "You remember the last time you saw your dad?"

I nodded, taken off guard by the question. I hadn't thought about my father in a long time, and it certainly wasn't a subject I'd expected George to raise out of the blue. "After Mom died. When he showed up at the funeral."

My parents had never married, but I had hazy memories of them living together for a brief period when I was little. Around when I was three or four, my father had taken off, leaving my mom to fend for the two of us alone. Though he hadn't been minded to stick around and do the hard work of parenting, he'd dropped back into our lives every so often on the excuse of spending time with his son, but only when he was down on his luck and needed money or a temporary place to stay. Those short bursts of paternal attention had been more than enough for me to form an impression of him as a selfish, small-minded bully we were better off without.

After my mother married George, my father's visits stopped altogether and my contact with him dwindled to an occasional postcard or letter. Until my mother's death, when he'd shown up to her visitation out of the blue.

"Drunk and making a scene," George said, as if either of us needed a reminder.

I'd been nineteen at the time. Although my father wasn't a small man, I'd grown up to be four inches taller than him and started to put on some serious muscle by then. As soon as he'd launched into his drunken tirade, I'd wasted no time taking the man in hand and bodily removing him from the premises.

It was the first and only time my half- and stepsiblings had ever seen my father, and I still remembered their shocked, pitying looks with a sense of embarrassment.

"You ever hear anything from him again after that?" George asked me now.

My jaw clenched as I stared down at the floor. "Not a word."

"Ever wonder why that is?"

"Not especially. I try not to think about him if I can help it."

"I never told you this, but he came to the house the day after the funeral, looking for you."

My head snapped up. "He did?"

"He guessed that your mama might have left you some money, and he was looking to shake you down for a share of it."

"That sounds about right." Always looking out for himself. That was my old man.

George studied me as he rubbed his fingers over his bushy gray beard. "Did you know he used to beat your mama?"

My jaw clenched again as I nodded. "I'm aware."

"Wasn't sure if you remembered."

I remembered enough. What surprised me was that George knew. I hadn't realized my mom had told him that much about her life before she met him. Showed how little I knew about their relationship, which had always struck me as a mutually beneficial social partnership instead of a love match. Though I did believe George had genuinely cared for her in his own way—just not the way a husband and wife were supposed to love each other.

"He ever hit you?"

"Once or twice." Not as much as he'd hit my mother. Not nearly as much as I wished I'd hit him outside the funeral home that day.

George gave me a long look before saying, "Kathleen wouldn't have wanted him sniffing around you and that insurance money she left you. So I made sure he never bothered you again."

"How'd you manage that?" I didn't know why I'd asked, since

I could guess exactly how. There was only one thing my father would have wanted, and George King had plenty of it to spare. "How much did you have to pay him?"

"No more than his absence from our lives was worth. It was a trifling sum as far as I was concerned, but it was enough to make sure he'd be taken care of for the rest of his life—on the condition he never attempted to communicate with you again."

I swallowed, oddly touched. "I don't know what to say."

George had always been good to me in his own sort of way. He wasn't an affectionate man or even a very likable one. I couldn't say that love played any part in our relationship, but loyalty certainly did. He'd always looked out for me and treated me like family—in some ways even better than he'd treated his own flesh and blood kids. He hadn't had to do that, especially after my mom died. But he'd done it anyway out of a sense of duty, which was something I could respect.

"You don't need to say anything," George told me gruffly.

"I should probably say thank you at least."

His shoulder twitched with a shrug. "That man's behavior wasn't your fault or your responsibility."

"I gotta say, it doesn't sit well with me that he's been living easy on your dime all these years. He doesn't deserve that kind of reward for his shitty behavior."

"The world's full of injustices everywhere you look. I did what I needed to do to take care of you like I promised your mother I would."

I understood George well enough to know he wouldn't want any messy displays of emotion or gratitude, so I swallowed the lump in my throat and kept my feelings to myself.

"Why are you telling me this now?" I asked. "Did he die? Is that why you asked me here tonight?" As I contemplated the possibility, I didn't feel anything at all. I literally couldn't care less if my father was alive or dead.

"Not exactly. Not yet, anyway."

"He's sick, then." Again, I felt nothing at the thought of it.

"He is," George confirmed with a grave nod. "I've had someone keeping tabs on him, making sure he doesn't violate his agreement, and he let me know a few months back that your father's health has been declining. I wasn't planning to tell you because I didn't think you needed to be burdened with it."

He paused, perhaps waiting for me to complain about his secret-keeping, but I couldn't find it in me to mind. When it came to my father, I was happy enough to be left in the dark.

After I failed to object, George continued. "But now your father's written me a letter that he asked I pass on to you. Under the circumstances, I figured I'd better do it."

George opened a drawer and extracted a plain white envelope that he set in the middle of his desk.

I stared at the familiar handwriting on the envelope like it might bite me. "What does it say?"

"You can read it yourself."

"I'd rather you tell me, if it's all right." I didn't want to know at all. Whatever it was, it wouldn't be good news. My father had never once brought good news into anyone's life.

George interlaced his fingers and rested them on the desk in front of him. "It says he's been diagnosed with ALS. You know what that is?"

I'd heard of it. Largely because of that Ice Bucket Challenge that had been all over social media a few years back. "That's what Stephen Hawking had." He'd just died from it not too long ago. It was hard to wrap my head around the idea that Stephen fucking Hawking and my dad had anything in common.

"That's right," George said. "We used to call it Lou Gehrig's disease, but your generation doesn't have any idea who Lou Gehrig was."

"He was a baseball player," I murmured. "There was a movie about him."

"*Pride of the Yankees*. Gary Cooper played him."

"There's no treatment for it, right? So my father's dying?" From what I knew, it seemed like a pretty bad way to go. Progressive loss of motor function until eventually you couldn't control your own body at all. I gripped my forearm and clenched my hand into a fist as I tried to imagine losing control of my own limbs like that.

"Apparently the average life expectancy is two to five years," George said. "Stephen Hawking was an outlier for living with it for so long."

"Is that all the letter says?" I had a bad feeling it wasn't. If that was all it was, George wouldn't have bothered telling me, right?

"Not quite." He looked uncomfortable, which didn't put me at ease. Whatever else was in that letter must be pretty fucking bad. "ALS is caused by a genetic mutation. Sometimes it happens out of the blue to people with no family history, and sometimes it's inherited from a parent."

Inherited from a parent.

My throat went dry as the words sank in. "You're saying there's a chance I could get it too."

"According to your father's doctor, there's a fifty percent chance you inherited the gene."

"Fifty percent," I repeated numbly.

Jesus.

Those were fucking *terrible* odds when you were talking about a fatal, untreatable disease, weren't they? I wouldn't even put money on those odds at the blackjack table, much less bet my life on them.

My hand shook as I reached for the whiskey George had poured for me. It burned like hell when I downed the whole thing in one gulp but not enough to wake me up from this nightmare.

Wordlessly, George went to the bar cart and came back with the bottle. He refilled my glass before sitting back down. "I know that sounds pretty bad."

A mirthless laugh bubbled out of me. "It does, yeah."

It sounded like the end of my life. I hadn't been prepared for that when I'd walked into this room tonight. But then I supposed no one was ever prepared for something like this when it happened.

"You've got to remember, son, even if you inherited the gene, it's not a guarantee you'll get the disease." George was attempting to be comforting, which I found disorienting and unsettling. My stepfather had never been the comforting type—even when my mother had been dying of cancer, George had reacted with the same gruff, detached efficiency with which he approached his business and everything else in his life.

He inclined his head at the letter he'd placed on the desk. "They did some kind of genetic test on your father and were able to identify the specific gene that caused his ALS. That's good news for you, because it means you can be tested to see if you have it or not."

I grabbed the envelope off the desk and fumbled the folded papers out. The first page was a typed letter from my father to George, which I assumed my old man must have dictated to someone, because the spelling and grammar weren't atrocious. It was also a lot more polite than I'd ever known my father to be, but maybe that was because he was writing to George, a man he was financially beholden to and who wasn't going to be pushed around by the likes of Wayne Rennie, lifelong fuckup and ne'er-do-well.

The tone was recognizably my father's, however. It was the same old passive-aggressive, *woe is me* tone he'd used in all the letters he'd sent me over the years, as if he was the aggrieved party and my mother and I had betrayed him by moving on with our lives. Only this time, instead of describing all the bad luck he'd had (never taking any responsibility for his own part in it, of course), he was detailing his symptoms, diagnosis, and medical outlook. All of it sounded legitimately fucking grim if he was to be believed, which I guessed he was. For once, there was no need to exaggerate his plight to drum up sympathy.

After that, he went on to explain the genetic testing he'd undergone and what his doctors said it meant for "his offspring." Those were the words he used. Not his son. *His offspring.* He'd given me a potential death sentence and hadn't even bothered to mention me by name.

The next page was a letter from my father's doctor, explaining in more precise medical detail the potential implications of having a parent diagnosed with amyotrophic lateral sclerosis and recommending a consultation with a genetic counselor to discuss testing. The final page was a pamphlet for a genetic testing service specializing in ALS.

When I'd finished scanning through it all, I folded the whole thing up to the size of a Tic Tac box and shoved it deep in the side pocket of my cargo pants, afraid I might throw up if I looked at it anymore. Then I took another drink of whiskey in a futile attempt to calm my nerves. "My father's going to need a lot of specialized care."

"You don't need to think about any of that," George said. "I'll make sure he's taken care of."

"You don't have to do that. He doesn't deserve it." My knuckles whitened around the whiskey tumbler. "You could leave him to fend for himself the way he left me and Mom. Let the bastard reap what he sowed for once in his cursed life."

"I'm not going to do that." George gave me a pointed look.

"And I don't think you'd really want me to either. Whatever kind of man he may be, he's your father."

"He's never been any kind of father to me."

"I'm well aware of that, but he's still your kin. And you're mine, so I'll see that the right thing's done whether he deserves it or not."

I stared down at my glass and swallowed thickly.

"Listen, son, we're going to do whatever it takes to get you through this. I don't want you to think you have to deal with this on your own. Whatever you need, you'll have it, you understand me?"

"Don't tell anyone." I met my stepfather's eyes. "I don't want the rest of the family to know."

George's forehead creased. It looked like he wanted to object, but after a beat he inclined his head. "If that's what you want."

"It's what I want. Obviously, if I get—" My tongue threatened to choke me when I tried to force the words out, and I had to stop and take a breath before starting again. "If I get sick, they'll have to find out. But until then, please don't tell anyone about this."

I didn't want to spend the time I had left with everyone I knew looking at me like I was dying. I wouldn't be able to stand that. It was bad enough I'd be looking at myself that way for the rest of whatever life I had ahead of me.

Now that I knew, nothing could ever be the same. Everything I'd thought my life might turn out to be had been snatched away in the blink of an eye. All those branching possibilities that used to spread out before me, sparkling with promise, had narrowed down to only two paths. Life or death. Sickness or health. A normal, happy life or a life cut short far too soon.

And there was nothing I could do about it. There was no treatment. No escaping this sentence. The dice had been rolled for me at the moment of my conception. My feet were irrevocably set on one of those two branching paths already. I just didn't know which one it was yet.

Did I even want to know? What was the point when I didn't have any control over my fate? I wasn't sure I could stand to know if the news was bad. How was I supposed to go on living my life knowing something like that was coming for me?

A fifty-fifty chance. The flip of a coin. Heads or tails. I tried to look at it with a glass-half-full attitude. There was a fifty percent chance I wasn't carrying the gene and I'd be fine.

But I couldn't pull it off. Not with something like this.

It felt like my life as I knew it had ended.

1

MAGGIE

The heat outside was preposterous. Utterly unreasonable. Downright inhumane. It felt like the inside of a mouth. In the five minutes it took me to haul my suitcases into my rental house from my leased car, I'd sweated through my shirt. I had to stick maxi pads inside my bra and starfish under a ceiling fan for fifteen minutes to recover.

Welcome to Texas.

It wasn't as if I'd never experienced summer in the South before, but it'd been long enough that I'd forgotten how punishing it was—how it made my brain fog, my limbs heavy, and my Northern blood sluggish in my veins. How did people function under these conditions? Humans had no business living here. It was a perimenopausal woman's worst nightmare.

Even during our worst summers, we'd never had heat this intense where I'd grown up. Fun fact: Buffalo, New York, was one of only a few cities in America that had never officially recorded three-digit temperatures.

According to my weather app, the temperature in Crowder, Texas, right now was "only" ninety-three, but it was expected to break 105 later this afternoon. What in the blasted hellscape?

Accounting for humidity, the heat index would be 112. Degrees! And that was in the shade! God knew what it would feel like if you were suicidal enough to be standing in the sun. I imagined squirrels bursting into flames on rooftops, streets turning to rivers of molten asphalt, and swimming pools boiling people alive.

Perhaps I was being the teensiest bit overdramatic. But cheese and crackers, it was hot! What I wouldn't give for a nice snowdrift to plunge myself into right about now. If this contract hadn't been so lucrative, I never would have let myself be lured to Texas in August. Thank the gods above for air-conditioning! More specifically, thank god the air-conditioning in my rental house seemed to be holding its own against the weather outside.

When you rented online, you never knew quite what you were going to get. Those well-framed photos that realtors and property owners posted could be diabolically deceptive. I'd been burned more than once over the years and was used to making do with all sorts of unsatisfactory living situations, but a faulty air conditioner would be a trial I didn't want to deal with in this kind of weather.

My consulting business required me to travel wherever my client companies happened to be located. Sometimes I'd only need to be on-site for a few days or weeks, and sometimes I'd be in my temporary lodgings for months on end. Over the last eight years, I'd done time in all manner of short-term leases and extended-stay hotels, from the luxurious to the horrific and everything in between. At this point, I'd pretty much seen it all. Whatever life handed me, I could deal with it. Even this ungodly heat.

The new contract I'd taken on would likely keep me here for the next six months, so I was relieved to find my rental house hadn't presented me with any unpleasant surprises. None that were apparent yet, anyway.

My options had been limited in a town of this size. This wasn't Manhattan or Minneapolis or even Mobile, Alabama. Crowder was a rural community seventy miles from Austin in a county with only one hospital and more cows than people.

The two-bedroom house I'd rented sat on a large lot in a quiet neighborhood five minutes from the office where I'd be working as of Monday. The house had been recently updated with fresh paint, new countertops, and modern appliances, and even had a detached garage to protect my car from the sun and elements. Most importantly, the air conditioner seemed to be aces, which would be crucial in the punishing heat of a Central Texas summer.

Amazingly, my next-door neighbor appeared unfazed by the heat outside. As I stood at my kitchen sink getting a drink of water, I could see him through the window, pushing a lawn-mower across his backyard. To each their own, I supposed. Maybe he was used to it, living here. At least he was wearing a straw cowboy hat and long sleeves to protect him from the sun.

From what I could see of him, he appeared to be an extraordinarily large man. It was hard to estimate height from a distance, but I'd put him well over six feet. He was broad as well as tall, barrel-chested with thick arms and even thicker legs, and carried himself with the posture and grace of an athlete. Given his size and the fact that we were in Texas, my money was on football. A former college player perhaps.

Our backyards were separated by a low chain link fence which afforded an unobstructed view of his property from my kitchen window. His house looked to be a mirror image of mine in its layout, down to the detached garage that sat at the near back corner of his lot next to mine. Our driveways ran in parallel between our two houses with only the fence and a narrow strip of grass separating them. His kitchen window faced directly onto mine but was mostly obstructed by miniblinds and the big silver pickup truck parked in his driveway.

His garage door was currently raised, however, displaying an impressive collection of weights and gym equipment inside. If he exercised in an un-air-conditioned garage during the summer, I could only assume the man must have some sort of superhuman immunity to extreme heat. As I watched him march back and forth across the length of his yard, I could see sweat stains darkening the fabric of his shirt, but otherwise he showed no signs of fatigue or discomfort. Definitely superhuman.

Realizing I'd been staring at the man through my window for several minutes, I dragged my attention away. Fascinating as my neighbor's lawn maintenance efforts were, I had work to do. My new client had couriered over a laptop this morning granting me full access to all their financial, HR, and internal communications systems. By Monday morning, I needed to know everything there was to know about how the company spent its money so I'd be ready to hit the ground running. I sat down at the dining room table with the new laptop and didn't think about my neighbor again until much, much later that night.

WHILE I WAS ADJUSTING to a new place, I always had difficulty sleeping. Predictably, the anticipation of starting a new job conspired with the strange bed and even stranger wildlife sounds outside to keep me awake. After several hours of fruitless tossing and turning, I got up and wandered aimlessly around the unfamiliar house.

When my ramblings brought me to the kitchen, my attention was immediately drawn to the window. More specifically to the light pouring out of my neighbor's open garage. He must be either a night owl or a fellow insomniac, because he was not only awake but exercising.

Shirtless.

He wasn't simply big. He was *built*. Tremendously built. The man had muscles stacked on top of muscles, all of them bulging and flexing as he did dips in his squat rack.

I couldn't tear my eyes away. Those triceps! Those back muscles! That ass! My god, his ass. It looked like someone had stuffed two basketballs inside the thin, clingy workout shorts that hung tantalizingly low on his powerful hips.

What an unexpected gift. If they'd included a photo of *this* view in the rental listing for my house, they could have charged several hundred dollars more. Maybe even a thousand.

Was it wrong to stand here watching a stranger through my window like this? It felt vaguely naughty. But it wasn't as though I was invading his privacy. Not really. He was out in plain sight with his garage door wide-open. In the surrounding darkness, the bright overhead light illuminating his every move might as well be a spotlight shining on a stage.

He had to know people would be able to see him. Was I supposed to be ashamed of looking out my own window at whatever happened to be there for me to see?

Wrong or not, I was helpless to do anything but stare, captivated, as he wrenched his massive body up and down, up and down, in a rhythm so hypnotizing I found myself counting along with his reps under my breath.

How could he possibly keep it up for so long? And yet he did. He kept going like some sort of machine, his muscles straining and limbs shaking as he pushed himself to the breaking point.

Imagine being that strong. Having that much power and vitality. It poured off him in waves I swore I could feel even from the safety of my kitchen. Truly, the man was a marvel of nature. Genetically blessed, certainly. But the level of control he exerted over himself—the self-discipline it must have taken to achieve this sort of perfection—was even more impressive than his god-given gifts.

It almost felt like he was punishing himself. Either that, or he was training for the Olympic dips team.

Honestly, why wasn't there an Olympic dips team? I'd watch the hell out of that event. There ought to be a channel where you could watch beefy, shirtless men doing dips twenty-four hours a day.

Finally, after an inconceivable number of reps, his giant, quivering arms gave out on him. He dropped to the floor, chest heaving as sweat dripped off his skin. When he grabbed a towel off the rack to dry his face and neck, I reached and touched my mouth to make sure I wasn't drooling.

That was the moment he finally turned around. I didn't know if he could see me standing in my dark kitchen, but I wasn't willing to take the chance. Spinning away from the window, I lurched sideways until I was safely plastered against the wall, out of his view.

Feeling naughtier than ever, I sucked in an unsteady breath as my pulse pounded in my ears. Had I been caught? God, I hoped not.

Even if I hadn't technically done anything wrong, I certainly didn't want my new neighbor to *know* I'd been watching him.

WHEN I GOT up the next morning, my extraordinarily attractive neighbor was outside working on his yard again. This time I only allowed myself a brief glance through the kitchen window, enough of a look to see that he was once more covered up by a hat and long sleeves as he attacked the edges of his driveway with a weed whacker.

He had surely gotten even less sleep than me—how did he have so much energy for yard work after that late-night workout? All I'd done was watch, and I still felt oddly drained by the experience.

Though that might have something to do with the vivid, X-rated dream I'd had after I finally fell asleep last night. Featuring my hot neighbor, of course. I'd barely even seen the man's face, but my imagination seemed to have no trouble filling in the blanks. My cheeks flushed remembering how I'd awakened with my heart pounding and the fading pulse of an orgasm vibrating through my limbs.

I continued to hear him outside over the next several hours, wielding various instruments of serenity-defiling ear torture, but I resisted the urge to look out the window again. The noise eventually stopped, and when I ventured out to the grocery store around noon, my neighbor was nowhere to be seen. Nor was he around when I returned home an hour later, dripping with sweat from my brief trek across the grocery store parking lot and the short drive home in a roasting hot car.

As I lugged my groceries inside, I was simultaneously relieved and disappointed not to have encountered him. I had no interest in getting to know my neighbors, not even the hot ones, and I definitely wasn't eager to introduce myself to the stranger I'd had an explicit sex dream about. And yet I couldn't help longing for another hit of the dopamine the sight of him provided.

At the very least, a better look at the man's face wouldn't be unwelcome.

―――

THAT NIGHT, once again, I had trouble falling asleep. Tomorrow would be my first day at the client site, and I had a lot on my mind. In particular, my meeting with the entire senior management team first thing in the morning. It was important I make a strong impression right off the bat to set the tone for our relationship going forward. I certainly wasn't thinking about my neighbor at all.

All right, maybe I was thinking about him a little. As I lay under the ceiling fan tossing and turning, I couldn't help wondering if he was out in his garage at that very moment. Did he work out every night at the same time? I was dying to know.

Eventually my curiosity drove me from my bed. As I padded into the kitchen, my heart sped up at the telltale glow of light pouring through the kitchen window.

He was out there again!

Shirtless like last night, but this time he was facing outward, toward the open doorway of his garage.

I hung back, trying to keep to the shadows in case he happened to glance at my window. He was doing biceps curls with a pair of enormous hexagonal dumbbells, alternating one arm with the other in slow, precisely controlled movements.

Although his veiny biceps and chest were surely an impressive sight to behold, I was most excited to finally have a clear view of his face. His mouth was set in an intimidating grimace of exertion, white teeth bared behind tightly drawn lips. Beneath a thick shock of copper-colored hair, his strong brow was lined by deep furrows of concentration and his long, angular jaw covered with matching reddish-brown stubble.

It surprised me to realize he was a redhead. I'd been so distracted by his body last night, I hadn't even noticed his hair color, though surely it must have been as obvious then as it was now. No wonder he covered up when he was out in the sun. His fair, freckled skin would be particularly susceptible to sunburns and skin cancer.

Dark blue tattoo ink covered the inside of his right biceps, one of his pecs, and the cap of his left shoulder, but sadly I was too far away to make out the details. I could see that more red hair swept across his chest, trailing into a thin line down the center of his abdomen. His stomach was firm but not flat. Instead of the sharply defined six-packs you saw on fitness magazine covers, his abs were thick bands of solid muscle that protruded slightly around his waist at the navel.

Involuntarily, I glided closer to the window, mesmerized by the fierce intensity of his expression as he sucked in one harsh breath after another. I had to wonder what his face looked like at rest or even smiling. It was hard to imagine, but I desperately wanted to know.

When he finished his set, he turned away to put the dumbbells in a rack along the wall. His shorts tonight were loose and black instead of gray and clingy, which didn't afford nearly as good a view of his glorious backside. Disappointing.

He stooped to retrieve a bottle of water off the floor and tipped his head back to chug several long swallows. After wiping his mouth with the back of his hand, he turned to gaze out the open door of his garage into the darkness, giving me my first look at his natural expression. His face was far less intimidating than I'd initially supposed. In fact, I'd go so far as to call it friendly. There was an inviting openness to his expression, even as he was still catching his breath from his last exercise set. Something about his wide, shapely lips and the lines around his eyes suggested someone who smiled a lot. I found myself drifting still closer as I tried to imagine what one of his smiles would look like. It seemed a shame he was out there all alone with nothing to smile at.

His head turned slightly, and his eyes seemed to focus on my window.

I froze where I stood, afraid to move for fear of drawing attention to myself. Could he see me standing here in the dark kitchen? I dearly hoped the reflections on the outside of the glass were enough to hide me from his view. I held my breath as his gaze lingered. It felt like he was looking right at me, but his expression didn't change. Surely if he'd seen me, he would have reacted somehow? Frowned or squinted or *something* at the sight of someone spying on him in the dark.

When he finally turned away, I stumbled out of the kitchen, clutching the doorframe as I released a ragged breath. My heart was in my throat and my chest was heaving almost as hard as his had been after he'd finished his curls.

Had he seen me? He hadn't, had he? No, of course not. He couldn't have.

It took me a long time to fall asleep after the adrenaline surge of nearly being caught. When I finally did, I was visited once again by intensely sexual dreams in which my athletic neighbor played a starring role.

AT EIGHT FORTY-FIVE on Monday morning, I strode into the corporate headquarters of King's Creamery wearing my traditional first day on the job ensemble: an immaculately tailored Alexander McQueen navy pin-striped power suit and comfortable tan pumps with my platinum blonde hair pulled into a sleek boss-babe low pony. The man at the security desk gave me an ID badge and directions to my new office before waving me toward the elevator bank.

As I stepped off on the eighth floor and strode past the glass-fronted conference rooms and executive offices, I ignored the curious looks cast in my direction. They had good reason to be curious about the appearance of a stranger in their midst, but they'd learn who I was and why I was here soon enough.

Finding my office with no trouble, I unpacked my laptop and stowed my purse away inside my new desk. I was making a last-minute review of my slides when the company's CEO appeared in the doorway of my office wearing jeans and cowboy boots with his thinning gray hair pulled back in a ponytail.

"You get settled in all right?" he asked in his gentlemanly Texas twang as I rose to shake his hand.

I'd met George King only once before, over drinks in the bar of the Driskill Hotel when I'd flown to Austin last month to discuss his company's needs and what I believed I could do for him. The impression I'd drawn from that conversation, as well as the extensive research I'd done on him and his company, was that he was a no-nonsense businessman with a razor-sharp edge lurking beneath his good-old-boy manners and deceptively casual style.

"Perfectly," I answered. "Is everyone in the conference room?"

"They are. Shall we get this show on the road?"

Grabbing my laptop, I accompanied him down the hall. "Do they know why I'm here? Have you told them anything yet?"

"Not a word. Thought I'd let you do the honors yourself."

That was good. It prevented misinformation and panic from spreading through the company before I had a chance to speak to the leadership team myself. When I didn't have to waste time combating people's preconceived ideas, things tended to go more smoothly. There was also an advantage in taking people off guard, so they didn't have a chance to take up a defensive posture ahead of time.

All eyes turned our way as George King indicated for me to precede him into the conference room. He'd called a mandatory special senior leadership meeting, which had undoubtedly set off all sorts of alarm bells, and I could read the apprehension on everyone's faces. I could also see many of them drawing their own conclusions about my purpose here based on the fact that I'd entered the room alongside their CEO. The most perceptive ones were drawing the correct conclusions and had already figured out what was coming.

Thanks to the research I'd done, I was able to put a name and title to every face before me and knew that several of the EVPs present were the CEO's children. King's Creamery was a family-owned business that had been founded by George King's grandfather in 1921. But it was George's leadership over the last thirty years that had grown it from a modest regional ice cream company to the second-best-selling brand nationwide.

"Good to see everyone made it," George said as he cast an appraising eye over his assembled leadership team. He gestured at me as I strode to the front of the room and plugged my laptop in to project my slides onto the screen. "This is Maggie Silvestri. I brought her in to take a look at our numbers."

Having delivered his brusque introduction, he claimed a chair at the back of the room and casually propped a cowboy-booted ankle on his knee.

"Good morning," I said, straightening to address the people seated around the table before me. I wasn't a small woman, and people often found my height intimidating, something I used to my advantage in situations like this. "I'm Maggie, and as George said, I'm here to assess the company's financial health."

I paused for a beat to let that sink in before dropping the next bomb.

"Today I'm going to show you that if you keep doing the same things you're doing now, King's Creamery will not exist in five years."

2

MAGGIE

Things went about as well as I could have expected over the next several days. I'd made a convincing case to support my dire forecast and laid out my preliminary hundred-day plan to diagnose where the company was losing the most money and identify ways to stanch the bleeding. The executive leadership had all walked out of that first meeting with a list of action items I'd assigned them. So far, most had been cooperating.

I encountered some minor resistance from a few quarters, but less than I'd expected and no more than I was prepared to handle. Most people seemed reluctant to incur George King's wrath by openly stonewalling the management consultant he'd brought in to fix the messes they'd made. It quickly became clear most of his employees were afraid of him, even his children, which in this instance worked in my favor.

But beyond that, most people seemed to understand the urgency of the situation and the necessity of what I had been brought to do. Treating me as the enemy wasn't going to save anyone's jobs if the company was headed for insolvency.

Most of my first week was spent conducting one-on-one

meetings with the EVPs to gather additional information that would allow me to assess where their budgets were going and how much money their efforts were generating for the company.

I was particularly impressed by George King's daughter Josie King, the EVP of marketing, and his adopted son Manny Reyes, the EVP of plant operations. Both struck me as extremely sharp, deeply invested in the company's future, and concerned for the well-being of its employees. That wasn't always the case with nepotism hires at a family company like this one. Family members were sometimes the biggest liabilities, which could make my job more difficult since they were usually immune from being laid off.

George King's son Nate King, the EVP of sales, was more of a wild card. When I met with him one-on-one for the first time Thursday, he appeared distracted, agitated, and intensely unhappy to be there. Nevertheless, he provided straightforward answers to all my questions without any obvious attempt at stonewalling. I came away from our meeting unable to guess how much he was likely to get in my way.

Nate King was far from the only unhappy person at King's Creamery that week. News of my purpose for being there had quickly rippled through the ranks of the company, creating a palpable atmosphere of anxiety. My ultimate goal was to put most of those worries to rest and save as many jobs as I could, but the fact that my presence was needed in the first place meant there was valid cause for concern.

Such was the reality of my job. I'd grown used to working in a climate of fear because I brought it with me everywhere I went. The nature of my consulting business meant that companies didn't call me in unless trouble already lay ahead.

Despite that, with only a few exceptions I found my new colleagues welcoming and pleasant. Under different circumstances, there were several I might have been able to see myself becoming friends with. But I didn't have the luxury of friends. Given my mission, friendship was a conflict of interest. Professional objectivity required a polite distance. Still, as the week wore on I grew increasingly optimistic that my time in Crowder might be relatively enjoyable.

Aside from the unbearable heat, of course.

I doubted I'd ever get used to roasting alive when I got into my car at the end of every workday after it had been baking in the sun for the last ten hours. But that wouldn't last forever. I expected to be here for the next six months, and my new colleagues had promised me the weather would be pleasant in October and November.

I looked forward to being able to go outdoors again then and explore some of the local sights once the outside world didn't resemble the surface of the sun. In the meantime, I fully intended to stay holed up in my air-conditioned rental house whenever I wasn't at the office. Fortunately, I had plenty of work to keep me busy in addition to my new hobby as a part-time voyeur.

My muscle-bound next-door neighbor continued to preoccupy me in my free time. Whenever I heard one of his doors slam or the sound of his truck pulling into the driveway, I couldn't resist peeking out my window to see what he was up to.

What else did I have to do for entertainment? There were only so many times a woman could rewatch *Magic Mike XXL* before it lost some of its charm.

To my disappointment, my neighbor stayed out all night long on Monday. Then on Wednesday evening, he had two male visitors who arrived in separate cars and didn't leave until after I'd fallen asleep.

I'd learned by then that he didn't work out every night. I only caught him in his garage twice more that week, on Tuesday and Friday. Other nights, when I crept to my kitchen window at the usual time, I was disappointed to find his garage closed up and dark.

In general, he seemed to keep highly irregular hours. My limited observations outside of my own work schedule failed to uncover any pattern to his routine. Did he have a job? A girlfriend? My imagination ran away with itself making up explanations. Maybe he was a hit man. In witness protection. Or perhaps an undercover agent for some shadowy government agency, foreign or domestic.

My curiosity had turned me into a forty-five-year-old Harriet the Spy. I was so invested in solving the puzzle of my neighbor's odd schedule, I was tempted to start recording my observations in a journal in case there was a pattern to be decoded. Except I feared committing my surveillance to paper would cross the line between a benign diversion and a genuine obsession.

I wasn't obsessed. I was merely curious. And bored. And possibly a little lonely.

And all right, maybe also a perv who enjoyed watching my attractive neighbor get sweaty in his gym. But my god, I was only human. No one who'd seen him back there working out would be able to blame me for appreciating the view.

Tragically, my second weekend in the house I didn't catch sight of him at all. He was home all day Saturday but never came outside, not even to work out. Then Sunday morning he left before I woke up and was still gone when I went to bed that night. So disappointing.

But the following Monday a major piece of the puzzle finally revealed itself! As I was leaving for work, my mysterious neighbor happened to be getting home from wherever he'd been for the last twenty-four hours. I backed out of my driveway just as he got out of his truck. There, on the back of his dark blue T-shirt, clear as day, were the words *CROWDER FIRE DEPARTMENT* printed in bold white and red letters.

Mystery solved! His irregular schedule and overnight absences suddenly made far more sense. My giant hunk of a neighbor was a firefighter. Of course he was. What else would someone who looked liked him be?

As I continued to back my car toward the street, internally celebrating my newfound knowledge, my neighbor glanced over his shoulder at me and raised a hand in greeting.

I didn't return the gesture. I was far too busy backing out of a driveway. Safety required me to keep both hands on the wheel—as he should know, being a first responder.

But he'd officially seen me now. I was no longer invisible. He definitely knew I existed.

―――

THINGS FELT DIFFERENT AFTER THAT. The veil between us had been breached. My neighbor went from being an object of my fanciful imagination to a real person with a real job who knew I was living next door. Now that his schedule had an ordinary explanation, I didn't need to be Harriet the Spy anymore.

At night, I lay in bed listening to the katydids and crickets as I watched the time tick toward midnight when he might be working out in his garage. But I didn't get up and slip into the kitchen to gaze out my window. It felt too risky, now that he knew I was here.

Sometimes I could even hear the faint clang of his iron weights, beckoning me, letting me know he was there to be seen. But I refused to give in to my base urges anymore. No matter how much I wanted to.

I couldn't control my dreams, however. He continued to haunt them regularly. They were still often X-rated, but I also dreamed of more mundane interactions with him. In one dream we were grocery shopping together. In another he gave me a ride in his big silver pickup truck and we listened to the Eagles on the radio. I woke up when he reached across the console to hold my hand.

Oddly, now that I'd ceased my covert peeping I began seeing more of my neighbor accidentally. When I stepped outside on Tuesday evening to retrieve a package from my porch, he happened to be unloading groceries from his truck. Once again he raised a hand in friendly greeting, and once again I didn't return the gesture, hurrying back inside instead.

I'd always had an instinctive distrust of overly friendly strangers. *Why* were they so friendly? What did they want from me? Why couldn't people leave each other alone to go about their business undisturbed? I didn't understand why Southerners considered their aggressive friendliness good manners. In most of the places I'd lived, forcing an unnecessary interaction on a total stranger was considered rude.

Besides, I wasn't here to make friends. I was here to do a job. I'd only be in town for a few months, so there was no point in getting to know my neighbors. If I needed anything to do with the house, I had the owner's contact information as well as that of the leasing agency.

Additionally, in a town this small where a large number of the residents were employed by my client, getting to know people was a risky proposition. The last thing I wanted to do was become friendly with someone whose job I might need to eliminate.

I didn't even know for certain that my neighbor worked for the fire department. It was an assumption based on a glimpse of a T-shirt he could have borrowed from someone else. Or he might be a volunteer firefighter. There was still a possibility he worked for King's Creamery in some capacity. In which case even a neighborly, passing acquaintance could present a conflict of interest.

It was a risk I wasn't willing to take. Far better to keep my distance and avoid any possible awkwardness or entanglements.

Unfortunately, this became more difficult as fate conspired to randomly throw us into each other's paths. On Wednesday morning, I barely managed to look away in time to avoid making eye contact when he emerged from his house as I was leaving for work.

I had no such luck on Friday evening, when he stepped out his front door as I was checking my mailbox. This time he didn't simply wave but also called out a loud "Hi there!" Pretending not to have heard him, I quickly went back inside and shut the door.

On Sunday, my neighbor decided to wash his truck in his driveway. I couldn't help but see him when I went into the kitchen for a cup of coffee. The man was right outside my window! Parading around in nothing but a pair of bathing trunks with his jaw-dropping muscles on full display in all their glory!

I felt like I was being tested. Worse, while I stood there momentarily paralyzed by the view, he looked up and caught me gaping at him. This time I knew he'd seen me, because he had the cheek to break into a crooked grin and give me a friendly wave.

Mortified, I turned on my heel and walked out of the room. Deciding I could do without additional caffeine, I avoided the kitchen until he took his half-naked body back inside his house.

I might need to invest in some curtains for that damn kitchen window.

MONDAY EVENING, not long after I'd gotten home from work, there was a knock on my front door. Since I was expecting a package I thought nothing of it, assuming it was the delivery driver dropping it off.

Instead, when I opened the door, I found myself face-to-face with my ridiculously hot neighbor, who was even taller and more massive up close than he'd looked from a distance. At six feet tall myself, I wasn't used to looking up at people, but he had to be nearly half a foot taller than me.

As he stood there cradling a parcel in an arm as big as a ham hock, he offered me a grin. "Hi! I'm Ryan McCafferty. I live in the house next door."

Taken completely off guard by his appearance on my doorstep, I found myself too tongue-tied to respond. I hadn't been prepared to face the specimen of physical perfection I'd been fantasizing about the last two weeks, much less be expected to have an actual conversation with him.

"You must be Margaret Silvestri," he continued, seemingly unperturbed by my silence. He had dimples on each cheek. They were mesmerizing, as was his smile. And his arms. And his everything. "Your package was left on my porch by mistake."

When he held it out, I managed to shake myself from my stupor enough to accept it and say, "Thank you."

"You're welcome." His thick copper eyebrows lifted slightly. "I said hi to you the other day, but you didn't say hi back. Maybe you didn't hear me."

Disconcerted, I pressed my lips together. As his statement didn't require an answer, I didn't offer one.

At my continued silence, his mouth twitched into a smirk as his light gray eyes twinkled. "I'm gonna take a stab in the dark and guess you're from out of town."

"That's correct," I answered, even more disconcerted by his amusement, which sparked in the air around him like fireflies.

If he noticed my irritation, he gave no sign of it. In fact, his smile had the temerity to grow even wider. "How long are you here for?"

"A few months."

"That's good."

"Why?" I asked, unable to fathom why he'd have feelings one way or the other about this information.

"It'll be nice to have the same neighbor for a while. Since Alli converted the house to a short-term rental we've had a lot of folks passing through. Most only stay for a few days or maybe a week tops. Alli grew up here, you know." When he raised one of his arms to gesture at the house, the sleeve of his T-shirt pulled so tight around his enormous biceps it looked like it was in danger of bursting open. But it also allowed me to see that the tattoo on the inside of his biceps was an hourglass. "This used to be her dad's house, but she had the whole place gutted and renovated last year after he passed away. She let me have a look around after the contractors finished. They did a real nice job with it, I thought. How are you liking it so far? Settling in all right?"

I'd been so busy staring at his arm during most of this monologue, it took me a second to realize he'd ended it with a question. "Yes, the house is fine."

His gaze felt like a hot stroke on my skin as it slid over me. "So what brings you to Crowder?"

"A temporary job," I answered, feeling a flush creep up my neck. I didn't like being the focus of his attention. Hypocritical of me, I realized, considering how much of my attention the man had occupied over the last two weeks. "Sorry, I've got food on the stove, so I really need to go."

"Oh yeah, sure." He nodded but made no move to take his giant self off my front porch. "I'm in that green house right there in case you want to borrow a cup of sugar." The sly twinkle in his eyes made it clear he wasn't talking about granulated sweetener.

"I don't bake," I said, trying not to roll my eyes.

"Or need a jar opened."

"I'm quite capable of opening my own jars, thank you."

His smile spread even wider. "If you need anything at all, I'm at your disposal."

"I appreciate that," I said, pushing my door closed. "Good night."

"Enjoy the rest of your evening!" he called out cheerfully as I shut the door on him. "It was nice to meet you, Margaret!"

When he was gone, I went straight to my laptop to check Ryan McCafferty's name against the King's Creamery employee database. It was a relief to confirm he wasn't on the payroll, nor was anyone else with that last name.

While I had my laptop open I considered googling him, but managed to talk myself out of it. I didn't need to know anything else about him.

In fact, I wished I'd never seen him at all.

THE NEXT MORNING, as I was getting ready for work, I heard an odd sound outside. It sounded like something scraping against the side of the house. Or perhaps inside the wall? Hoping it was squirrels or maybe a cat messing around in the bushes, I pulled on a robe and grabbed the pepper spray from my purse before venturing out the front door to investigate.

As I approached the side of the house, a giant, hulking shape loomed up in front of me. It took me a harrowing second to identify the hulking shape's face as that of my neighbor, Ryan.

"Oh my god!" Clutching my chest, I lowered the pepper spray I'd nearly doused him with. "What are you doing here?"

He blinked at me, arching a single eyebrow as that disconcerting expression of amusement curved his lips. "It's Ryan, remember? I live next door?"

"I know *who* you are. What are you doing in my yard?"

"Watering." He hefted the coil of hose dangling from the crook of his mighty arm to illustrate. "Is that pepper spray?"

"I didn't know who was out here, did I?"

His smile ebbed. "Sorry. I didn't mean to scare you."

"You didn't," I lied, attempting to muster some dignity while standing in the front yard in my bathrobe.

Piercing gray eyes swept over my face, seeing far more than they should. I didn't enjoy the feeling.

"Why are you in my yard watering at six thirty in the morning?" I asked huffily. I'd been outside for all of ten seconds, and beads of sweat were already forming on my forehead.

Finally tearing his gaze from me, he went back to dragging the hose across the front yard. "Alli asked me to keep an eye on the house for her."

"Isn't there a service that takes care of the yard?" I'd been told they would come every Wednesday. But since they always showed up while I was at work, I hadn't actually seen them, only the results of their labor in the freshly shorn grass and trash bags left at the street.

"There is," Ryan confirmed. "But it hasn't rained for over six weeks, and I wanted to make sure this old pecan tree gets a deep root watering so we don't lose it." He shot me a wry look. "I don't have to though, if you're willing to risk this big tree falling on the house where you're sleeping."

"I wouldn't want that," I agreed, swatting at a mosquito buzzing around my face. "But I can do it myself if you tell me what needs to be done."

Ryan shook his head as he continued to haul on the hose. "I don't think Alli would want that since you're a paying tenant.

And I wouldn't want you getting yourself all dirty before work. I'll be out of your hair as soon as I finish laying out this soaker hose. Then we need to let the water run for an hour so it penetrates the roots."

I tried not to stare at his flexing biceps and forearms as he arranged the hose in a wide circle around the tree. When he bent over, taunting me with a view of his spectacular backside, I swallowed and looked away. "I can turn it off before I leave for work."

"I'd appreciate that and so would the tree." He shot a curious look my way. "What kind of job is it that brought you to town, anyway?"

"How often do I need to water the tree like this?" I asked, ignoring his question. My work was covered by an NDA, and although it didn't prevent me from naming my client, answering one question would invite others, which I preferred to avoid. My presence at King's Creamery had already inspired enough alarm, and I didn't want to hasten its spread around town.

"The once should be good. Hopefully we'll get some rain before too much longer and we won't have to do this again." Straightening, he squinted at me as he brushed his palms off on his jeans. "You're not very friendly, are you?"

I crossed my arms, bristling at his rudeness, but also trying to blot my underboob sweat. "I'm friendly to my friends. I don't like answering nosy questions from strangers."

I hadn't always been like this, cold and sharp-tongued, keeping everyone at a distance. I'd had to learn the hard way to keep my feelings hidden behind thick, barbed armor that had taken me years to build up. But it served its purpose well, protecting me from hurt and disappointment.

Experience had taught me there was no purpose to be served in pretending to make friends with any of my temporary colleagues, acquaintances, or neighbors. Not when I'd be leaving here in a matter of months, and we'd never see or think of each other again. There was no point pretending the reality was otherwise.

"We're not strangers. We're neighbors." His tone held a note of reproach.

"Only temporarily," I replied as I swatted at another mosquito. "That's not the same as friends."

"It's not the same thing as strangers either."

I couldn't continue to look at him with his unfairly attractive body and reproachful eyes and try to carry on a conversation in my now sweat-soaked bathrobe while being feasted on by bloodsucking insects. "I have to finish getting ready for work. I'll turn off the water before I leave."

Without waiting for him to respond, I walked back into the house with as much pride as I could muster under the circumstances and only a moderate pang of guilt.

3

RYAN

Margaret Silvestri was a tough nut to crack, but I'd always enjoyed a challenge. She tried to act as if she didn't like me, but I knew better. I'd seen her watching me through her window.

Not just once either. On at least three occasions I'd spotted her there in her kitchen late at night, shrouded in shadow as she'd watched me exercise. She must have thought I couldn't see her. All I'd been able to make out was a vague, almost ghostlike figure, but I'd known she was there. And I knew she'd liked what she saw enough to come back for more.

So she could play like she wasn't interested in me all she wanted. I knew her dirty little secret. I knew she liked to look at me when she thought I couldn't see her—which meant I also knew that pretty rose-petal flush that colored her chest and neck every time she had to talk to me wasn't because I annoyed her. It was because she was thinking about my body and how much she liked it.

I was fine with that because I liked looking at her too. She'd caught my eye the very first time I'd seen her strutting across her front yard to check her mailbox. Strut was the perfect word for the way she walked. Driven by purpose, shoulders back, her proud chin thrust in the air and her hips and ponytail swaying with every long, swift stride in those killer heels she wore to work every day.

I enjoyed watching her strut in those heels the same way she enjoyed watching me sweat in the gym—on a purely aesthetic level. I appreciated the flash of her shapely calves beneath her prim business skirts, the sashay of her hips, and the take-no-prisoners confidence she projected. But I especially liked that she was tall and big like me.

Well, not quite like me, but a better match to my size than most women I encountered. She wasn't some fragile slip of a thing I might break if I wasn't careful. Margaret's ample hips were exactly the right size for my big hands to hold on to, and her breasts looked generous enough to fill my palms to overflowing.

Not that I'd been sitting around thinking about her breasts.

Much.

In any case, it wasn't as if I planned to do anything about it. I wasn't looking to start anything up with my new neighbor or anyone else for that matter.

Mostly, I just enjoyed pushing her buttons. Her determination to ignore my existence only intrigued me further. What did the woman have against saying hello? Would it kill her to return a friendly wave? Or even—god forbid—deign to offer a smile? Given that she'd been peeping at me through her windows for the last two weeks, I couldn't resist taking her behavior as a dare.

So maybe I'd washed my truck in my driveway Sunday just to fuck with her a little. I'd given her something to look at on purpose to see what she'd do. I hadn't been disappointed either. When I'd caught her leering at me through her window and waved to let her know she'd been caught, she'd been so embarrassed she'd turned and fled the room.

I probably would have left it at that if fate hadn't intervened to deliver one of her packages to my door the next day. Sure, I could have left the misdelivered box on her porch while she was still at work, but it wasn't in my nature to let such a lucky happenstance go by without milking it for all it was worth.

I'd enjoyed how flustered she'd gotten when she found me on her porch. She didn't strike me as a woman who flustered easily, so I took it as a compliment. It had amused me to see how my attempt at making friendly small talk had driven her to distraction. Poor Margaret hadn't been able to get rid of me fast enough.

After that first one-sided conversation, I'd gone home and given my former neighbor Alli Meckel a ring to ply her for information about her current renter. Just out of curiosity. I hadn't had any particular aim in mind by it.

All she'd been able to tell me was that Margaret had booked the house for six full months. Remembering my offer to help keep an eye on the property, I happened to mention the old pecan tree out front might need some extra TLC to help it through the drought we'd been having, and I'd be happy to see to it if Alli liked.

I hadn't been trying to rile Margaret up when I'd gone over there this morning. I felt properly bad about giving her a scare, but I couldn't say I'd disliked seeing that sharp temper of hers. As much as I'd enjoyed making her flustered before, there was something about the way her cold blue eyes flashed with heat and her voice took on that crisp, commanding timbre that went straight to my balls.

The woman walked and talked and carried herself like someone who was used to giving orders and being obeyed, and I liked it. I liked it a lot.

Margaret Silvestri reminded me of a prickly pear cactus. A vibrant, colorful flower protected by sharp spines to keep people away from her sweet, tender fruit. At least I liked to imagine there was something sweet and tender hiding underneath that prickly exterior of hers. For all I knew, she was spines all the way down. Even though I'd sworn off women, there was a part of me that wanted to find out.

"Are you chopping those onions or making sweet love to them, Big Red?"

I pulled my head out of my ass and glared at Gareth, who was cooking dinner for B shift at the firehouse. "You can't rush an artist, G."

He returned my glare with a cocky grin. "I can and I will. If you don't hurry it up, my garlic's going to burn."

Gareth made lunch and dinner for our crew every shift. We used to trade off cooking duties, but since he was far and away the best chef among us and he actually enjoyed it, we'd decided by unanimous vote that he should take charge of all the cooking. Anything to avoid ever having to eat Quincy's tuna casserole again.

No sooner had I finished dicing the onions than Gareth swept the cutting board away and scraped them into the Instant Pot. He'd snagged it at an after-Christmas sale last year and taken up a collection from all three shifts to cover the cost. I swore the man loved that appliance more than his own mother. The only time I'd seen him close to committing violence was when one of the guys on A shift had failed to clean the lid after making corn chowder.

"Quince, preheat the oven to 425 and throw the cast iron skillet in there," Gareth said as he stirred the onions and garlic together. "Jamal, how's that chili paste coming?"

We all pitched in to help with prep and take care of the cleaning-up when Gareth cooked. I suspected that was why he liked playing chef so much—he got to boss us around *and* get out of doing dishes.

"All ready," Jamal said, setting the blender jar next to the Instant Pot. The eye-watering scent of pulverized ancho and pasilla chiles combined with the smell of frying onions and garlic.

"Hey, what's this?" Quincy asked, leaning around Gareth. She grabbed the two cans of beans off the counter and wrinkled her nose. "You're not putting beans in the chili."

"I surely am," he shot back.

"No way. You don't put beans in chili. Every Texan knows that."

"I'd care if I was entering a chili cookoff, but I've got six mouths to feed on a budget and Big Red over there eats like a buffalo training for an ultramarathon. Beans are a cheap way to make the food go farther."

It was true that because of my size and training regimen, I required more calories and protein than anyone else on the crew. On account of that, I always tossed extra money into the chow fund, plus I kept a tub of protein powder in the station kitchen so I could supplement with shakes between meals.

Quincy looked to Jamal for help. "Back me up here, Einstein."

"Well," Jamal said, looking thoughtful, "chili is shorthand for chili con carne, which was first introduced to the Americas by immigrants from the Canary Islands who'd been resettled to San Antonio by the government of New Spain. Traditionally, it was a tangia-like stew made with meat, chili peppers, and onions flavored with a cumin-heavy spice blend resembling the Berber seasoning style of Morocco. No beans."

And that was why Jamal had earned the nickname "Einstein" around the station. The guy was as smart as a whip and had all sorts of knowledge tucked away in that bald head of his.

"Don't care," Gareth said, unmoved by the culinary history lesson. "I'm the one rattling the pans, so I decide what goes in the chili. If you don't like it, Quince, you're free to do the shopping and cooking next shift."

"No!" Jamal and I barked in unison, causing Gareth to cackle.

Please god, never again. Quincy's cooking damn near qualified as a war crime under the terms of the Geneva Convention.

"Where's the probie?" Quincy asked, looking around for Justin, our probationary firefighter. "Let's see what he thinks."

"He's out in the barn washing the booster truck," I said. "And rookies don't get a vote."

She turned her big eyes on me in a plea for support. "Come on, LT, you're not seriously going to let G-Man commit this offense against Texas chili on your behalf, are you?"

I shrugged as I dried off the cutting board. "I like beans. Nothing wrong with a little extra fiber and protein."

"There, see? The lieutenant's spoken. Gimme those." Gareth made a swipe for the beans Quincy had taken hostage.

She deftly spun out of his reach. "Maybe we should ask the cap what he thinks and let him be the tiebreaker."

Giving a warning shake of my head, I arched a quelling eyebrow at her. "What Cap thinks is he doesn't want to be bothered with petty nonsense when he's in his office doing paperwork."

"Fine." Sighing dramatically, Quincy relinquished the beans to Gareth. "I tried to save you from yourselves. Don't blame me when they revoke your Texan cards."

Gareth pushed the beans toward Jamal. "Drain these for me, will you?"

"Sure thing," Jamal said, clearly not that fussed about the prospect of beans in his chili. He looked over his shoulder at me as he fetched the can opener. "Hey, so, Ayesha's got this cousin who's just moved to town and doesn't know many people here besides us..."

I gritted my teeth, already knowing where this was headed. People were constantly trying to set me up on dates. No one wanted to believe that a single man like me who was pushing forty might want to stay single. No matter how many times I reiterated my stance on the matter.

"I was thinking maybe you wouldn't mind showing her around a little," Jamal went on. "You could take her out one night to introduce her to some of the hot spots. Just so she'd know someone else in town. What do you say, Big Red? I'd owe you one."

Sneaky of him trying to frame it as a favor for a poor, friendless relative, but I wasn't falling for it. "I'm busy," I said gruffly, yanking open the fridge.

"I didn't name a specific day," Jamal said.

"Doesn't matter." I grabbed the buttermilk, eggs, and butter Gareth would be needing for the cornbread and elbowed the fridge closed. "I'm busy every night for the next thousand years not going on a blind date with your wife's cousin."

Quincy snorted. "Told you he wouldn't go for it. If he wouldn't let me fix him up with my hot bisexual friend with the tongue ring, he's not going to say yes to Ayesha's cousin, no matter how needy you make her sound."

"Look," I said, "I'm sure she's lovely—"

"She is lovely," Jamal said. "I think you'd really like her. She's a pediatric speech therapist who does CrossFit competitions. I'm talking seriously fit."

"I'll go out with Ayesha's cousin," Gareth immediately volunteered.

"Not a chance," Jamal shot back.

"Why not?" Gareth asked, all innocence. "You know I'll show her a good time."

"That's what I'm afraid of, and then you'll never call her again. My wife would spike my coffee with laxatives if I let you anywhere near her cousin." Jamal directed a hopeful look at me. "Tina's a good person with a good heart. She deserves a man who's going to treat her with respect."

I folded my arms across my chest. "I'm respecting her by refusing to waste her time pretending I have any interest in dating when I don't."

"I just don't understand why you've gone off dating altogether." Jamal frowned as he rubbed his chin. "You used to date all the time, so it's not as if you don't like women."

"Yeah, what exactly is the deal with you these days?" Quincy said, giving me a puzzled look. "It'd be one thing if you were into playing the field like Gareth, but I don't see you hooking up with anyone either. If you don't do casual sex and you don't do relationships, what do you do?"

"Himself," Gareth quipped as he added the rest of the chili ingredients to the Instant Pot. "Man's in a monogamous relationship with his right hand."

When I offered him my middle finger, the smartass winked at me.

"Seriously though," Quincy said, refusing to give up. "Did you have a bad experience or something? Do I need to go kick some hoe's ass for breaking your heart? Give me her name and I'll round up a posse."

Touched as I was by her offer, I shook my head. "It wasn't because of any one thing or any one person. I just got tired of looking for Mrs. Right and never having anything to show for it. Why bother when I like my life fine the way it is? The whole dating thing's more trouble than it's worth to me these days."

It was the best explanation I could offer. At least it was a kind of truth, even if it wasn't the real reason. That truth stayed locked away inside me—I didn't talk about it with anyone, not even my closest friends or family. And honestly, after so many dating disappointments over the years, I'd almost found it a relief to give up on the idea of finding a partner. At least I didn't have to confront my failures anymore.

Quincy studied me, her too-perceptive eyes narrowing. "Yeah, sorry, but that sounds like a load of bullshit to me. You expect me to believe you just gave up? Because you got *tired*? I'm not buying it. The Ryan McCafferty I know doesn't quit things that easily."

"She's right," Jamal said, giving me a speculative look. "That doesn't sound like you."

I set my jaw and stared them down. "Maybe I just realized I don't want it that bad."

That was a lie. I wanted to find the love of my life and settle down as much as anyone. Possibly even more than most. I just hadn't ever found the right woman, and now it was too late.

What if I fell in love and then got sick? How could I let a woman commit herself to me when there was a fifty-fifty chance I was carrying a ticking time bomb in my DNA? A fifty-fifty chance she'd have to nurse me through a debilitating illness and end up a widow. What kind of thing was that to do to someone you loved? Every morning I woke up and wondered if this was the day my first symptom would show up and seal my fate. No way was I inviting someone else to live that nightmare with me.

"Leave him alone," Gareth cut in. He shot a cranky look at Quince and Jamal as he locked the lid onto the Instant Pot. "Not everyone needs another person to complete them. Just because you two are happy being tied to someone else doesn't mean the rest of us want to be. Hell, half the couples in the world are fucking miserable together. Maybe the world would be a happier place if more people stayed single instead of feeling pressured to partner up."

Quincy opened her mouth to retort, but never got the chance. An electronic tone sounded over the fire station's alert system as a red light began flashing on the ceiling overhead. We all went still, listening as the voice broadcast over the intercom dispatched Engine 1 and Ladder 1 to the address of a reported house fire.

I'd been saved by the bell. Literally.

I switched off the oven as Quincy, Jamal, and I headed to our trucks while Gareth hastily shoved the perishables back in the fridge before following us. Dinner would have to wait until we got back.

I could only hope by then our interrupted conversation would be forgotten.

4

RYAN

"You're such a sweetheart for doing this," Mrs. Salinas said from behind me as I climbed the ladder I'd set beneath the smoke alarm in her kitchen. "There are some tasks you just need a strapping young man to do for you."

The Crowder Fire Department offered free smoke alarms, battery changes, and fire safety checks for its elderly and disabled residents on request. The city provided the batteries and alarms, but us firefighters volunteered our time to the program on our days off. Some of the guys complained about having to do it, but I didn't mind. Not having a family of my own meant I had the free time to spare, and I liked to keep busy.

"I'm happy to be of service, ma'am." I was fairly certain the septuagenarian was admiring my ass, but I didn't hold it against her. She could look all she wanted so long as looking was all she did. I'd had one or two randy seniors make actual passes at me, and it had been an uncomfortable experience for everyone involved.

"Don't you ma'am me," she retorted pertly. "Call me Claudia or you'll make me feel old."

Chuckling, I cast a grin over my shoulder and gave her a

jaunty salute. "Yes ma'am, Claudia." After I'd popped a fresh battery in her smoke alarm, I climbed down from the ladder and cast my eye around her living room ceiling. While I was on one of my house calls, I always offered to do any other simple tasks that required climbing a ladder, like changing out air filters and light bulbs. "When's the last time you had your air filter changed?"

"Oh, goodness," Claudia said, twisting her arthritic hands together. "Not since the last time I had to call the repairman out."

I'd figured as much from the dust buildup on the grill. "If you've got a new one handy, I can change it out for you now."

"You're an absolute angel." Beaming a grateful smile at me, she shuffled off to get the filter.

"Do you have a brush or a broom I can use?" I called out after her as I moved the ladder into the living room. "I can clean off this grill while I'm up there."

"In the pantry," she shouted from somewhere in the back of the house.

Whistling to myself, I found a broom and mounted the ladder again. It only took me a few extra minutes to clean the grill, swap out her filter for her, and sweep up the dust I'd knocked onto the floor.

"I don't suppose you'd like some coconut tres leches cake?" she asked as I emptied the dustpan into the trash. "I've got some left over from my book club last night, if you've got time to stay for a piece."

I looked into her hopeful, eager face and smiled. "I happen to love coconut tres leches cake."

She was my last house call of the day, and I had nothing else planned that couldn't wait a half hour. A lot of the folks we visited led solitary lives, and I didn't mind spending a little extra time with them if they wanted the company.

Claudia's cheeks flushed with pleasure as she bustled around getting the cake out while I washed my hands. We sat at her little formica dinette table, and I ate my cake—which turned out to be fucking delicious, by the way—while she talked about her late husband's love of gardening and their grown daughter who was a lawyer in California.

"How long ago did your husband pass away, if you don't mind me asking?" In all the pictures of him I'd seen around the house, he'd looked fairly young.

"Oh, it was over twenty years ago. He was only fifty-one. Colon cancer. Not a pretty way to go, though I suppose none of the alternatives are especially pretty, are they?"

"Not really," I agreed, fidgeting in my seat. "I imagine it must have been hard though, losing him so young like that."

Her thin lips pursed as she brushed crumbs off the placemat in front of her. "It was, but looking back now I feel blessed to have had the time together that we did. Not many people can say they were truly happy in their marriage. I'm one of the lucky ones who can."

I nodded mutely, pushing the last bit of my cake around on my plate as a lump filled my throat.

"I notice there's no ring on your finger," she commented.

"Nope. Never been married." Shoveling the final bite of cake into my mouth, I pushed my chair back and carried my dishes to the sink.

"Never? A kind, handsome man like you? I can't believe no one's snapped you up."

Time for me to go.

Turning on the water, I hurriedly rinsed my dishes and stacked them in the sink. Maybe I could make a graceful exit before she got around to saying the thing I suspected was coming next...

"I have a niece who's about your age," Claudia said as soon as I shut off the water.

Damn.

"She just got divorced last year. If you're interested—"

"I really need to get going," I said, heading into the living room where I'd left my ladder. "Thank you for the delicious cake, Claudia. Remember to call and have us come back to replace those batteries again in a year."

She trailed me to the front door. "I've got a single nephew too, if that's more your speed."

"It's not, but I appreciate the thought. You take care." With an awkward wave, I hustled my ass out of there before she could force any phone numbers on me.

On the drive home, I tried to feel grateful there was no one waiting for me or placing demands on my time and attention. The rest of the day was mine to do with as I pleased. While I contemplated what I wanted to do with my big fat empty Saturday afternoon, I had trouble mustering a cheerful attitude. There were a few projects around the house that needed doing, but I wasn't feeling particularly motivated to tackle any of them. Honestly, I wasn't feeling like doing much of anything.

Margaret's garage door was open when I pulled into my driveway, which I thought nothing of. But as I was hauling the ladder out of the bed of my truck, a loud crashing sound came from somewhere inside the garage. Shielding my eyes from the bright sunlight, I peered into the shadowy interior.

I caught a glimpse of a blonde ponytail moving around behind her car. There was another loud crash, followed by a string of colorful curse words.

"Everything all right in there?" I called out as I abandoned the ladder to walk around the hurricane fence dividing our properties.

"Yes, fine, thank you," came her tersely shouted reply.

As I strolled up her driveway the crashing noises continued, accompanied by additional muttered curses. I found Margaret in the back corner of her garage, wielding a mop like a poleax as she attacked something on the floor.

"What on earth are you up to?" I asked, mesmerized by the sight of her all glistening and sweaty with her damp navy tank top plastered to her torso and her long legs on display in a pair of white linen shorts.

"I'm trying to kill something before it kills me." Resting her mop on the floor with a grimace, she wiped the sweat off her forehead and gestured into the corner.

"What kind of something?" I asked, moving closer. "Is it a snake?"

"It has way too many legs to be a snake, but it's bigger than any insect has a right to be."

Coming alongside Margaret, I peered into the corner. "That's a centipede."

"I've never seen one that big before."

"Me neither."

She glanced at me with a look of surprise. "I thought maybe they were all that big here, since everything's supposedly bigger in Texas."

"I mean, I've seen big ones before, but usually they're only four or five inches. This fella looks to be eight or nine, wouldn't you say?"

She shuddered. "If you want to get down there with a ruler and measure the horrific creature, be my guest."

"I'll pass, thanks. Texas redheaded centipedes are notably aggressive and have a mean bite."

Margaret lifted her mop again with an expression of grim determination. "Right then, back to killing it."

Much as I admired her mettle for taking on the giant centipede by herself, I wrapped my hand around the mop handle to stay her attack. "Hold off on that. Let me call someone."

"Who?" she asked, lowering the mop again. "An exterminator? A big-game hunter? Or a monster slayer, perhaps?"

"Someone even better than that." Bending down, I snapped a picture of the critter with my phone. After texting the photo to my half-brother Wyatt, I called his number and held the phone to my ear.

"Yo, what's up?" he said when he answered. "Why are you texting me photos of an ugly-ass bug? Is this supposed to be some kind of threat?"

"Are you with your girlfriend right now?"

"Yeah."

"Show her the picture."

Margaret gave me a questioning look, and I lowered the phone, putting it on speaker so she could hear. A few seconds later, Wyatt's girlfriend, Andie, came on the line.

"Did you just take that picture?" she asked. "Where are you? Is it still there?"

"I'm in the garage of the house next door to mine," I told her. "And I'm looking at it right now."

"How big is it?" Andie asked excitedly. "It looks big."

"Seven inches, maybe. Want to come get it?"

"We'll be right there. Keep it in your sight."

"Who was that?" Margaret asked after I'd disconnected the call.

"My brother's girlfriend works at the state park nearby. She loves this kind of thing."

Margaret's lip curled slightly as she cast a sideways glance at the centipede. "Really?"

I shrugged. "To each their own, I guess."

"So we're just supposed to hang out here with the giant nightmare bug and wait?"

"They're only ten minutes away. I can babysit Mr. Too Many Legs by myself if you want to go inside." It was hot as hell in the garage. I wouldn't blame Margaret one bit for heading back into the AC.

She looked tempted but shook her head. "I'll wait with you. It's *my* giant nightmare bug, after all."

"Suit yourself." I leaned back against the door of her SUV and crossed my arms. Did I do it because I knew it emphasized my biceps? Nah. I was only trying to get more comfortable. The fact that Margaret's gaze darted downward to skim over my arms was just a bonus.

"Are you a firefighter?" she asked, her eyes lingering on my chest.

I glanced down at my Crowder Fire Department shirt, then back up at her with a deadpan expression. "How'd you guess?"

The corner of her mouth twitched. "I took a wild stab in the dark."

Huh. Look at that. She'd actually made a joke, albeit a dry one. Had that mouth twitch been a smile trying to break free of her perma-frown? If so, it'd be the first time she'd ever smiled at me. I felt my lips curve in a responding smile of their own.

"So you rescue kittens from trees as well as giant centipedes from garages," she said, still not quite smiling, but not not-smiling either.

"I have in fact rescued a few kittens, but this is my first centipede rescue. Can't wait to write it down in my saved animal journal tonight."

Her lips did that twitching thing again as she cocked her head. "Firefighters don't really rescue cats from trees, do they? I thought that was a myth."

"We'll rescue anything from anywhere: cats, dogs, people, livestock, you name it. We're equal opportunity rescuers."

"How noble of you." Her tone was crisp and mocking—no,

not mocking, I decided. *Teasing*. That must be why it sent a twist of warmth through my chest.

Either that or it was just too hot in this fucking garage.

"What's the most interesting animal rescue you've ever done?" she asked, leaning against the car next to me.

"Besides Mr. Too Many Legs here, you mean?" I rubbed my jaw as I thought about it, enjoying her sudden show of interest after weeks of pretending to ignore my existence. "Depends on your definition of interesting, I guess. I've evacuated all sorts of pets from residential fires—guinea pigs, hamsters, and even an iguana once."

"I had a pet chameleon when I was a kid."

I raised my eyebrows in surprise. "Do they make good pets?"

"Not really. They're solitary and don't like to be handled."

Talk about pets resembling their owners. I wisely kept that thought to myself, however. "What was its name?"

"Chameleonardo da Vinci." Her lips curved all the way into a real smile at last, one so pretty and unexpectedly sweet it startled the breath right out of my lungs.

I let out a cough and cleared my throat. "You must have been an interesting kid."

She shrugged wordlessly as she stared straight ahead. In the silence that followed, I watched a drop of sweat slide from her throat down her chest and disappear inside the cleavage of her low-cut tank top.

"We had to pull a horse out of a swimming pool once," I volunteered, unwilling to let the conversation die out.

Her expression softened as her head swung toward me again. "Poor thing."

"Me or the horse?"

"The horse," she said with a huff that could have been either annoyance or amusement. It was hard to tell with her.

"It turned out all right in the end. The owner installed a

fence around their pool after that, and the horse lived happily ever after."

"That's nice to hear. I imagine your stories don't always have happy endings."

"No, not always."

A lot of our runs turned out to be either false alarms or minor emergencies with good outcomes, but then there were times you rolled up on the worst day of someone's life. Those were the days that were hard to shake off afterward.

Margaret didn't say anything, but I felt her eyes follow my movement as I reached up to rub the sweat off the back of my neck.

I gave her a sidelong look. "So do I ever get to know what it is you do for a living? Or is it still top secret?"

Her lips pressed together as she turned her face forward, giving me her profile. "I'm a management consultant."

"Is that like where companies bring you in to tell them how to manage their business better?"

"Something like that."

"Do you have to travel a lot?"

"I go wherever my clients are."

"You don't mind being away from home that much?"

"No."

"So no partner and kids back home missing you?"

"Do you want some water?" she asked abruptly, letting me know I'd pushed my luck too far. "It's awfully hot out here."

"I wouldn't say no, if you're offering."

"I'll be right back." She slipped past me on her way out of the garage, making sure to keep plenty of distance between us. "Don't lose my giant centipede while I'm gone."

Shamelessly, I watched her stride away, appreciating the luscious roundness of her ass and how much of her long legs were on display in those shorts of hers. I couldn't help myself. It was like the woman was true north and I was a goddamn compass fixated in her direction. I didn't know what it was about her that got to me so much. I wasn't usually this helplessly horny for women I barely knew.

Maybe horniness was the explanation. Possibly it had been too long since I'd let myself feel the touch of a woman, and my neglected libido was wreaking its revenge.

Contrary to what Quincy thought, I hadn't been completely celibate since my self-imposed moratorium on dating. I'd indulged in the occasional discreet hookup when the right circumstances presented themselves. Unfortunately, the right circumstances didn't come along all that often in a town of this size. I was too afraid of getting someone's hopes up and inadvertently hurting their feelings. How were you supposed to tell a woman you're not interested in anything but meaningless sex without sounding cruel? Call me old-fashioned, but I'd never gotten the hang of it.

All this was to say, it had been a spell since I'd gotten my rocks off with anyone other than myself. Gareth's crack about my right hand had landed disconcertingly close to the mark. That had to be the reason Margaret Silvestri was getting under my skin so much. My biological urges were making their demands known.

I heard her back door slam and looked up as Margaret strode toward me carrying two plastic bottles of water. That damn tank top she was wearing was too fucking much, the way it hugged her full, round breasts like a leotard. I had to forcibly tear my eyes away from the sight of them swaying with every step as she approached.

"Here," she said, thrusting one of the waters at me.

"Thanks." Our fingers touched when I took it from her, and my stomach bottomed out like I'd brushed against a live wire. Her sharp intake of breath made me wonder if she'd felt it too.

Or maybe she just disliked me that much. The way she snatched her hand back, you'd think I'd tried to bite her.

It was too hard to know why I made her so uncomfortable. Could be she was embarrassed about spying on me. Or maybe it was because she thought I was beneath her. Just a dumb meathead who was only good for looking at. It wouldn't be the first time someone had written me off because of my size and shape.

It didn't usually bother me. If people chose to jump to the wrong conclusions based on my appearance, that was their problem, not mine. I was secure enough in who I was not to need validation from small-minded strangers.

Yet it bothered me to think Margaret might feel that way about me. It bothered me a lot. I wanted her to think better of me. But I also wanted to think better of her than that.

I watched her turn away from me as she twisted the cap off her bottle and lifted it to her lips. God help me, but my gaze jumped to her breasts again when she arched her spine to tip her head back. Here I was getting all high and mighty about her leering at me when I was just as guilty. What a fucking hypocrite I was.

Gritting my teeth, I wrenched my water open and guzzled down half the bottle to wet my dry throat. As I was wiping my mouth with the back of my hand, I saw Wyatt's pickup truck pull into my driveway. Stepping to the edge of the garage, I lifted my hand to greet him and Andie.

"Thanks for coming," I said as they walked up Margaret's driveway toward me.

"Thanks for calling," Andie replied, squeezing my arm and tugging me down to her level so she could kiss my cheek. "Where is it?"

The girl had a one-track mind when it came to rare native wildlife. The creepier and crawlier it was, the more she liked it. I'd make a joke about that explaining her interest in my brother

Wyatt, except he wasn't the least bit creepy or crawly. He was a handsome charmer who worshipped the ground Andie walked on and had ever since they were kids.

Margaret came forward and introduced herself to Andie. "Hi, I'm Maggie."

I stared at her in surprise as she shook hands with Andie and then Wyatt. It hadn't even occurred to me she might be a nickname sort of person.

Margaret—Maggie—showed Andie and Wyatt where the centipede was. Andie had brought a plastic container with a screen set into the lid, and she squatted down next to the creepy-crawly.

"Oh, look at you," she cooed lovingly. "What a beauty you are."

Maggie came back over to stand by me as Andie bravely attempted to corral the angry and quick-moving centipede into the container while it did its best to bite the shit out of her. Wyatt looked on fretfully, offering lots of unhelpful advice that Andie didn't need.

While the two of them were occupied with the centipede, I shot Margaret a sideways look. "Maggie, huh?"

She shrugged. "It's what my friends call me."

"Right," I said. "Gotcha, *Margaret*."

It shouldn't get to me. What did I care? We weren't friends. She'd told me as much to my face the last time we'd spoken.

"I didn't mean..." Margaret's fingers touched my arm hesitantly as if she was afraid it might burn her. "You can call me Maggie or Margaret. I like either."

"Got it!" Andie shouted triumphantly as Wyatt cheered. She held up the container to show off the giant centipede, who was futilely trying to climb out of his slippery plastic prison.

"Goddamn, that fucker is ugly," Wyatt said, taking the words right out of my mouth. "Good job, babe."

Margaret shuddered when Andie brought it over to show it off. "What are you going to do with it?"

"I'll take it out to the park and release it somewhere it won't bother anyone."

"You're not going to keep it as a pet?" I teased her.

"Jesus, don't give her any ideas," Wyatt said. "I'm not sharing a house with that thing."

Andie grinned at him and shook her head. "Lucky for you, they're pathologically unsociable."

I cocked an eyebrow at Margaret. "Now who does that remind me of?"

If I didn't know better, I'd swear that was a smile playing on her lips.

5

MAGGIE

King's Creamery's issues weren't as straightforward as I'd hoped. So far, I hadn't turned up any major, obvious areas of waste that could be eliminated. Sure, I'd identified plenty of places where processes could be streamlined, head counts trimmed, and belts tightened, but none of it was significant enough to make more than a dent in the problem.

Well, drat.

I was due to give a status report to the CEO, COO, and CFO on Monday. I'd hoped to impress them by presenting a simple fix for the company's revenue problem, but that was looking less and less likely.

Still hoping to pull a rabbit out of my hat, I'd been holed up in my house all weekend working on my report. But it was Sunday afternoon now and my brain was tired. I was doing more staring off into space than anything as I sat at the dining room table I'd been using as an office.

The noise coming from next door wasn't helping my concentration. My neighbor Ryan was apparently hosting a backyard party. I'd started hearing car doors and chattering voices an hour ago. Shortly thereafter the music had started up, and now there was cheering and shouting happening as well.

Getting to my feet, I stretched the kinks out of my back and wandered into the kitchen to see what was going on. Ryan was definitely having a get-together of some kind. Almost a dozen people had gathered in his backyard.

But it wasn't like any kind of party I'd ever seen before. For one thing, they were all wearing kilts. Every single one of them was swathed in a different colored tartan like some sort of Scottish meeting of the clans. For another thing, they were all enormous. None were quite as tall as Ryan, whose height and red hair made him easy to spot. But they were all exceptionally thick and muscular, even the three women I counted in the mostly male group.

As if that wasn't odd enough, they all seemed to be standing around drinking beer as they watched one of the men heave a block of metal straight up into the air by the thick ring attached to it. Everyone cheered as the weight flew upward and reversed direction. I pressed my hand to my mouth, cringing as it seemed to plummet back to earth directly at the thrower's head. The man, who sported a beard and long hair worthy of a rock star, stayed where he was and calmly watched over his shoulder as the weight landed safely several yards behind him.

I lowered my hand to my chest, where my heart was still racing, and saw Ryan peel off from the group and bend over to open a cooler. As he straightened with a beer in his hand, he happened to glance my way and catch me watching him through the window.

A now-familiar—and not entirely unpleasant—prickling sensation stole over my skin as our gazes clashed. Just like the day when he'd been washing his truck, he broke into a grin and waved at me. This time, however, I was more prepared for it—and for the way his smile made my belly clench. Instead of fleeing like a coward, I stood my ground and lifted my hand to return his greeting.

His grin grew wider as he made what looked like a come-here gesture. My forehead furrowed in confusion, and I shook my head.

Undeterred, he pointed at me and repeated the gesture. In case that wasn't clear enough, he set his hand to the side of his mouth and bellowed, "Hey, Margaret! Come over and have a beer!"

I felt my ears grow hot as Ryan's guests all turned to see who he was shouting at. And yet I found myself strangely tempted to take him up on the offer. I'd been here over a month without socializing other than at the office, and I was tired of staring at the inside of my house. In addition, the weather had been steadily improving throughout September, and this afternoon was the closest thing to a pleasant temperature we'd had since I'd arrived.

Why not take Ryan up on his offer? It wouldn't kill me to be friendly for a few minutes. I could certainly use the break. My mind made up, I slipped into a pair of sneakers and stepped out the back door where I was greeted by the smell of grilling meat.

Ryan grabbed a second beer out of the cooler and ambled over to meet me as I walked across my driveway to the fence between our yards. He moved with impressive grace for someone of his size, like a man in perfect command of every muscle in his body. Speaking of muscles, the sleeves of his navy blue T-shirt had been cut off into a muscle shirt, exposing the glorious, freckled caps of his shoulders. With his giant arms on display, the whole red plaid kilt and white knee socks aesthetic was far sexier than it had any right to be.

"You actually came out," he said, twisting the cap off the beer bottle before handing it across the fence. "I can't believe it. I didn't think you would."

I accepted it with thanks as my gaze lingered over the tattoo on his left shoulder, which I could see now was an intricate Celtic knot design. "My curiosity got the better of me. What's going on over there?"

"What? This?" He hooked a thumb at the gathering behind him. "Just an informal meetup of our local Highland Games club."

"Highland Games as in Scotland? Isn't that where people toss a telephone pole?"

His lips quirked with amusement. "It's called a caber, and it's not quite as big as a telephone pole. But that's one of the events, yeah."

I raised an eyebrow as I sipped my beer. "You're not planning to practice doing that in your backyard, are you?"

The sound of his deep, rumbling laugh sent a warm buzz through my whole body. "Definitely not. One of the guys has a farm he lets us use to practice the caber, hammer throw, sheaf toss, and weight for distance."

"*Sheep* toss?" I asked incredulously.

"Sheaf," Ryan corrected, choking down another laugh. "It's a burlap bag stuffed with straw."

"But you really throw hammers? At what?"

"At an empty field. The point is to see how far you can throw it, not to hit anything."

Encouraging shouts from the group behind him had him turning around to watch as one of the women got ready to throw the weight next. I smiled at the back of Ryan's shirt, which said *KEEP TEXAS KILTED*. When the woman sent the weight flying up in the air, Ryan let out an ear-piercing whistle of approval.

"Has anyone ever dropped that weight on their head?" I asked, trying not to visibly flinch.

He took a drag of his beer as he turned back to me. "I'm not gonna say never, but I've yet to see it happen. It's a lot safer than it looks from a distance."

"I certainly hope so. And this is what you all do for fun?"

"This is practice, but most of us compete in Highland Games around the state. There's a local one coming up in November that we're training for."

"I had you pegged as a football player. Scottish Games never even crossed my mind."

"I played some football in high school. Didn't like it all that much. This is more my speed."

"I guess that explains your tattoo," I said, letting my gaze fall on his bare inked shoulder. "I hope you're wearing sunscreen with all those freckles."

"Don't tell me you're concerned about my well-being, Margaret. Someone might consider that neighborly behavior." He cocked his head toward the group of practicing athletes. "Want to come give the weight a throw?"

"No thank you. I have a rule against throwing heavy things in the air above my head."

"At least come over and meet everyone." His gray eyes twinkled. "You can watch me throw when it's my turn."

I very much wanted to see that, far more than I was willing to let on. But I wasn't so sure about meeting everyone else. "I've got a lot of work to do for tomorrow. I should probably get back inside."

"Come on, stay for a few more minutes. There's venison sausage on the grill if you're hungry."

My nose wrinkled as I realized that was what the delicious odor was. "Bambi sausage?"

"Don't knock it till you've tried it. Shane makes it himself with his own secret blend of seasonings, and it's the best damn sausage I've ever tasted."

"That's okay. I don't really—" I broke off when Ryan reached across the fence to cup my elbow with his big hand, and the shock of his touch brought my brain function to a screeching halt.

"Stay for a little while." His fingertips only exerted the lightest of touches, but the small contact rippled through me like an electric current, swamping me with heat.

Helpless to resist, I let myself be guided along the fence and onto his driveway. He kept his hand on my arm, his fingers skimming over my skin as he escorted me into his backyard and over to the picnic table by the grill. Even then, he didn't let go as he set his beer down and unfolded a packet of foil, spearing a bite-sized slice of sausage with a plastic fork.

"You have to try this." His eyes locked with mine, his expression encouraging and expectant as he held the fork in front of my face.

Did he intend to feed the sausage to me himself? Surely not. Our superficial acquaintance didn't meet the level of intimacy required for putting food directly into each other's mouths to be considered acceptable.

I should reach up and take the fork from him. Except my free hand was attached to the arm he was still holding, making my blood feel thick and hot as lava in my veins, and I couldn't seem to make myself move it.

My mouth opened with the intention of politely declining the proffered food, but instead I found myself opening wider when he moved the fork closer. Gingerly, he placed the bite of sausage just inside my lips, and my teeth closed around it as he slid the fork free. At that point I had no choice but to eat it.

A smile danced in Ryan's eyes as he watched me swallow. "Well? Best sausage you've ever tasted, right?"

I wanted to deny it, but I couldn't. Bambi or no, it was delicious. "It's all right," I managed in an unsteady voice.

The way his cheeks dimpled made me feel light-headed. "Told you you'd love it."

"It's not as bad as I expected" was all I was willing to concede.

His lips curved as we stared at each other for a long moment while I fought the urge to return his smile.

What am I doing? I had no business flirting with this man. Nothing good could come of it. I needed to get control of myself and walk away.

I edged backward, about to make my apologies and escape. But before I could, Ryan was hailed by his friends calling out that he was up next.

"Come on," he said, shepherding me toward the waiting onlookers. "Come watch me throw."

Well. I couldn't very well leave *now*. What would be the point of *that*?

"Everybody, this is my new neighbor, Maggie," he announced when we reached the others. "Maggie, this is everybody." Having completed this expansive introduction, he removed his hand from my arm finally and walked over to the weight, leaving me on my own surrounded by strangers.

"Hello," I said, offering a polite smile to the group.

Their answering greetings were friendly, although I felt many a curious eye lingering on me as I turned to watch Ryan. I couldn't help wondering if any of them worked for King's. Were any of their names part of the head count I'd been studying all weekend?

Ignoring their stares, I focused on Ryan as he bent to pick up the weight by the metal ring. He hiked his kilt up with his left hand, exposing a pair of black bike shorts as he braced his palm on his enormous thigh, answering any question I might have about what he was wearing under his kilt. His face set in a frown of concentration as he swung the weight between his legs. Once...twice... On the third time he popped his hips and extended his arm overhead as he let the weight fly. It arced upward, reaching what I'd estimate to be a height of fifteen feet before landing on the ground behind him.

I joined in the applause as everyone cheered, impressed as much by the grace of Ryan's throw as by the obvious show of strength.

"You ever throw before?" asked a man standing beside me.

"No, never," I answered, looking over at him.

He was one of the smaller men present, leaner than some of the others and of a height with my six feet, though he was still impressively burly by any ordinary standard. His face had a boyish handsomeness to it that I imagined made him quite popular with the ladies around town, and his cocky smile said he knew exactly how good-looking he was.

"You've got a good body for it," he said, brazenly looking me up and down.

"Jesus, Gareth, could you be more of a d-bag?" said the woman standing on his other side. She was only a little shorter than me with thick, muscular thighs showing between her miniskirt-length kilt and pink knee socks. "Don't mind him," she told me. "He's not housebroken yet."

"What?" Gareth spread his hands to protest his innocence. "Tell me she doesn't look like she'd be a natural."

"It's true. You've got the perfect proportions for it." The woman leaned across him, casually shoving him back with her shoulder as she thrust her hand out at me. "I'm Kenzie, by the way."

"Maggie," I said, shaking her hand. Her grip was firm, callused, and chalky. "Nice to meet you."

"Seriously, if you ever want to give it a try, we'd love to have you. We could always use more women in the sport."

"I don't really think it's my thing."

"Never know until you try it," Gareth said.

"Are they trying to recruit you?" Ryan asked, appearing at my side.

Kenzie shrugged. "I was just telling Maggie we'd be happy to teach her the basics if she ever wants to come to one of our training seshes."

One of Ryan's eyebrows lifted as his gaze settled on my face. "Let me guess: she said no, didn't she?"

I gazed back at him without answering, since he hadn't directed the question at me. And he wasn't wrong, which irked me. I didn't like that he thought he knew me so well.

"It was worth a shot," Kenzie said.

"You should bring her to the park next weekend to watch us practice the Braemar stone," Gareth suggested.

"She won't want to do that." Ryan's eyes drilled into me. "I'm sure she's got better things to do."

I got the sense he was baiting me, attempting to provoke me into agreeing. The annoying thing was it made me want to say yes, just like he knew it would. "I know what you're doing, and it's not going to work."

"I'm not doing anything." Ryan's expression was placid. Pure innocence. Utterly infuriating.

"I should get back to work," I said. *Because you're making me feel light-headed and reckless, and I need to leave before I accidentally flirt with you more than I already have.* "Thank you for the beer and the throwing demonstration."

Ryan's chin dipped. If he was disappointed, he was a master at hiding it. "Anytime, Maggie."

"It was nice to meet you," I said to Gareth and Kenzie before shooting a final glance at Ryan. "Try not to drop any weights on your head, Freckles."

The smile that curved his lips made my heart give an ill-advised squeeze. Before my mouth could run away with me again, I turned and made my way back to my house, trying not to think about the fact that Ryan's eyes were on me as I walked away.

6

RYAN

Twenty minutes earlier than expected, I knocked on my brother Manny's door. I was there to babysit so he could take his wife out to celebrate their anniversary tonight, but I'd showed up early hoping to get a few minutes with him before they left.

He wasn't my brother by blood, but he might as well have been. We'd been best friends most of our lives, much like my stepfather and Manny's dad had been best friends. When Manny was ten, his parents had died in a boating accident, and my mother and stepfather had adopted him. Manny and I were the same age, so that and the fact that we'd both been outsiders brought into the King family—me as George King's stepson and Manny as his adopted son—had bonded us together as kids.

Of all my step- and half-siblings, Manny was the one I was closest to. As much as I loved my two half-brothers, Tanner and Wyatt, they were seven and nine years younger than me, and I'd always felt more like a parent to them than a brother. Especially after our mom died. George wasn't the most nurturing father in the world, so I'd tried to look out for them the way our mom would have if she'd been around.

When Manny flung open the door, the harried expression on his face told me I'd made the right call coming early. "You're a lifesaver," he said, fumbling with the buttons on his shirt as he stood back to admit me. "Seriously. You have no idea how much we appreciate this. I could kiss you."

"It's not a problem." I tapped him on the stomach as I edged past him into the entryway of the house where he lived with his wife, Adriana, and their two kids. "You missed a button."

He looked down and muttered a curse he was forced to bite off when his three-year-old daughter appeared.

"Uncle Ryan!" she squealed at the top of her lungs as she flew at me like a guided missile.

I scooped her off the floor and dangled her in front of my face. "Wait a second," I said, squinting at her. "You look kinda like my niece Isabella, but you're way too big to be her. Who are you?"

"I'm Isabella!" she shouted.

"You sure about that?" I asked, settling her on my hip as I carried her into the living room.

"Yes!" Giggling, she smacked her tiny hands on my cheeks. "It's me! I'm Isabella."

"In that case, you know what time it is, don't you?"

"What time is it?" she asked, her eyes growing wide and serious.

"It's time for...*bear kisses!*" I let out a growl as I rubbed my stubbly face against her cheek while she shrieked and laughed, pretending to fight me off.

Once I decided she'd had enough—or that I'd had enough, anyway—I set her down on the floor, and she tore out of the room shouting, "Run away! The bear's after me!"

"Where's the baby?" I asked Manny, who'd followed us into the living room and was tucking in the tails of his shirt after finally managing to get his buttons straight.

"Adriana's giving him one last feeding before we go."

I eyed Manny, evaluating him for signs of more than just the usual exhaustion. "How've you been? Haven't seen you in a few weeks."

Not since we'd gone to lunch last month right after he'd found out that George King was actually his biological father. Not only that, George had known all along and never said boo to anyone—including Manny. And he probably never would have if Tanner hadn't stumbled across an old paternity test and spilled the beans.

It had been a bit of a bombshell, to say the least. Although Manny had seemed to handle it fairly well, all things considered. Especially after George explained that Manny's parents had asked him to be a sperm donor because of fertility troubles, and it had been kept a secret at their request. Knowing he wasn't the product of an affair had made the whole thing easier for Manny to swallow, though I still wondered if he had any lingering resentment over being kept in the dark.

I'd tried to put myself in his shoes by imagining how I'd feel if I suddenly found out George was my biological father after all these years. But my situation was too different from Manny's. Given the kind of man my real father had been and the genetic legacy he'd stuck me with, I'd be too fucking relieved to feel anything but happy.

"I'm sorry," Manny said, giving me a guilty look. "Things have been crazy busy the last month."

"So the same as always, then?"

Between his job, his wife, and his kids, Manny didn't have a lot of time leftover for anything else these days, including me. I wasn't resentful, but I missed him. I had plenty of friends, but few truly close relationships. It wasn't my way to open up, so all most people ever saw of me was the cheerful, even-tempered exterior I let them see.

The truth was, I'd been feeling increasingly lonely recently. Even Tanner and Wyatt didn't need me as much as they used to now that they both had serious girlfriends to keep them company. I was as happy for them as I was for Manny, but it felt like everyone was leaving me behind. Most people would partner up eventually and start families of their own, but that would never be me. They'd all get busy with their own lives, and I'd still be all on my own. I'd tried to make my peace with it, but sometimes reality still stung.

"No, it's worse than usual. Things at work have been..." Manny grimaced and shook his head when Isabella skipped back into the room and dumped an armful of toy ponies at my feet.

"What?" I prompted as I let her tug me down to the floor. "Tell me."

I'd never had any interest in going to work for the King family business like Manny had, so we didn't talk about the company all that much. But if something at work was stressing him out, I wanted to hear about it.

He sank onto the couch with a sigh. "I assume you've heard revenues have been trending down for a while?"

"I heard." A lot of George's kids worked for the company, so I heard things here and there. Nate hardly talked about anything else, even in the family group text. "Is it really that bad?"

"It's pretty bad, yeah."

Isabella thrust a pony and hairbrush into my hands, and I got to work brushing its mane. "Layoffs bad?"

"We don't know yet, but I'm guessing yes. It's bad enough that George and Terry brought in an outside management consultant to advise them."

My head jerked up at the title. "What's her name?"

"Maggie Silvestri." Manny gave me an odd look. "How'd you know it was a her?"

"She's renting the Meckel house next door to me."

"You know her?"

"Just a passing acquaintance. She didn't tell me who she was working for." I'd wondered if the creamery might be the client who'd brought Maggie here, but it hadn't occurred to me she'd be reporting directly to George. She must be a pretty big deal if he'd brought her in personally.

"She's supposed to be some kind of expert at turning companies around when they're in trouble."

"By laying people off?" If that was the case, it explained why she was so reluctant to make friends with anyone. I wouldn't want to make friends with people either if I was the one who decided whether they got to keep their jobs or not.

"Among other things, but yeah, it's definitely one of the scenarios on the table. Assuming she can't find other ways to reduce costs and increase revenue."

"Sounds like she's got her work cut out for her."

"We all do. She's analyzing every department's spending from top to bottom, so she's got us all running ragged trying to justify every dime we spend."

"Sounds like a real pain in the ass."

"It is. I mean, I get why it's necessary, but with the extra work plus worrying about what's going to happen to the people who work for me, it's been a rough few weeks. Employee morale's been in the dumpster since word spread about why she's here."

"I can imagine."

Unhappy with my technique, Isabella confiscated my brush and pony with a disapproving tut and climbed into my lap to demonstrate the proper grooming of plastic toy ponies. "Not like that. Like this."

Keeping one eye on Isabella's lesson, I addressed Manny again. "So other than the work stuff, how've you been doing? How are things between you and George these days?"

"All right, actually."

I raised an eyebrow as I studied him, trying to decide if he was telling the truth, or telling me what he thought I wanted to hear.

Manny held his hands up. "I swear. After I got over the initial shock, it didn't feel like such a big deal."

"You really mean that?" I asked as I picked up one of Isabella's extra brushes and ran it through her wavy black hair. She'd inherited her mom's curls and rich bronze complexion rather than Manny's stick-straight hair and lighter golden skin. It was funny I'd never noticed how much he resembled the other King kids. Now that I knew, it was obvious that he shared their long noses, angular jaws, and that charming King smile.

"It's all water under the bridge at this point," he said with a shrug. "What does it really matter who my DNA donor was? As far as I'm concerned, Manuel Reyes is still my dad and always will be. But George stepped up when I needed him, and that counts for a lot."

I nodded in understanding. For all his flaws, George had been there for me in a big way too. Enough that he'd earned the right to my understanding and some forgiveness for a lot of his mistakes. "You're not running out to change your name to King, then?"

Manny snorted. "Hell no. I'm happy being a Reyes, thanks. Although I think Nate's afraid I will. He's been acting weird ever since he found out."

"That doesn't surprise me." I divided a brushed section of Isabella's hair and started to braid it. She loved to have her hair played with, so it was a good way to keep her still and distracted while her dad and I talked. "Nate sees everything as a competition he's terrified of losing."

He was one of four kids from George's first marriage to Trish Buchanan, the woman he'd divorced before he married my mom. The two oldest kids were long gone: Chance had died nearly twenty years ago, and his twin brother Brady had run off to be a musician and cut ties with the family. That had left Nate to fill the hole left by Chance, who'd been expected to take over the family business one day. Nate had spent every day since then killing himself to please his father and prove himself worthy.

But both Manny and Nate's younger sister Josie had given Nate a run for his money and risen to a comparable level of seniority in the company. Knowing how unpredictable George could be, I wouldn't even venture to guess which one of them he was most likely to name as his chosen successor.

Since Manny was a year older than Nate, the recent paternity revelation made him the first-born biological son—at least out of the ones who were still around—for whatever that was worth. I doubted it made much difference for George's plans, but it was easy to imagine the news had thrown Nate for a loop after he'd devoted all of his adult life to the idea that he was the heir apparent.

"I feel bad for him," Manny said. "He's so emotionally invested in the company, it's like it's the only thing he cares about. He doesn't have any kind of life outside of work. That's no way to live."

"It's not a recipe for happiness, that's for sure." I glanced up as I smoothed the braid I'd put in Isabella's hair. "You think Nate resents you?"

Manny shook his head. "It's not that. He's just...on edge. We all are, but Nate seems to be taking everything as some sort of personal failure on his part."

"That boy desperately needs to get laid," Adriana said, walking into the room with their son, Jorge, propped on her shoulder.

"There's my nephew," I said, holding out my arms. "Hand him over."

"Have at it." Adriana passed him down to me. "I need to go grab my shoes."

Nestling Jorge into the crook of my arm, I bent down for a sniff of his sweet baby head. "I can't believe how fast he's growing. It feels like yesterday I was catching this tiny, wriggling newborn with my very own hands to welcome him into the world."

Manny rolled his eyes. "You're never going to stop rubbing that in my face, are you?"

"Not a chance," I said, making a silly face at the baby as he gurgled and drooled.

I'd delivered Jorge myself after Adriana's water broke at the grocery store. My engine crew happened to be the first on scene in response to the panicked store manager's 911 call. That baby had been in such a big hurry to come into the world there hadn't even been time to transport them to the hospital. Manny had barely made it there in time to witness the birth of his son along with the rest of my crew.

"You sure you're up for this babysitting challenge?" Adriana asked me, coming back into the room with a pair of high heels dangling from her fingers. "Jorge's teething, so he's extra fussy."

"Absolutely." She and Manny didn't get to go out for a romantic night together very often. They deserved a break to enjoy a relaxing, adults-only meal without fending off spit-up or temper tantrums. "Isabella's gonna be my deputy and help me take care of her baby brother, right?"

"Uh huh." She looked up from her ponies and nodded with utmost seriousness. "I'm the big sister. That's my job."

"See?" I told Adriana. "We've got everything under control."

"You're a saint," she said as she slipped on her heels. "Not many single men would volunteer to take on an infant and a potty-training toddler solo."

"It's not a big deal," I said with a shrug. "I love kids. Especially these kids."

She and Manny couldn't understand how much I loved hanging out with their kids. Being with them was the closest I'd ever get to having the family of my own I'd always wanted, so I took advantage of every opportunity I had to see them.

Who knew how many years I even had left when I'd be able to play with these kids? Maybe I'd be around to watch them grow up, but there was a chance I wouldn't. I had to enjoy being their uncle while I still could.

7

MAGGIE

The office they gave me at King's Creamery was on the executive floor at the top of the corporate headquarters building. Because my work often involved confidential, delicate, or unpleasant conversations, I was off to myself at the far end of a row of offices occupied by the senior members of the legal department. Which meant I didn't tend to get people strolling past my office unless they were specifically coming to see me.

The next meeting on my calendar wasn't until after lunch, so I was surprised to see Josie King, the EVP of marketing, striding past the glass wall of my office. When she stopped at my open door, I could tell at once from her grim expression that something was wrong. Something big enough that she'd felt the need to seek me out in person rather than send an email.

"Sorry to interrupt," she said. "I need to talk to you about something urgently."

I gestured her inside. "Of course."

Josie closed the door behind her, and I braced myself for bad news as she perched on one of the chairs facing my desk and smoothed her black pencil skirt. Her stylish appearance set her apart from most of her colleagues at the creamery. Like me, she favored designer suits and sky-high heels that emphasized her tall, slim frame and looked more like something you'd expect to see on Madison Avenue than in the corridors of a Texas ice cream company known for its small-town roots and hippie vibe. Her fashion sense was less surprising when you knew she'd spent most of her career rising through the ranks at major ad agencies in Dallas and then Manhattan before coming back home two years ago to take over marketing for her family's company and build an in-house ad agency.

"I just got off the phone with a business reporter from the Austin newspaper," Josie said. "He wanted a comment for a story that's going to run in tomorrow's paper."

"What's the story?" I asked as my sense of foreboding increased. I'd never once known it to be a good thing when a reporter asked for a comment on a forthcoming story.

"It's about the company's financial troubles and the expense-cutting measures we're allegedly planning in the face of declining revenues. He claims to have an inside source who told him we're discussing a major restructuring that would include closing the Crowder plant and relocating the corporate headquarters to our distribution facility in Oklahoma."

"That's categorically untrue," I said. "Unless those discussions are happening without my involvement."

"The source specifically attributes the plans to you."

"Then his source is full of shit, because I haven't made any such recommendation. I haven't even completed enough of my analysis to be anywhere near ready to propose something that big."

"I'm afraid that's not all," Josie said with a grimace. "The article includes an extensive profile of you and your work as a consultant that describes how you've come into other companies and gutted their head count, putting thousands of people out of work over the course of your career. At one point you're referred to as the 'harbinger of death.'"

I cast my eyes to the ceiling with a sigh. "Lovely. Although I've been called far worse, I suppose." Just not in a story printed in a major newspaper. That would be a personal first.

Josie offered me a tight, sympathetic smile. "The whole thing reads like a hit piece, and I have no idea where it's coming from. I was hoping you might have some idea."

"I wish I did. There's no shortage of people out there with reason to harbor a grudge against me, unfortunately." The claim that I'd put thousands of people out of work wasn't an exaggeration. That most of those people would have lost their jobs anyway without my intervention didn't change the fact that I'd been responsible for making the call to eliminate certain jobs in order to save others. "What's your sense of this reporter? Is he just fishing? Do you think he'd go so far as to make up a source?"

"I don't think so," Josie said. "I've dealt with him before, and he's always been reasonable and professional. I have to assume his source is feeding him false information."

"Okay, but he's not going to take some loose cannon's word for it without any corroboration, is he?"

Josie's lips pressed into a tight line. "He says his source provided him with copies of internal communications that back up his claims."

"That's impossible." No such communications existed. Or if they did, I'd never seen them. They certainly hadn't come from me.

She looked down at her phone and swiped her finger across the screen. "I convinced him to email me what he had so I could offer a comment on it. Let's see if he's sent it yet... Here we go. I'm forwarding it to you so you can see for yourself."

Pulling my laptop closer, I tabbed to my email and waited for the forwarded message from Josie to download. It took a few seconds, because it contained several image attachments that turned out to be screenshots.

"Shit," I said when I saw what they were. Because they had come from me after all.

"I've never seen these before," Josie said as she squinted at the email on her phone. "Do you recognize them?"

"Yes," I admitted, rubbing my forehead. "I wrote them."

Her hazel eyes snapped to me as she raised her perfectly shaped brows. "Explain."

"They're from the presentation packet I prepared for my preliminary meeting with Terry Goodrich when we were first discussing the possibility of an engagement." Terry was the company's COO and the man who'd first reached out to express interest in my consulting services. I'd spoken with him on the phone several times before he'd set up a virtual meeting for me to make a formal pitch that he could pass on to the CEO. Only after that was I flown out to meet George King in person to receive his seal of approval.

"So it was before you actually started working here?"

"Correct. I didn't have access to any of the company's internal reports or systems yet. I was working from publicly available information when I created this presentation."

"Well that's something, I guess."

"These screenshots have been taken completely out of context. They're not recommendations, but hypothetical examples of the different kinds of solutions I'd be capable of overseeing. These particular slides were meant to illustrate projected timelines for varying scopes of reorgs *if* they should be deemed necessary."

"Right. Okay." Josie's brow furrowed as she chewed her lower lip. "So who's seen this presentation besides Terry Goodrich?"

"I sent it to Terry, and he forwarded it to the CFO, Bruce Pollard, when he invited him to sit in on my virtual presentation.

I assume it was also sent to your father at some point. That's all I know about."

"Have you shared it with anyone outside the company?" Josie asked. "Anyone at all?"

"Definitely not."

"All right, so I need to identify everyone who's had access to it internally."

"I'm sorry," I told her. "I never meant for those slides to be taken this way."

"I don't think it's your fault. It sounds like we've got a Benedict Arnold in our midst trying to stir shit up, which isn't something you could have foreseen or prevented."

"Do you think you'll be able to stop the newspaper from publishing the article?"

"Based on what you've told me, I doubt it. If I could claim the documents were outright fakes, that'd be one thing. All I can do is try to explain the context, and I'm not sure that'll be enough to put him off the story."

"But there's no story there. The conversations they're claiming to have knowledge of haven't even happened yet."

"Let me ask you this: Is there any possibility you'll propose closing the Crowder plant or relocating corporate HQ? Can you tell me with one hundred percent certainty that it's not on the table?"

I hesitated, giving her question serious consideration. Based on what I knew so far, my instincts told me such measures would neither be necessary nor the most effective solution to the company's problems. But I still needed more data before I could finish doing all my cost-benefit analyses. As much as I wanted to give Josie the guarantee she was looking for, I couldn't rule out the possibility entirely. "It would be premature for me to make that kind of judgment at this point."

She sighed, her polished veneer cracking a little. It wasn't often that she let her emotions show, but I could see how troubled she was by the situation. "If that's the case, I can't refute the claims outright. Not if there's a chance we might end up going that route. False reassurances will only bite us in the ass even harder later."

"So what will you do?"

"We'll have to try and reassure people somehow without lying to them." She offered me an implacable smile as she got to her feet. "But you let me worry about that. It's my problem to manage."

"I'm sorry for my part in what's happening."

"It's not your fault," she said, pausing at the office door before opening it. "But I'm afraid it's going to make your life here a lot more uncomfortable for a while. The article sets you up as the villain who's going to kill the town of Crowder. People around here aren't going to take that lightly."

LEAVING the house this morning had been a mistake.

Ever since the article about me in the Austin paper had hit front porches and newsstands yesterday, I'd been subjected to whispers and dirty looks. Josie's attempt at damage control—a company-wide email from George King himself denouncing the article's claims as baseless and wildly premature—didn't seem to have done much to change hearts and minds. All day at work on Friday, I'd felt side-eyes and accusing glares follow me through the halls of the office.

I should have known better than to come to the grocery store this morning. I should have holed up in my house all weekend until emotions had cooled more. I'd known the article would provoke a negative reaction, but I hadn't realized how strong the impact would be. I'd thought I could handle it.

I was wrong.

I'd underestimated how quickly and thoroughly news traveled in a small town like this. And how much hostility people would feel free to express to my face.

The stares started up as soon as I walked through the automatic doors of the grocery store. As heads swung in my direction, more than one expression hardened with recognition. The online version of the article had helpfully included a full-color headshot of me taken from my website. My face had become locally famous overnight.

Ignoring the unfriendly glares, I edited my shopping list down in my head as I grabbed a small shopping cart. Instead of doing the full shop I'd planned, I decided I'd just grab a few necessities, just enough to get me through the next several days. I wouldn't have come at all, but there was currently nothing in my house to eat except Cheerios dust, a hunk of moldy cheese, and two stale heels of a loaf of bread.

In the produce department, three different people stopped in their tracks to give me the evil eye as I hurried past. I heard one of them mutter "fucking bitch" under her breath as I seized avocados at random without even bothering to check for mushiness.

More resentful stares and whispers followed me as I rushed through the store, but I kept my head down and endeavored to tune them out. I understood their anger, even if I believed it was misplaced. They were frightened for their livelihoods and those of their loved ones. Contrary to public opinion, I wasn't uncaring. I'd always been deeply aware of the impact my recommendations had on the lives of real people and their families, and I carried that burden heavily.

Not that it mattered to the people who lived here. If King's Creamery relocated, it wouldn't just be the people employed by the company who'd suffer. Such a move would devastate the town's tourism trade, real estate market, and entire commercial economy. There wasn't any business here that wouldn't suffer from the loss. The disinvestment, unemployment, and diminished tax base would quickly turn Crowder into a ghost town, another victim of rural blight.

There was no way to explain to the people around me in this grocery store that I was hoping to avoid such an outcome. Or that if it did come to that, it would be a last resort undertaken only because the company's demise was otherwise inevitable. If things stayed the way they were, King's Creamery would go out of business anyway and take the town with it.

The people who were staring daggers at me as I hastened through the frozen foods didn't know that. They didn't know *me*. So I tried not to take their hatred personally. They were reacting out of fear based on the distorted facts they'd been given by what should have been a trustworthy news source. Who could blame them for being upset?

I turned into the pasta aisle, my final stop before I could make my escape from the resentful looks. Dropping a package of spaghetti into my shopping cart, I attempted to make my way toward the checkout, but found the aisle blocked by two carts that had stopped alongside each other.

A middle-aged couple and a youngish man in a green baseball cap appeared to be responsible for the two inconveniently placed carts. The three of them eyed me with similarly cold expressions, making no effort to get out of the way as I slowly pushed my cart toward them.

"Excuse me," I said in my politest voice. "I just need to get by."

"What do you think you're doing here?" the younger man challenged.

I met his hostile gaze, refusing to betray any reaction despite the prickling hairs of alarm on the back of my neck. "I'm trying to buy some groceries, if you don't mind."

"We do mind, actually," said the older man. "We mind a hell of a lot."

"You're not welcome here," the younger man said.

"I'm happy to leave if you'd let me get by."

"I want to ask you a question first," the woman shot back. "What's it like to have no soul?"

Ignoring her, I turned my cart around to go the other direction but found two men had entered the aisle behind me. They stood shoulder to shoulder watching me with their arms crossed. Their unfriendly expressions told me they wouldn't be inclined to let me pass that way either.

All my escape routes had been cut off. I was trapped.

8

MAGGIE

"You think you can swan into town with your big fancy salary and kill everything we've worked our whole lives for? You think we're going to stand by and let you do that?"

Clenching my jaw, I gripped the strap of my shoulder bag as I turned around to face the older man behind me who'd just spoken. I had my pepper spray inside my bag if things got really bad, but I didn't want to believe that anyone would go so far as to physically attack me in the middle of a crowded grocery store on a Saturday morning. A woman watching the situation unfold from the far end of the aisle had a toddler in her shopping cart. Surely no one would allow things to get that ugly with children around.

Still, my amygdala insisted on reminding me that people could be unpredictable and unreasonable. You could never really know what was going to inspire a stranger to violence, especially when they felt emboldened by the support of onlookers. Mobs could quickly get out of control and behave outside the bounds of reason.

"What do we have here?" asked a rumbling, deep voice behind me.

I glanced over my shoulder and felt a surge of relief at the sight of my neighbor, Ryan the fireman, standing by the endcap at the aisle behind me.

But my relief was quickly displaced by a flicker of uncertainty. What if Ryan was just as angry with me as everyone else? I had no claim on his loyalty and no right to expect that he'd take my side against his own town. Maybe he was here to express his displeasure too.

When the two men blocking that end of the aisle swiveled their heads to look at him, Ryan greeted them both with a genial nod. "Roland. Nick. What's up?"

"Nothing," one of them mumbled as Ryan ambled toward them.

They didn't look nearly as intimidating with Ryan bearing down on them. In fact, unless I was mistaken, they looked a little worried. And guilty, like they'd been caught doing something they knew was wrong.

Ryan strode straight down the center of the aisle, leaving them to get out of his way. Which they did, backing up against the shelves awkwardly as he brushed past.

His gaze fixed on me, and all the geniality faded from his expression. "What's going on, y'all?"

"We're just having a friendly chat," the older man behind me answered before I could say anything.

"Doesn't look all that friendly to me." Ryan came to stand next to me, his towering bulk a reassuring presence at my side as he focused on the man who'd spoken. "Looks to me like you've got a woman cornered, Gene. Five against one by my count."

"We're only talking," the woman snapped defensively.

"Is that right? What are you talking about?" Ryan's tone was mild, but there was an unmistakable note of censure in it. "Are you rolling out the welcome wagon, Sheila? Showing the lady here what Crowder hospitality is like?"

"Something like that," she muttered, refusing to meet his eye.

"You know who this is?" challenged the younger man in the baseball cap, puffing up his chest in a show of bravado.

Ryan laid his big hand on my shoulder, sending an unmistakable signal to everyone present that I was under his protection. "I know exactly who she is."

I wanted to resent being relegated to the role of a powerless maiden who needed the protection of an alpha male. But since I was still coming down from my initial adrenaline spike of alarm, I couldn't manage to feel anything but grateful for the comforting weight of Ryan's hand and the warm press of his arm at my back. I was glad he'd happened to be here and was apparently willing to stand up for me.

His gaze narrowed as it traveled over the three ringleaders of the grocery store posse. "It occurs to me, Dale, now that you've brought it up, maybe we should all go around and introduce ourselves by our first and last names. Just to make sure Maggie here knows exactly who everyone is."

From the way they all paled at the suggestion, I guessed at least some of them were employed by King's Creamery. They'd been counting on anonymity to protect them, but if Ryan revealed their names, I could ensure they lost their jobs.

Dale's eyes narrowed with contempt as they zeroed in on Ryan. "Why are you sticking up for the likes of her, McCafferty? Are you getting a piece of that ass or something?"

Ryan's expression went hard as his eyes blazed with anger. "Ex-*cuse* me?"

Despite the small flinch he betrayed at Ryan's fury, Dale

stubbornly refused to back down. "That's the only reason I can think why you'd choose to stand there defending that woman. You saw that article in the *Statesman* yesterday, didn't you? You know she wants to move King's Creamery to Oklahoma and put everyone in town out of work?"

Ryan continued to stare daggers at Dale. "You really believe that's true? I gotta say, I'm surprised any of you would take the word of some out-of-town reporter when you know as well as I do that around here the buck stops with George King and no one else. Nobody's doing anything at that company unless it's at his behest, so it seems to me your concerns are better directed to George than Ms. Silvestri here. But even if she was the Wicked Witch of the West like you want to believe, that doesn't make it all right to gang up on a woman like a pack of dogs. I'm ashamed of all y'all for behaving this way."

An uncomfortable silence followed this speech. We'd drawn quite an audience by that point. A group of onlookers hovered at the end of the aisle, watching the scene unfold from a safe distance. I suspected if I looked over my shoulder, I'd find even more spectators gathered behind us.

The older man, Gene, spoke up again, the lines of his grizzled face set in a grim expression. "I've worked at that plant my whole life, just like my father before me. You know that, Ryan."

"I do," Ryan said solemnly.

"I'm five years away from claiming my pension." Gene turned his head, addressing his next rueful words to me. "What am I supposed to do if they lay me off now?"

I had no answer to give him. There was nothing I could say to put his well-founded fears to rest. I couldn't tell him that King's Creamery was on track to file for bankruptcy before he ever saw a cent of his pension. Even if I wasn't constrained by an NDA, I doubted he'd believe me if I told him I was trying to protect him and the other employees from something like that happening. Especially when it was unlikely I'd be able to save every job. My good intentions and justifications would count for nothing to the people who were let go.

"I wish I knew," Ryan answered when I remained silent. "But what you're doing right now isn't helping anything. What did you think—that you could intimidate some poor woman into leaving town and that would solve everything? I thought you were smarter than that."

"We just wanted her to know who it is she's hurting," the woman piped up.

"I think it's safe to say she knows exactly who you are, but I'm not sure it helped your case the way you thought it would." Ryan gave her a disdainful look as he let his words sink in. "Now if you'll all excuse us, we'll be going." With that, he turned his back on them, leading me along with him.

He took charge of my cart, pushing it toward Roland and Gene, the two sentries blocking the aisle behind us. They shuffled into a single file, allowing us to get past while the assembled spectators melted away, pretending a sudden, urgent disinterest in us.

I followed behind Ryan in numb silence as he navigated my cart to the registers. The grocery store seemed to have fallen unnaturally quiet, and the sound of the Dave Matthews Band song playing over the speakers was jarring in its cheerfulness.

When we got in line and Ryan proceeded to put my groceries on the belt, I snapped myself out of my daze enough to help him. The cashier and bagger darted uneasy looks at both of us as they scanned and bagged my purchases.

Meanwhile, my heart was still pounding in my chest with an overload of emotions: discomfort and dismay that it had happened, relief that Ryan had intervened, shame that I'd needed him to, irritation that he now perceived me as someone in need of rescuing, and guilt for feeling so irritated when I should be grateful to him.

It was too much to process with so many eyes on me. The receding surge of adrenaline had left my fingers feeling numb and shaky, and I dropped my credit card when I tried to insert it into the reader. Ryan caught it before it hit the floor and handed it to me, which compounded my embarrassment and irritation.

You're fine, I reminded myself. *It's over now and nothing bad actually happened.*

In all likelihood, nothing all that bad would have happened even if Ryan hadn't stepped in. At most I might have endured a few uncomfortable minutes of angry words before they'd gotten it out of their system and let me go on my way. It wasn't as if I'd been in any real danger. There was no reason to be this upset.

"Thanks very much," Ryan told the cashier cheerfully when she handed me my receipt. He took charge of my cart again before I had a chance to and steered it toward the door. Once we'd made it outside, he paused beside a display of fall-colored chrysanthemums to squint at me in the bright sunlight. "You okay?"

"I'm fine. Thank you for your assistance." In an attempt to recover my wounded pride and regain control of the situation, I reached for my shopping cart. "I can take it from here."

Because the man was a perpetual nuisance, his sharp eyes homed in on the lingering tremor in my hand. He arched a gently admonishing eyebrow, refusing to give up my cart. "I'm walking you to your car, Maggie. Deal with it."

Concluding it was fruitless to argue, I set out across the parking lot with Ryan pushing the cart in my wake. He even insisted on loading my bags into the back of my SUV, crowding me out with a look of mortal offense when I attempted to do it myself.

When he'd finished, he shut the tailgate and turned to face

me. As his eyes swept over my face, his expression twisted with worry.

I had to look away. I couldn't handle how handsome he was when he was being all concerned and protective. It conjured unwanted fantasies of being cared for and pampered by this sweet giant of a man, and I couldn't meet his eye while I was imagining such a thing.

His hand touched my shoulder again, causing my heart to flutter in a way that had nothing to do with adrenaline. "Hey…"

"I'm fine," I reiterated before he could ask me again. "It's fine."

"The fuck it is." The unexpected harshness of his tone drew my eyes back to him. "They shouldn't have done that to you. There's no excuse for it." His whole body vibrated like a spring under tension while he fought to contain his anger. "I'm sorry you had to deal with that."

"They're not your responsibility and neither am I." Realizing how sharp and ungrateful I sounded, I endeavored to soften my tone as I added, "But thank you for stepping in regardless."

"Let me drive you home."

"That's not necessary. I told you I'm fine. No harm done."

His gaze excavated my expression, doubtless seeing far more than I wanted him to. "What if we make a deal? I'll pretend I believe you if you let me do it anyway?"

I stuck my chin out, refusing to give in. My pride had taken enough hits for one day. Foolish romantic fantasies aside, I didn't need babying from anyone. "I appreciate your concern, but I'll be driving myself home."

Mutely shaking his head, he stepped aside and gestured his acquiescence. I turned my back on him, climbed behind the wheel, and closed the door. Ryan shoved his hands deep in his pockets, watching me with a frown on his face as I backed out and drove away.

As soon as I was out of his sight, I let out a deep breath. But the anticipated sense of relief at finally being alone never came.

Instead, the loss of Ryan's company left me feeling cold, and I found myself impetuously wishing I'd taken him up on his offer. The bitter taste of regret coated the inside of my mouth the whole drive home.

9

RYAN

I let Maggie drive away by herself like she wanted. Only after she'd pulled out of the parking lot and disappeared from sight did I walk back to my truck and drive off after her.

Technically, I wasn't following her, since we were both going to the same place. It wasn't my fault we lived next door to each other. Still, I drove at a more leisurely pace than usual so she wouldn't think I was doing it on purpose. God forbid I should commit the unforgivable crimes of looking out for her or trying to be nice.

She'd already closed up her garage and gone inside by the time I pulled into my driveway, but I could see her SUV through the window in the door. Reassured that she'd made it home safely, I went inside my own house, determined to spend the rest of the day minding my own damn business.

Margaret Silvestri's problems were not my problems. I tried to remind myself that she was a stuck-up out-of-towner who'd made it clear she didn't want anything to do with me.

Except it didn't help. I couldn't stop thinking about her no matter how hard I tried.

It was easy to understand why Maggie kept to herself so much, if this was what it was like for her everywhere she went. People looking at her with anger and distrust, treating her like some kind of boogeyman. What sort of life was that? Constant travel, always keeping herself isolated, never staying long enough to put down roots. It must be lonely as hell.

The more I let my thoughts go down that path, the more it bothered me to think about her all by herself next door. She'd tried to hide it, but I knew she'd been shaken up by the scene in the grocery store. A person shouldn't be alone after an upsetting experience like that. I lasted all of ten minutes before I shoved my shoes back on and trudged across the lawn to knock on her front door.

I'd just check on her real quick like any decent neighbor would. Just to make sure she didn't want any company after all. Which, knowing her, she definitely wouldn't. And then I'd be able to leave her alone knowing I'd fulfilled my civic duty.

Damn, she was taking a long time to open the door. Long enough that I started to envision all sorts of emergency scenarios, which my imagination had no problem providing given how many I'd walked in on after seventeen years of answering 911 calls.

I raked a hand through my hair, starting to sweat despite the mildness of the weather, and pounded on the door again, louder than before. "Maggie!" I shouted. "It's Ryan. If you're in there, answer the damn door."

A few seconds later, I heard the scrape of the chain and the click of the deadbolt sliding back. Only then did it occur to me her door didn't have a peephole. Of course she hadn't answered my first knock. Not when she couldn't see who was knocking.

The door opened a few inches, and Maggie peered out at me. "What do you want?"

"That's how you answer the door? Do they not have any manners at all where you were raised?"

She opened the door a little wider—just enough so she could glower at me more effectively. "You're seriously going to stand there and lecture me about good manners today of all days?"

It shouldn't have made me want to smile, but after I'd worked myself into a fit of worry, it was such a relief to see her back to her prickly old self that I couldn't help it. "Fair enough. Now invite me in."

"Why would I do that?"

"Because I'm not your enemy, Maggie. And because it's the neighborly thing to do."

She continued to glower at me. After emitting a deep, aggrieved sigh she finally stepped back to open the door all the way.

"What if I don't want company?" she said as I sidled past. "Why can't it be neighborly to respect my desire to be left alone?"

"I usually find when people claim they want to be alone is when they need company the most."

My gaze wandered around the living room, which I'd last seen just before Alli started renting the place out. She'd gutted the whole house, stripping out the ancient wall-to-wall carpet, painting the rooms trendy colors, and replacing her dad's old furniture with modern furnishings and decorations. After she'd finished with the place, it'd looked like something you'd see on Instagram.

It still looked sort of like that, but if a pack of slovenly college students had been squatting here for a year. I couldn't believe that one person had managed to generate this much clutter in such a short time. The nice furniture was all hidden beneath a layer of dirty dishes, empty water bottles, delivery boxes, blankets, pillows, and what looked to be an entire closet's worth of discarded clothes. Had the woman never heard of hangers?

Given how impeccably well put-together Maggie always looked, the state of her house was a shock. I'd assumed she was the sort of woman who not only folded her undergarments neatly but arranged them alphabetically by color. When in fact she was the sort who tossed them haphazardly onto the floor. That would teach me for assuming.

"The presumption that you know what I need better than I do is patronizing and offensive," she said, interrupting my visual inspection of her living room.

"Yes, I'm a real villain for caring enough to check on you after a traumatic experience." I picked up the half-empty glass sitting next to the vodka bottle on the coffee table and gave the clear liquid a sniff. Definitely vodka, which confirmed how not-fine she was if she'd come home and immediately poured herself a glass of straight vodka.

She snatched the glass out of my hand and began angrily gathering up dirty dishes with hands that were still shaking. *God dammit.* It was all I could do not to bundle her up in a hug. I would have, too, if I didn't think she'd scratch my eyes out for trying it.

"It wasn't that traumatic," she tossed over her shoulder as she disappeared into the kitchen. "Thanks for your concern, Dudley Do-Right, but I'm fine."

"Yeah, you keep saying that," I muttered, grabbing up the dishes she'd left behind and following after her.

Maggie's kitchen was in the same shape as her living room. Dirty dishes overflowed from the sink onto the counters, fighting for space alongside empty takeout containers. The trash can that stood in a corner of the room overflowed with still more takeout containers stacked in a precarious tower.

My eye twitched. "Was your house invaded by thirteen

hungry dwarves and a stoned wizard? Or does it always look like the aftermath of a kegger?"

"I've been working a lot, okay?" She shot a glare over her shoulder as she yanked open the dishwasher. "And don't you dare pass judgment on my housekeeping after forcing your way into my house uninvited."

"I forced nothing." I raised my hands in innocence. "I merely suggested you invite me in, which you did."

"I did no such thing." Scowling at me, she jerked one of the cabinets open and began shoving the clean coffee mugs from the dishwasher inside.

I didn't want to care about Maggie Silvestri, and she quite clearly didn't want me caring about her. Unfortunately for both of us, that ship had already sailed.

When I saw someone in need, I couldn't just walk away without trying to help. I'd once stopped my truck on a highway shoulder and dodged through traffic to rescue a snapping turtle from the road even though the ungrateful son of a bitch had done its best to bite my fingers off. Maggie would have to work a lot harder than that bastard snapping turtle if she wanted to scare me off.

"Aren't you going to offer me a drink?" I asked when she slammed the cabinet shut.

She snorted as she grabbed clean plates out of the washer. "What? You want some vodka?"

"It's customary to offer an invited guest whatever you're drinking." I got down a clean glass for myself and picked up the vodka bottle.

"I did *not* invite you," she grumbled.

"You stepped back and held the door open, which is a universally recognized gesture of invitation. Everyone knows that." I topped off her glass and held it out to her. "At least now you won't be drinking alone."

She accepted it without meeting my eyes. "Thank you."

The words came out so softly, for a second I wasn't sure I'd even heard her right. I probably shouldn't have wanted to pump my fist in triumph over two little words, but it felt like a major victory.

Cautiously, I touched my fingers to her arm, still a little worried she might try to bite them off like that snapping turtle. "Come on, leave the dishes and let's go sit. It's too late to keep me from seeing what a slob you are."

To my surprise, she let me guide her back into the living room without resistance. Although she did give me a mutinous look as she shifted pillows, blankets, and clothes aside to clear a space on the couch. "If I were to go over to your house right now it'd be pristine, would it? You're a regular Marie Kondo, I suppose?"

"Compared to you? That would be a yes." In truth, I was kind of a neat freak, and the state of Maggie's house made me fidgety. I was barely restraining myself from launching into a cleaning frenzy. Given how defensive and proprietary Maggie was about...well, everything, I suspected my intervention would piss her off even more. "Are you by any chance related to Oscar the Grouch of the Sesame Street Grouches?"

She snorted in what I was almost certain was a bitten-off laugh and gestured for me to sit. Enjoying the fact that one of my jokes had finally managed to amuse her, I perched myself on the space she'd cleared on the couch. A soft, flowery scent I assumed to be her perfume wafted up from the stack of pillows mounded against the arm of the couch next to me.

The room's only other seating was an armchair covered with clothes (including a couple of bras I was trying not to look at), so Maggie had no choice but to share the couch with me. She sank back against the cushions, releasing another cloud of that pleasant, flowery scent, and propped her bare feet on the edge of the coffee table.

Her toes were painted a bright Barbie pink, which I didn't expect. I'd only ever seen her wearing dark or neutral colors. Her wardrobe seemed composed entirely of navy blue, black, and varying shades of gray. She was wearing a black blouse today, in fact, with a pair of cropped jeans that showed off her ankles and the lower part of her shins. Even the bras I was definitely not looking at were plain beige and black. And yet her toes were the brightest pink I'd ever seen, an incongruous blaze of cheerful color she'd been keeping hidden underneath her austere outward appearance.

She sat beside me in silence, staring at the wall opposite the couch. Probably trying to pretend I wasn't here until I eventually got bored and left. If there was going to be any conversation, it was up to me to initiate it.

I took a sip of vodka as my gaze wandered around the room again. "Were you just watching *John Wick*?" I asked when I noticed the movie paused on the TV screen.

"It suited my mood for some reason."

"Solid choice." I could see how she might find it cathartic to watch Keanu Reeves unleash hell on everyone who'd wronged him for two solid hours.

"You don't have to worry about me," Maggie said. "I really am fine."

I turned my head to study her, frowning as I took in her slightly hunched posture and the way she was cradling her glass in both hands. "Forgive me if I don't think anyone should be fine after what just happened to you."

One of her shoulders lifted in a careless shrug. "People get upset when their livelihoods are threatened. It comes with the job."

"Are you saying that kind of thing happens to you all the

time?" I hated the thought of that. A lot more than I had any right to, considering it was her life and had nothing to do with me.

"No, not all the time. Every company's situation is different. But it's not the first time I've been confronted by unhappy employees. I'm used to being hated." She said it lightly, but with a wry smile that tore a hole in my chest.

My hand curled into an impotent fist beside my thigh as I tried to imagine what it must be like for her. "And you expect me to believe you're okay with that?"

Another small shrug. "I can't control other people's feelings."

"Sure you can. Human emotions are notoriously easy to manipulate. That's the whole basis of advertising and public relations." My stepsister Josie had once explained to me all the psychology that went into ad campaigns, and I'd been appalled. Now that I knew, it was easy to spot everywhere. She'd ruined Super Bowl commercials for me forever.

Maggie swiveled her head to give me a look so weary it made me want to pull her into my arms so I could protect her from all the shit she had to put up with. "Then maybe I just choose not to care."

Did she think I couldn't see how brittle she was? How much hurt and loneliness lay hidden behind her cold expressions and overly sharp words? Whether she admitted it or not, she was desperately in need of a friend.

"But you do care," I said. "Otherwise you wouldn't be drinking vodka at noon on a Saturday."

"What if I'm a closet alcoholic? Maybe I drink vodka every day at this time."

I gave her a long, hard look. "Are you really so afraid of admitting you're upset that you'd rather have me think you're an alcoholic? Is that your actual play here?"

"Fine. It upset me, okay?" The words sounded like they'd

been dragged out of her against her will. "I don't enjoy feeling helpless."

"You don't say," I deadpanned. "I never would have guessed that about you."

The glare she directed at me was undermined by the smile ghosting over her lips. "Honestly, why do people seem to like you so much? Because I find you incredibly annoying."

My mouth spread in a smile. "You'd certainly like me to think so, but I happen to know it's all an act."

"See, that's your problem right there," she said. "You think you know better than everyone else."

"Oh, and you don't?"

"Only when I'm right," she shot back, but her eyes were shining with amusement rather than irritation.

My smile widened as an unfamiliar warmth slid into my chest and filled it up. "That's what I like about you, sweetness. How meek and humble you are."

Maggie snorted and lifted her drink to her lips.

The silence she fell into felt more comfortable this time, like she'd given up resenting my presence. Maybe she'd even started to appreciate the company a little. It was hard to tell with her.

"Do you want me to tell you their last names?" I offered as my mind turned once more to the assholes who'd tried to intimidate her at the grocery store.

A little line appeared between her brows. "To what purpose?"

"That's up to you." If she'd hated feeling powerless at the store today, it was a way to give her back some of her power.

"What if I had them all fired on Monday?" Her eyes narrowed as they looked into mine. "Would you be okay telling me their names in that case?"

I took a second to ponder that and decided I could live with it. "Yes, if that's what you think is the best thing to do. What they did was totally out of line. Bad choices should have consequences sometimes." I was still feeling pretty outraged on Maggie's behalf—a lot more than she seemed to be.

She stared down at her drink with a pensive frown. "Don't tell me," she said after a moment. "I'm not interested in retribution, and I don't want anyone to lose their jobs."

"That's ironic, considering."

Her gaze snapped to mine. "What does that mean?"

"Just that everyone's convinced you're eager to put the whole town out of work, when you're not even willing to get three bullies in trouble they brought on themselves."

"Does that 'everyone' include you?" she asked.

"I stood up for you, didn't I?" It bothered me that she felt the need to ask. Hadn't I shown her by now I was on her side?

She stared back at me. "Maybe you were just defusing the situation like the do-gooder you are."

"Nothing I said was a lie."

She took this in. "You haven't even asked me if the article was true."

"I don't need to."

"Why not? What if I'm everything it said I was? Would you still be so nice to me if I was pushing to relocate King's Creamery away from Crowder?"

It was almost like she wanted me to hate her. Or maybe she was so used to being hated she had a hard time believing anyone might actually have her back. I had a feeling life had thrown her so many jabs she was always braced for the next one.

"Wait, so I'm being nice to you now?" I said, crooking a grin. "I thought I was being annoying."

"I'm serious," she said.

"I don't think that's what you're doing," I answered truthfully.

"Why not?"

There were a lot of reasons, not all of which I was eager to admit. Confessing that my secret infatuation with her had inspired an instinctive trust probably wasn't going to win me any points with her. So instead I gave her the easiest explanation. "Because George King's my stepfather, so I like to think I'd know if there was any truth to that article."

"What?" Maggie's eyes went wide as dinner plates. "Are you fucking kidding me?"

10

MAGGIE

"The CEO of King's Creamery is your *stepfather*?" I gaped at Ryan. How could I not know he had a family connection to my boss? "Why didn't you *tell* me that?"

His brow scrunched into furrows. "You make it sound like I've been trying to hide it, but it's not like we've exchanged personal information or family histories. Why would I tell you who my stepfather is when you wouldn't even tell me what company you were working for?"

Shit, he was right. If I'd been more forthcoming, he might have volunteered the information sooner. "I just wish I'd known."

"Why?" He shifted on the couch to face me more fully. "What would you have done different?"

Good question. Would I have done anything differently? I'd already been trying to avoid him, not that I'd been successful. It wasn't as if I would have talked about my work any more or less than I already had. Realistically, knowing who Ryan was wouldn't have changed anything. Except it did somehow. Or at least it felt like it did.

"Would you have been nicer to me if you'd known?" he asked.

"No, probably not," I admitted.

A smile quirked his lips. "Didn't think so."

The man's dimples were a health hazard, but I refused to let them distract me from the subject at hand. "How involved are you with the company?"

He wasn't on the payroll, I knew that much for sure. But he'd more or less implied he had insider knowledge. How much did he know exactly? Had he been talking to his family about me all this time?

"Not at all," he said. "And I never have been. I don't have shares or any kind of financial connection to it, if you're worried about that. All I know is what I hear from the family."

"From your stepfather, you mean?"

Ryan shook his head and downed the last of his drink with a grimace. Straight vodka didn't seem to be a favorite of his. "George never talks to me about the business. I hear stuff from Manny mostly. Sometimes Josie or Nate."

"They're your stepsiblings," I said as I struggled to comprehend the implications. Ryan was related to three of the company's top executives as well as the CEO. "I've been working with them for the last month and never had any idea you were family."

He shrugged as he leaned forward to set his glass on the coffee table. "That's the thing about small towns. Almost everyone's related to each other somehow or other, if not by blood then by marriage. And even if they're not related, they've still probably got some kind of history or connection."

"Are you close to them?" I asked, finding it difficult to imagine Ryan hanging out with either Nate or Josie King.

His brow furrowed slightly as he appeared to weigh his

words. "To Manny, yes. My mother was married to George when they adopted him, so we grew up together."

"What about Nate and Josie?"

When Ryan reached up to scratch his neck, I couldn't help admiring the thick cords of muscle that disappeared inside the collar of his T-shirt. Or the way his shirt clung to his enormous chest and shoulders. His body was unlike anything I'd ever seen before and a permanent distraction that made it difficult to think straight around him.

"They lived with their mom, George's first wife," he said, "so we're not as close. But we're still family. We see each other at holidays and special occasions."

"And the brother who came over with his girlfriend to catch the centipede? Wyatt?" Now that I thought about it, there was a definite King family resemblance there. George's company bio listed seven biological children in addition to Manny Reyes, but I hadn't bothered to learn the names of the ones who didn't work for him. I couldn't recall there being any mention of a stepson.

"He's my half-brother," Ryan said. "One of two kids my mom had with George."

"I really need a Wikipedia page for your family."

He chuckled. "Yeah, we're a messy bunch. Christmas shopping is a nightmare, let me tell ya."

"So what have they told you?" I asked. "Have you talked to them about me?"

His eyebrows pulled together as he looked away.

"You don't have to answer that," I amended, realizing it wasn't fair of me to expect him to share private conversations. "I shouldn't have asked."

"No, it's okay." One of his big shoulders twitched as he scratched his head. "All I really know is that revenues have been down, and it's serious enough that George brought you in to assess the situation. Manny said you're supposed to be an expert at this kind of stuff and they're counting on you to turn things around. He told me the article was a load of clickbait horseshit."

Now I was the one who looked away. "It wasn't all lies. I have been responsible for thousands of layoffs."

"Sounds like a lot of pressure, being the one who has to make the hard decisions with so much hanging in the balance."

"It is a lot of pressure. But that's the job."

"And getting harassed at the grocery store is just part of the job too, is it?"

I glanced over and found Ryan's face set in a frown. "I'm just lucky they didn't have their torches and pitchforks on them," I said, trying to make a joke.

He didn't smile. "I don't know why you keep trying to act so casual about this. You don't have to pretend it doesn't bother you. Not with me."

I did though. It was how I'd learned to cope with it. I didn't know how to do anything else. "It's easier to pretend than admit the truth."

"Yeah," he said softly. "I get that."

I could see in his eyes how much he did understand. A flicker of something dark and haunted stirred in the gray depths—something he usually kept well hidden behind his friendly smiles and easygoing manner.

He dragged his gaze away and rubbed the back of his neck. For the first time since I'd met him, Ryan looked uncomfortable in his own skin. Whatever pain he was hiding, it made my throat tighten to see it.

I almost asked him about it, but I didn't think he'd want me to. He'd just said as much, hadn't he? He preferred to keep his troubles to himself, just like me. The least I could do was respect that.

"I am sorry they jumped to conclusions about us," I said, changing the subject.

"What do you mean?" he asked with a puzzled expression.

"When that guy Dale thought we were sleeping together."

Ryan's frown lines deepened. "I don't care about that."

"It seemed like you did. I was worried you might have a girlfriend who'd be upset by that sort of rumor."

"I don't have a girlfriend."

I tried not to show any reaction to this information, since it had nothing whatsoever to do with me. "Right. Well, either way, I don't blame you for being upset. Who would want to be romantically linked with public enemy number one?"

"Fuck that," he said with surprising vehemence. "I was angry because he thought it was an appropriate question to ask and because he assumed it was the only reason I'd stand up for you. But I don't give a fuck if people think we're together. They can think whatever they want if it makes them think twice about harassing you again."

Have mercy. The man was even hotter when he went all growly and sweary.

"Lucky for me you were there to put the fear of god in them," I said. For once I wasn't trying to be combative, but it seemed to upset him.

"They *respect* me. There's a difference."

"You're right," I said. "It did seem like they looked up to you. Fear is what they feel about me."

Ryan's lips pressed together as he gave me a long, appraising look. "Why do you do it?"

"My job?" I said, feeling judged. "Because I'm damn good at it."

"I'll bet you could be good at anything you set your mind to."

"Maybe, but this is what I've built a highly successful business around, and I'm not going to walk away from it just because it's hard sometimes." I shouldn't care what Ryan thought of me, and yet I did anyway. "I know it seems like I must be cruel and heartless to want to do this job—"

"I don't think you're either of those things," he said.

"You're one of the few, then."

My quip seemed to upset him even more. "Listen to yourself, Maggie. How can you be happy like that?" He sounded so aggrieved that I realized he wasn't judging me at all. He was just trying to understand.

I tried to explain it without being defensive this time. "I like fixing things that are broken. In a way, what I do is like being a surgeon. I find the diseased tissue and cut it out so it doesn't kill the whole patient. People think I'm here to eliminate jobs, but my goal is always to save them if they can be saved. When I manage to do that, it makes me feel good. That's why I do it."

"So you're helping people," he said.

"I'm trying to."

"But you're the one they blame if they lose their jobs. Doesn't it bother you to be the focus of so much resentment?"

"Better me than someone who doesn't take the responsibility seriously. Companies lay people off all the time for terrible, stupid reasons, hurting people without a second thought. At least when I'm the one who makes the recommendation, I know it's the right call—the one that will do the least harm."

"You're an impressive woman, Margaret Silvestri." The admiration in Ryan's eyes was entirely too much.

Be still my heart. If I wasn't careful, this man was going to melt it.

"Says the guy who charges into burning buildings to save pet guinea pigs," I replied, unable to resist smiling.

"I never said I wasn't impressive too." His sexy smirk filled my head with all sorts of dirty, inappropriate thoughts.

"Why don't you have a girlfriend?" I blurted out, unable to

help myself.

The smile slid from his face. "What do you mean?"

"Everyone likes you, you're kind, friendly, sociable, gainfully employed, and you're...well..." I gestured at his body rather than attempt to describe it. "I'm sure you know what you look like."

His smirk returned as he propped his elbow on the back of the couch. "What do I look like? Tell me."

"Stop fishing for more compliments and answer the question. Why are you single?"

"I could ask you the same question."

I shook my head. "You know as well as I do it's not the same for women my age."

"You say that like you're not smoking hot."

My stomach tightened with pleasure at the compliment, but I didn't acknowledge it. "I'm forty-five, run my own successful business, and I'm not afraid to speak my mind. Most men find at least one of those things off-putting, if not all three."

"Then most men are idiots," Ryan said.

"That's certainly been my experience." I narrowed my eyes, determined not to let him change the subject. "What's your excuse?"

"Why do I need an excuse?" He shrugged. "Maybe I like being single."

"Do you?"

"Is there anything wrong with that?"

"No, of course not," I said. "I happen to like being single too. I just find it hard to believe that none of the single women around here have tied you up and stashed you in their basement."

"We don't have basements in this part of Texas," he said with a wink. "And I never use restraints without agreeing on a safe word first."

Wow. Okay.

"You really like being single?" I said, trying not to visualize that scenario in intricate detail.

"Dating's a lot of hassle. And for what? I don't want to get dragged into a serious relationship at this point in my life. I'm set in my own habits now. I have no interest in changing the way I live to make room for someone else's annoying habits."

"That pretty much sums up how I feel too," I said, nodding.

Ryan arched an amused eyebrow as he glanced around my messy living room. "That's a shocker."

I threw a pillow at him, which he effortlessly batted aside with his massive forearm.

"Now you're making even more of a mess," he said, grinning.

"Maybe you're single because you're a neat freak."

"Maybe so," he agreed and propped his head on his hand. "Now tell me why you're single."

His attractiveness was becoming a serious problem. It was hard not to stare at the strong line of his jaw and the soft, perfect curve of his lips when they were so close to me like this. How was I supposed to have a rational conversation with a man who looked like Ryan staring at me the whole time?

I swallowed, trying to remember what he'd just asked me. *Right, why am I single?* "Because I like it better than I liked being married."

He looked surprised. "You're divorced?"

"Is it that hard to believe someone would marry me?"

"No," he said with a frown. "It's hard to believe someone would let you go."

Be careful with this one, I thought. *He's trouble.*

"For someone who doesn't date, you sure are quick with a line," I said.

"I'm *retired* from dating," he said. "But I did more than my fair share before I hung up my hat." He smiled. "And that wasn't a line."

I rolled my eyes. "Don't waste your breath. It's not going to work."

Lies. It was already working. But I'd rather eat my own handbag than admit that to him.

"Anyway," I said, making myself look away from him and his dangerous face. "I definitely don't miss providing unpaid care and labor, or compromising my happiness for someone else's comfort."

"Wow, you make marriage sound terrible," Ryan said. "Please tell me more so I can have my life choices validated."

"It wasn't all bad," I said and took a drink of vodka. "I got a pretty great sister-in-law out of it. We're still good friends. I suppose there were some other nice things about it, but eventually they got outweighed by all the bad ones."

"How long were you married?"

"Six years." The whole experience was long enough ago now I didn't even feel bitter anymore. Not the way I used to. That chapter of my life was so distant the memories had all gone filmy and soft-focus. "The only thing I really miss about it is the easy access to sex, but honestly, we weren't even having that much after the first year."

"That's a goddamn travesty," Ryan said.

"Isn't it?" I took another drink. "Sex is overrated anyway."

"If that's what you think, you've been having sex with the wrong men."

The way Ryan was looking at me made part of me want to scoot away from him and another part of me want to throw myself at his face and kiss him just to see if those lips were as soft as they looked. The second part of me clearly wasn't very smart or sensible.

"Is there a right kind?" I asked.

He shook his head. "Now you're just making me feel sad for you."

"I suppose you think you're the right kind of man," I said, trying to sound disdainful rather than hopeful.

"Well I sure wouldn't let you walk away thinking sex is overrated."

I stared at him, and he stared back unblinking. *Well, shit*, I thought, not doubting for a second that was true but also really wanting to find out for myself.

No. Bad idea.

Or...was it a good idea?

Ryan leaned in closer, and my pulse kicked up. "You know what I think we should do, sweetness?"

"What?" I asked, feeling dizzy.

"Start the movie back up and watch *John Wick* together."

I blinked, then frowned. "You want to watch a movie?"

"It's a great movie. I can't think of a better way to spend my afternoon than hanging out here with you watching it."

"Yeah, okay," I said with a shrug, and Ryan broke into a grin as he leaned forward to grab the remote.

I sank back against the couch, mostly feeling relief with only a little disappointment. Which meant it was just as well he hadn't tried to follow through on his flirting. He was way too hot and charming. I didn't need that kind of complication in my life.

Halfway through the movie, Ryan suggested we order pizza. While we were waiting for it, he went next door and came back with a six-pack of beer that we drank with our pizza as we watched the rest of the movie. When it was over, he gathered up all the empty bottles, thanked me for letting him watch the movie, and took himself and the bottles home.

Even though it hadn't started well or ended the way I'd expected, it still turned out to be one of the most enjoyable days I'd had in a long time.

How pathetic was that?

11

MAGGIE

Ryan showed up at my door again the next day. This time with a paper bag from the local hardware store. Apparently, he'd called my landlord and gotten her authorization to install a peephole in my front door. No amount of telling him it wasn't necessary would dissuade him from installing it right then and there.

It was pretty sweet, actually, how concerned he seemed to be about me. I'd be lying if I said it wasn't reassuring to know he was looking out for me. It'd been so long since anyone had, I'd forgotten how nice it felt.

That wasn't something I could afford to let myself get used to though. Ryan McCafferty was a unicorn. An outlier skewing the data. Tempting as it might be to let my guard down around him, it was too risky. I had to keep my walls in place so they'd be there when I needed them.

Therefore, I didn't invite him in after he'd finished the job. I didn't suggest we watch *John Wick 2* and order another pizza, even though I thought about it.

Instead, I offered Ryan a bottle of water and my thanks.

Then I bid him goodbye and swallowed down my feelings of regret as I watched him walk back to his house.

That night I heated up a personal-size frozen pizza and watched *John Wick* 2 alone with an annoying sense of dissatisfaction. Even though I tried not to, I thought about Ryan the whole time, wishing he was sitting next to me, cracking jokes and pointing out all the unrealistic parts of the fight scenes like he'd done yesterday.

Monday morning I woke earlier than usual, giving myself extra time to get ready for work as I prepared to leave my house for the first time since the confrontation in the grocery store. I'd had to prove myself to the world over and over to get where I was, and I'd be damned if I'd let anyone intimidate me. Today *I* would be the one doing all the intimidating. Maintaining an image of flawless professionalism was one of the key tools in my arsenal, so I armored myself for the day by dressing to kill in my best Armani power suit, my favorite crocodile Jimmy Choo Love pumps, and my boldest red Dior lipstick for added slay-all-day badassery. Because nothing said "get the fuck out of my way" like a bold red lip.

Ryan's truck was already gone when I stepped out of my house. That meant he was probably working one of his twenty-four-hour shifts and wouldn't be home until tomorrow morning after I'd left for work. Disappointment set in at the realization I wouldn't see him again for at least the next two days.

Irritated with myself for caring, I batted my disappointment away like one of those pesky fruit flies that kept trying to drown themselves in my half-full wineglasses. Ryan's comings and goings were of no consequence to me. It didn't matter a single fat fig if he'd be gone for the next twenty-four hours or the next twenty-four days. Either way, I had no plans to see him and no reason to think about him at all.

Thus resolved, I got in my car and drove to work. On the way there, a woman in a minivan flipped me off at a traffic light. But I didn't let her get to me. Her juvenile gesture couldn't permeate my hard, polished shell.

I held my head high as I strode through the parking lot and into the King's corporate headquarters—the very headquarters I'd been accused of wanting to relocate—showing no emotion as heads turned my way and whispers followed in my wake.

From now on, nothing was going to get to me. I refused to let it.

OF COURSE THE universe decided to try me. No surprise there. The only surprise was that it waited two whole days to do it, lulling me into a false sense of security before springing its next attack on my peace of mind.

Save for the one lone bird-flipper on Monday, there'd been no further incidents of overt hostility. Things remained tense around the office in the aftermath of the news article, but that was as much to do with the investigation the COO had launched into the source of the leak as with the rumored downsizing. Now that several days had come and gone with no big, dire announcement, the initial wave of panic had died down to a low background hum of unease.

Foolishly, I was feeling pretty good when I walked out of my house on Wednesday morning to find a message spray-painted onto the street in front of my rental house.

The word *BITCH* had been written on the asphalt in giant orange letters. A pair of arrows pointed helpfully at my house in case there was any question who the bitch was. Not especially creative or eloquent, but it got the point across.

Somehow they'd managed to find out where I lived. So that was a fun new thing to worry about.

At the sound of a door slamming, I glanced over my shoulder to find Ryan headed my way. It was the first I'd seen of him since Sunday afternoon, and although now was not an appropriate moment to notice how hot he looked, I couldn't help myself. He was a walking wall of cut, beefy muscle sporting a sexy, just-rolled-out-of-bed look in a pair of gray knit shorts and a white undershirt so thin I could see the tattoo ink on his pec through the fabric.

"Everything okay?" he asked as he hopped the ditch that ran along the street.

I gestured to the graffiti. "Someone left me a love letter last night."

His face flushed bright red with anger when he saw it. "What the fuck?"

"I guess my fan club has escalated to defacing public property."

Ryan set his hands low on his hips, cocking his head like he was studying a brainteaser. "What's that symbol on the end supposed to be?"

I'd had the same question when I'd first seen it. The handwriting was clear enough, but the art skills of my secret admirer left something to be desired. It had taken me a moment to recognize it as a crude attempt to draw a skull and crossbones. But I didn't want to tell Ryan that because he'd likely overreact. So I pressed my lips together and said nothing, hoping he wouldn't figure it out. But of course he did. I saw the moment he worked it out.

His expression went thunderous, but he locked it down again almost before I'd registered it, clenching his jaw as his gaze darted to me. "Shit, Maggie."

"It's probably just teenagers making mischief." I shrugged, trying to pretend it didn't bother me. If he suspected I was scared, he'd get even more overprotective.

Ryan's cheek hollowed as he chewed the inside of it. He avoided shaving on his days off, so he was sporting a layer of stubble this morning, adding to his scruffy hotness. "I don't think so. Teenagers tend to be a lot less coherent in their graffiti."

"You think it was adults because they spelled 'bitch' correctly?"

He flinched slightly when I said the word bitch, which I found adorable. "Not just the spelling—the fact that it's legible and the message is so straightforward. Teens like to be cryptic. Plus, that fluorescent orange paint is the same kind used in construction. Something tells me this was done by grown-ass adults."

"Adult being a relative term, obviously," I said.

Ryan's thick arms crossed over his chest as his brow furrowed. "I don't love that they know where you live."

His worry for me shouldn't have been so attractive, but my stomach stubbornly insisted on fizzing despite the less-than-pleasant circumstances.

"I'm sure my landlord won't be happy either," I said. "I hope she doesn't ask me to move out because of this."

I wouldn't blame her if she did, but I'd have to move into one of the nearby motels, which was unappealing for a number of reasons. Comfort, for one. But also security. I'd feel a lot less safe in a motel surrounded by strangers instead of here with a nosy, overprotective fireman next door. Not to mention, I wouldn't be able to see so much of Ryan if I moved. Or any of Ryan at all, probably. Not that I should care about that. But I did.

"I'll talk to her," he said. "You don't need to worry about that."

"It's not your problem to handle, Dudley Do-Right."

His eyes locked with mine, his determined expression brooking no argument. "And yet I'm going to handle it anyway."

"You're exasperating, you know that?"

The corner of his mouth crooked. "I think the words you're looking for are, 'Thank you, Ryan, for being so helpful.'"

"Thank you for being so helpful," I said with sincerity.

His smile brightened for a second, showing off his dimples before it faded into a worried frown again. "Have you considered hiring extra security while you're here?"

I could probably get King's Creamery to foot the bill under the circumstances, but it felt like an overreaction to a little graffiti. "It's just some petty vandalism. Whoever did this, I doubt they intend any real harm."

"They better not." Ryan held his palm out and wiggled his fingers. "Give me your phone."

"Excuse me?"

"I'm going to put my number in your contacts, so you'll have someone to call in case they come back to give you any more trouble."

"If that happens, I can simply call the police."

His eyebrows arched. "You're confident they'd hurry to your rescue, are you? Do you know how many members of the city police department and county sheriff's office have friends and family employed by the creamery?"

I hadn't thought of that. *Well, shit.* Now I'd be worrying about getting pulled over on my commute to and from work.

"In any case, I'm only twenty steps away. I can get to you a hell of a lot faster than any police cruiser." Ryan wiggled his fingers again.

"Fine." As I unlocked my phone and handed it over, I wondered if he'd actually counted the steps between our front doors.

"If you hear any odd noises or see anything at all suspicious, you don't hesitate to call me, no matter what time it is." He glanced up from typing in his info to punctuate this instruction with a stern look. "Don't worry about waking me up. My sleep schedule's all over the place because of my shift work, so I'm often up at odd hours of the night."

I was all too aware of that from his late-night exercise habit. My chest grew warm remembering how I'd shamelessly watched him through my kitchen window the first couple of weeks I'd lived here, before I knew him. I could still hear him out there clanging weights around in the middle of the night several times a week, but I refused to let myself get out of bed to spy on him anymore.

Ryan handed my phone back, and I saw he'd put himself in my contacts as "Dudley Do-Right."

I shook my head as I typed out a quick text message: *Dear Dudley, thanks for worrying about me. —Maggie*

"There," I said as I hit send. "Now you've got my number too. Don't abuse it."

He gave me one of those crooked grins I liked more than I ought to. "I was going to write it on the wall of the men's room at Dooley's bar, but since you asked so nicely, I guess I'll refrain."

"Always the gentleman."

"You know it." His gaze took a very ungentlemanly journey down my body, pointedly checking out my hip-hugging gray Max Mara sheath dress and red Prada pumps. I fought to maintain an indifferent facade as his lips curved in an appreciative smile that made my belly erupt in flutters. "You need to get to work, I'm guessing."

Right. Yes. Work. I'd been about to leave when I'd spotted the graffiti. "What do you think I should do about this?" I asked, indicating the vandalized street.

"I'll handle it," Ryan said. "Don't worry about it."

"You like to handle things, don't you?"

The corner of his mouth twitched. "And you don't like to give up control."

"And yet you keep expecting me to."

"Maybe I just like to watch you squirm."

My mouth opened with a retort that died on my tongue when Ryan's focus snagged on my lips. The way his lids lowered caused heat to bloom under my wool dress despite the pleasantly cool October weather this morning.

"You should just give in and let me take charge," he said, still staring at my lips as he shifted subtly closer. "You know you want me to."

He was too much—his body too big, his voice too deep, his gaze too taunting and arousing at the same time. He knew it too. He could read me way too well, which was another problem.

I pushed out a breath and made myself take a step back. "Since I really do need to get to work, I guess I'll let you have your way this time."

"Thanks," Ryan drawled with a self-satisfied grin. "That's generous of you."

"You're welcome." I fought a smile and lost the battle. My defenses were good for nothing against this man.

12

MAGGIE

By the time I got home from work that evening, Ryan had already installed security cameras around the outside of my house. He was up on a ladder in the backyard, adjusting one pointed at my back door when I pulled into my garage.

"Are those real?" I asked, peering up at the small white camera he'd mounted under the eave.

"Yes, they're real," he said as he climbed down from the ladder.

"I thought they might be dummy cameras to scare people off."

"Any self-respecting delinquent can spot a dummy camera a mile away. These are motion-activated spotlight cameras with infrared night vision. If anyone comes near the house, they'll find themselves literally under the spotlight as well as recorded in the act. And if that's not enough of a deterrent, check this out." He whipped his phone out of his pocket and tapped the screen. "Go walk toward your back door."

I raised my eyebrows but did as requested. When I got a yard away from the door, a loud, recorded voice screeched, *Warning.*

You have triggered the perimeter alert system. Your movements are being recorded.

"Wow. That should be annoying enough to scare anyone off."

Ryan came over and held his phone out so I could see the screen. "Smile. You're on *Candid Camera*."

Sure enough, there the two of us were, captured on impressively clear video. The camera had a wide lens that covered a lot of the backyard close to the house, including a full view of the back door and anyone who might be standing in front of it. Or just inside, for that matter.

"You installed the app on your phone?" I said, frowning. "Does that mean you'll be able to watch me come and go?"

An odd smile played over his lips. "You got a problem with me watching you?"

Uhh...shit. Did he know I'd watched him working out in his garage?

"My kitchen window looks directly onto your driveway and backyard," he continued, still smiling. "It's not like I can't already see your comings and goings if I want."

"I suppose that's true," I said, relaxing slightly.

"But if you're uncomfortable, I'll delete the app and have Alli change the password so I can't access it. I just thought you might feel safer if I could keep an eye on the house when I'm at work. But I wouldn't want to watch anyone without their permission."

"No, it's fine," I said as a fist of guilt pressed into my chest. "You're right. It's probably a good idea for you to have access to the cameras."

Ryan nodded, still giving me that odd smile. "I'll text you the login info so you can use the app on your phone too. It's pretty self-explanatory, but let me know if you need help setting it up. I'm happy to come over and walk you through it."

"I'm sure I'll be able to figure it out."

"Just so you know, Alli will be able to access the cameras as well. So don't go trying to smuggle any contraband or unlicensed pets into the house."

"So noted." I looked up at the cameras and frowned. "How much did all this cost? I should pay you for it."

"Alli's covering it. I convinced her it was a good investment to keep a closer eye on her short-term renters. Plus it gets her a discount on her insurance."

"And she agreed? Just like that?"

He grinned. "I can be pretty convincing."

"Yes, I'm aware." I went to unlock the back door, eager to get inside and take my shoes off. "Thank you for doing all of this. I really do appreciate it."

"I like hearing you say thank you." Ryan followed me into the kitchen without waiting for an invitation. "Speaking of my awesome powers of persuasion…"

"Oh no." I set my bag on the kitchen table with a sigh. "What now?"

"Just hear me out. You don't even know what I'm about to suggest. Maybe it'll be something you actually like." He opened my fridge like he lived here and surveyed the contents.

"Is it?" I asked as I stepped out of my shoes.

Helping himself to a bottle of water, he shut the fridge and rounded on me. "I don't want to seem cocky or anything, but I'd like to think so."

It was impossible not to find the man charming, especially when his dimples were showing. "Just tell me."

"Remember on Saturday when Dale assumed we were together? And I said I was fine with it if it makes people less likely to harass you?"

"Yessss." I already had a bad feeling about where this was going.

Ryan guzzled a long drink of water and swiped his hand across his mouth before continuing. "I want you to come out with me on Saturday night. Somewhere public where everyone will see us together."

I took an involuntary step backward as I shook my head. "Oh, no. No, thank you. I prefer not to subject either of us to that sort of attention."

He came over to stand directly in front of me, giving me an appraising stare. "What are you going to do? Barricade yourself inside your house for the next few months?"

"Yes? Why not? It's working great for me so far." Taking off my heels had been a mistake. Ryan was easier to deal with when the height difference between us was less pronounced. Now that I was barefoot, he towered over me in a way I liked far more than I should. It was a rare novelty to encounter a man so much taller than me.

"Please," he said. "You're desperately lonely and going stir-crazy on your own. Admit it."

"I am *not*." Bristling, I planted my hands on my hips. "I'm doing fine, thanks."

Ryan shifted closer. Close enough that I could smell the intoxicating mix of soap and sweat rising off his skin. A few more inches and our chests would be touching. "You can't hide in your house alone all the time, Boo Radley."

I swallowed thickly, dizzy with the urge to run my fingers down his arm to feel how firm the muscles were. "Sure I can. I happen to love my own company. It's my preferred company, in fact."

"Of course it is." He shook his head in amusement. "Look, you're the one who said everyone in town likes me. And you're right, most people do. More importantly, they trust me and respect my judgment."

"Are you just bragging on yourself now?"

"If everyone sees that we're together, it'll make them question their assumptions about you."

"Or it'll make them question their assumptions about *you*. Have you considered that?"

He shook his head. "Impossible."

"You're very sure of yourself."

"Yes, I am." His lips tugged to the side as his bottomless silver eyes pinned me in place. "That's why you and I are going to start dating."

The breath left my lungs. "Sorry...*what*?"

"You and me. Officially a couple. Going out together where everyone in town will see us."

"Um..."

"In case it's still not clear, I'm asking you to go out on a date with me, Maggie."

My stomach tried to flip over, but I sternly ordered it to cease and desist. Now was no time to get carried away. "You don't date. You told me that yourself."

"That's true," he said. "But I'm making an exception for you."

"Why?"

"To help you out."

"Why would you go to so much trouble to do that?"

He cast an exasperated look at the ceiling before focusing on me again. "It's not that much trouble to take you out on a few dates. Maybe I just enjoy being helpful, okay? It's not like I'm talking about a serious relationship. You're only in town for a few months, and we've already established that we both like our space, so there's no risk of either of us getting clingy." He paused. "And maybe while I'm helping you out, you can help me."

Ah, here we go. I knew there had to be a catch. "How exactly will I be doing that?"

"By getting everyone who's constantly hassling me about being single and trying to set me up on dates off my back for a while. They won't be able to matchmake if I'm dating you. Come on. You've got to admit it's a great plan."

"It's ridiculous," I said.

He drew back in mock offense as if I'd slapped him across the face with a white silk dinner glove. "Wow. Ouch."

"I don't mean it like that."

His eyebrows ticked upward. "You know I'm considered quite a catch in this town, right?"

Of that, I had no doubt. "You can't possibly be serious about this."

"Why not?"

"I can think of at least two dozen reasons off the top of my head. Would you like me to list them in order of relevance or alphabetically?"

"I don't want to hear any of them, Negative Nancy. Look, we're friends, right?" When I opened my mouth to respond, he pointed a warning finger at me. "You better not say no, or I'll get my feelings hurt."

"We're friends," I conceded. "Sure."

"So we already know we like each other."

I tilted my head and squinted at him. "Do we?"

A smile pulled at his lips. "Hush. We like each other. Deal with it."

I tried not to smile in response and utterly failed. "Look, it's nothing against you personally. I'm just not into the whole 'going out in public' thing."

I wasn't sold on the dating thing either, to be honest. No matter how attracted I might be to Ryan, I questioned the wisdom of getting involved with anyone in the short time I was here—whether or not it was real or just for show, which I wasn't actually clear on.

But Ryan wasn't giving up so easily. "Look, this happens to be a great town, and you haven't seen any of it since you've been here. That's a damn crime, is what it is. You need someone to take you out and show you around who commands enough respect that people will mind their business and leave you alone to mind yours."

I gave him a skeptical look. "You think that's going to be enough, do you? People will leave me alone because I'm with you?"

"If they see me glaring back at them when they try to give you dirty looks, then yeah, I think they'll reconsider their fucking life choices. And hey, who knows? Some folks might even be inclined to give you the benefit of the doubt for having the good taste to go out with me."

"There's that modesty I admire so."

His smile quirked wider. "It's like politics, right? You get the endorsement of some respected local bigwig, and you'll win voters' respect just for winning his."

"As long as you don't have an inflated idea of your own importance," I said with a roll of my eyes.

"Go out with me, Maggie. Saturday night. Let me show you a good time."

I should say no. This plan of his was more likely to make things worse for him than to help me. For his sake, I didn't want Ryan getting further tangled up in my problems. And for my own sake, I didn't want to get further tangled up with him. I had a feeling it would be hard to give a man like him up once I let myself get involved with him. Even so, part of me wanted very much to let Ryan show me a good time, and that same part of me also wanted to get my body very literally tangled up with his.

"You want to show everyone how tough you are, don't you?" he prodded, sensing my weakening resolve. "You're not going to do that hiding away in this house. They'll think they've intimidated you, which will embolden them to keep going."

Just say yes.
But I shouldn't.
But I *wanted* to.

"Prove you're not afraid by going out with me on Saturday night," Ryan said. "Otherwise I'll know you're too scared to stand up for yourself."

"Fuck you." Damn him for always knowing exactly how to push my buttons.

His face spread in a grin. "That's more like it. There's that fire I'm talking about."

"You're infuriating."

"So you've mentioned." He leaned closer and bent his mouth to my ear. "Say yes, Maggie. Prove me wrong."

My heart fluttered as I felt his body heat radiating through me. We were so close I couldn't believe we weren't actually touching.

"One date," he murmured in a devastatingly low voice. "Go out on one date with me and see how it goes. If it's a disaster or you hate it, I promise I'll leave you alone like you want."

Leave me alone? Who was I kidding? That was the last thing I wanted.

Oh, the hell with it.

"Fine," I said. "Okay."

The smile that lit up his face made the bottom fall out of my stomach. *Dangerous.*

"Saturday night," he said, still smiling as he backed toward the door. "You're going to want to get yourself a pair of cowboy boots if you don't have any already."

"What? No way. I'm not doing that." What kind of date was he planning to take me on? "I'm not doing anything that requires cowboy boots."

"Oh yes you are, and you're going to love it. Trust me."

I must have been out of my mind to agree to this. *Heaven help me.*

13

RYAN

Was this plan of mine a huge mistake? Possibly. Did I give a shit? Apparently not, because I couldn't stop smiling as I walked across my front yard to pick up Maggie for our date on Saturday night.

My smile froze in place when she opened the door. For a moment I was unable to do anything but stare at the jaw-dropping sight of her. It was the first time I'd ever seen her hair unbound, hanging in soft yellow waves that brushed the tops of her shoulders. On top of that she was wearing a ruffled floral sundress that showed off cleavage so deep it made my eyes water. I'd never seen Maggie in anything so soft or brightly colored, and the shock nearly stole my breath away as my gaze traveled downward, taking in the tiered skirt that fluttered around her knees, showing off her brand-new boots.

Oh, how we'd gone back and forth on those boots. She'd fought me tooth and nail on them, but I'd refused to back down. Our destination tonight was a key part of my plan. If we wanted to make the biggest splash possible, there was only one place in town to go, and you couldn't go there without proper boots.

Knowing how uneasy she was being out in public, I'd offered

to escort her to the western wear store on Main Street. But she'd turned me down, insisting she could manage for herself. Stubborn woman.

I didn't know where she'd gotten the plain red roper boots she wore, but goddamn, they looked perfect on her. Everything about her looked perfect. She had no way of knowing it, but I'd always had a weakness for women in red shoes. Ironically, ever since my Sunday school teacher had told us that good girls never wore red shoes.

A wrinkle formed between Maggie's brows as I stood there gaping at her like a man who'd lost his senses. "Is it that bad? Tell me the truth."

That snapped me right out of my trance. "What? No! Are you kidding? You look incredible."

"I feel ridiculous."

"Are there no mirrors in your house? Because you look fucking gorgeous." I reached for her hand and brought it to my lips. It'd been a long while since I'd taken anyone on a date, but my instincts were ingrained enough to remain intact.

Her eyes widened at the compliment—or maybe at the kiss. Regardless, I took immense pleasure in her momentary speechlessness.

"You ready to go?" I asked, releasing her hand. Once she'd locked the door and tucked her keys in her bag, I rested my palm on her back to lead her to my truck. "Nice boots. Where'd you get 'em?"

"I drove up to Austin today. They were the least ugly pair I could find."

I could tell by the slight curve of her lips that she was baiting me, and I chose not to rise to it. "They look good on you. You wear them like a natural."

Her nose wrinkled, and I laughed as I opened the passenger door and offered to help her up. After a brief hesitation, she placed her hand in mine and stepped onto the running board to hoist herself into the seat.

My gaze dropped to her legs as her skirt rode up above her knees. Just that little glimpse of her bare thigh sent a hot electric pulse straight to my dick. As soon as she'd gotten herself situated, I shut the door and covertly adjusted myself inside my jeans.

"Are you ever going to tell me where we're going that requires cowboy boots as part of the dress code?" she asked when I climbed behind the wheel next to her. She'd been trying to pry the destination of our date out of me since Wednesday, but I'd refused to answer her questions because I didn't want her making her mind up against it in advance. "It's not cow-tipping is it? Because I have an ethical objection to playing cruel pranks on defenseless animals."

I snorted as I reached for my seat belt. "No animal that weighs two thousand pounds is defenseless."

"All the more reason not to taunt them."

"We're not going cow-tipping."

"Is it a barn-raising?"

I gave her a disbelieving look. "Is that what you think people do around here on a Saturday night?"

"How am I supposed to know?"

When I started the engine, the sound of country music filled the car and I saw Maggie's nose scrunch again. "Let me guess. You don't like country music?"

"Not particularly, no."

I laughed again as I backed out of the driveway. "You're gonna love King's Palace."

"That's where we're going tonight?"

"Yup."

"What is it?"

"It's a local landmark," I said. "People come from all over the state to go there."

"That doesn't tell me what it is. Are you going to make me google it?"

"It's a country-western dance hall."

Yet again, Maggie's nose wrinkled in distaste. "We're not dancing."

"Oh yes we are."

"I'm serious."

I cocked an eyebrow at her as I paused at a stop sign. "So am I. If you want the people of this town to give you a fair shake, this is how you do it."

"By dancing for them?"

"By showing them that you're one of them."

"But I'm not one of them," she said.

"That's the whole reason we're doing this—to make 'em think otherwise." I cast a sidelong glance at her. "How are your dancing skills?"

Her chin tipped up. "Adequate."

"Can you two-step?"

"No."

"Not to worry," I said. "I'll be glad to teach you."

She rolled her eyes. "Does George King own King's Palace too?"

I shook my head. "His father bought the building in the fifties and converted it into a dance hall, but one of George's brothers runs that side of the business, including the folk festival old Earnest King founded."

"The King family has their fingers in everything around here, don't they?"

"You don't even know the half of it."

George King held seats on the city board of development and

the police citizens advisory board in addition to having handpicked allies placed on pretty much every other local board, commission, and committee to make sure his interests were represented. My illustrious stepfather had the mayor, city council, county judge, commissioners court, and most of the other business owners in town in his pocket, not to mention the ear of our state legislators, congressperson, both US senators, and the governor's office. Almost nothing happened in Crowder without George's okay.

That was one reason I was so angry about the way people were scapegoating Maggie. They all knew damn well she wouldn't be able to do a single thing without George's full blessing. But everyone around here was too afraid of George to direct their anger his way. It was easier to attack an outsider—and a woman, at that—than the man who actually held all the power.

"What kind of relationship do you have with George?" Maggie asked. "Are you two close?"

"We're family," was all I said, disinclined to take a deep dive into our complicated history.

"Stepkids don't always feel that way."

When I glanced at her, she had her face turned to the window. "Are you speaking from experience?"

Her shoulder twitched with a shrug. "I have a stepmother and half-siblings I barely know. They're technically the only family I have left, aside from a few cousins, but we haven't spoken since my father's funeral five years ago."

"I'm sorry to hear that." Because she'd offered me something personal, I offered her something in return. "I was six years old when my mom married George. He treated me a hell of a lot better than my own father ever did." I tried to keep the bitterness out of my voice to avoid provoking more questions, but Maggie's head swiveled sharply my way, letting me know she'd seen right through me.

Instead of asking about my father, she surprised me with her next question. "But you didn't want to go into the family business?"

"I had my own dreams, and they didn't include going to work for George." Seeing how much pressure he put on his own kids and the way he used his money and power to control people convinced me I was better off making my own way in the world.

"Did you always want to be a firefighter?"

"No, not specifically. I just knew I wanted to help people instead of sell them stuff." I switched hands on the steering wheel as I shifted in my seat. "I got my bachelor's degree in social work."

"How'd you end up in the fire department?"

"During my internships, I noticed that people often found my size intimidating, especially when they were already in a vulnerable position. It made it harder for me to win their trust. I figured I should do something where I could put my size and strength to good use, so I applied to the fire academy."

"You really are Dudley Do-Right."

"Did you always want to be a management consultant?" I asked, trying to move the conversation off of me.

Maggie huffed out a wry laugh. "Yes, that's what every child dreams of. Being a management consultant."

"So what'd you want to be?"

"A ballerina."

I grinned as my mind helpfully supplied an image of Maggie in a formfitting pink leotard and tights. "You would have made a good one."

"I wasn't slim enough," she said. "Or talented enough to compensate for not being slim. I also wanted to be a florist for a while."

"A florist? Really? I've never heard that one before."

"I guess I thought it sounded nice, being surrounded by flowers all day."

"It does sound nice," I agreed, shooting her a smile.

When I slowed down and put on my turn signal, Maggie peered through the windshield at the building ahead. "Is that it?"

"That's it."

The truck bounced over a pothole as I turned into the dirt patch that served as the parking lot of King's Palace. The outside of the barn-like building wasn't much to look at with its rusty tin siding and rows of narrow windows. It had originally been built by German immigrants in the late eighteen hundreds as a community center that hosted Saturday night dances and Sunday morning sermons. These days it filled more or less the same function minus the preaching. A hundred years later, it was still the hottest spot in town on Saturday nights, hence why I'd brought Maggie here.

The parking lot was already halfway to full. The band wouldn't take the stage until eight, but a lot of people liked to get here early to stake out a table, drink, and get barbecue from the food truck outside while they waited for the dancing to start.

"It's not what I expected," Maggie said once I'd parked and cut the engine.

"What'd you expect?"

"Something flashier. And cheesier. And less rustic."

"I told you it was a landmark. It's one of the oldest buildings in town still standing." I climbed out of the truck and walked around to open her door.

Once again, she accepted the hand I offered her, and once again my eyes lingered on her legs as she hopped out onto the dusty ground. This time I kept hold of her hand, threading our fingers together as I shut her door.

A Darius Rucker song spilled out of the open doors and windows of the hall, and the smell of pit smoke perfumed the cool evening breeze. It was the perfect weather tonight for coming here—not too cold and not too hot.

"Are you really going to make me dance?" Maggie asked as we wended through the rows of cars.

"I really am," I confirmed with a nod. "But don't worry, I'm going to butter you up with food and beer first."

There were people milling around outside the open hangar-style door of the hall, standing in line for food, and sitting at the cluster of picnic tables next to the food truck. As we approached, I sensed Maggie tense beside me, bracing for their reaction.

"You sure this is a good idea?" she murmured. "It's not too late to forget the whole thing and leave."

I turned my head to cock an eyebrow at her. "I didn't take you for a quitter."

"I'm just not convinced this is worth doing."

No one seemed to have noticed her yet, but I imagined it was just a matter of time. Tugging her closer, I draped my arm around her shoulders. "That's because you haven't tasted the handmade German sausage yet. Trust me. It's worth it."

We started getting looks as soon as we got in line. First one head then others swiveled in our direction, more than one doing double-takes as people recognized Maggie and realized she was with me. You'd think I'd shown up with the Bride of Frankenstein on my arm the way they were gawping at us.

I knew some of the faces, but not all. Buck Peterson, whose dad owned Peterson's Plumbing, stood toward the front of the line with Kyle Browning, the assistant manager at the HEB. Cindy Diaz, who I'd gone on a few dates with five years back, was right in front of us with Delilah Green, a nurse I knew from the hospital. And I recognized a couple of my stepbrother Cody's friends among a group of college-aged kids at one of the picnic tables.

A hush fell over the crowd like someone had pulled sound-deadening curtains around us. I felt Maggie shift closer to me and gave her shoulder a gentle squeeze.

Everyone was staring now, even the woman taking orders inside the food truck. And not a single face looking at us was friendly.

Well, I'd wanted attention.

We definitely had it now.

14

MAGGIE

Ryan's pleasant, relaxed expression didn't waver as he met the unfriendly stares directed at us, but I could feel the tension vibrating through him. He pulled me even closer, tucking me against his side to send an unambiguous message to everyone watching, making sure they all knew we were here as a couple.

My arm snaked around his waist as I leaned against the solid shelter of his body, grateful not to be alone. Of course, I wouldn't be here at all if Ryan hadn't goaded me into it.

Why had I ever agreed to do this? Clearly it had been a terrible idea. These people didn't want me here. That was plain from the sneers on their faces. Ryan's presence at my side wasn't enough to deflect this much animosity.

He seemed to sense it at the same time I did. As I felt the muscles of the arm around me contract like a catapult readying to launch an attack, a lead weight settled in my stomach. I never should have let Ryan put himself in the middle of my problems. He might be big and strong, but he didn't strike me as a man who enjoyed violence. I dearly hoped I hadn't dragged him into a situation where he might feel obligated to raise his fists against his friends and neighbors to defend my honor.

While I was trying to figure out how to forcibly drag him back to the car before anything bad happened, Ryan's gaze settled on the two women standing just in front of us in line. He smiled as he bobbed his head in a cheerful nod, ignoring the taut atmosphere around us. "Hey, Cindy. Hi, Delilah. Good to see you."

They blinked several times, taken off guard, before they pulled themselves together enough to offer a subdued greeting in response.

Ryan directed his attention to the front of the line next, raising his hand in a wave. "Hey there, Kyle! You get any more babies born at the store recently?"

The inquiry was met with a murmur of whispering and shuffling up and down the line, but whoever Kyle was, he didn't answer.

"Hey, Buck," Ryan called out next, unfazed. "How's your dad been doing?"

A man in a blue checked shirt reached up to push back the brim of his cowboy hat. "Still working himself too hard. Same as always."

"You tell him I said he needs to take it easy. We don't want him giving us any more scares."

Amazingly, Ryan's friendly patter seemed to be defusing the tension. People were already turning away to resume their own conversations, having lost interest in us when we didn't immediately provide the hoped-for drama. A few prying eyes continued to dart in our direction, but they no longer felt quite so menacing.

As the line shuffled forward, Ryan's attention returned to the women in front of us. "How's your mom, Cindy? I heard she had a hip replacement."

"She's doing well," the Latina woman answered as her eyes flicked to me. "Getting around much better these days."

"I'm glad to hear it. You give her my best." Ryan shifted his gaze to the Black woman next to Cindy. "Haven't seen you at the hospital in a while, Dee. You change departments or something?"

"I've been working up in the ICU the last month," she replied, giving me an openly curious stare.

"Sorry, where are my manners?" Ryan said. "This is my friend Maggie. Maggie, this is Delilah, and this is Cindy."

"Pleased to meet you both." I offered them my hand as if everything was completely normal and we were all just having a pleasant chat.

"So are y'all *together*?" Delilah asked, putting it right out there. "Like, *dating*?"

"That's right." Ryan dragged me against him and smacked a kiss on the top of my head as Cindy and Delilah stared at us in wonder.

As for me, I was too awed by the wall of hard, lovely-smelling muscle I found myself crushed against to say anything at all. When Ryan released me, it left me so light-headed I had to clutch the back of his shirt for balance.

As he continued to make conversation with Cindy and Delilah while we waited for our turn to order, his hand slid down my back and squeezed my hip like it was something he'd done a million times before. I said very little, content to let him take the conversational reins as I quietly marveled at the feel of his enormous back muscles under my hand. After a while, I even forgot to notice the stares we continued to get as people walked by or got in line behind us.

Once Cindy and Delilah had gotten their food, Ryan let go of me to give them each a hug before they headed inside. By that point, I was starting to think he'd been right after all. Maybe he was so likable he could make people forget how much they hated me.

"They seemed nice," I said, watching the two women whisper to each other as they walked away. Speculating about me, no doubt.

"They are nice. Most everyone around here is when they don't let their emotions make them lose all sense of reason." Ryan draped his arm around me again and leaned in close to whisper in my ear. "Now's when you admit that I was right."

The tickle of his warm breath sent a shiver down my spine. I was becoming more accustomed to the physical contact, but not so much that I was unaffected by it.

"The night's not over," I reminded him, unwilling to concede so soon. We hadn't even gone inside yet. I didn't want to think about how many more people were in there and how many of them were predisposed to hate me.

"That's fine," he murmured, smiling as his hand smoothed down my arm. "You can tell me later. I'm more than happy to wait."

Warmth spread through my chest as I gazed up at his handsome, dimpled face and twinkling eyes. For a moment, I very nearly forgot who I was and who he was and that this was something we were doing for show. Fortunately, the arrival of our food brought me back to my senses as Ryan stepped forward to retrieve our order.

Passing me one of the styrofoam containers, he laid a hand on my back to guide me inside the dance hall. "In we go."

It was much bigger than it looked from the outside, a vast, vaguely cross-shaped space with a pitched beam ceiling, weathered wood floors, and antique tin signs decorating the exposed frame walls. Rows of long tables packed with people filled up the area immediately inside the door. A stage sat at the opposite end of the room with a bar off to one side and pool tables on the other. In the middle of it all was a large open space for dancing.

We paused inside the door as Ryan surveyed the rows of tables. There had to be at least a hundred people here already—maybe even two hundred. I suspected it would get even more crowded as the night wore on. Over half the long tables were occupied with rowdy groups of people eating, drinking, and shouting their conversations over the country music blaring from speakers mounted around the room.

The size of the crowd inspired a fresh wave of apprehension. It was one thing for Ryan to distract and charm a few dozen people standing around outside, but that wouldn't work with a crowd like this, especially when it was so noisy even he would have trouble making himself heard.

Once more taking my hand in his large, callused one, he led me down one of the aisles between two rows of bench seats. A chorus of voices hailed him by name as we neared a group of smiling people, a few of whom I recognized from the gathering in Ryan's backyard two weeks ago. They shifted down the benches to make a space for us to sit in the middle of their group.

"Everyone, this is Maggie," Ryan announced as he stepped over the bench. "Maggie, this is Kenzie, Ozzy, Casey, Gareth, Quincy, Tina, Ayesha, and Jamal."

I smiled at the assembled group, feeling slightly overwhelmed but relieved to be surrounded by allies. The more big, strong friends Ryan had around him, the less likely it was that anyone would try to start trouble.

He helped me climb over the bench to squeeze in between him and Kenzie, the female Highland Games athlete I'd spoken to in his backyard. We greeted each other as I sat down next to her.

Gareth, who I'd also met that day, pulled an icy beer out of a bucket and leaned across the table to offer it to me with a grin. "It's nice to see me again too, right, Maggie?"

Kenzie scowled at him as she grabbed the beer out of his hand and passed it to me. "Seriously, dude, are you even capable of interacting with a woman and not flirting with her?"

He flashed an extra-dazzling smile. "This isn't flirting. It's just my natural charm."

The woman sitting next to him jabbed him with her elbow. "You're such a dork, Gareth." She turned to me with a sunny smile. "Hi, I'm Casey, Gareth's roommate. And this is my brother, Ozzy."

The rumpled, curly-haired man on Casey's other side gave me a wave as he shoveled a handful of fries in his mouth. I recognized him as one of the throwers I'd seen in Ryan's backyard.

"Sorry about Ozzy," Kenzie said. "He's got the table manners of a four-year-old."

Ozzy stuck his tongue out at her, showing off a mouthful of half-chewed french fries.

Kenzie's nose scrunched in disgust. "Nice, *Oswald*. Way to prove my point."

"You asked for it, *Rose*," he shot back with a cheeky grin, earning himself a death glare from Kenzie.

"Don't be a butthead." Casey elbowed her brother, who elbowed her back hard enough to shove her into Gareth.

"Hey!" Gareth shot Ozzy a warning glare as he put a protective arm around Casey. "Don't make me separate you two."

"Don't start none, won't be none," Ozzy said with a shrug.

"Anyway," Kenzie said, turning to me again, "we're all a bunch of uncouth children. Are you sure you don't want to join our Highland Games club?"

I smiled, charmed by their youthful exuberance, as most of them appeared to be ten to fifteen years younger than me. It'd been so long since I'd socialized with anyone other than work colleagues, I'd forgotten what it was like to hang out with people who weren't worried about appearing professional. "Does everyone here do Highland Games?" I asked, glancing around the table.

"Not me," Casey said. "I'm just a hanger-on."

"Since the day she was born," Ozzy quipped, and Casey flipped him the bird.

Gareth pointed at the woman on his other side and the man sitting next to Ryan. "Quincy and Jamal work with me and Ryan at the fire station, but they both refuse to come throw with us because they're losers."

This statement inspired a vigorous argument to break out between the firefighters and the throwers, with Gareth gleefully egging both sides on.

Ryan leaned toward me as the debate raged around us. "You okay?"

"Yeah, I'm good," I said, surprised how much I was enjoying myself.

"Sorry, they can get a little boisterous sometimes."

"Did you know they'd be here?"

His lips curved into a smile. "I may have made a few calls and begged-slash-badgered them into meeting us here tonight. Hope you don't mind."

"Not at all," I said. "It was a good idea."

"I'm pleased you approve." Ryan gave me a wink as he flipped the lid of my food container open. "You better eat up. You're gonna need your strength on the dance floor later."

While I ate my brisket sandwich and fries, I listened to Ryan's friends banter back and forth. Despite my inclination to stay quiet, they kept drawing me into their conversations, asking my opinions on various points of discussion or questioning me about my background and travels—although I did notice they delicately avoided the subject of my job and the work I was doing for the creamery. I continued to get a few obvious stares from some of the people seated around us, but no one felt inspired to come over and say anything while I was surrounded by Ryan's stronger-than-average friends.

I was most of the way through my second beer and feeling nice and relaxed by the time the band took the stage at the far end of the hall. So much so, I didn't even argue when Ryan announced it was time to go dance. We all got up, save Quincy and Tina, who both declined and volunteered to stay with the purses and save our table.

Ryan clasped my hand, grinning as he pulled me toward the quickly filling dance floor. "Ready to get your two-step on, sweetness?"

"If I must," I said, studying the couples who were already dancing.

"Two-stepping is as easy as walking. I'm sure you'll be fine."

"I'm sure I will." It looked straightforward enough, a simple quick-quick-slow-slow pattern danced over six beats in four-four time. Piece of cake.

Ryan wore boots with heels as thick as mine, so when he pulled me into dancing position, I was eye level with his chin. With my left hand resting on his enormous biceps, it was all I could do not to caress it through his checked shirt as he explained the steps to the dance.

"You ready to give it a try?" he asked, and I nodded.

Mirroring his movements, I stepped back with my right foot as he stepped forward with his left. Two one-beat steps followed by a pair of two-beat steps. Repeat ad infinitum. Easy.

Ryan's eyes narrowed as he led us into the counterclockwise stream of dancers. "You've done this before."

"Nope," I said. "I've never two-stepped in my life."

"Then how are you this good at it so quickly?"

"I have some dance experience," I said with a shrug. Like a couple of decades worth of tap, ballet, and contemporary dance lessons, plus several semesters of ballroom dance in college.

Ryan wasn't a bad dancer either. For his size, he was impressively light on his feet. "What kind of experience?" he said. "You didn't learn this doing ballet."

"I did musical theater and dance in high school and college."

His blink of surprise morphed into a slow grin. "I sure would've liked to see that."

"Alas for you, you never will." Never mind that I had recordings of a few performances saved on DVD. They were buried in a box in my closet back home, and Ryan never needed to know they existed.

His brows pulled together as he steered us around a sweet, slow-moving elderly couple. "So why'd you act like you hated dancing? Or is it just dancing with me you find abhorrent?"

"It's the country-western part that put me off. Dancing with you is fine."

"Just fine, huh? That's all I get?"

I rolled my lips together, trying not to smile. "You're fishing for compliments again."

"That's exactly what I'm doing," he said. "Don't leave a man hanging."

"Dancing with you is better than fine," I conceded.

"How much better? Come on, I'm needy."

It was impossible not to smile at his playful, twinkling expression. "If it wasn't for the music, I might go so far as to call it actively enjoyable."

"Actively enjoyable?" he drawled. "Wow. Such effusive praise. Be still my heart."

I shook my head, laughing at his dramatics. "What if I said this is the most fun I've had in a long time? Is that better?"

"Much." His eyes softened as he smiled at me, and my heart

went *ping* against my rib cage. "I'm going to make a country-western lover out of you yet," he said and lifted his arm to spin me

I laughed as I came out of the spin and gripped Ryan's biceps again. "Doubtful."

If I wasn't mistaken, some of the glances being directed at me now looked more jealous than hostile. I felt like the friendless outcast who'd been asked to prom by the most popular guy in school.

"What musicals were you in?" Ryan asked, still smiling. "I want to be able to imagine it properly."

"I played the lead in *Kiss Me Kate*."

"Of course you did," he said. "I'll bet you absolutely killed as Lilli."

My eyes lifted to his in surprise. "Why Freckles, don't tell me you're a musical theater fan?"

"What? I can't have layers?" He cocked his head to the side with a smirk. "I'm not all country music and throwing weights around, you know. What else have you been in?"

"I was the Witch in *Into the Woods* and Miss Hannigan in *Annie*."

"I think I'm sensing a theme there," he said, raising an eyebrow.

"Yes, well, I tended to get typecast because of my height."

"That's not something I can relate to at all," Ryan said dryly.

I studied him. "Does it ever bother you the way people react to you because of your size?"

"It is what it is. Not like I can blame them."

"It does bother you," I said, still watching him.

A muscle ticked in his jaw. "I don't like making people feel afraid of me."

"That's where you and I differ. I happen to love it when people are afraid of me."

"I'll bet you do," he said as his lips quirked.

"It's not exactly the same though. No one's afraid I'll physically hurt them. They're just afraid I won't let them push me around the way they're used to being able to intimidate and walk over most women."

"That's true." He wasn't smiling anymore. "I don't like bullies, and I don't like it when people assume I am one because of my size."

I considered Ryan in silence for a moment as we circled the dance floor. "Is that why you're so dead set on helping me? It triggered your protective instincts when you saw me getting harassed?"

"I like helping people," he said, meeting my gaze. "Even when they don't want my help."

"I'm not a horse trapped in a swimming pool. I can take care of myself."

"You think I don't know that? You're one of the most badass, capable women I've ever met. But that doesn't mean you should always have to fight your battles alone. There's nothing wrong with letting someone else back you up occasionally."

I swallowed and looked away. "I guess I'm not used to anyone volunteering for the job."

"Well you'd better get used to it," he said, squeezing my hand. "As long as I'm around, I've got your back."

Before I could think of a reply, Ryan lifted his arm and spun me again before smoothly lowering me into a dip. He pulled off the move with enough confidence that my dance training kicked in and I relaxed in his arms, trusting him to hold me up as he bent me back toward the floor.

"See?" he said after he'd pulled me upright again. "It's not so bad, is it?"

"No, not *so* bad," I said as my heart beat an erratic rhythm in my chest. I wasn't sure if we were talking about dancing or learning to trust him. Both were turning out to be a lot easier than I'd anticipated.

"So what do I have to do to get you to sing for me?" he asked, his lips quirking.

I laughed and shook my head. "Get me a lot drunker than I am now."

His eyebrows rose as he broke into a grin. "That can be arranged."

———

RYAN and I danced three songs before Gareth requested to cut in. When I shrugged my assent, we traded partners and Ryan whisked Casey away.

Gareth was a competent dancer and a perfect gentleman, despite his playful flirting, but I found myself missing Ryan's company. My eyes kept seeking him out among the other couples circling the floor. As often as not, I'd find him looking back at me. He and Casey never seemed to be too far away. I suspected he was keeping close in case anyone decided to give me trouble.

After Gareth, I danced with Jamal and then Ozzy. The whole time, Ryan stuck close by as he danced with Ayesha and then Kenzie, keeping a protective watch over me. Finally, after my dance with Ozzy, Ryan reclaimed my hand for himself.

"Did you pressure them into doing that?" I asked, happy to be in his arms again.

"Doing what?" he said, frowning slightly.

"Asking me to dance."

He shook his head. "That was all them."

I narrowed my eyes at him, trying to decide if he was lying.

"I swear," he said. "I never even suggested it."

"If you say so."

"You know, Maggie, you might need to accept that some people actually find you likable. You're not the hideous ogre you think you are."

"I don't think I'm a hideous ogre. I'm a heartless, intimidating, extremely hot ogre."

Ryan laughed. "I'll give you two of those things."

"Which two?" I asked, lifting my eyebrows. Now I was the one fishing for compliments.

"Hot and intimidating," he answered without hesitation. "Obviously."

"You've never been intimidated by me though."

"I'm not easily intimidated," he said with a cocky grin. "Besides, I know something no one else knows."

"What's that?"

He leaned in until his lips brushed my ear. "Underneath that tough exterior you're secretly a softhearted marshmallow."

I wanted to deny it, but his low, rumbly voice sizzled through me, melting my insides into oozy-gooey marshmallow fluff. Ryan pulled back, his eyes crinkling warmly as they held mine, and I decided I didn't care if he made me into a marshmallow.

When the song came to an end, I was forced to admit I needed a restroom break and asked him where to find them.

"I'll take you," he said.

"I don't need you lurking outside the ladies' room, thanks. Just point me in the right direction, and I'm sure I'll manage." No one had bothered me yet, and I was feeling more confident that Ryan's plan was working as intended. Surely no one here would chance his wrath after seeing us dancing together.

For a second I thought he'd argue, but instead he pointed out the hallway beside the bar where the restrooms were located. "I'll be waiting by those high-top tables, okay?"

"You're very sweet, you know that?" Surprising both of us, I rose on my toes to kiss his cheek. Then I skedaddled before he could react.

As I was washing my hands after exiting the stall, two women entered the ladies' room chatting boisterously back and forth. I kept my head down, hoping they wouldn't notice me, but an uneasy prickle crept down the back of my neck as their conversation died out.

Lifting my gaze to the mirror, I found them both staring at me and making no effort to hide it. When I shut off the water and crossed to the paper towel dispenser on the wall, the taller woman, a brunette, advanced on me.

Her outward expression was pleasant enough, but that didn't necessarily mean anything here in the South where smiles and pretty manners could be just as malevolent as active aggression.

"Do you mind if I ask you a question?" she said in a thick Texas accent.

What's it like to have no soul? The accusation the woman had leveled at me in the grocery store clanged in my head as I straightened my spine, bracing for a confrontation.

Tonight had been fun for a while, but it'd been foolish of me to think my good luck would last.

15

MAGGIE

I drew my armor around me, prepared to accept the woman's censure. She could say whatever she had to say, but I didn't have to let it affect me. I could receive her anger with compassion, letting her get it out of her system, and walk out of here just as strong as I'd walked in. No matter what the people of this town thought of me, I wouldn't allow myself to be hurt by it.

Fixing a polite smile on my face, I lifted my eyes to meet the woman's gaze. "What can I do for you?"

"You came here with Ryan McCafferty, right? Are you two, like, *dating*?"

Her question was so far removed from what I'd been expecting, it left me momentarily speechless. "Um," I said eloquently as the paper towel I'd yanked on shredded in my hands, leaving me holding two tiny dots of soggy paper. "Oh...well..."

The entire purpose of tonight's outing had been to make everyone think Ryan and I were dating, but I found myself hesitant to answer in the affirmative. It was one thing to go through the motions of a date, letting onlookers draw their own conclusions, but another thing entirely to answer a direct question with a lie.

It would be a lie, wouldn't it? Ryan hadn't been shy about the fact that he found me attractive, but he'd also made it clear he had no interest in getting romantically involved with me or anyone else. When he'd claimed me as his date to the women in the food line, he'd been putting on a show, right? To make people believe he was off the market.

As I waffled, struggling to pry more than a square inch of paper towel from the clutches of the infernal dispenser, the woman yanked the plastic cover off the front and held a handful of folded towels out to me. "Here you go, honey. They always fill these dang things up so full you can't get them out to save your life."

"Thank you," I said, accepting the paper towels.

"Let me guess. Things with you and Ryan are complicated, right?" The woman exchanged a knowing look with her ponytailed friend. "It always is with Big Red."

"Big Red?"

"Ryan. Don't get me wrong, he's totally the sweetest guy in the world. But he can be hard to pin down. I'll bet you know what I mean, huh?"

I didn't have the slightest idea what she meant. I hadn't even known Ryan went by the nickname Big Red. But this woman seemed to know him well. *Intimately* well. "Did you and he go out?"

Nodding, she hooked her thumb at her friend. "We both did, actually."

"You both did," I repeated. "Wow."

What were the odds, considering he allegedly didn't date? Then again, Ryan had implied the no-dating thing was a more recent development. How many exes did he have running around this town exactly? In a dating pool this small, maybe you ended up getting around to everyone eventually. Maybe that was the real reason Ryan had given up dating. He'd already run through the whole pool of eligible candidates.

"I'm Stephanie, by the way," the brunette said, then gestured at the woman with the ponytail. "This is Lori."

"I'm Maggie," I said.

"Oh, yeah, we know who *you* are," Lori said brightly. "I imagine everyone around here does."

Stephanie turned to Lori. "How long's it been since you and Ryan were together? Must be over ten years back now, right?"

Lori frowned as she thought about it. "Closer to fifteen, I'd say. Brett and I are coming up on our ten-year anniversary, if you can believe it."

"That's right!" Stephanie shook her head in wonder. "Y'all had such a beautiful wedding. It was a real shame about all the food poisoning."

Lori nodded sadly. "I still can't even look at a deviled egg. Easter just doesn't feel the same without them."

Stephanie turned back to me. "Anyway, I guess it was about three years ago that Ryan and I went out."

"You know, I've always wished I'd tried harder when we were together," Lori said wistfully. "I only broke up with him because I thought he wasn't that into me. I never felt like I had his full attention.

"Exactly," Stephanie said with a nod. "Like he could take or leave the whole relationship, right? Like it was just something he was doing to pass the time."

"Phoning it in, more like," Lori said.

"Except in bed," Stephanie added with a grin.

"Oh yeah. My god!" Lori laughed as she fanned herself. "The things that man could do to me—best sex of my life. Don't tell my husband I said that though. He'd never recover."

They both cackled as I stood there feeling lost. The things

they were saying sounded nothing like the Ryan I knew. Except the part about him being excellent in bed, which I found easy to believe despite my lack of firsthand knowledge.

But phoning it in? Not giving them his full attention? That hadn't resembled my admittedly limited experience with him so far. If anything, he'd given me too much of his attention.

"I'm sorry, look at us just standing here babbling at you," Lori said, blushing a little. "You must think we're nuts."

"No, it's fine," I said as I tossed my paper towels in the trash.

"We're just nosy," Stephanie said. "But honestly, hold on to Ryan if you can. Good for you if you manage to pin that man down. It's way past time someone did."

"Okay." I edged toward the door, eager to escape this bizarre conversation. "Well, nice to meet you."

"Buh-bye!" Stephanie called after me as I fled the ladies' room.

I liked to think I had a finely honed radar for women who were pretending to be nice while trying to undermine me, but neither of them had set off my alarms. As far as I could tell, they genuinely were just nosy, like Stephanie had said. The fact that I was dating Ryan was apparently far more interesting to them than anything else I'd been accused of. *Weird.*

"Everything okay?" Ryan asked when I found him waiting for me as promised.

"Everything's fine." I craned my neck to peer in the direction of the bar. The two beers I'd had earlier had already worn off. "Do they have anything to drink here besides beer?"

He laid his hand on my shoulder and turned me back toward him with a frown. "What's the matter? You look spooked."

"Nope. Not spooked." I offered a smile to reassure him. "I made a couple of new acquaintances in the bathroom."

His frown grew deeper. "Who? What do you mean? Did something happen?"

I lifted his hand off my shoulder and squeezed his fingers. "Nothing bad. They're old friends of yours, apparently. Stephanie and Lori?

Ryan's face froze. "Stephanie Gift and Lori Halperin?"

"I didn't get their last names, but they seemed nice."

"What did they say?"

"Oh look, there they are now." I waved as they walked through the bar.

"Hey, Ryan!" they called out in singsong voices, waving back.

"Apparently you dated both of them." I turned back to him with a smile. "They were *very* complimentary."

"You said you wanted a drink, right?" He took me by the arm and steered me toward the bar.

"Exactly how many of the women here tonight have you dated?"

He cleared his throat as we got in line. It was hard to tell in the dance hall's multicolored lighting, but I was almost certain he was blushing. "A few."

"So more than just those two, then?"

"Mmhm," he mumbled without looking at me. "What do you feel like drinking? I can't vouch for the wine selection, but they've got some decent whiskey back there."

"How many more?" I asked.

"Hard to say." He shifted his weight from foot to foot. "It's a big place. I don't know who all's here tonight."

"Make a guess." It was wrong of me to enjoy his discomfiture so much, but I couldn't help it. "Five? Ten? More than that?"

"Why are you so interested?" he asked, rounding on me.

"Why are you so embarrassed?"

His eyes narrowed. "What did they say to you in the bathroom, exactly?"

My smile grew wider. "I told you, they were *very* complimentary."

"What does that mean?" He was definitely blushing. *Bless.*

"It means they were nice," I said. "Answer my question."

He looked away and cleared his throat again. "Three others that I've noticed."

So five in total. That was a high concentration of ex-girlfriends in one building. No wonder he was so nervous. "Will you point them out to me?"

"No, I will not."

"Have you dated any of the women we were sitting with earlier?"

"No."

I found myself relieved by that, since they were all considerably younger. "What about the two women we talked to in the food line?"

"One of them," he admitted.

"Which one? Cindy or Delilah?"

"Cindy," he said. "Now stop trying to embarrass me and tell me what you want to drink."

"I'll have whatever you're having."

"I'm driving, so I'm having water."

"Then I'll have water too," I said.

"I thought you wanted something stronger?"

I shrugged. "I don't want to drink alone."

When we made it to the bar, Ryan greeted the pretty dark-haired bartender by name and ordered two shots of Four Roses bourbon and two bottles of water.

While she was getting our drinks, I leaned in to speak into his ear. "Did you use to date her too?"

He sliced a look at me. "Keep it up and I'm going to think you're jealous, sweetness."

"You'd like that, wouldn't you?"

His lips quirked as he leaned in even closer. "I would, yeah." The feel of his warm breath on my face sent a wave of tingles down my back and between my legs.

The bartender lined our drinks up, and Ryan produced two twenty-dollar bills and pushed them at her with a smile and a *keep the change*. When I tried to protest that he should let me pay for something, he growled and shoved the two bottles of water at me before picking up the shots.

"I'm the one who asked you out on this date. I'm paying for it."

I followed him to an empty high-top table. "I thought this wasn't a real date."

"What makes you think that?" he asked as he set the shots down and took the waters from me.

"Isn't that what you said? It's just for show?"

"Just because we want people to see that we're on a date doesn't mean it can't be a real date."

"*Is* it a real date?" I asked, confused and conflicted. I wouldn't have agreed to this if I'd believed his intentions were romantic. But now that we were here, I found myself wishing it *was* a real date.

"We're dressed up, we're out together, eating and drinking and dancing. What's the saying? If it walks like a duck and farts like a duck, it's a duck." He pushed one of the shots toward me. "Have at it."

I knocked it back and set the glass down, enjoying the happy warmth that unfurled through me as the alcohol sank in. "Maybe it's all an act," I said as I gazed up at him, savoring every detail of his face. Lord, the man was irresistible. "Maybe you don't mean any of it."

Ryan's eyes locked onto me with the intensity of a cheetah who wanted to hunt me down on the Serengeti. "What would I need to do to make you think I meant it?"

I was still processing *that* question as he settled his large hand over mine on the table. There'd always been a flirtatious element to our banter, but the addition of touching escalated it to a whole new level.

"I suppose you'd have to kiss me at the end of the night." Saying the words aloud drove home just how badly I wanted him to do it. My gaze dropped to his mouth as I imagined what his kiss would feel like.

"That's a good point," he said as his fingers stroked the inside of my wrist. "You should keep an eye out for something like that. See if it happens and report back to me with your findings."

As much as I enjoyed his teasing, what I really wanted right now was a straight answer. "Are you planning to kiss me?"

"You'll have to wait till the end of the night to find out." His voice was low and doused with promise. Releasing my hand, he pushed the second glass of whiskey toward me. "Drink your other shot."

"That one's yours," I said.

He shook his head. "I got them both for you. I'm driving."

"But I told you I didn't want to drink alone."

"You're not alone. I'm right here, aren't I?" To illustrate the point, he shifted closer—close enough that his arm brushed against mine.

Unhelpfully, my mind chose that moment to remind me what Lori had said about Ryan's skills in the bedroom. Best sex of her life, she'd claimed. And Stephanie had seemed to agree.

"Are you trying to get me drunk, Freckles?" If so, it would take a lot more than two little shots of whiskey.

"I'm trying to make sure you have a good time, sweetness. Is it working?"

Yes.

Instead of answering his question, I downed the other shot

of whiskey. "Do you *want* to kiss me?" I challenged, fueled by a fresh infusion of liquid courage.

Holding my gaze, he reached up and stroked his fingers over my cheek as he pushed my hair behind my ear. "What do you think?"

I swallowed, every nerve ending in my body ablaze. "I think you do."

"Do you want me to?"

"Yes." I couldn't be bothered to pretend otherwise anymore. I wanted it too much.

Ryan leaned in, and I held my breath, wondering if he was going to kiss me now. But his lips moved to my ear instead of my mouth. "Are you ready for me to take you home?"

"Yes." I jerked my head in an eager nod. "Yes, I am."

16

RYAN

I didn't know what the fuck I was doing. No, that wasn't true. I knew *exactly* what I was doing. I just didn't know how to make myself stop.

How was I supposed to resist a woman like Maggie when she'd as much as admitted she wanted me? Strong as I was, I wasn't strong enough for that.

Guilt needled at me as we drove toward home. I'd been leading her on all night, letting my craving for her get the better of me. Writing checks I shouldn't cash. I hadn't been able to help myself. She'd been so damn responsive, giving as good as she got. I could tell she liked the push and pull between us as much as I did, that it excited her the same way it excited me.

Christ, I hadn't even touched her yet and my whole body felt like it was on fire.

Squeezing the steering wheel, I dared a glance at her. She was staring out the window with her legs crossed and her knee jiggling impatiently.

Five minutes later, I pulled into my driveway and cut the engine. Without looking at Maggie, I jumped out and walked around to open her door. She beat me to it, hopping down before I could offer my hand. Our eyes clashed for a charged moment before she dodged around me and set off for her house, leaving me to decide whether to follow her—or not.

Not following wasn't a possibility. No matter how conflicted I might be, there was no way I wasn't going to walk my date to her door.

I trailed behind, shamelessly staring at Maggie's backside as she strode ahead. When she got to her porch, she spun around and waited, watching me approach. I stepped onto the porch and stopped in front of her, still waging a war with myself.

Maggie's lips twitched as her gaze swept over my face, and I felt that twitch all the way down in my groin. Those expressive lips of hers were too goddamn much. All night long they'd been taunting me, every cheeky twist and confident curve hitting me like a punch to the solar plexus. The desire to taste them was so strong I had to clench my hands into fists to hide the way they were shaking.

"I had a good time tonight." Her tone was deceptively mild, projecting a nonchalance I knew she didn't feel any more than I did. "Thank you for taking such good care of me."

"I didn't do all that much," I said, equally casual, as if I couldn't care one way or the other what happened next. As if I wasn't standing there fighting a losing battle against the impulse to push her up against her front door and crush my mouth to hers.

We were back to playing our game again. Circling around each other. Pretending indifference and daring the other to break first. But Maggie's eyes gave her away. Her bright blue irises had been swallowed up by midnight black pupils that betrayed her desire. It stole another block from the teetering Jenga tower of my willpower.

"Yes you did," she said and turned her back to me as she dug in her bag for her house keys.

My gaze traveled down her body, drinking in the swell of her hips and the lush roundness of her ass.

God, I wanted her.

If I was a better man, I'd say good night right now and go home before anything else could happen between us. But I wasn't that better man, because instead of walking away and putting a stop to this, I stepped up right behind her.

Maggie stilled, the hand clutching her keys frozen in midair halfway to the lock. I'd stopped just short of touching her, but she could sense how close I was. Her sharp intake of breath told me that.

I pressed both my hands against the door, caging her between them. My nose pushed into her hair, and I inhaled a lungful of that pretty, flowery scent I'd been catching whiffs of all night. "Tell me something, sweetness. When's the last time anyone took care of you?"

The way she pushed back against me, seeking more contact, gave me the answer before she spoke. "I can't remember."

I trailed my fingers up her arm to her shoulder. "That's what I thought."

It was easy to guess from the walls she'd constructed around herself that she'd been disappointed too many times. It made me angry to think about it.

"You're a magnificent woman, Maggie." I moved her hair aside, baring the back of her neck. "You deserve to be cherished."

When I pressed my lips to her skin, a shiver vibrated through her body into mine. That small fracture in her composure threatened to topple me with a wave of dizziness. She wanted me badly enough that her ironclad self-control dissolved at my touch. What would it be like to break down all her walls? Who would she be underneath it all once she was bared to me completely?

I skated my hand around her rib cage as I dragged my mouth down her neck. She tasted like sin, sweet and luxurious. Like a temptation I wouldn't be able to resist now that I'd sampled it.

But it was okay because Maggie wasn't the sort of woman to get clingy, not when she was only here for a few months before she moved on to her next job. She was far too practical and independent to let herself get attached to someone like me. I doubted she'd even glance in the rearview mirror when she'd left me and this town behind.

It would be all right if we enjoyed each other's company for a little while. The only one in danger of getting hurt here was me. Right at this particular moment, I couldn't seem to give a fuck about that.

My hand spread over her stomach, holding her against me as I pressed a kiss to her temple. "I can feel you trembling."

"Ryan." The way she said my name sounded like *please*. Faint and shaky. Imploring.

As if I could say no to her now, even if I wanted to.

If I was being honest, we'd passed the point of no return long before this moment. We'd been racing down the road toward this inevitable outcome since I'd proposed to take her on a date. Maybe even before that. Maybe since I'd first noticed her watching me through my window.

"Do you want me to touch you?" I asked.

"What do you think?" she said, throwing my earlier words back at me.

A laugh rumbled out of me as I kissed her jaw. "Maybe you should invite me inside, then."

Maggie sprang forward and shoved her keys in the lock.

Once she had it open, she twisted around and seized me by the arms, towing me inside.

I kicked the door closed behind me as I crowded her up against the nearest wall. "I still haven't heard an actual invitation."

Her eyelids fluttered when my hips pinned hers. "Would you like to come in?" she murmured, letting her purse fall to the floor.

"Yes. Very much." Smiling, I buried my face in her throat.

A sigh escaped her when I sucked at her delicate, sweet-tasting skin. Or maybe that was me who'd sighed. It was hard to know at this point. I felt like I was floating above my body, untethered from it yet still somehow rooted in my fleshly desire.

My hands drifted over her hips and up the sides of her waist, stopping just below the swell of her breasts. I felt her ribs expand as she arched her back, straining toward me, eager and impatient. Instead of giving her what she wanted, I teased my thumbs along the band of her bra while I kissed my way down to her collarbone.

With a huff of frustration, Maggie covered one of my hands with hers and dragged it up to her breast.

I nipped her gently as I let out a chuckle. "It's like that, is it?"

Drawing back, I gazed down at her as I palmed her breast. Just as I'd thought, it more than filled my large hand. Her dark eyelashes fluttered against her cheek when I rolled her nipple between my thumb and forefinger.

"You think you want to be in control, do you?" I pinched her harder, and her head fell back against the wall with a whimper.

God, that whimper. So damn needy and inviting. I'd be hearing it in my fantasies from this moment forward. Every time I thought of Maggie, I'd think of that sound.

I slid my other hand into her hair, tugging a little as I cupped the back of her head. "Or would you rather give up control and let me do things to you? I think maybe you'd like that even more."

She drew a ragged breath, her eyes searing into mine. The hazy look she'd gotten told me how much she liked it, even if she wasn't willing to say it out loud. Not yet, anyway. She was too proud and stubborn to submit so easily. But I knew I could get her there. And I knew how much she wanted me to.

A slow smile spread over my face. "Yeah, that's what I thought. You like the sound of that, don't you? You'd like to let me have my way with your beautiful body."

Flames bloomed in her cheeks as she squirmed against my dick, nearly making my eyes roll back in my head. I was so hard I felt like I could punch through a fucking wall.

Leaning in, I flicked my tongue against her ear. "You're getting wetter just thinking about it, aren't you? I'll bet your panties are fucking drenched, you want it so bad."

A tremor went through her, and she arched against me with a moan.

"Tell me I'm wrong, and I'll stop." My fingers stole inside the neckline of her dress, dancing over her silky bare skin. "Is that what you want? You want me to stop?"

"No." Her protest shuddered through her whole body like it had been forcibly wrenched out of her against her will. "Don't stop."

Roughly, I shoved her dress off her shoulder and scooped her breast out of her bra. "Gorgeous," I murmured, licking my lips as I kneaded the pillowy mound. "Just like I knew it'd be."

When I leaned down and touched the tip of my tongue to her bare nipple, she melted against me. Pressing my open mouth against it, I banded my arm around her waist to hold her up and keep her locked against me.

I drew her nipple into my mouth, alternately sucking and licking as her fingers slid through my hair. The rougher I was, the more she writhed against me, seeking more of that electrifying friction between us. Our lust had gone from a steady drip to an open floodgate. Neither of us had any choice at this point but to let the torrent sweep us away.

Mercilessly, I ground the hard jut of my erection against her. "You feel that? That's what you do to me, sweetness."

Her hands dragged down my chest and over my stomach, clawing at my shirt. When her questing fingers dipped inside the waistband of my jeans, my cock throbbed to the point of agony. But it'd just have to keep on suffering, because that kind of play wasn't part of my plan.

Grabbing Maggie's hips, I spun her to face the wall and locked my arm around her middle. "Be still," I hissed as I grabbed a fistful of her skirt and hiked it up.

All due credit to her self-control, she went still as a statue, even as I stroked my hand up her thigh.

"I'm going to give you what you want," I said, "but you're not allowed to move. That's the deal." I could feel her legs quivering as my fingers skated higher. "If you move, I stop. You understand?"

Her head jerked in a nod.

"That's a good girl," I said as I shoved her skirt up around her waist and out of my way. "You're so good at this. You want me to touch, don't you? You're aching for it."

"Yes," she whispered, leaning back against me. "Please."

When I brushed my knuckles over her underwear, she let out a gasp and her whole body jerked like she'd been shocked.

"How long has it been since a man's touch has satisfied you, Maggie?"

"I don't want to tell you," she said, her thready voice barely a whisper.

"You have to." I cupped her mound, flexing my fingers over the soaking wet fabric. "Unless you want me to stop, that is."

"Years," she bit out, bracing her hands against the wall. "Three. Maybe four."

"That's way too long," I said. "No wonder you're so desperate for it. But don't worry, I'm going to make you come." I found the swollen bud of her clit through her underwear and circled it with my index finger.

Her head fell back against my shoulder as she let loose another one of those delicious whimpers. I fucking loved how well matched we were in size, as if she'd been custom-made for me.

"You need it so bad, I can tell. You're dying to open yourself up to me." I hooked her thigh with my left hand and lifted it up, spreading her wide. "You're going to let me do whatever I want to you. As long as I make you come, you're mine to take as I see fit. Isn't that right?"

A shudder racked her frame, but she didn't resist or deny it. She liked it too much to protest.

I rewarded her by shoving my hand inside her underwear. The thin, stretchy fabric had plenty of give to it, allowing me ample room to maneuver as I dragged my fingers through her slick folds. Her relieved exhale disintegrated into a moan when I flicked her clit with my thumb.

Growling in approval, I sucked at her neck while I explored her with my fingers, taking my time to learn her body and note her reactions to every touch and motion.

"Is this a fantasy of yours, Maggie? Giving up control and letting a man take you however he pleases?"

When she didn't answer, I let my hand go still between her legs. She whimpered and rolled her hips, trying to rub herself against my fingers.

"What did I say about moving?" I growled, nipping her neck.

She made a frustrated noise but went still.

"That's better." My tongue darted out to lick the spot I'd nipped. "I think it is your fantasy, and you don't want to admit it. You know how I can tell? Because you get even wetter when I talk about it."

We both groaned when I worked a finger inside her. Jesus, she was so fucking hot and tight. I closed my eyes as I imagined what it'd feel like to bury myself inside her, how hard she'd squeeze my dick as she came around it.

I wanted that. I'd give almost anything to have it.

Almost.

Shoving my own desires aside, I rubbed the heel of my hand against her clit, giving her the friction she needed while I pumped my finger inside her.

"Oh god." She was shaking now, her breaths coming out in rough pants. She was close, teetering on the edge of losing control. It was a beautiful thing to witness. Even better than I'd imagined.

My own self-control was fraying along with hers. Much as I wanted to draw out this encounter, I wasn't strong enough to make her wait anymore. "You feel so good," I murmured, kissing her neck as I stroked her faster, increasing the pressure. "You're so fucking hot like this. So perfect."

She fell over the edge with a bitten-off cry, her whole body tensing. I felt her walls clench around my finger with every pulse that shuddered through her, leaving her lax and trembling in my arms.

"There you are. I've got you." I lowered her leg to the floor, holding her tight as she sagged weakly against me. Her face turned to nuzzle into my neck, and I closed my eyes again as I placed a tender kiss on her forehead.

She was so sweet and pliable in this state. More than

anything, I wanted to lift her into my arms, carry her into the bedroom, and spend the rest of the night lavishing her with attention. The last thing I wanted to do was let her go.

Fuck, I'm in trouble.

The thought propelled me out of my lust-soaked daze. I needed to leave before I let things go too far. The lines I wasn't supposed to cross existed for a good reason. It wasn't just myself I risked by ignoring them.

I hadn't been prepared for the way this woman unraveled me. She'd strutted into my life on those incredible legs, flashed those challenging eyes, and I'd been under her spell ever since. But if I let her get close, she'd see the truth I'd been trying to hide from everyone. Underneath the surface I was a broken wreck of a man with an uncertain future. I wasn't what she needed or deserved.

As soon as Maggie could stand under her own power, I spun her around and backed her against the wall.

I ached to cover her mouth with mine, but I couldn't afford to. I couldn't even let myself look her in the face or I might lose my resolve. Instead I pressed my lips to her forehead, stroking my hands down her arms as I drew in a slow breath, inhaling her rich, sweet scent as I reminded myself that I had nothing to offer her. "I enjoyed the hell out of that."

Her hands squeezed my biceps. "Me too."

"And now I'm gonna go."

"Now?"

The surprise and disappointment in her voice tore at my chest.

It's for the best. It's for her own good.

"Always leave 'em wanting more. That's my motto." Cupping her jaw, I laid a final, firm kiss on her cheek. "Good night, sweetness. Don't forget to lock up behind me."

I forced myself to let go of her and walk out, putting much needed distance between us. Once I'd closed the door behind me, I only paused long enough to listen for the sound of her deadbolt shooting home, so I'd know she was safe.

As soon as I heard the telltale click, I trudged a path back to my house, wondering how big of a mistake I'd made tonight.

17

MAGGIE

So. That happened. I wasn't sure how to feel about it.

Up until the moment Ryan had abruptly said good night and walked out, everything had been going great. Better than great. More like stupendous.

I had no idea what to make of his hasty departure. Despite giving me the best orgasm I'd had since Obama was in the White House, Ryan had left me feeling strangely unsatisfied. I'd barely even gotten to touch him. As much as I'd enjoyed being the recipient of his concentrated and *highly* skilled attentions, I really would have liked a chance to get at that body of his.

Leave 'em wanting more indeed. Mission damn well accomplished there.

But was that the real reason Ryan had left? Or had he regretted letting things get physical and used that as a flimsy excuse to make a quick exit?

Admittedly, my gut wasn't always the most reliable in these kinds of matters, but right now it was coming in firmly for the latter. There'd been something off about Ryan's exit. He'd shifted gears too quickly and been in a little too much of a hurry to get away from me.

He hadn't even kissed me on the mouth, which I'd only realized after he was gone.

That was pretty weird, right? I'd told him he'd need to kiss me at the end of the night to convince me it was a real date. And then he hadn't.

What was that about? Did it mean tonight hadn't been a real date after all? Was an orgasm Ryan's way of letting me down easy? Or was it supposed to supersede a kiss?

I couldn't tell if I'd been dissed or not, which meant I had no idea how I should act around him after this. Was he done with me? Were we dating now? Or was it some other murky third option that involved orgasms but no relationship?

I *hated* not being sure of myself. Damn him for making me feel that way.

On top of that, I was disappointed the evening hadn't lasted longer. I'd wanted to spend more time alone with Ryan. I'd wanted more of *him*. I'd wanted to at least kiss him, dammit, and touch more of that body of his, and give as good as I got. I'd wanted to make him feel as much pleasure as he'd given me.

I tried to tell myself I should be grateful for Ryan's expedient departure. He'd done me a favor by removing himself without expecting reciprocation. I ought to be ecstatic, not up in my feelings because he hadn't kissed me.

But *why* hadn't he kissed me?

———

WHEN I GOT up the next morning, after a restless night of sleep and self-recrimination, Ryan's truck was gone. If he was working a shift today, he'd be gone for the next twenty-four hours. That meant there'd be no chance of seeing him until tomorrow night.

Good, I thought. Just as well. I could use a cooling-off period to kick these feelings I shouldn't be having to the curb. Some distance to help me disinvest myself in Mr. Ryan McCafferty.

An hour later, he texted me.

I had a really great time last night.

Of course.

Right when I'd resolved to put my walls back in place, he'd tossed a grappling hook over them. Why were men like this?

I stared at the text, debating how or if I should respond. The detached, logical part of me said it would be best to pull the emergency stop and end things between us now, before it got too complicated.

Too late, said the not-so-detached part of me. *It's already too complicated.*

All the more reason to end it. Ryan was a distraction I didn't need. Look how he'd already messed with my confidence. Honestly, getting involved with him was the last thing I wanted.

Liar, the voice in my head whispered. Getting involved with him was exactly what I wanted. More than I'd wanted anything in a long time.

Impulsively, I typed a reply to his text and hit send before I could think better of it.

Did you?

I regretted it immediately. It sounded passive-aggressive, needy, and pitiful. Everything I didn't want to be. See what Ryan was doing to me? Turning me into a weak version of myself I despised. What had happened to being detached and logical? I was supposed to be a sensible person.

I scowled at the screen as it mocked me with the information that my message had been delivered. It wasn't too late to tell Ryan I wasn't interested in seeing him anymore. All I had to do was type another text telling him that.

Except my fingers refused to do it, the traitorous appendages. Seconds passed, then minutes, and no reply came from

Ryan. No little dots appeared on-screen to let me know he was typing. All I got back from him was silence.

Why had he even bothered to text me in the first place?

And now I was upset about that too. *Dammit!* I hated that he made me react this way. He shouldn't have so much power over me.

Angrily, I tossed my phone onto the couch and switched on the TV. There was plenty of work I could be doing, but I wasn't in the mood to deal with any of it right now. I flipped through the various streaming services, searching for something to watch, but nothing appealed. I wanted to distract myself but didn't actually feel like watching anything.

Thirty minutes later, I'd resorted to retail therapy and had my laptop balanced on my knees as I squinted at lipstick colors online. When my phone rang next to me, I sighed and reached to shut the sound off, assuming it was a spam call.

It was an incoming call from Ryan.

I bit down on my lip, only hesitating for a second before answering it. "Hello?"

"Why do you answer your phone like you don't know who's calling?"

"Hello is a perfectly normal way to answer a phone," I shot back in irritation. "Why are you calling me?"

"Am I not allowed to call you?" he asked, sounding confused.

"No, you are. I'm just surprised you did."

"Why wouldn't I want to call you? And why don't you believe I had a good time last night?"

"I never said that." Curse that whiny, passive-aggressive text. What had possessed me to send that?

"Something's wrong," he said. "Tell me what it is."

I couldn't very well tell him that I was angry because he'd made me care more than I wanted to. That he was too irresistible. That I wanted him more than I should, more than was safe, because it made me weak and vulnerable. Telling him all that would be exposing too much. It would only make me weaker and more vulnerable.

"Nothing's wrong," I said.

"You're a liar."

Of course he saw right through me. Of course he did. That was the whole problem, wasn't it? How well he seemed to understand me. Infuriating.

"Is there a reason you called?" I asked. "Other than to harass me, that is?"

"Yeah. I wanted to hear your voice."

Oh. I squeezed my eyes shut, trying not to feel anything. My heart was not melting at the soft sincerity in his voice.

"Is that okay?" Ryan asked.

"Yes. It's fine."

"There's that word again. You can't give me more than just fine?"

"It's nice, all right? Is that better?"

His low, husky chuckle pulled a smile to my lips against my will. "You're amazing for my ego, sweetness."

"I had a good time last night too," I said. Because it was the polite thing to do and also the truth.

"I'm glad to hear it because I wanted to talk to you about our next date."

"Is there going to be a next date?" I asked, super casual, like I was fine either way and my pulse hadn't leaped at the mere suggestion.

"Why wouldn't there be, since we both just said how much we enjoyed the last one?"

"I wasn't sure if further dates would be necessary."

"Oh no, they're necessary all right." He went silent for a beat. "Don't tell me you thought we were one and done."

When I didn't respond right away, he swore under his breath.

"You can't seriously think, after I got you off like that last night, that I'd want to walk away without seeing you again."

"Maybe that's how you operate," I said, carefree as an ocean breeze. I wasn't the least bit invested either way. "You did leave pretty abruptly. How am I supposed to know?"

"I had a shift today." He sounded remorseful.

Hairline fractures were forming in my detachment. "You could have said as much. You could have said something more than goodbye."

"You're right. I'm sorry. The truth is..." He swallowed so hard I heard it through the phone. "The truth is I had to get out of there before I lost my self-control and stayed up all night making you come over and over."

I sucked down a gulp of air. "Oh."

"Yeah, *oh*," he said, his voice rough as sandpaper.

"Aren't you at work right now?"

"Yeah, I'm standing in the middle of the station with the rest of the crew listening to every word I say. They're all waving for me to tell you hi from them, by the way."

A smile quirked my lips. "You're messing with me."

"Of course I am," Ryan said. "I waited until I could step outside to call you in private because I'm not a dumbass."

"That's a relief."

"I'm sorry if the way I left made you think I didn't have a good time," he said, growing serious again. "Because I promise you the exact opposite is true. You wouldn't believe the cold shower I had to take last night. I thought I was going to get frostbite before my dick went down."

"Good to know," I said, although I felt a little bad for him.

"Now that we've cleared up how I feel, how do *you* feel? Do you want to go on another date with me?"

"I..." Yes. Yes, I did. But should I? Going on more dates was no way to disinvest myself.

"Maggie?"

"Obviously, I find you attractive," I said, still hedging.

"Obviously," he repeated dryly. "Just in case you had any lingering doubts, I find you insanely attractive as well."

"Thank you. That's nice to hear."

"So we've established we're hot for each other. Does that mean you're game for a second date? Or is there some other reason you don't want to go out with me?"

"I just wouldn't want anyone to get the wrong idea," I said. *Meaning me. I'm anyone.*

"What idea would that be?"

"That this is more than it is." I took a breath. "Neither of us is interested in anything serious, right? You don't want a relationship, and I'm only here temporarily. Getting involved would be impractical." *There. Distance.* I'd done it.

"I'm proposing a date, not a commitment," he said. "It doesn't have to be complicated."

Doesn't it? I thought. And then I thought, *maybe not.*

"It's kind of ideal if you think about it," he went on. "We both want the same thing."

"Which is?"

To have lots of hot sex. That's what I want.

"To see each other without the pressure of it turning into anything serious or long-term. Simple, easy, no complications. Isn't that what you want?"

In other words: hot sex with no attachment. "Yes," I said. "Exactly."

"Perfect. So we're in total agreement."

Everything he was saying sounded reasonable. Rational. Sensible. I gave in and stopped trying to fight it. "In that case, I'm fine with a second date."

"Don't get carried away with the enthusiasm."

I bit back a smile. Why was his pouting so cute? It shouldn't be cute, but it was. "You know what I mean."

"Yeah, but I'd still like to hear you say what you mean instead of saying it's just fine."

"I'd like to go out with you again," I said, feeling a giddy thrill at the prospect. "If that's what you want."

"That's what I want," he said with a smile in his voice. "So it's decided. How about Friday night?"

"Friday night works." I closed the browser tab on my laptop, no longer feeling the need to console myself with emotional support lipstick. Not when there was sex with Ryan on the horizon. "Where are we going this time? Will it require shopping for a specialized costume again?"

"Yeah, as a matter of fact. You don't have a PVC allergy, do you? If so, we'll need to make sure the fetish shop has natural rubber bodysuits in stock."

I laughed at the thought of squeezing myself into a PVC catsuit. There wasn't enough baby powder in the world. "You're messing with me again."

"Unfortunately yes," he said. "Because I'd love to see you in fetish wear."

"In your dreams, Freckles."

"You can count on that, sweetness." The low, husky voice he'd dropped into rippled through me like a heat wave. "But for Friday, wear whatever you'd wear out to dinner at a nice restaurant."

"Is that what we're doing?" I asked. "Going out to a restaurant?"

"You'll have to wait and find out when we get there."

"You can't just tell me now?"

"I could," he said, "but I like surprising you too much."

I didn't want to admit it, but I liked it too.

18

MAGGIE

The spreadsheet on my computer screen blurred into indecipherable shapes before my eyes. I couldn't seem to concentrate, and it was all Ryan's fault.

Since our phone conversation yesterday, I hadn't been able to stop thinking about him and our upcoming date. I was actually giddy with anticipation, which was something I hadn't felt about a date in...longer than I could remember at this point. I'd missed it, that hopeful sense of potential, the fizz of nervous excitement when you were infatuated with someone.

That was all this was, I'd decided. Infatuation. Which was fine because infatuation wasn't the same thing as attachment. It wasn't real or meaningful or complicated. It was a temporary high that would dissipate on its own in time.

But it was certainly fun while it lasted.

A knock on my open office door dragged my attention back to the present. I looked up to find Josie King standing in my doorway and instinctively braced myself for bad news.

Her smiling expression didn't telegraph bad news, however. "Are you busy?" she asked, letting me know that whatever she wanted wasn't that urgent.

I let myself relax as I waved her in. "I could use a break." When she shut the door behind her, I raised a curious eyebrow. "What's up?" I asked as she sank onto one of the chairs facing my desk.

Crossing her legs, she interlaced her fingers and rested them on her knee. Her smile twitched wider as her gaze fixed on me. "So...you and my stepbrother, huh?"

I opened my mouth and promptly shut it again, unsure how to respond.

Technically, my personal life was none of Josie's business. Ryan had no legal connection to King's Creamery, and therefore my relationship with him didn't pose a conflict of interest. I wasn't required to disclose the details of my personal life to anyone at the company.

I suspected she wasn't here out of professional interest, however, based on the way she was smiling. And since the whole point of going out with Ryan had been to call attention to our relationship, it would be pointless to deny it.

Except, once again, I found myself hesitant to claim our relationship as genuine. Given our mutual disinterest in a serious attachment, Ryan and I weren't headed for long-term couple-dom. As much as I'd come to like and respect Josie over the two months we'd been working together, I didn't feel good misleading her about my intentions toward a member of her family.

"I take it you heard we went out on a date Saturday night?" I said carefully.

"Everybody in the whole damn town has heard about it by now," she said. "You two caused quite the stir stepping out together like that."

I shook my head in amazement. "News really does travel fast around here, doesn't it?"

"Never underestimate the Crowder gossip mill," she said. "I

don't know if you're aware, but Ryan happens to be one of this town's most sought-after and elusive bachelors. Any change in his relationship status ranks as major news around here. The fact that the first woman he's dated in years happens to be *you*, of all the people he could have chosen, makes it even more juicy."

"I'm glad I can offer the town busybodies some entertainment." I had to hand it to Ryan. He'd been dead right about the amount of attention we'd attract.

"So?" Josie leaned forward, her expression eager. "What's the deal? Are you into my stepbrother? How did you two even meet? I want to know everything."

"Are you asking as my professional colleague or as Ryan's stepsister?" I said, still treading cautiously.

"I'm asking as your very nosy friend who promises not to let anything you say leave this room." Josie made a cross over her heart followed by a zipping motion across her lips.

"We're neighbors," I said, smiling. "I happen to be renting the house next door to Ryan's."

"Interesting." She propped her chin in her hand. "Tell me more."

"There's not that much else to tell. Every time we'd run into each other, Ryan was very friendly."

"Yeah, he's like that." Josie's mouth pulled to one side. "He's also very good-looking—or so most women seem to think, anyway. I don't see it myself, having known him since we were kids. But he's obviously very, um, large. And muscly."

"Yes. I couldn't help noticing that as well."

"I'll bet," she said, smirking.

"I'm afraid I was a little unfriendly to him at first," I confessed as I pinched the bridge of my nose. "I didn't have any interest in getting to know my neighbors, which Ryan seemed to find barbarous."

Josie laughed. "He would. People around here don't understand what it's like to live in a high-density city. If everyone in Manhattan was always stopping to shoot the shit and chat each other up the way we do here, it would be unlivable. No one would ever get anywhere or have any peace."

"Exactly!" I said, feeling vindicated. "Why would I want to drop everything I'm doing to make meaningless small talk with a total stranger just because we happened to walk past each other?"

"So you were rude to him." Josie looked delighted. "He probably loved that."

"He did seem to take it as a personal challenge," I said, warming at the memory. "The more I tried not to talk to him, the more he insisted on talking to me."

"So how'd he finally win you over? Or did he just wear you down?"

"Oh, well..." I pressed my lips together, not wishing to rehash the scene in the grocery store, which I'd refrained from reporting to avoid getting anyone in trouble. "Remember how someone painted graffiti on the street in front of my house?" Since it had involved actual vandalism, I had reported that incident to both Josie and HR in case the situation escalated into a security threat.

"Of course!" Josie said, slapping the heel of her hand against her forehead. "If you're neighbors, Ryan would have seen it. That must have kicked his protective instincts into hyperdrive."

I smiled. "He called my landlord and got her to pay for security cameras that he installed around the outside of my rental house himself."

"That sounds like him all right." Nodding, she leaned back against her chair. "He's a big ol' mama bear, always looking out for everyone else."

"I think he's taken me on as his own personal charity case. It was probably pity that motivated him to asked me out."

Josie tilted her head at me. "I don't think so. Ryan helps people every day, but you're the first woman who's tempted him out of his self-imposed dating moratorium in a long time."

"We've been on one date. Let's not get ahead of ourselves."

"Too late," Josie said, shaking her head. "Half the town is planning your wedding, and the other half has gone into mourning because you've taken Ryan off the market."

I pinched the bridge of my nose again. "Of course they are."

"The good news is, from a PR standpoint you couldn't have picked a better piece of arm candy to improve your image around here. Everyone adores Ryan. He's probably rolled up in his fire engine and helped half the people in town at one time or another. He's universally beloved."

"That is convenient," I said, poker-faced.

"If we're lucky, whoever fed the *American-Statesman* that hit piece on you will think twice before messing with my brother's girlfriend."

"I take it Terry hasn't found the source of the leak?"

Josie shook her head. "IT said they couldn't narrow down who might have accessed the file." She folded her arms and smiled at me. "I'm not going to ask for any gross details, because Ryan's my brother and *ugh*. But are you seeing him again?"

"We're going out again on Friday," I admitted.

She brightened. "So you two are date-*ing*. As in ongoing and potentially serious."

I shook my head, not wanting her to get her hopes up. "I'm only here for a few months, and neither of us is looking for a relationship."

"Did he say that?"

I nodded. "We're only hanging out casually."

"Hmm." Josie frowned.

"What?"

She shook her head. "Nothing."

It was obviously *something*. I opened my desk drawer and pulled out a bag of Trader Joe's peanut butter pretzel nuggets that I'd picked up when I was in Austin.

"Want some?" I offered, setting them on the desk in front of her.

"Oh, you *are* a temptress." She plunged her hand into the bag and popped a pretzel nugget in her mouth with a happy sigh. "God, I miss living in a city with a TJ's."

I said nothing as I took a pretzel for myself. Either she'd decide to tell me what was on her mind or she wouldn't.

"It's funny," she said after helping herself to another pretzel. "Ryan and I have always been polar opposites. I used to be laser-focused on my career with no interest in tying myself down, but Ryan always struck me as a natural family man. He was practically a second father to his half-brothers after their mother died, and you should see how great he is with Manny's kids. I remember him telling me once when we were younger how much he wanted to get married and have a big family of his own one day, but then he never did."

That didn't sound at all like the man who'd claimed to be too set in his ways to make room in his life for a partner. I wondered what had changed his mind.

"But now we've both flip-flopped," Josie went on, crunching thoughtfully on a pretzel. "I'm the one thinking about marriage, and it sounds like Ryan's embraced the bachelor life."

"You're thinking about marriage?" I said, raising my eyebrows with interest.

"Thinking about it. Not doing it." She shoved another pretzel in her mouth with a sigh. "Not anytime soon, the way things are going.

"Do you have a prospect in mind?" I knew nothing at all

about Josie's personal life other than what I'd pieced together from her résumé.

"I did. Still do, I guess. But I'm not sure he feels the same way. I'm starting to suspect I've hitched my wagon to the wrong horse. *Again*." She smiled tightly as she smoothed her ponytail over her shoulder. "Seems to be a habit of mine."

"Maybe he'll come around," I said, hoping for her sake it was true.

"Maybe." She didn't look optimistic. "Anyway, whatever it is you've got going on with Ryan, congratulations. He's a good catch."

That might be, but this fishing trip was strictly catch-and-release. I'd be tossing Ryan back into the lake so he could wriggle away to once more enjoy his freedom.

"Can I ask you something?" I said.

Josie's eyebrows lifted. "As your professional colleague or as Ryan's stepsister?"

"As my friend," I said. "And also a bit of the other two."

"Hit me," she said, gesturing for me to continue.

"Do you think your father's heard about me and Ryan?"

She let out a snort. "Oh, yeah. Dear old Dad knows everything that happens in this town. I wouldn't be surprised if he knew before you did."

I didn't find that the least bit comforting. "How do you think he'll feel about it?"

"Ah, well, that's more difficult to predict. Dad's not the sort to share all his thoughts and feelings—unless he's unhappy with you, then he'll definitely let you know exactly what he thinks."

"So if he doesn't say anything…"

"You're probably fine." Josie offered me an encouraging smile. "The good news is Dad's never butted into Ryan's life the way he does with those of us in the line of succession. Lucky bastard." Her smile took on a wry twist. "Now, if you were dating me or Nate, you'd need to watch your back—not that you'd want to date Nate unless you have a thing for angry robots."

I smiled. "And here I was thinking he was only that way around me because he didn't like me."

"Oh, no, he probably doesn't like you," Josie said. "But it's not personal. He doesn't allow himself to like anything. My brother suffers from a terminal case of stick up his ass, the result of an obsessive need to please a father who can never be pleased." She shot me a warning look. "I didn't say any of that though."

I mimicked her zipping motion over my lips. "Not a word leaves this room."

She leaned back in her chair and flicked a pretzel crumb off her dress pants. "The sad thing is, Nate wasn't always like this. When we were growing up, he was a lot easier to bear. Almost fun sometimes, even." Her faint smile faded into pensiveness. "It was only after our brother Chance died that Nate turned into a single-minded automaton."

"That is sad." I knew George King's eldest son had died in a car accident when he was still in college—there'd been a big fundraiser last month for the Chance William King Memorial Foundation. It wasn't hard to guess that he'd been the one groomed from birth to follow his father into the family business, and his unexpected death had left the unprepared younger son scrambling to take his dead brother's place. "Poor Nate."

Josie nodded. "Dad put a lot of pressure on him. He put pressure on all of us, but Nate volunteered himself as whipping boy with self-destructive gusto. I, on the other hand, got the hell out of here as fast as I could."

"And yet you eventually came back," I pointed out.

"I did, didn't I?" Her lips twisted to the side. "Making it in the real world turned out not to be as rewarding as I'd hoped."

"How so?"

"It was a confluence of events, really." Her shoulder twitched as she examined her manicure. "A bad ending to what I'd thought was a good relationship at the same time a shithead boss was making the career I loved into a living hell. Plus a lot of my friends were moving out of the city and starting families. It made me question what I was doing with my life. The grind that used to seem so important started to feel pointless. I guess I got worn down." She glanced up with a wry smile. "Or maybe I wanted to feel like a big fish in a little pond."

"I've read your résumé," I said. "You were a pretty big fish in a big pond."

"Not big enough to avoid being a pawn in someone else's power trip." She reached up and flicked her ponytail off her shoulder. "It was disheartening to realize that no matter how much I accomplished or how hard I fought my way up the ladder, there'd always be some bigger fish pushing me around."

I nodded in understanding. "Why do you think I started my own consulting business?"

"You were smart," Josie said. "I came running home to Daddy."

"As far as I've seen, your father didn't give you anything you hadn't earned on your own."

"That's true," she agreed, forcing cheer into her expression. "There are some people who say otherwise, but honestly, fuck them. By the time I dragged myself back here, I'd developed a thick enough skin that I don't give a shit what my father or anyone else thinks of my choices." Her smile died on her lips. "Poor Nate never got there, unfortunately for him. He cares too much about everything. That's his problem."

I'd never thought about Nate that way, but it helped make sense of his uptight personality. He continually pushed himself and everyone else too hard, chasing an impossible state of perfection. He'd probably never learned to roll with the punches or shrug off defeats. Not with his father constantly reminding him of every shortcoming and judging him against the memory of a brother who'd never had a chance to make mistakes of his own.

"But I didn't just come back home for the job," Josie said. "As much as I used to hate it when I was young, I missed being part of a tight-knit community where everyone knows everybody else."

My nose wrinkled. "I'm glad you're happy here, but I couldn't stand living in a place like this long-term."

"Don't be so sure," she said, wagging her finger at me. "This town has a way of sneaking up on you and getting under your skin."

I snorted. "Now *that* I can believe."

Josie laughed and shook her head at me. "I used to think I loved living in the city too. But I'm telling you, Maggie, there's something special about a town like this. There's a sense of connection you get here that I've never felt anywhere else. Like I'm really part of this place instead of just someone who happens to live here. Trust me, you stick around long enough and you'll feel it too."

I suppressed a shudder at the thought. Lucky for me, I wouldn't be here that long.

19

RYAN

"So it is a restaurant," Maggie said when I parked in the lot next to Post Oak Lodge. "You could have just told me as much."

I tossed a wink at her as I shoved my door open. "Where's the fun in that?"

She waited for me to come around and give her a hand out of the truck. The dress she'd worn tonight was a clingy, low-cut black number that did amazing things for her figure. Once again she'd worn red shoes, as if she knew what they did to me. When she carefully stepped down in her killer red heels, I didn't even pretend not to be ogling her gorgeous legs.

"You look fucking amazing." I interlaced our fingers together once she had both feet on solid ground. "I like those shoes a lot."

"Thank you." A smile plucked at her shiny, plump lips as her eyes traveled down my body. Her bright red lipstick perfectly matched her shoes and both made me equally horny. "You're looking quite handsome yourself."

The feel of her appreciative gaze made my gut tighten. It was all I could do not to tug her into my arms and lay a kiss on her right then and there. But I'd promised myself I'd keep things between us slow and casual. Shoving my tongue down her throat before we'd even gotten inside the restaurant was neither slow nor casual.

I needed to keep myself on a tight rein, so I didn't lose my head completely. Boundaries. Restraint. Discipline. She already had too much of a hold on me. If I let myself go, I'd be absolutely fucking lost and there'd be no coming back.

Making myself take a step away, I led Maggie toward the restaurant, eager to be in polite company where there'd be less temptation to touch her the way I wanted to.

"The decor is...interesting," she commented as we walked through the bar to the maître d' stand.

I glanced around us at the log cabin walls, exotic animal-pelt barstools, and hunting trophies ringing the ceiling. "Is that supposed to be a nice way of saying you hate it?"

Post Oak Lodge was the nicest restaurant in town, but with all the traveling Maggie had done it must seem provincial to her. The best Crowder had to offer couldn't compare to big-city restaurants with celebrity chefs and Michelin stars. Nothing our town had to offer was good enough for someone as accomplished and well-traveled as Maggie.

It helped to be reminded of that. We were a pit stop for her, me included. It was the only reason I felt safe letting myself do this with her. There was nothing here that could tempt her to stay, not when she had so many reasons to leave.

She squeezed my hand, her soft smile letting me know she hadn't meant any offense. "No, it's just very Texas."

I couldn't argue with that. The decor had a lot in common with George King's tastes, though it felt more appropriate for a restaurant specializing in steaks and wild game than a family home.

When the maître d' showed us to our table, I stopped

Maggie before she could slide into the booth. "Sit on this side, next to me."

She gave me an odd look but sat where I indicated and scooted over so I could squeeze in beside her.

After the maître d' had left us with our menus, I leaned in to speak quietly in Maggie's ear. "We want to be seen together, and we want everyone to know we're on a date."

The spectacle we'd made at King's Palace last weekend seemed to be having the effect I'd hoped. Maggie hadn't experienced any further incidents of harassment, but we needed to keep up appearances. I'd specifically requested a table in the main room when I made the reservation for tonight. The side of the booth where we sat faced the doorway, so we'd be visible to everyone walking through the crowded restaurant.

"Good thinking." Maggie turned her head to gaze at me, and I became aware of how close we were sitting. Painfully aware. Her mouth was near enough to taunt me, I could smell her perfume with every inhale, and mere inches separated our thighs under the table.

I hadn't thought this through well enough.

As if reading my mind, her red lips tilted with a smile. "Cozy."

In need of a distraction, I picked up the wine list. "Do you want to get a bottle of wine?"

"Will you help me drink it?"

"Afraid not," I said. "I'll be sticking with water tonight."

Her lips pursed. "Because you're driving?"

"That's right, but don't let that stop you."

A tiny wrinkle formed between her brows. "So you never drink when you're driving? At all?"

"Depends," I said, flipping open my menu.

"On what?"

"On how long it's going to be before I have to drive and whether I'm responsible for someone else's safety."

"Is it because you're a first responder that you're so cautious about drinking and driving?"

"That's part of it." I pretended to study the menu, even though I'd been to this restaurant enough that I knew it by heart. "I've definitely seen way too much of what happens when people get careless."

"And the other part of it?"

I kept my eyes on the menu as I answered. "I had a stepbrother named Chance who was killed by a drunk driver. I guess it made an impression."

"Right, of course," she said, her voice soft with sympathy. "Josie mentioned him the other day."

"She did?" I looked up, surprised that Josie had brought up Chance with someone outside the family. Or anyone at all, frankly. She and Nate didn't talk about their older brothers much.

Maggie nodded but didn't say anything else.

The subtle tightening of her mouth told me she didn't feel comfortable telling me anything else about her conversation with Josie. As it happened, I wasn't eager to talk about my family either. I slid the wine list over. "You should get whatever you want to drink without worrying about me."

"What if I promised to linger over dinner for at least two hours? Would you have a drink then?"

I didn't like disappointing her. Taking her hand under the table, I lifted it to my lips and brushed an apologetic kiss over her knuckles. "No, because I'm your designated driver tonight. If you suddenly weren't feeling well or needed to leave for an unexpected reason, I'd want to be able to get you home safely."

"You're disconcertingly responsible, you know that, Dudley?"

Laughing softly, I released her hand and looked down at my menu again. "You're not the first person to tell me that."

"What about after you take me home? Will you have a drink with me then?" Her voice had dropped an octave, and I felt her gaze on me like an inviting caress.

A bolt of heat shot through me as I locked eyes with her. "If you offer me one, I'll be more than happy to take you up on it."

Her mouth opened, then snapped shut again as she looked past me.

"Evening, Ryan!"

I turned away from Maggie to greet the server standing at my elbow. "Evening, Christie. How've you been?"

I was pleased to see she was working tonight. Christie Kimble and her mother were two of the town's most notorious gossips, which was another reason I'd brought Maggie here. News of our date tonight was certain to spread like wildfire now that Christie had seen us together.

"I've been good." Her smile grew wider before her gaze shifted to Maggie. "I've been real good."

Maggie straightened her spine in response to Christie's scrutiny. Her fingers twitched on the tablecloth like she wanted to clench them into a fist, and I laid my hand over hers.

Christie tracked my movement like a bird of prey as I slid my fingers between Maggie's. "What can I start y'all off with to drink?"

"I'll have a vodka martini," Maggie said with an unruffled smile. "Extra dry with a twist, please."

Christie's gaze darted back to me. "You want anything besides water tonight, Ryan?"

"No thank you, I'm good as I am." I turned to smile at Maggie as I stroked her fingers. "But we'd love to hear the specials."

While Christie recited tonight's off-the-menu items, I kept my focus on Maggie, idly toying with her hand. After she'd finished her sales pitch, Christie said she'd give us a minute to make up our minds and scuttled off to place our drink order—and most likely text her mother and everyone else she knew to tell them what she'd seen.

"Did you date her too?" Maggie asked when Christie was out of earshot.

I recoiled a little at the question. "No. She's too young for me."

"She's not that young. How old are you?"

"Just shy of forty, and she's barely out of her twenties."

Maggie shrugged as she slipped her hand out of mine to reach for her water. "Most men wouldn't see that as a problem."

"Well I do."

She considered me for a moment. "You're five years younger than me. The age gap doesn't bother you?"

"Five years isn't as much of a gap as ten. And there's a big difference between a woman in her twenties and one in her forties."

"Yes, there is."

"I know what I like, and it's not younger women." I let my eyes sink lower, indulging in a slow perusal of Maggie's figure as a smile tugged at my lips. "Does it bother *you*? Being seen with a younger man?"

Mirroring my smile, she conducted her own study of my body. "Not in the least."

"Glad to hear it." I reached over and opened her menu for her. "If you're wondering what's good here, the answer is everything. But the South Texas antelope steak is a favorite."

We passed the next few minutes discussing the menu. Maggie expressed skepticism of all the gamier options and announced her intention to order the beef tenderloin, despite my endorsement of the antelope. I decided I'd get the wild game mixed grill so she could at least sample the more exotic meats, which she only agreed to consider, depending on how appetizing the food looked when it came out.

We were still haggling over it when Christie came back. She rested her hand on my arm as she leaned over to set the martini glass in front of Maggie. "Y'all know what you want to order?"

While I communicated our choices, Maggie casually lifted my arm and draped it around her shoulders, nestling herself against me. My mind catalogued every sensation—the warmth of her body, the press of her thigh against mine, the soft nudge of her breast—as I struggled to hold on to my train of thought.

Christie's eyes were wide as moons as she repeated our order back to us. As soon as we confirmed she had it right, she swept our menus off the table and hurried off, looking downright discombobulated.

I arched an eyebrow at Maggie. "Not that I'm complaining, but was your sudden urge to cuddle inspired by something other than my magnetic sex appeal?"

"She was flirting with you right in front of me."

My brow furrowed in confusion. "No she wasn't."

"You're not really that naive, are you?"

"I guess I am, if taking our dinner order counts as flirting."

Maggie made a scoffing noise. "She put her hand on your arm."

"She was just leaning across me to set your drink down."

"Servers don't just casually touch customers under ordinary circumstances. Her breasts were right in your face—don't tell me you didn't notice that."

"No, I noticed all right," I admitted with a grimace. "Even though I tried really hard not to."

"You didn't think it was unusual for a woman you're not dating to thrust her breasts in your face?" She was looking at me like I was thick as a post. Which I was starting to think I was.

"I thought it was an accident."

Her eyes rolled to the heavens. "That was no accident. It was a test."

"A test for who?"

"*Us*. You to see if you'd take the bait, and me to see if I'd defend my territory."

I crooked a grin. "I'm your territory now, am I? I thought that sort of retrogressive attitude was frowned upon in enlightened society."

It earned me another eyeroll. "She wanted to see if I would react when she flirted with my date."

"That's why you plastered yourself against me. To mark me as your property." I pulled her closer, liking the sound of that. I also liked that Maggie's hand was now resting on my thigh.

"Yes. Otherwise she might have thought we weren't on a serious date. But since she's gone now…" She started to shift away, but I tightened my hold, keeping her right where she was.

"Not so fast. I like having you here. As long as you're not uncomfortable?"

"Definitely not uncomfortable," she said, resting her head on my shoulder.

Enjoying this unexpectedly cuddly version of Maggie, I smoothed my hand down her back and settled it on her hip. "So did I pass the test?"

A soft laugh vibrated through her. "Yes, you were appropriately clueless about her flirting and didn't offer her any encouragement. Well done."

"Whew. That's a relief. I'd hate to think I was going around unknowingly encouraging anyone." I still wasn't sure there'd been any real flirting, but Maggie probably knew what she was talking about better than me. "Wait, so every time a woman accidentally touches me, does that mean she's flirting with me?"

She lifted her head from my shoulder to see if I was serious. When she saw I was, her lips quirked in amusement at my ignorance. "More often than not. Most women don't go through the world touching men unnecessarily unless they're either in a relationship or want to be."

"Huh." The information put a different spin on a lot of social interactions I'd had in the past. Now that I knew, I sort of wished I could go back to being blissfully oblivious.

"You never realized that?" She laughed, finding my naivete hilarious.

I shrugged. "I'm a big guy. I figured I was in the way and people had a hard time avoiding me."

Maggie's laugh grew loud enough that several diners at neighboring tables turned their heads to see what all the merriment was about. It was a beautiful thing to see her so happy and unrestrained, and even better to know it was for me. "They have a hard time avoiding you all right, but not because you're in the way. It's because they're trying to cop a feel of those big muscles."

I cast a pointed glance at the hand she had on my thigh. "The way you're doing right now, you mean?"

Her fingers flexed, making my dick twitch in greedy anticipation. "Yes, exactly like that."

I cleared my throat and took a sip of my water. At this rate, I wasn't going to make it through dinner.

A saucy smile curved her mouth as she leaned forward to retrieve her martini. She settled back against me and lifted the glass to her lips.

My thumb lightly stroked her waist as I watched her. "Speaking of women, there's something I've been wondering about for a while. With all your wisdom, maybe you can shed some light on it for me."

She arched a suspicious eyebrow at me. "Why does this feel like a trap?"

I offered her a placid smile. "I don't know, sweetness. Why are you so paranoid?"

"Because I don't trust you."

I knew she was teasing, but her words sank uncomfortably into the pit of my stomach. The ugly thought that I was using her for my own selfish needs whispered in the back of my mind.

Was I? Or was I projecting my insecurities onto her? Maggie wasn't the sort of woman to let herself be pressured into anything she didn't want to do, and she was as disinterested in a permanent entanglement as I was. The fact that she was here with me right now meant it was where she wanted to be. For the moment, at least.

Her expression softened as she gave my thigh a gentle squeeze. "You know what I mean."

I forced a smile and covered her hand with mine, subtly sliding it away from my dick. "I hope so."

She laced our fingers together. "Ask me what you wanted to ask."

Leaning back, I angled my head to make sure I had a good view of her face before I asked my question. "What does it mean when a woman spies on you through her window at night when you're working out in your garage?"

She flinched so hard she sloshed martini out of her glass and down the front of her dress.

Stifling my laugh, I rescued the glass from her hand before she lost more of her drink. "Careful, people will think you have a drinking problem."

"You *knew*." She directed an accusing glare at me as she grabbed a napkin to blot the front of her dress.

"Here, let me do that for you." I relieved her of the napkin and pressed it to her damp breasts, enjoying myself thoroughly.

"Stop feeling me up in public," she hissed, snatching the

napkin away from me. "I can't believe it. All this time, you knew. Why didn't you say anything?"

"I think the more important question is: Why did you do it?"

She drew her shoulders back as her expression grew defensive. "You were on display in plain sight. It was hard not to see you."

"But you didn't have to keep looking, did you? You didn't have to stand there in your dark kitchen watching me. You didn't have to keep coming back night after night to watch in secret."

Her lips pursed in chagrin. "You could see me."

"You know what I think?" I leaned in and brushed my nose against her cheek as I let my voice drop lower. "I think you liked what you saw. You did, didn't you?"

A shiver went through her, and her fingers tightened on my thigh. "You know I did."

I fought to hold still when she drew back to look at me. Her pupils were as wide and dark as the heavens as they gazed into mine.

A smile played at the corners of her mouth. "You know what I think? I think you wanted to be seen. You liked knowing I was looking at you."

I licked my lips, suppressing my own shiver. "I did."

Her smile grew wider. "So I guess we're even, then."

20

MAGGIE

My stomach fluttered with a mix of nerves and anticipation the whole drive home from the restaurant. This was it, finally. The part of the date I'd been looking forward to all week—getting Ryan alone and all to myself.

Sitting so close to him at dinner had been the sweetest kind of torture. The heat of his body soaking into mine, combined with all those little touches and light brushes against my skin, had kindled a slow-burn inferno inside me. My blood was positively humming in my veins by the time we pulled into his driveway.

The sudden silence that descended when Ryan cut the engine made the air inside the truck feel heavy with expectation. Instead of jumping right out of the cab like usual, he shifted in his seat to face me.

His gaze settled on me like a hot stroke over my skin. "Are you going to invite me in for that drink now?"

I swallowed, fighting the urge to throw myself at him right here and now. "Maybe you should invite *me* in for a drink. You've been inside my house multiple times, but I've never been invited inside yours."

Something that looked like discomfort flickered across his face. "You're not missing much."

"I'd still like to see it," I said as I reached across the console and slid my fingers up his thigh.

Ryan made a sound in the back of his throat and leaned over to unbuckle my seat belt. A big hand curled around the nape of my neck, pulling me closer so he could kiss the corner of my jaw. "I don't have anything to drink at my place right now," he murmured as he trailed his index finger down my sternum.

Distantly, I wondered at his reluctance to invite me into his house, but I wasn't inclined to press the issue and ruin what was looking to be a very promising evening.

That's exactly what he's counting on, a voice whispered in the back of my highly preoccupied brain as Ryan's hand slid inside my dress.

Fortunately, I wasn't so far gone that I failed to remember the new cameras mounted around my house when he started to push my neckline down. "Hey," I said and caught his wandering hand. "Are any of those security cameras you installed pointed at us right now?"

"Shit," he muttered, letting me go and drawing back. "Are you going to invite me in for that drink or not?"

Briefly, I considered asking him why he didn't want me in his house. But the drumbeat of lust pounding in my ears was a far more pressing concern. I wanted Ryan and didn't really care where I had him as long as it was private and camera-free.

"All I have is wine and vodka."

His gaze focused on my mouth. "I'll drink anything you've got."

My tongue darted out to wet my upper lip, and I saw his

pupils darken. "Would you like to come in and have a drink?" I said, feeling slightly faint.

"I thought you'd never ask."

He helped me climb out of his truck and trailed me to my front porch. This time, he kept his distance as I opened the door and gestured for him to follow me inside.

"What'll it be?" I said as I set my purse down on the way to the kitchen. "I've got a bottle of red open, but there's tonic and limes in the fridge if you'd rather have a vodka tonic."

"I'll have whatever you're having," he said, ambling behind me with his hands jammed into his pockets.

I took the lazy way out and filled two wineglasses while Ryan's gaze took in my bare counters and empty sink.

"You cleaned up," he said as I handed him his glass.

"I am capable of it on occasion."

"You do that just for me?"

My jaw tightened. "I did it for me. I don't clean up for men." *Not anymore.*

He lifted his eyebrows at my terseness but kept quiet.

"Sorry," I muttered into my wine. "Sore subject."

"I don't expect you to clean up for me," he said.

"Good, because I'm not going to change for you or anyone else." I'd made a promise to myself after my divorce. No man on earth was worth compromising or diminishing myself. Been there, done that, got the emotional baggage to prove it.

"I wouldn't want you to." Ryan ducked his head to catch my eye. "Just to be clear, I like you exactly the way you are. Hard edges, messy habits and all."

The man was a natural-born charmer who always knew the exact right thing to say. Except when he said things like that, it didn't sound like a line. It was easy to believe he meant it. Too easy. *Dangerously* easy.

I didn't trust myself around him. That was the problem. The

attraction between us was so strong, so overpowering, I couldn't think straight when I was with him. All my good sense, my logic, my rationality went out the window as soon as I looked into his eyes. I had the unsettling sense he'd be able to talk me into anything he wanted to. Even more unsettlingly, part of me was absolutely okay with that.

An odd smile played over his face as he sipped his wine.

"Why are you smiling like that?" I asked.

Ryan looked up at me, his dove gray eyes soft and guileless as they held mine. "Because you're beautiful, and I'm happy to be here with you right now."

This guy was definitely too good to be true. He had to be, saying things like that. How did he do that? Just say things so tender and direct as if it didn't cost him anything?

He didn't even have to touch me to make a mess of me. I was standing here with my heart pounding and my legs shaking, and he hadn't even kissed me yet.

Why hadn't he kissed me?

He leaned a hip against the counter, watching me. "Tell me what you're thinking right now."

"I'm wondering what we're doing here."

"I thought we were having a drink."

"Is that all?"

The corners of his lips quirked. "Hopefully not."

"You've never kissed me on the mouth."

His face went carefully blank. "I haven't?"

"You know you haven't," I said. "Why is that?"

Ryan moved closer and took my wineglass, setting it on the counter with his. His gaze settled on my face again, and his tongue dragged across his lower lip, taunting me. "If you want me to kiss you, sweetness, all you have to do is ask."

"Kiss me, then."

He brought his hand up to cradle my jaw. I held my breath as he tilted his head and leaned in with maddening slowness. His lips were so close now, only a breath from mine. And yet he still wasn't kissing me. I would have stomped my feet in frustration if my legs hadn't felt so unsteady beneath me.

"That sounded more like an order than a request," he said in a voice halfway between a growl and a purr.

"Please kiss me," I whispered weakly. My whole body felt like it was made of liquid.

A smile curved Ryan's lips as he brushed them over my mouth in a soft, closed-mouth kiss that wasn't the least bit chaste. In no hurry whatsoever, his lips caressed mine, exploring their shape with gentle, insistent presses while his hands moved over my body in a way that felt almost worshipful. *Cherishing*, just like he'd said I deserved.

I let out a sigh when he drew back to gaze at me with eyes as dazed as I felt. His thumb traced my jawline until it found my fluttering pulse, and he smiled and captured my lips again, this time with urgency instead of softness.

The luscious taste of him washed over me as his mouth devoured me in savoring slides. I let myself fall into him, drowning in the devastating heat of his tongue and rough friction of his stubble. It was too wonderful. Too unexpectedly perfect.

Until he pulled back again, his face flushed as his eyes held mine. We stood there staring at each other with our chests rising and falling in shallow, rapid breaths.

"More," I said and grabbed the front of his shirt with both hands to drag him closer. My blood surged as our mouths crashed together, and I kissed him with everything I had, arching against him, aching to get closer and feel his hard body against mine. He groaned and kissed me back like he couldn't get enough. His greedy hands traveled all over me, squeezing and fondling, rough rather than reverent.

Without warning, Ryan broke off the kiss and took a swift step back, leaving me standing on my own, breathless and dizzy. Teetering slightly, I reached out to steady myself on the counter.

There was something feral in his eyes as he stared at me. It reminded me of a wolf stalking a lamb that had wandered too far from the herd.

"Take off your underwear," he said, licking his lips.

The gruff command sent a tingling shock through me. I didn't think twice before fumbling under my skirt and shoving the lace down my legs.

"Leave the shoes on," he said when I started to step out of them.

I did pause then, looking up to see if he was serious. "Really?"

"You have no idea what the sight of those shoes on you does to me," he said in a voice gone hoarse.

I stepped out of my underwear, leaving on my red stiletto heels as requested. "What does it do to you?"

"Makes me want to bend you over the kitchen table, spread your pussy with my fingers, and eat you out until you come all over my face. It's pretty much all I've been able to think about all night."

"Oh," I whispered as the air rushed out of my lungs. It was like he'd unlocked a hidden door to my secret desires, the ones I'd buried deep, unwilling to acknowledge their existence even to myself.

And yet he knew. Somehow he saw right through me. My protective walls were nothing more than transparent film to him, as fragile as a soap bubble. It was terrifying to be known so intimately, but also unbelievably thrilling.

"Oh? That's all you've got to say?" The corners of Ryan's mouth curled with mischief. "Don't get shy on me, sweetness. Tell me how you feel about that."

"I feel good about it. Extremely good."

"Extremely good, huh?" He held out his hand. "Get over here, then."

When I slipped my hand into his, I could feel it shaking before his fingers tightened around mine. It was even more of a turn-on, knowing he was as excited and off-balance as me.

He jerked me against him, just rough enough to let me feel how strong he was. Instead of frightening, it was electrifying to glimpse a fraction of the power he kept so carefully in check.

Ryan's big hands slid over my body, handling me like something that belonged to him. Because I did. There was no pretending otherwise. The lust surging through my veins made my body pliant and my brain tractable. I was more than willing to do whatever he asked in exchange for the pleasure he promised.

He spun me around, and his fingers encircled my throat as he pressed his mouth to the back of my neck, pushing the strap of my dress aside to kiss a tender trail along the curve of my shoulder.

Just as I started to relax against him, he pushed me down onto the kitchen table, laying me out on my stomach beneath him. I rested my cheek and palms against the cool laminate surface and prayed the table was sturdy enough to support my weight as Ryan positioned me the way he wanted me.

He leaned in so the hard jut of his cock pressed between my ass cheeks. "Feel that?" he said, grinding against me. "That's what you do to me. I've been hard as a rock all night."

I pushed back into him with a needy whimper. I'd never done anything like this before, never *felt* anything close to this thrill. Never knew I could love dirty talk and being manhandled this much.

"Look how eager you are. You're ready for me, aren't you?" He stepped back and shoved my skirt up around my waist. The sudden cool air on my exposed skin made me shiver as he ran his callused hands over my backside. "Fuck me, I wish you could see yourself right now. These perfect, lush ass cheeks and that swollen pussy just begging to be filled."

I closed my eyes and imagined it, how indecent I must look in this position with my legs spread lewdly and everything on display. I could feel my pulse throbbing in my clit as I pictured Ryan towering over me, about to have his way with my body.

"Spread your legs," he said, nudging them apart. "Nice and wide for me."

My thighs quivered with anticipation as my high heels scraped over the hardwood floor. When I felt the first light touch of his fingertips between my legs, I jerked like I'd been shocked.

Ryan laid his palm on my back to steady me. "God, I love how bad you want it," he said and slowly pushed two fingers inside me.

I moaned in relief as he eased in and out. His fingers were so thick it felt almost as good as a cock, especially when he went deep enough to stroke the aching place that made me gasp and shudder.

"You're so goddamn wet," he murmured as he continued to pump his fingers inside me. "I make you that way, don't I? Tell me it's for me."

"Yes," I gasped. "It's you. You make me wet."

"What about when you watched me through the window? Did I make you wet then?"

My face flushed, but the words tumbled out of my mouth freely. "Yes, so wet. I couldn't help it. Looking at you always gets me hot."

"Jesus," he said and dropped to his knees behind me. His fingers withdrew and then both his hands were running over my ass again, squeezing and kneading before sliding lower. My breath hitched as he dragged his fingertips through my cleft and spread it apart. "Look at you, you're beautiful. I'll bet you taste even better than you feel."

I moaned in response, excitement zinging through me at the thought of what he must be seeing up close like this. Not to mention how close his *mouth* was to me. It felt like the most erotic thing I'd ever experienced. When his thumb grazed the underside of my clit, I bucked my hips at the sudden, intense jolt of arousal.

"You like that, do you?" Ryan's thumb ghosted over the sensitive spot, his agonizingly light touch spreading pleasure through my body. "Feels good when I do that?"

I opened my mouth to tell him just how good it felt and beg him not to stop, to keep touching me right there, and to do it even harder, *oh god please harder*, but he spoke again before I could.

"Do you want me to lick it?"

"Guhhhh," was all I could manage in response.

"I'm sorry," Ryan said, a tease in his voice, "I couldn't quite understand that."

"Yes!" I shouted, and I heard him chuckle.

But then he wasn't laughing anymore, because his face was pressed between my legs and his tongue was busy doing other things. A ragged gasp tore out of me when he flicked his tongue over my throbbing clit, lightly at first, followed by a slow, ruinous sweep that left me shaking and babbling. Words I was only half conscious of saying spilled out of my mouth, all to the effect of *more* and *harder* and *please for the love of god don't stop*.

Obediently, he hooked his fingers around my hips and gave me everything I wanted, lapping and rubbing and stroking with ruthless intensity while the aching pressure inside me built and grew to the point where I didn't think I could stand it anymore. But Ryan kept going, firm and insistent, showing no mercy until I was sobbing his name over and over.

He slid a finger in me to stroke that sweet, perfect spot, and I fell apart, crying out loudly as my orgasm rolled through me, wave after wave of pure, mindless ecstasy.

Ryan stroked me through every last aftershock until my legs finally crumpled beneath me, then he swept me into his arms, cradling my trembling body in his lap as he sat on one of the kitchen chairs. I sagged against him, weak with pleasure as he brushed my hair out of my face.

"Satisfied looks good on you," he murmured, smiling softly as he peppered my face with tiny kisses.

That was the moment I knew Ryan McCafferty was going to ruin me. Not because of the oral sex, although it had been phenomenal. But because of the careful way he was holding me and the tenderness of those little kisses.

I'm in so much trouble, I thought as I closed my eyes and curled into him.

21

MAGGIE

Ryan didn't stick around for long after giving me that mind-blowing orgasm on my kitchen table. He didn't leave as abruptly as the last time, but he didn't linger either.

I didn't protest or question him. As much as I would have liked him to stay, spending the night together would have been asking for trouble. I could already feel myself sliding down a slippery slope with him. Liking him too much. Wanting him too much. *Feeling* too much.

We were supposed to be keeping things simple and easy. Uncomplicated. Casual. That was what we'd agreed to.

He was right to leave. We needed to get good at saying goodbye, so it wouldn't hurt so much when we had to do it the final time.

Ryan had to work a shift the next day, but on Sunday he offered to bring over takeout for dinner. We ate enormous burritos with the best salsa I'd ever tasted and watched *Atomic Blonde*.

And by "watched" I mean we got distracted making out on my couch. Which turned into dry humping, which led to him pushing me back against the cushions and eating me out until the movie ended three orgasms later. As the credits scrolled, Ryan pulled me upright, kissed me sweetly, and said good night.

When I didn't hear from him all day Monday, I told myself it was for the best. He was doing the right thing by keeping some distance between us.

It was safer that way. We shouldn't see each other every night. I shouldn't even *want* that. I *liked* my alone time and my space. I didn't want a man hanging around all the time, getting in the way.

Except I wanted *this* man around.

Safe didn't feel good. It sucked, actually. Spending the evening by myself wasn't all it was cracked up to be when I knew how much more fun I'd be having if Ryan was here with me. It didn't help that I could see his truck parked in his driveway, taunting me with the knowledge that he was home.

It was driving me crazy that we still hadn't had actual sex yet. I must have picked up my phone a dozen times to text Ryan and ask him to come over. But I talked myself out of it every time, refusing to cave. *Go Team Willpower.*

At nine o'clock, Ryan showed up at my door unannounced. When I let him in, he pulled me into his arms and kissed me breathless. Then he picked me up and carried me into my bedroom. So much for willpower.

"Take off your clothes," he said, stepping back after he'd set me down by the foot of the bed. He hadn't even said hello or asked how my day was. He'd just carried me to the bed like a caveman and ordered me to strip.

God, it was hot.

This was it, I thought. We were finally going to have sex. My pulse fluttered wildly as I pulled my T-shirt over my head. I wasn't wearing a bra, and Ryan's eyes went hazy as they focused on my now-bare breasts.

His tongue darted out to wet his lower lip. "Now the pants."

I untied my pajama pants and pushed them down to the floor.

"Underwear too."

After I'd tugged them off I said, "Now it's your turn."

His lips pulled into a quicksilver grin. "You'd like that, wouldn't you?"

"Yes, that's why I said it." I still hadn't seen him naked, which I considered a monumental injustice. I needed to see what he was packing in those jeans and get my hands on it.

Heat shot through his expressions, but he shook his head. "I've got something else in mind first."

My stomach tightened with excitement. "What?"

"Get on the bed."

I didn't have to be asked twice. As I lay back on the mattress, Ryan exhaled a sharp breath and advanced on me, pushing my legs apart so he could kneel between my knees. My skin tingled like it had been electrified as his gaze traveled worshipfully over my naked body.

"God, you're amazing." He lowered his weight onto me, holding himself up with one arm while his other hand cupped my breast.

His tongue darted out to lick my nipple, and I hissed with pleasure as I sank my hands into his hair. Glancing up at me with a smile, he covered my nipple with his mouth and sucked hard enough to make me arch off the bed with a whimper of pleasure-pain.

"I've been thinking about you all day," he said as he soothed my tortured flesh with soft, gentle licks. "Thinking about all the things I want to do to you."

Desire pulsed between my thighs, and I pulled his head up so I could kiss him. My tongue plundered his mouth as his big body pressed down on me, and I wrapped one of my legs around his waist.

Still kissing me, he reached up to tug my ponytail out, then plunged his fingers into my hair and clenched them into a fist. It was exactly the right amount of rough, the way he pulled my head back, and it made me think of something I wanted to do very much.

Dragging my mouth down his neck, I slid one of my hands between us and flicked open the button on his jeans.

"Maggie." His voice sounded choked.

Good. I wanted to make him lose control for a change and give him the kind of pleasure he was so good at giving me.

His hand tightened in my hair when I yanked on the zipper of his jeans. "What are you doing?"

I blinked up at him and licked my lips. "I'm going to suck you off."

"You don't need to do that."

"I want to." I reached up to cradle his jaw, stroking my fingers over his cheek. "I want to take care of you the way you take care of me."

He covered my mouth with his, and I sighed as our tongues tangled together. But when I tried to reach for him again, he caught my hands in a steel-strong grip.

"I told you, I've got plans for you tonight. Stop trying to distract me." He stretched my arms above my head, pinning my wrists against the pillow. "No using your hands. I want them to stay right here. Can you do that, or do I need to tie you up?"

A tremor of excitement shuddered through me, but I didn't especially want to wait while he went in search of something to use as restraints. *Another time.* Smiling, I gripped the bottom of the headboard to show him how agreeable I was.

"Good girl." He grasped my chin and brushed a light kiss to my lips before pushing himself off me.

"Where are you going?" I asked as he crawled over to the edge of the bed. Ignoring me, he yanked the bedside table drawer open. "Oh, I don't actually keep condoms in—"

I broke off as I remembered what *was* in that nightstand.

"I knew it," Ryan said as he rummaged around in the drawer where I kept my personal, private, *intimate* things. "Damn, look at all these. This is quite the collection you've got."

"Hey," I said, feeling my face flush bright red. "I didn't give you permission to look in there."

"How's this one even supposed to work?" he said, ignoring me as he held up my Volta clitoral vibrator, which I had to admit looked a bit like a demented Daffy Duck.

I pushed myself upright. "Ryan—"

"Margaret." He turned and arched a stern eyebrow. "You're not supposed to move."

"You're snooping through my drawers without permission!"

"Are you telling me you *don't* want me to use any of these toys on you?"

I snapped my mouth shut and swallowed, suddenly wanting that *very* badly.

"That's what I thought." An unbearably smug grin spread across his face. "Now get your sweet ass back where I put you."

I lay back and gripped the headboard again, fighting the urge to squirm with impatience as Ryan went back to browsing through my sex toys. "There are more in the drawer below," I said.

"That right?" He tossed an approving glance over his shoulder before opening the next drawer. "Well, hello, look at all you fellas."

I closed my eyes and tried to summon my zen. Unfortunately, it was currently offline and not responding to message requests.

"Which one of these two should I fuck you with?" Ryan said.

When I opened my eyes, he was holding a sleek purple rabbit vibe in one hand and my spiral-shafted G-spot vibrator in the other.

"Is that glitter?" he asked, squinting at the spiral vibe.

"It's supposed to look like a unicorn horn," I said, feeling like I might faint. I couldn't decide if I was more turned on or mortified. Possibly equal amounts of both. "You know, because it's a spiral shaft. And because a unicorn is what women call the perfect partner because he's elusive and mythical." My face grew even hotter. "It's called the Screwnicorn."

"Right." Ryan grinned, dropping the rabbit back in the drawer. "The Screwnicorn it is."

Oh god oh god oh god. I felt like I was going to explode as he crawled over to me and knelt between my legs again.

His gaze skimmed over my body. "You look pretty when you blush."

"Are you really going to use that on me?" I asked weakly as I eyed the vibrator in his hand.

He looked down at it, rubbing his thumb along the shaft, then back up at me. "You want me to, don't you?"

I bit my lip. "Yes."

"That's what I thought." He set the unicorn down and smoothed his hands up the insides of my thighs. "But I'll make sure you're good and ready first. All you have to do is make sure you keep those hands exactly where they are."

My hips lifted off the bed of their own accord, straining for his touch. I was so worked up, it was a miracle my whole body wasn't levitating off the bed.

"Don't worry," he murmured as he bent down and wrapped his arms around my thighs. "I'm going to take care of you. I promise."

RYAN HAD another twenty-four-hour shift at the firehouse the next day. I didn't hear from him again until Wednesday night. This time he waited until almost ten o'clock before he showed up at my door.

Once again, he swept me off my feet and seduced me into letting him have his way with me. I'd never known anyone who took so much pleasure in giving head. The man was a cunnilingus machine. Why try to fight it when it felt so good and I wanted what he was offering? I wanted it badly enough that it crowded all the other things I wanted right out of my head.

It shocked me how much I liked letting Ryan take charge and call the shots in bed. I'd never known how hot it could be to relinquish control. There was a hedonistic thrill in submitting to him and letting myself be lavished with attention until I was so lust-addled and orgasm-drunk I couldn't think, or resist, or do anything at all except enjoy the feeling.

Who wouldn't like that?

But every time Ryan walked out afterward, he left me feeling unsettled. I couldn't shake the sense that we were on a roller coaster with a gaping hole in the tracks ahead. The first part of the ride was thrilling, but any second now the bottom was going to fall out.

The red flags were all over the place if I let myself look for them. Like how difficult I found it to say no to him. Or the fact that it felt like he was holding something back from me. Or maybe it was that he was holding himself back. He'd given me untold orgasms but hadn't let me give him any yet. I'd never known a man with so much self-control when it came to foreplay. He loved to tease and torture me, so much so that we still hadn't had intercourse. I told myself he was playing the long game, withholding sex to stoke the desire between us until the tension was so unbearable it'd be truly explosive when he finally did give in, but part of me couldn't help wondering if he had another reason for avoiding it.

The most worrying thing of all, however, was how much I thought about Ryan and missed him when we were apart. It scared me a little, how much he had come to matter to me in such a short span of time, but I didn't have any reason to think he felt the same way. The ease with which he walked away after hookups told me he'd have no trouble letting me go when the time came. If only I could say the same.

Thursday night, Ryan knocked on my door at nine thirty.

This is becoming a habit, I thought as he crowded me up against the wall and crushed his mouth to mine.

What had happened to distance? We'd seen each other five of the last seven nights. That didn't feel very casual.

"Miss me?" he asked in between long, drugging kisses.

"Yes," I said, because I had. Too much.

His big hands gently cupped my face as he stroked his thumbs over my cheekbones, gazing at me with eyes so warm and inviting I could drown myself in them. "Good, because I missed the hell out of you."

This man...god. This was the problem right here. It wasn't just the sex that was addictive. That, I could have handled. It was all the small, sweet things he did and said. An achingly gentle touch. A soft, fond look in his eyes. Those heart-melting moments of tenderness when it felt like I meant something special to him. When he made me want to believe I did.

Ryan's mouth caught mine again in a kiss that sent my thoughts scattering and my heart pounding. It was like this every time. I kept expecting the infatuation to fade, but it had only grown more intense.

The solid thickness of his cock pressing against my stomach served as a compelling reminder of all the things I wanted that we hadn't done yet. The things he kept withholding from me.

I hadn't even seen him naked yet or managed to get my hand around his cock for more than a second or two. Every time I went for it, he threw a sexy distraction at me.

As much as I enjoyed Ryan's sexy distractions, I wanted his penis to join the party. It seemed only fair, considering how much pleasure he'd showered on all the various parts of my body. There wasn't an inch of me he hadn't seen, touched, and tasted. Now it was my turn to get some. Or rather, *his* turn.

I snaked a hand between us and cupped him through his jeans. A shudder went through him, and he dropped his head to my shoulder with a groan. Emboldened by his reaction, I stroked the hard column of his cock.

His hands locked around my wrists in a grip exactly the right amount of too tight. He held them captive behind my back as he pressed me up against the wall and covered my mouth with his, kissing me with the same urgency beating in my chest. By the time he dragged his mouth away from mine, I was panting and writhing against him.

He kissed my neck before moving up to my ear with a growl. "I need you naked."

Desire spiraled outward from my belly as he released my wrists to cup my ass with his hands, lifting me off the floor like I weighed nothing. I wrapped my arms and legs around him while he carried me to the bedroom. When we got to the bed, he set me on my feet and slid his hands under my shirt to cup my breasts.

I knew where this was headed. If I let Ryan have his way, I'd be on my back with his head between my thighs again. Appealing as that was, tonight I had my own plans for him.

"No," I said, pushing his hands off me as I stepped back.

He gave me a questioning look. "No?"

"I want you to take off your shirt."

"You do, huh?" A sly smile curved his lips. "Come over here and take it off for me, then."

That's more like it.

I was on him like a cat on a mouse, shoving his T-shirt over his head and tossing it to the floor. I'd seen his chest before, but only through my window from a distance. I knew his body was impressive, but I wasn't prepared for how it would affect me up close and personal.

Enraptured, I pressed my palms to his chest, pushing my fingertips through his chest hair as I explored the wide expanse of bare skin. Ryan's pecs were squares of solid muscle, the left one covered by a tattoo of a butterfly. I licked my lips as I followed the thin trail of red hair down to the thicker patch of fur low on his stomach.

"Hey, my eyes are up here, sweetness."

My gaze stayed right where it was. "You're magnificent."

"Glad you think so." His massive arms wrapped around me, bringing us chest to chest.

God, the feel of his bare skin all around me was sublime. Why hadn't I made him take his clothes off sooner?

I pressed my face into his neck and closed my eyes as I breathed in his clean, intoxicating scent. My hands smoothed over the solid columns of muscle in his lower back while I kissed a trail across his collarbone and down to his tattoo. I could feel his heart beating under my lips, racing as fast as mine was. When I flicked my tongue over his nipple, he shivered and slid his hands into my hair.

"Pants off," I said, hooking my fingers into his waistband. If I didn't get my hands on him soon, I was going to burst a blood vessel.

"You first." He plucked at the drawstring on my pajama pants. "I need to touch you."

I caught his wrist and pushed his hand away. "You'll have to wait. It's my turn now."

Tonight I was going to see what happened when he gave up control and let himself go. I wanted to know if I could make Ryan lose his composure the way he'd systematically dismantled mine.

"I don't like waiting," he said, his eyes flashing with carnal intent. "Not when it comes to you."

Quick as lightning, he broke free of my grasp and pushed me back onto the bed, lifting my shirt up as he pinned me beneath him.

Even when he was rough, Ryan was always so *careful* with me. It made my heart flutter, the way he made sure his weight didn't crush me too much as he held me down and licked a circle around one of my nipples.

The man had me trapped, and I couldn't pretend I didn't love it. My body flushed with excitement at the feel of all those hard muscles pressing down on me. Covering me. Touching me everywhere it was possible for our bodies to touch.

Except he was still wearing too many clothes. I wanted all of him touching all of me with nothing in between.

I tried to slide my hands down to the cock throbbing against my hip, but he casually captured them and held both my wrists imprisoned in one big hand. Then he went back to leisurely savoring my breasts as if we had all the time in the world, when time was what we didn't have enough of. There could never be enough time.

"I want to feel you," I said, squirming beneath him.

"I'm right here." He held my gaze as he slid his hand down the front of my pajama pants and under the waistband of my underwear. "Feel that?

"Unnngh," I said as he circled my aching clit.

"How about that?" he asked and slipped a finger inside me.

"Yes." My hips bucked when he stroked my G-spot, and I clenched my teeth. "I want you inside me."

"I am inside you." His voice was as rough and tight as I'd ever heard it. "God, you're beautiful like this. I love getting you off."

"Then get me off by putting your cock inside me so we can both get off." I knew he relished the seduction, but I'd been well and truly seduced by now. I was more than ready to take things to the next level. "Ryan."

"I like the way you say my name," he murmured as he slowly fucked me with his fingers.

If this had been a real, serious relationship, I could understand him wanting to go slow. I still wouldn't like it, but at least it would make more sense. But why take things so slow when we were allegedly keeping this casual? We were working against a timetable here, and I didn't want to waste precious minutes not banging each other's brains out.

"Why do you always have to be in control?" I asked, frustration edging into my words.

Ryan went still. "I don't."

"Could have fooled me."

He released my wrists and withdrew his hand from my pants. "I take control when I'm with you because it's what *you* like. Don't pretend you don't."

"But what do *you* like?" I said. "I don't even know."

He'd always been able to read me as if I had an instruction manual printed on the surface of my skin. But he wasn't so easy to decipher. All I'd seen of him was what he *let* me see. Which wasn't much.

"I like getting you off." He shrugged lightly, but he wasn't looking me in the eye. "I'm not that complicated."

I didn't believe that for a second. The feeling he was keeping something from me reared its ugly head again. "What if I want to be able to do that for you? The whole point of sex is mutual pleasure. It's not mutual if you're always giving and never receiving."

"You don't need to worry about me," he said tautly. "Watching you come gives me plenty of pleasure. Trust me."

"But it doesn't get you off. You haven't gotten off once in all the times we've been together." I frowned at him as uncertainty reared its ugly head. "Is there a reason you don't want to have sex with me?

His eyebrows pulled together. "No, of course not."

"It feels like there is. Are you not attracted to me enough?"

He drew back with a look of disbelief. "You think I'd bury my face in your pussy night after night if I wasn't attracted to you?"

"I'm starting to wonder."

"Margaret." Ryan's eyes grew soft as he cupped my face. "You're so fucking beautiful, I can't get enough of touching you."

"Good to know." I slid my hands around his neck. "I can't get enough of you either, so take off your pants and let's have sex."

He didn't move.

"What's the problem?" I said, letting go of him.

"I can't."

"You can't?" I blinked, struggling to understand. From everything I'd seen and felt, his plumbing seemed to be working fine. I could feel it right now in fact, rock-hard and pulsing against my leg. "Is there something wrong...physically?"

"It's not that," he said, sounding irritated. "I *can*, I just don't want to."

At my flinch, his expression crumpled with regret.

"No, Maggie, listen—"

I tried to push him off me, but it was like trying to shove a mountain. "Get. Off."

The second he sat up, I scrambled off the bed and paced to the far corner of the room.

"I didn't mean it like that." He sounded distraught. "I shouldn't have said that."

"How exactly did you mean it?"

He swung his legs over the edge of the bed and scrubbed his hands through his hair. "Look, I know it sounds like a cliché, but I promise it's got nothing at all to do with you. It's a thousand percent me."

"What is?"

"I just don't like..." He shook his head and looked away.

"Sex?" That didn't seem right though. He seemed like a man who liked sex very much. More than most, even.

"Being vulnerable in front of someone else." His voice sounded tortured, like the words had been dragged out of him against his will.

My heart ached at the pain and loneliness I heard in his confession. "I've let you make me vulnerable. Over and over again."

"You liked it," he said with an accusatory look.

"I did. But it stops being fun if it's all one-sided."

He sighed and tipped his head back to glare at the ceiling. "I'm not good at casual sex."

The implausibility of that made me want to laugh, but I held it back. "From what I've seen, you're very good at all kinds of sex."

"Fooling around is one thing. I can do that without it meaning anything. But if I let myself cross certain lines, my head starts to get in the way." He scowled as if the words tasted bad in his mouth. "I guess I've got some old-fashioned ideas I haven't been able to shake."

"So you're saying you can do all manner of intimate things to me with your fingers and mouth and that's fine because it's just *fooling around*, but putting your penis in my vagina without a commitment is a bridge too far? Am I getting it right?"

"It's not about that," he said, refusing to look at me. "It's about whether or not I let myself come when we're together. Letting go like that with someone else makes me feel too much."

For a second I could only blink. "That's why you won't let me touch you? You're afraid to let me get you off because..."

Because he might develop feelings for me.

Ryan stared down at his hands, which hung loosely between his knees. "It's not something you need to worry about, okay? I've got it under control."

"Right." Control. Of course. My heart pounded, pushing the blood through my veins too quickly. Suddenly this thing we'd been doing felt all too real. Complicated. *Serious.*

He looked at me with pleading eyes. "I don't want to talk about this anymore. Let's just go back to doing what we've been doing. It was working great."

"Was it?" I reached up to rub my chest. "I don't think so."

"Maggie." He stood and moved toward me. "Come on, just let me keep making you feel good. I like doing that. Let's just do that, okay?"

I jerked away as he reached out. "No."

I couldn't go back to that, letting him take me apart inch by inch while he kept himself locked up tight. Every time I permitted him to chip away at my defenses, I fell deeper down the rabbit hole. If we kept going, I'd be lost down there by myself with no protection at all.

Ryan dropped his hand. "This doesn't have to be a big deal unless you make it one."

"What if you let yourself have feelings?" I said against my better judgment. "What would happen then?"

His lips pinched. "That's not what this is. We agreed. No complications."

We had agreed to that. I'd been right there with him because

I'd thought it was what I wanted. Now I wasn't so sure. "What if we renegotiated the agreement?"

He shook his head. "You're leaving in a few months."

"We could try to figure something out. See what happens. Maybe we can find a way to make it work." I didn't know how or what. All I knew was if he said he wanted it, I'd be willing to try anything. I didn't want to let him go.

"A relationship's not an option for me." The hard edge in his voice left no room for debate. "I told you that before."

He certainly had. What had I thought? That he'd magically get over his aversion to commitment and welcome me into his life with open arms? That all those soft looks and gentle touches had actually *meant* something? Of course they hadn't. He was a charmer. He'd been charming me.

"Right," I said, feeling like I'd been hit by a baseball pitch. "Okay."

I couldn't let him see how much it hurt. This was on me, not him. I was the one who'd gotten carried away. How stupid of me.

I'd allowed myself to want something impractical. If Ryan had wanted it too, I would have been willing to try for it anyway. But he didn't. So that was that.

What I wasn't going to do was keep banging my head against this wall. I needed to minimize the damage.

"In that case..." I drew in a breath, steeling myself to say the words. "I don't think we should see each other anymore. We need to end this."

22

RYAN

Maggie's words hit me like a thunderclap, making my heart pound in panic. I didn't want to lose her. I wasn't ready yet. We were supposed to have more time than this. Months more.

"No, come on," I croaked, my throat feeling thick. "Don't say that."

She shook her head, her expression turning to ice before my eyes. "This is a bad idea. It was always a bad idea."

"I promise you don't need to worry about me getting attached. I can handle this." Lies. Every word of it. But I didn't care what happened to me. She'd be gone by then and never needed to know how I felt.

Her only response was a dark, bitter laugh that hit me square in the pit of the stomach.

"You don't have to do this," I said, fully begging now. "Nothing has to change."

I need you. Don't make me give you up yet.

"You're wrong." She paused to draw a harsh breath as if it was an effort to get the words out. "We can't keep on like we have been and expect to just walk away. Maybe if we were different people we'd be able to do it, but it's not going to work with us."

"You don't know that," I said, still in denial even though deep down I knew she was right. We'd always been playing with fire.

"I do, actually." Maggie lifted her eyes to mine with a sorrowful smile. "I care about you, Ryan. That's the problem. It's not just you that's in danger of developing feelings. Because I already have, you see."

All the air left my lungs as I stared at her in shock. I'd never expected to hear her say that. I'd assumed she wouldn't get attached. I'd thought she'd be safe. This wasn't supposed to happen.

"I should have stopped this long before now, but I liked you so much," she said, every word embedding itself in my skin like sticker burrs. "I never should have let it start in the first place. I knew better, but I lied to myself that it'd be okay." Her voice betrayed a quaver as pain leaked into her stoic expression. "Maybe you can handle this, but I can't."

My chest caved in on itself as guilt swamped me. I'd done the thing I never meant to do. I'd told myself it was only my own heart I was putting at risk. But the truth was I'd been taking advantage of Maggie all this time, using her to relieve the emptiness inside me. I'd convinced her to let me in by offering to be her protector, but I was the one who'd hurt her.

The knowledge of what I'd done tormented me even more because of how badly I longed to give Maggie what she was asking me for. I would've happily handed her my heart on a platter if I could have. There was nothing in this world I wanted more than to be with her for real and try to make this relationship work, damn the challenges.

But I couldn't take the risk. If I let her commit herself to me and I got sick, I wouldn't just be breaking her heart. I'd be ruining her life. Condemning her to suffer through my illness along with me, but her lot would be far worse than mine because she'd be the one left behind to grieve alone and try to pick up the pieces after I was gone.

"You're right," I said with a finality that almost did me in.

"I am?" The tiny catch in her voice was so subtle I doubted many people would even have noticed it. But I could read her well enough to know she was hurting so much she might as well be doubled over in pain. *Because of me.*

"Yes," I forced myself to say, driving the knife deeper. The fact that it was a mercy killing didn't make it easier. "This was a mistake. We need to end it now."

I watched her take that in, pulling her shoulders back as she straightened her spine. Standing tall and strong and coldly beautiful, the way she'd looked the first time I'd met her. Too proud to let anyone in.

A fresh wave of guilt snaked through my gut at the memory. She would have been a lot better off if I'd never spoken to her at all.

"Okay," she said with a brisk nod. "I guess that's it, then."

Silence coiled thickly in the air between us as we stared at each other. Knowing this was probably the last time I'd ever be this close to her again, I let myself take one last, long look, committing every perfect detail of her face to memory.

"I'm sorry," I said, hating myself for hurting her.

Her hard expression didn't waver. "Me too."

Without another word, I grabbed my shirt off the floor and saw myself out.

"I FEEL guilty asking you to do this," Adriana said as she backed her Suburban out of her garage.

I glanced over at her with a frown. "Why? You know I don't mind."

The two kids were strapped into their car seats in the back, and Isabella was "reading" a board book to her baby brother. Her chattering monologue as she made up a story to go with each of the pictures of farm animals filled up the silence while Adriana backed out onto the street of their quiet neighborhood.

She and Manny owned one of the big, new brick-fronted houses in the fancy development that had gone up on the west side of town a few years back. When I was a kid I would have called it a mansion and assumed they were rich, but that was before my mom married George King and I learned what real rich looked like.

"I hope you mean that," Adriana said. "It's not like I can't do it by myself." She was taking Isabella to the pediatrician today for a checkup and had asked me if I'd come along to help manage the kids in the waiting room.

"Just because you can doesn't mean you should have to." As I said the words, I couldn't help thinking of Maggie and reached up to rub my chest, which ached every time my mind rubber-banded back to her. Five miserable days had passed since I'd walked out of her house, and the pain hadn't gotten any less acute. "It's a handful trying to manage both of them by yourself."

"I could have asked my mom, but frankly I prefer your company. You don't nag me nearly as much." The corners of Adriana's eyes crinkled as she tossed a glance my way. "Besides, we haven't seen enough of you lately. I keep meaning to have you over for dinner, but Manny and I can't seem to do anything but collapse on the couch in the rare moments when these two gremlins aren't running us ragged."

I stared at her profile as she concentrated on the road ahead. She looked thinner, but that could be from normal loss of baby weight. The exhaustion shadowing her eyes and lining her face wasn't new, but it seemed more pronounced than the last time I'd seen her.

"How have you been doing?" I asked. "It must be hard on you to have Manny working longer hours right now with the new baby."

Her shoulder twitched in a shrug. "It's not great, but we're managing. This is the glamorous life I chose when I decided to be a stay-at-home mom."

"It's okay to admit it if you're having a hard time. No one's going to blame you for struggling with all the stress you're under."

She laughed. "You've met my mother, right? The woman who raised five kids while running a restaurant and still managed to have perfect hair and makeup every day?"

"Adriana," I said gently. "You can tell *me* if you're having trouble. Postpartum depression can start anytime in the first year after birth."

"Hey, you're supposed to be less naggy than my mom." She flicked me a smile. "I'm fine. Really. It's just run-of-the-mill lack of sleep. Some days I'm crankier than others."

"You'd tell me if it was more than that, wouldn't you?"

"I promise," she said, reaching over to give my hand a quick squeeze. "You've seen my cervix. There's no secrets between us now."

I looked out the window as a knot of guilt formed in my esophagus. What right did I have to expect Adriana's honesty when I wasn't willing to share my own troubles with the people closest to me?

"Don't worry about me," she went on. "I'm hanging in there. Manny's good about taking charge of the kids as soon as he gets home so I can have a break. And any day now Jorge's going to start sleeping for more than five hours at a time. I just know it."

"I'm a good sleeper," Isabella piped up from the back seat. "Aren't I, Mama?"

"Yes, baby." Adriana smiled at her in the rearview mirror. "You're an excellent sleeper. Even when you were as little as your baby brother, you always slept through the night."

"Maybe you could have a talk with your brother about letting your mom sleep more," I said to Isabella.

"Okay," she said brightly, and proceeded to lecture him about it in an adorably serious tone.

"You know," I said to Adriana, "I'm always happy to come watch them on my days off so you can sneak in a nap or some time for yourself."

"I appreciate that," she said, her eyes crinkling again. "I'll let you know."

"I'm serious. I don't mind."

I could certainly use the distraction right now. Anything to keep me from moping around my house, beating myself up over the way things had turned out with Maggie. I couldn't forgive myself for getting involved with her in the first place. My attraction to her had overthrown my good sense. It filled me with shame to remember how carelessly I'd flirted with her. I'd let myself get caught up in the challenge of the chase without stopping to think about the consequences. It had been a selfish, stupid thing to do, leading her on like that when I knew I couldn't pursue a relationship.

I'd convinced myself that Maggie would be safe, that she wasn't in any danger of developing feelings for me. I'd believed it because I wanted to believe it, when I should have known better.

Sure, when I first met her I'd thought the only thing either of us felt was simple sexual attraction. But it hadn't taken me long to see beyond the surface she presented to the world. I should have backed away then, but I was too busy falling for her by that point. I'd lied to myself about the risks to justify taking what I wanted.

A fresh wave of shame and guilt bubbled up, and I rubbed my chest again.

Adriana glanced over at me with a frown. "I worry sometimes we take advantage of you. You're always so willing to help, but you never let us do anything for you in return."

"I don't need much," I said. "Anyway, spending time with you and the kids is a treat, not a chore. It might be different if it was someone else asking."

"Still, you've probably got better things to do with your time than babysit for us."

"Not really."

"What about this new girlfriend I keep hearing so much about? Isn't she keeping you busy?"

"She works as much as Manny," I said, pretending my chest didn't feel like one big bruise. "Anyway, we're not that serious."

I hadn't told anyone I wasn't seeing Maggie anymore. I'd spent all day Sunday with Tanner and Wyatt, helping out with the renovations to the bookstore Tanner had bought, and I'd dodged all their questions about Maggie without letting on that we'd broken it off. In part because I didn't want the people who'd been harassing her to hear about it and think the coast was clear to start that shit back up again. But also, more selfishly, because I didn't want to talk about it. Telling people would invite a landslide of questions I wasn't prepared to answer. And I didn't need anyone throwing me a sympathy party when I was the one who'd been an asshole.

It was easier to let everyone think we were still seeing each other casually and downplay it until it no longer seemed remarkable that things had fizzled out. No dramatics and no fuss, the way I preferred it. No one needed to know how fucked-up I was over her.

"That's too bad," Adriana said. "Why not?"

I rolled my shoulders so she wouldn't see them stiffen. "She's only going to be around for a few months," I said. "There's no future in it."

"You never know. Circumstances can always change."

"Yeah," I said, not wanting to prolong the conversation by arguing. All the wishful thinking in the world wasn't going to change anything between me and Maggie.

"Mommy! Uncle Ryan!" Isabella shouted from the back seat.

"Yes, my darling," Adriana answered.

"I'm going to read you a book now. You have to listen, okay?"

"You got it." I tossed a grin over my shoulder, grateful for the change of subject. I was going to buy that kid an irresponsible amount of candy later. "Read away."

Isabella launched into a rambling, nonsensical story about a puppy who was giving a dance recital which was attacked by bunnies and then they all went to live in a castle with a princess who was building a robot. Or something. To be honest, I only managed to halfway follow along, although I doubted it would have made much more sense even if I'd given it my full attention.

While Isabella's story devolved into singing gibberish words at the top of her lungs, I stared out the window at the familiar buildings along Main Street. But all I could see was Maggie's face in my mind, her lips swollen from kissing me, her disheveled blonde hair falling across her cheek, and the hurt shining in her eyes when I said I didn't want her.

You had to do it, I told myself for the millionth time. *It was for the best.*

Maybe after a million more I'd start to believe it.

23

MAGGIE

The problem with dating and then breaking up with your neighbor was you couldn't get away from him. He was right next door every day, reminding me of his existence. Making sure I couldn't forget how I'd humiliated myself.

If I looked out my kitchen window, I'd see his big stupid truck parked right outside. Taunting me. Bringing up memories I'd rather forget.

Every time I stepped outside my house, I had to pray we wouldn't run into each other. It'd been over a week since our breakup, and I still couldn't stand the thought of coming face-to-face with him again. So far I'd lucked out, but I figured it was just a matter of time.

The cameras Ryan had installed around my house served as another nagging reminder of him. I wondered if he still had the app on his phone and if he ever watched me come and go. Maybe he used it to avoid running into me.

I'd debated texting him to request he delete the app. But in the end I'd decided against it. Frankly, I loathed the thought of having even that much contact with him. Plus, despite everything, I still felt safer knowing Ryan could keep an eye on my house in case I had any more trouble. Especially once word got around that we were no longer dating.

Although, as far as I could tell, he hadn't told anyone yet. The news hadn't made its way to Josie anyway, based on the fact that she'd asked me yesterday how things were going with Ryan, and not in a sympathetic, *sorry for your breakup* kind of way. I'd told her something vague about not having seen him for a few days, and then I'd lied about having a meeting to get out of the conversation.

I didn't know why Ryan wasn't telling people, but I wasn't going to be the one to do it. The longer it took for everyone to figure out we weren't a couple, the longer I could enjoy the protection of my connection with him. I was afraid when people found out, there'd be a backlash. With my luck, the whole town would decide I'd mistreated their favorite son and was even more of a villain. They'd probably come for my head.

That wasn't something I looked forward to dealing with. Especially not while I was still smarting from Ryan's rejection, which I was finding harder to put behind me than I should have, given how brief our involvement had been.

It wasn't as if I hadn't been rejected by men before. It had happened enough that I'd taught myself not to take it personally. Or I thought I had.

This was different. I couldn't simply tell myself it was because Ryan was shallow or insecure or arrogant and therefore not worth my time. He wasn't any of those things. His opinion mattered to me a lot more than I'd realized. When he'd said he didn't want to have feelings for me, it left some shrapnel behind. And I couldn't even be mad at him because he'd been right to do it.

Ryan had been the smart, logical one in all of this. It had been delusional of me to suggest that we should try for something more. I'd forgotten where I was and who he was. I'd forgotten who *I* was. All immutable facts that made any possibility of a lasting relationship between us impossible.

I should be grateful to him for keeping a clear head and sticking to his boundaries. Maybe one day I would feel grateful. For now, I was too busy being hurt that he hadn't lost his head over me the way I'd lost mine over him.

Ah well. Lesson learned. This was what I got for getting to know one of my neighbors. *Never. Again.*

Speaking of the neighbor I was desperately trying to forget, a familiar squeak of hinges alerted me that he'd opened his garage door. A late October cold front had turned the weather crisp and lovely this week. While my dinner had heated in the microwave, I'd cracked the kitchen window to let in some of the fresh, cool air outside. Then I'd poured myself a glass of wine and sat down to eat, trying not to think about the things Ryan had done to me on this kitchen table.

He just had to choose this precise moment to work out in his damn garage. The window was right behind me. If I turned around, I'd be able to see him out there.

And he'd be able to see me.

I stayed where I was and attempted to ignore him by reading a book on my phone while I finished my dinner. Except my focus and my appetite had both evaporated the moment I heard Ryan outside. All I could do was sit there listening to the clang of weights and the heavy thump of the barbell every time he set it down.

If I closed my eyes, I could picture him perfectly. The red-faced grimace of exertion on his face, the way the veins in his arms bulged as his muscles strained, the beads of sweat forming on his brow. The butterfly tattoo on his chest that I'd traced with my tongue the last time we'd been together.

I just about jumped out of my skin when a loud crash rattled the windows of Ryan's garage as if he'd dropped the barbell from a much greater height than usual. Reflexively, I stood and went to the window to make sure everything was okay.

Ryan stood facing his squat rack with the barbell at his feet. He teetered oddly for a second, then he started to topple, and I watched in horror as he went over like a felled tree.

Time seemed to slow down as he took a clumsy, staggering step and reached out for the rack, trying to catch himself. His shin caught the barbell at his feet, and his hand grabbed uselessly at empty air as he pitched forward. Ryan's forehead hit the rack with a sound I felt in the pit of my stomach as he crumpled to the floor.

24

MAGGIE

I was flying out my back door before I'd even made a conscious decision to move. Broken pecan shells bit into the bottoms of my bare feet as I sprinted across the driveway and scaled the low chain link fence, in too much of a hurry to run all the way around.

Ryan lay frighteningly still on the floor of his garage, canted half on his side and half on his stomach with his legs splayed across the barbell. Panic twisted my insides as I dropped to my knees beside him, repeating his name over and over in a desperate plea for him to be okay.

Blood welled from a gash at his hairline where he'd hit the rack, the beads of crimson stark against his unnaturally pale skin. The sight of his chest moving filled me with relief as I pressed my hand against his cheek. His eyelids fluttered in response to my touch, and he let out a low moan.

Too late, I realized I'd left my phone on my kitchen table in my rush to reach him. Cursing my thoughtlessness, I glanced desperately around the garage as I patted Ryan's shorts pockets, hoping he'd brought his phone out to the gym with him.

I spotted it sitting on a chair against the wall and surged to my feet. It was password protected, but I managed to activate the emergency SOS settings and call 911 as I sank down next to Ryan again. The call was answered more quickly than I expected, and I fought to keep my voice calm as I described the situation to the operator.

Ryan's eyes had opened by then, but he appeared dazed and unable to focus as he lay there blinking slowly. As soon as the 911 operator assured me EMS was on the way, I shoved Ryan's phone into my back pocket and bent over him anxiously.

"Ryan?" I pressed my hand against his cheek as I peered into his face. "Ryan, baby, it's me."

He tried to speak, but the words were slurred and unintelligible. It scared the shit out of me. Swallowing down a sickening churn of panic, I forced myself to take deep breaths as I silently prayed for the ambulance to hurry.

The blood from the gash on Ryan's head had started dripping onto the floor, so I leaned over to grab his gym towel off the rack. He flinched when I pressed it to the wound and lifted his arm, trying to push me away.

"Ryan, hey. It's Maggie," I said, clasping his hand and squeezing it. "Shhh. It's okay."

Finally, his eyes seemed to focus on me. He jerked back like he'd been startled and tried to push himself upright.

"Hey, no, please don't move," I begged as he shook off my attempts to keep him from getting up. Even injured he was impossibly strong. "You need to stay still, okay?"

Ignoring me, he rolled onto his hands and knees, then lurched precariously to his feet. Terrified he was going to fall again, I fastened myself against his side, knowing full well I wouldn't be able to stop him if he went over. The best I could hope to do was cushion his fall by throwing myself beneath him.

"Where'd you come from?" he whispered, looking at me like he'd never seen me before. "Who are you?" His eyes went wide with panic as he stared around him in a state of confusion. "You can't tell them! You can't tell anyone!"

"Ryan, it's me. It's Maggie." My voice cracked as my fear increased. "I'm your friend, remember? I live next door."

He reached up to touch his forehead and blinked at his fingers when they came away covered in blood.

"Come on, you need to sit down. Can you do that for me?" To my tremendous relief, he let me guide him to a chair against the wall.

Once I had him seated, he looked up at me and frowned. "Maggie?"

"That's right, it's me," I said, blinking back grateful tears as I used a corner of the towel to wipe the blood away from his eyes.

"What are you doing here?"

"You passed out while you were lifting and hit your head on the rack. You don't remember?"

He shook his head, winced, and lifted his hand to his injury.

"Stop that," I said, pushing his questing fingers away. "Be still. I need to keep pressure on your head wound."

"I passed out?"

"Yes."

"Were you here?"

"No, I was in my kitchen with the window open. I heard you drop the weights and looked outside just in time to see you fall over."

For some reason this made him agitated. He grabbed the towel away from me and tried to stand up.

"What do you think you're doing?" I managed to shove him back down on the chair before he could get his feet under him for leverage. "You shouldn't be walking around right now."

"I need to get a bandage and some ice for my head."

"You need to be still while we wait for the ambulance. You shouldn't have even gotten up from the floor."

"I don't need an ambulance."

"You were unconscious and disoriented, Ryan. For all I know, you're still disoriented."

He glared at me from beneath the towel he held to his bleeding head. "I'm fine. It's just a flesh wound."

I glared right back at him. "We'll let the paramedics decide that when they get here."

"I'm a certified EMT—I can decide for myself. And I don't want anyone I work with finding out about this, so you're not calling a fucking ambulance."

"Too late. I already called and they're on their way."

"Fuck," he hissed under his breath, growing even more agitated. "Are you serious? You have to call them back and tell them it was a mistake."

"I'm not doing any such thing. The fact that you were unconscious long enough for me to call 911 is enough reason to let them come check you out."

"Where's my phone?" He cast his eyes around wildly. "I'll call them myself."

"You will not." I didn't understand why he was getting so worked up about this. Was he really so proud that he couldn't accept medical care from his colleagues when he needed it? Sure, maybe they'd haze him about it later, but that didn't justify taking chances with a head injury. As a certified EMT, he should fucking know that.

"Goddammit, Maggie—"

Whatever Ryan had been about to say was interrupted by the sound of an approaching siren. He dropped his head into his hands as it grew louder.

"Fuck," he muttered under his breath. "Fuck, fuck, fuck."

A moment later, a big red fire truck rumbled to a stop in front of the house. Three firefighters in navy blue pants and shirts climbed out, and I went to wave them into the garage.

They all greeted Ryan by name as the one at the front of the group crouched in front of him to peer at his head wound. "We heard you took a little spill, McCafferty. You couldn't wait until after we'd finished dinner to crack your head open?"

"It's just a cut," Ryan muttered with an embarrassed grimace. "Sorry to waste everyone's time over nothing."

"He was unconscious for close to thirty seconds," I told them. "It wasn't nothing."

The two firefighters hanging back exchanged a silent look, and the male one headed back to the truck while the female one knelt at Ryan's side and unzipped the bag she'd brought.

Meanwhile, the one in front of Ryan was already rummaging in his own bag. "Since we're already here, we might as well assess you to make sure it really is nothing. What do you say?"

Ryan grimly nodded his assent, and the two firefighters proceeded to take his vitals and pose a series of questions to assess his mental and physical condition. When they began asking him about the specifics of the accident, Ryan was unable to recall anything at all about it.

"The last thing I remember, I was deadlifting. Then, next I knew, I was sitting in this chair with Maggie holding a bloody towel to my head."

I filled them in on everything I'd seen, including Ryan's confusion and slurred speech when he first regained consciousness. He'd avoided looking at me ever since the firefighters had arrived, and he continued to do so as I answered their follow-up questions. I couldn't tell if he was still mad at me for calling 911 or just uncomfortable having me around.

In that time, the fire truck out front had been joined by an ambulance, yet another fire truck, and a red fire department Suburban. I counted more than half a dozen blue uniforms milling around next to the fleet of emergency vehicles, which even I had to admit seemed like overkill.

Before long a pair of county paramedics joined the firefighters in the garage. The female firefighter continued to talk to Ryan and monitor his vitals while the male firefighter wandered off to talk to the two paramedics out of earshot. Much discussing and consulting ensued as they stood on the driveway deep in conversation. When they eventually returned, the male firefighter addressed Ryan.

"So look, your vitals are all outstanding, but I've got concerns about your TBI. I think it's likely you've got at least a mild concussion, and that laceration could use stitching."

Ryan's scowl had deepened as his colleague delivered his assessment. "You want them to transport me, don't you?"

"Yeah, I do."

"What if I promised to follow up with a doctor first thing tomorrow?"

The firefighter shook his head. "I know it's a pain in the ass, but we all agree it's a good idea under the circumstances."

"I could refuse transport."

"You could, but the deputy chief is standing out there at the end of your driveway, and that's not going to look good for you or us. So I really hope you aren't that stupid."

"Fine," Ryan muttered with a scowl. "But I'm walking onto the bus on my own two legs."

The two paramedics exchanged shrugs before one of them answered. "As long as you promise you won't get dizzy and pass out. Because there's no way any of us are catching your heavy ass, and I don't wanna have to explain how you got a second TBI on our watch."

I hovered off to the side as the firefighters packed up their gear and the paramedics prepared to escort Ryan to the ambulance.

"Do you mind following him to the hospital?" the male firefighter asked me as he hoisted his bag over his shoulder. "Since he doesn't remember getting the injury, it'd be helpful if you could tell the doctor everything you told us."

"Of course," I said. "I'm happy to."

The paramedics had already helped Ryan to his feet. He didn't look my way or say a word as they led him out of the garage and down the driveway to the waiting ambulance. As soon as the firefighters had all cleared out, I lowered the garage door and hurried into my house to grab my shoes and purse so I could drive myself to the hospital.

Only after the last emergency vehicle had pulled away did I remember I still had Ryan's phone in my back pocket. Recalling how reluctant he'd been to seek treatment for what the EMTs had clearly considered a serious injury, I made an executive decision I suspected he wouldn't thank me for.

Like any good first responder, Ryan had his medical information and emergency contacts set up on his phone so they could be accessed without the password. I pulled them up and called the first name on the list.

"Hey," a man's voice said cheerfully when he answered. "Can I call you back? I'm in the middle of something right now."

"Is this Tanner?" I asked.

"Yes." He sounded rightfully perplexed to find a stranger calling him from his brother's number. "Who's this?"

"My name is Maggie. I'm Ryan's next-door neighbor. I'm calling because you're listed in his phone as his emergency contact, and he's had an accident..."

THE LOCAL HOSPITAL bore the King name. Of course it did. As I parked my car in the lot outside the ER, I wondered how much money you had to donate to get your name on a whole-ass hospital.

The King money seemed to have been well-spent, because King Hospital had one of the nicest ERs I'd ever seen. Warm faux-wood floors, skylights to let in natural light, plenty of clean, comfortable chairs, and a play area for children made the space seem almost pleasant in spite of the unpleasant circumstances that brought people here.

Tanner had been as good as his word when he promised me he'd let the rest of Ryan's family know what had happened. Several of the Kings had beaten me here and taken over a corner of the waiting room already. I identified Nate, Wyatt, and Andie among the small group. There was a tiny blonde woman with them I didn't recognize, but I guessed the bearded man who looked like a toned-down version of Wyatt was probably Tanner.

They hadn't noticed me walk in, so I went to speak to the woman behind the glass-partitioned reception desk. As soon as I mentioned Ryan's name and explained why I was there, she grew markedly warmer and assured me the doctor would come out to talk to me in a bit.

"Maggie!" I turned and found myself swept into a hug by an anxious Josie. "Oh my god. Tanner told me what happened. Thank god you were there. Have you heard anything yet?"

"I just got here," I said. "The EMT said the doctor would need me to answer questions about Ryan's accident."

"It must have been terrifying. Are you okay? You're probably in shock. Come sit down, and I'll introduce you to the rest of the family." Josie grasped me by the arm and marched me over to the other Kings. "Everyone, this is Ryan's girlfriend, Maggie."

Shit. I'd forgotten everyone still thought Ryan and I were dating. But I wasn't sure I felt comfortable announcing our breakup to his loved ones without consulting him. He'd had his own reasons for proposing the charade after all, and I didn't want to make things more difficult for him right now. Nor was I convinced a hospital waiting room was an appropriate place to break that kind of news.

So I kept my mouth shut and tried to smile as I received a tense greeting from Nate, followed by hugs from Wyatt and Andie, who remembered me from the centipede incident. When Josie introduced me to Tanner and his girlfriend, Lucy, they both hugged me as well, offering profuse thanks for calling them.

"I brought Ryan's phone with me," I said, remembering I still had it. "I should give it to one of you for safekeeping."

"You hang on to it," Josie declared with authority. "Give it back to him when you see him."

Okay. I guessed I was staying until Ryan was able to receive visitors. For my own peace of mind, I was grateful for an excuse to stay. But I wasn't convinced Ryan would be so happy to see me.

My guilt increased with every family member who arrived at the emergency room and accepted my presence there as though I was Ryan's devoted girlfriend. Over the next fifteen minutes, I was introduced to Ryan's two youngest stepsiblings and George King's wife. When George himself arrived, he acknowledged me with only a somber nod before wandering off to take a phone call.

Manny and his family were the last to show up. Given what Ryan had said about how close he and Manny were, I thought he might have at least told Manny about our breakup. The emotional hug Manny gave me and the enthusiasm with which he introduced me to his wife and kids appeared to refute that theory, however.

So there I sat, surrounded by the entire King clan as we waited anxiously for news about Ryan. Josie had assumed the role of event organizer, assigning different family members to make phone calls and procure various snacks and beverages while we waited.

"Good news," she said, checking her phone as she sat down next to me. "Carter says he'll be out in a few minutes to talk to you and give us an update."

I looked up from the coffee she'd insisted Ryan's stepbrother Cody bring me. "Carter?"

She nodded as she sipped her own coffee. "My boyfriend's an ER doctor here. He's in with Ryan right now."

"That's handy."

Her mouth tightened. "Tonight it is. The rest of the time it means he's either working or exhausted from working. We barely see each other even though we live together."

"I'm sorry," I said, remembering what she'd said about hitching her horse to the wrong wagon. "That must be hard."

"I can't really be upset about it when he's saving lives, can I? It's what I get for falling in love with a doctor."

When Carter came out a few minutes later, Josie introduced me to him. He had a warm smile and a friendly, disarming manner that made him easy to like. Despite Josie's intimation of problems in their relationship, Carter looked at her like she was the best thing he'd seen all day, and she looked at him the exact same way.

He wrapped a comforting arm around her shoulders as he addressed the family members who'd clustered around him. "Ryan's doing just fine right now, aside from a pretty gnarly headache. We're monitoring his vitals, but everything looks good so far. I'm going to order some tests and keep him under observation until we get the results. I should be able to tell you more in a few hours."

"Can we see him?" Tanner asked.

"Not right now," Carter said. "The bump he took on his head has left him with some sensitivity to noise and light. I'd prefer to keep him quiet and let him get as much rest as he can manage. But he says to tell everyone he's doing great and not to worry about him. He also says you should all go home, but I told him that was probably wishful thinking."

Once he'd delivered his update, Carter kissed Josie on the cheek and motioned for me to follow him. We sat in a pair of empty chairs in a quiet corner of the waiting room while he asked me a series of questions about Ryan's injury and behavior in the aftermath.

"It was scary to see him that disoriented and slurring his speech," I confessed as Carter made notes on everything I'd told him.

"I'll bet it was," he said, offering a sympathetic smile. "But it's fairly normal after a loss of consciousness."

"It's bad that he lost consciousness though, isn't it?" That was the impression I'd gotten from the EMTs and paramedics.

He tucked his pen and notepad back into the pocket of his scrubs. "It's something that needs to be taken seriously, but in the majority of cases, people who experience a brief loss of consciousness fully recover. And it's a really good sign that the alteration of mental status only lasted for a few seconds." He gave me another smile as he pushed himself tiredly to his feet. "Try not to worry too much."

No chance of that, but I appreciated his attempt to allay my anxiety.

By the time I rejoined the Kings again, even more people had arrived, a few of whom I knew. Gareth, Quincy, and Jamal had showed up with some other members of the fire department, as had Casey, Kenzie, Ozzy, and some more faces I recognized from Ryan's Highland Games club.

It was a good thing the ER wasn't busy tonight and the waiting room was so spacious, because Ryan's fan club occupied fully a quarter of it. As the night wore on, more concerned friends trickled in while others trickled out and came back with food and trays of coffees that they handed around to everyone. Manny's daughter was having the time of her life with so many people willing to play with her, and the baby was passed from person to person until he fell asleep in his carrier.

You'd almost think it was a happy social gathering to see everyone laughing and enjoying each other's company. Except for the way people kept checking the time. Or casting worried glances at the door that led to the treatment rooms. Or occasionally letting their smiles slip as they stared off into space. Whenever anyone came out the door that led to the ER treatment rooms, all conversation momentarily fell silent in case it was someone bringing news about Ryan.

The sense of community was unlike anything I'd experienced in my life. I supposed it was the difference between small towns and bigger cities. There were a lot of downsides to being intimately mixed up in your neighbors' lives, but there was something to be said for the way people here showed up for each other in times of trouble.

Or maybe it was all down to Ryan and the kind of person he was that he'd inspired so much loyalty. It was really something —to see everyone who'd been brought together by their love for him. And here I was, right in the middle of them, made to feel like I belonged despite my efforts to hold myself apart.

What really surprised me was how much I liked the feeling. I hadn't realized it, but being here surrounded by Ryan's friends and family was exactly what I'd needed tonight. I *wanted* to belong here with them, even though I knew I didn't.

This stupid town had gotten to me. I'd tried to resist, but it'd wrapped its aggressively friendly arms around me and left an indelible impression.

I suspected I'd be carrying a piece of this place around with me long after I left here.

25

RYAN

"Exercise-induced vasovagal response," Carter pronounced after he'd gotten all my test results back. "Happens to weightlifters more than you'd think."

As luck would have it, Josie's boyfriend had been on shift at the ER tonight and had gotten all my tests fast-tracked for me. I'd received the VIP treatment all around because I knew pretty much everyone who worked in the ER. Unfortunately, it had also meant a steady stream of people popping in to check on me when all I wanted to do was curl up in a ball and hide under the covers in a dark, quiet room.

"The kind of weight you lift, it's not that surprising," Carter said as he made notes on my chart. "I'd tell you to knock off the heavy lifts, but I doubt you'd listen, would you?"

"I don't know," I mumbled, rubbing my throbbing head. "I'm not real eager to do this again anytime soon."

Carter walked over and flicked off the overhead lights in the treatment room they'd put me in. God bless him. Josie had picked a good one. "Maybe try not to hold your breath, anyway. Either that or surround yourself with pillows so you'll have a softer landing next time you vagal. You really do not want to get a second concussion."

"I've never vagaled out before. Is there a reason it happened this time?" I had to force the words out past the lump of fear in my throat. What if this was it? The first sign of ALS rearing its ugly head.

"Some people are more prone to it than others," Carter said with a shrug. "It's not usually connected to a serious health problem. It could have been dehydration, or it could be that your body's reactions are simply changing as you age. It happens to even the best of us."

"So there's nothing I should be worried about? Nothing in any of my test results that seemed off?"

"As far as I can tell, you're in the peak of health—disgustingly so, I might add." Carter gave me a considering look. "Is there something specific you're worried about?"

"No, just checking," I said quickly. "Like you said, I'm not getting any younger."

I couldn't very well ask Carter if passing out could be linked to ALS without telling him about my family history. And I couldn't do that because I didn't want it in my medical records. Not to mention, I didn't want him spilling the beans to Josie. Maybe Carter took patient confidentiality seriously enough that he wouldn't, but I couldn't trust my sister's live-in boyfriend to keep a secret like that from her.

"I wouldn't worry about it," he said. "If it happens again or you experience any more symptoms, let me know and I'll refer you to a cardiologist. But let's give you time to recover from that concussion first."

That was good to hear, but it didn't entirely neutralize the acid rising in my stomach. ALS might not be obvious. I couldn't necessarily expect Carter to pick up on something so obscure based on a few standard tests. Especially when my concussion could be masking other neurological symptoms.

Basically, I was still scared shitless and low-key having a panic attack.

"Right now, I'm more concerned about the gang of rowdy friends and relatives who've taken over the waiting room," Carter said. "Josie's been blowing up my phone for updates, and I'm afraid they're going to riot out there if I don't let your family see for themselves that you're okay. There's only so long you can say no to people whose name is on the building."

I tried to hide my chagrin. The last thing I wanted right now was a roomful of relatives fussing over me, but it couldn't be helped. "I guess you better let them at me, then."

———

THE ER TREATMENT room was barely big enough to contain everyone who'd been allowed back to see me. Carter had limited visitors to immediate family, so there were only nine people crowded into my room: Manny, Nate, Josie, Tanner, Wyatt, Cody, Riley, George, and Maggie.

I hadn't expected Maggie to come in with my family. I knew she'd been asked to follow me to the hospital and answer Carter's questions about my accident, but I'd hoped she'd gone home after that.

In all the commotion, I'd forgotten everyone still thought she was my girlfriend. They probably hadn't given her a chance to leave. It looked like Josie had more or less dragged Maggie into my room, and I could tell she was uncomfortable. That made two of us.

Not only was I embarrassed that Maggie had seen me pass out, I felt bad that she'd been obligated to come to my aid and then gotten stuck sitting around the hospital all night with my family. On top of that, it was just plain painful to see her again under any circumstances.

I missed her so much it felt like I'd broken a rib that ached every time I breathed. With everything else going on, I couldn't handle it. I was barely holding it together as it was.

I'd been a total dick to her earlier when I should have showed her some fucking gratitude for looking after me. It was one more thing I felt like shit about, but I hadn't exactly been at my best. Thanks to the concussion, I was having trouble regulating my emotions. Which was another reason I *really* didn't want Maggie around. I couldn't trust myself not to say shit I didn't have any business saying to her. Like begging her to let me kiss her one more time.

Looking at her face hurt too much, so I avoided making eye contact with her while everyone else clustered around me. Apparently she felt the same way, because she hung back, doing her best to stay out of my eyeline. I should have been grateful, but it only made me feel worse.

With my head hurting, it was hard to follow the conversation around me and field my family's well-meaning questions. Every sound was like a needle poking into my brain. It was all I could do not to snap at them to shut the hell up.

"Maybe you'll have a wicked Frankenstein scar." Riley had perched herself on the edge of my gurney and was peering at the bandage on my forehead. "How many stitches did you need?"

"Just a few," I said, pulling her questing hand away from my face and giving it a squeeze. "I doubt I'll be that much scarier-looking than I already am."

"But why'd you pass out in the first place?" she asked. "I didn't understand what Carter said about that."

"It's nothing to worry about," I assured her despite the worry gnawing at my insides. "It doesn't mean I'm sick or anything."

I hope.

"Vasovagal syncope is just a fancy doctor term for fainting," Carter said as he drew the long curtain that separated my room from the hallway. "It's a reflex of the nervous system that triggers a sudden drop in blood pressure—kind of like how possums play dead when they get scared."

"Did you get scared by something?" Riley asked me.

"No, kiddo." I squeezed her hand again. "That's not why I fainted."

"Sometimes our bodies overreact to certain situations and trigger syncope when it's not an emergency," Carter explained. "If you've ever known anyone who faints at needles, that's what's going on."

"There was a guy at summer camp who fainted once when he hit his funny bone," Cody said.

Carter nodded. "There you go. Another thing that can trigger the vagal reflex is holding your breath and straining, which is exactly what weightlifters do on heavy lifts. You wouldn't believe how many of them faint on the platform during competitions."

"So it could happen again?" Tanner asked with a frown.

"It's not something that's likely to happen again," I told him. "It was just a fluke that it happened this time."

"Maybe you shouldn't be lifting such heavy weights," Nate said.

"At least not without someone around to spot you," Wyatt added.

"I'll keep it in mind," I promised.

"So is he getting out of here tonight or what?" Manny asked Carter.

"I can let him go home as long as he's got someone to stay with him for the next twenty-four hours to monitor his concussion symptoms in case they worsen."

I groaned at the thought of having someone in my space

shadowing my every step when all I wanted was some quiet and privacy. "Come on, doc. That's not really necessary, is it? I feel fine."

Carter gave me a look that said he knew I was full of shit and in a lot more pain than I was letting on. "With your concussion, I'm afraid it's nonnegotiable."

"I'll do it," Tanner volunteered.

"No you won't," Wyatt said, giving him an odd look. "You've got other stuff to do tonight. I'll babysit the big guy."

"No offense to either of you," Josie interjected, "but I'm thinking Ryan would rather have his girlfriend take care of him than one of his little brothers."

My alarmed gaze jumped to Maggie, who'd been silently lurking at the edge of the room like she wanted to disappear. Her head snapped up at Josie's words, and her eyes locked with mine for the first time.

Quietly panicking, I groped for a plausible excuse to reject Josie's perfectly reasonable suggestion. "Oh, uh, that's..."

"Of course I'll do it," Maggie said, gazing back at me with an expression I couldn't parse. "If that's all right."

"Wyatt doesn't mind," Josie answered, thinking she was helping. There was no reason for her to think this wasn't what I wanted.

"It's cool with me if you want to take care of Grumpy Gus," Wyatt said with a shrug. "You'll probably make a better nursemaid than me, to be honest."

"I'm happy to do it," Maggie said, still looking at me.

Well, fuck. There was nothing I could say without getting into a whole conversation I frankly didn't have the emotional fortitude to deal with right now.

Maybe I'd be able to convince Maggie she didn't need to stay with me for the whole twenty-four hours. Seeing how she was right next door, I could check in with her via texts and avoid a live-in babysitter. I might actually get more privacy with her looking after me, since I doubted she'd want to spend any more time with me than she had to.

"Good," Carter said. "In that case, now's a good time for everyone else to say good night to Ryan so he can get lots of rest to heal that brain of his."

"Hang on," Wyatt said. "Real quick before we go, Tanner's got something to tell everyone."

Tanner gave a sharp shake of his head. "Now's not the time."

"Oh go on." Wyatt gave Tanner's shoulder a shove. "We could use some good news."

"What is it?" Nate asked, frowning.

"Yeah, you can't leave us hanging now," Manny said.

Tanner hesitated, darting a questioning look at me.

"Let's hear it," I said with an impatient wave of my hand. "Spill already."

He ducked his head, the shy one in the family who'd always been uncomfortable in the spotlight. "Well, the thing is…" His cheeks flushed as a smile spread across his face. "Lucy and I got engaged tonight."

"No shit?" I grinned despite the stab of pain in my head at the clamor of excited reactions to the news. Damn. Tanner was getting married. Good for him.

When everyone else had finished congratulating him, I pulled him in for a hug.

"That's the best thing I've heard in ages," I muttered as my eyes got watery. "I'm really happy for you."

"Shit, you're not crying, are you?" Tanner asked in alarm.

"Maybe a little," I said, dragging my hand across my eyes. Stupid concussion, throwing my emotions into a tailspin. "I can't believe I ruined your big night. You should be celebrating with your fiancée, not sitting around a hospital. Tell Lucy I'm sorry, okay?"

"So Wyatt, when are you going to propose to Andie?" Manny asked as he slung an arm around him.

Wyatt shrugged and exchanged a secretive smile with Tanner. "Who knows? I guess we'll have to see what happens."

"All right. Time's up." Carter waved his arms to shoo everyone out. "I hate to be the fun police, but visiting time is over."

"Sorry to mess up everyone's Friday night," I said as they made their goodbyes and started filing out. "I appreciate y'all coming, but you can go home now. And tell everyone else out there to clear out too. I mean it." I gave Josie a pleading look as she approached my bedside. "I'd rather not have a crowd waiting for me when I leave."

"Don't worry." She squeezed my arm as she leaned over to kiss my cheek. "I'm on it."

Aside from Maggie, who'd retreated to a chair on the far side of the room, George was the last to leave. He hadn't said a word the whole time he'd been in my room, which didn't surprise me. He might act gregarious in business and social situations when it benefited him, but I knew from experience that he retreated into stoicism whenever things got emotional.

He paused at my bedside, gazing down at me with a grim expression. "You okay?"

I could tell he was worried about more than just my mild concussion, the same as I was.

"I'm good," I told him, uncomfortably conscious of Maggie watching us.

George nodded and gave me an awkward pat on the arm. "You know what to do if you need anything."

I stared up at the ceiling as he walked out, trying like hell to hold myself together. My emotions were all over the map, and I was dangerously close to losing my shit. Which I absolutely could not allow to happen in front of Maggie.

Carter squeezed my ankle on his way out. "I'm going to go start your discharge paperwork and try to get you out of here as soon as I can. Be back in a bit."

And then he was gone. Leaving me and Maggie alone together.

Fuck.

26

MAGGIE

Silence fell like a ton of bricks as soon as Ryan's room emptied.

It was just the two of us now. Alone. With no buffers or distractions. *Fabulous.*

Unwilling to be the first to speak, I elected to study my fingernails, feigning an intense interest in my manicure.

More than a minute passed before Ryan's deep voice cut across the quiet. "You don't have to do this, you know."

I looked up and found him staring at me. It was hard to know how much of his tense, pinch-lipped expression was due to his headache and how much was due to me. "No one forced me into it. I volunteered."

He grunted and looked away. "I thought you might have felt obligated."

"My feelings are my business."

The way he flinched made me regret my tone. I was here to help his recovery, not put him on the defensive. Harassing a man with a traumatic brain injury was cold-blooded even for me.

"All I mean," I said more softly, "is you don't need to worry about me or what I'm feeling right now. It's my turn to worry about you for a while."

"Is that why you're doing this? To pay me back?"

I sat up straighter and crossed my legs. "That makes it sound like some sort of revenge."

"Is it? You looking forward to going all Nurse Ratched on me?" His wry smile lacked any humor.

"You haven't given me any reason to want vengeance, Ryan."

"Haven't I?"

An iron band tightened around my chest at the empty flatness of his eyes. "Quite the opposite, actually."

He turned his face to the far wall as though my answer wasn't what he'd wanted to hear. Or maybe he just didn't want to look at me anymore.

I was having some trouble in that area myself. Looking at Ryan reminded me how much I still wanted him. How much I still cared about him, even after he'd rejected me. If he offered to take me back right now, I'd probably say yes. I had no pride left when it came to this man.

It was also hard to see him lying on a hospital gurney, looking so drawn and fragile. It reminded me how frightening it had been to find him unconscious on the floor of his garage. My arms ached to wrap themselves around him like a protective shield and never let go again. Which was obviously impractical, not to mention unwanted by him.

"I'm afraid I'm not much of a Florence Nightingale," I said, desperate to fill the strained silence. "You might have been better off with Wyatt."

"That kid killed so many Tamagotchis, Tanner started calling him Dr. Kevorkian." Ryan's lips pulled to one side as his gaze flicked toward me. "Your bedside manner couldn't possibly be that bad."

"I'll do my best not to forget to feed you."

He closed his eyes, breathing heavily through his nose. I could tell he was in a lot of pain—more than he wanted anyone to know. He'd mostly managed to hide it while his family was here, but now that they'd gone he couldn't keep up the act.

"Can I do anything?" I asked quietly.

"No," was his grunted reply.

Rising from my chair, I crossed to his bedside and leaned over him to switch off the reading light on the wall behind him. Plenty of light from the hallway still spilled under the curtain divider, but at least it wasn't glaring right above his head. As I drew back, Ryan's fingers closed around my wrist.

"Maggie." His voice was raspy and thick.

Loosening his fingers, I placed his hand at his side and squeezed it gently. "Try to get some sleep."

"I won't be able to."

"Try to sleep anyway, okay?" I trailed my fingertips over the furrows cutting across his forehead, and they smoothed away as his eyes fell closed.

"Yeah, okay," he mumbled.

Thoughtlessly, I bent to kiss his forehead, only managing to stop myself at the last second. I hesitated, fighting the instinct to press my lips to his skin, and very nearly lost. But my better judgment prevailed in the end.

Drawing myself up straight, I retreated to my chair and resigned myself to silently watching over him from a distance.

"LISTEN," Ryan said as I pulled my car into my garage an hour later. "About all that stuff Carter said—"

"I hope you're not about to try and convince me to ignore your doctor's discharge instructions." I'd been given a list of symptoms to watch out for and thoroughly briefed on all the things Ryan wasn't allowed to do until his headache abated.

"No, of course not," he said. "Not ignore it. Just...take it with a pinch of salt."

I gave him a disbelieving look as I shut off the car.

"You know how doctors are," he went on as if he thought I was actually that gullible. "They have to be overly cautious about everything to protect themselves from malpractice and whatnot."

Ignoring him, I got out and walked around to open the passenger door.

"I don't need help getting out of the car," Ryan snapped when I offered my hand.

"Suit yourself." I stepped back, watching closely for signs of dizziness as he stood up and slammed the car door shut. "Take it slow in case you get light-headed."

He scowled at me as he stalked out of the garage. "I told you, I'm fine."

"Sure you are." I hit the button to close the garage door as I followed him.

"I don't need to be babied. That's what I'm trying to say."

"No one's babying you. I'm taking reasonable precautions, dictated by a doctor, for someone who's suffered a concussion."

Ryan stopped so abruptly I nearly crashed into him, then rounded on me with a surly glare. "You're hovering."

Despite my current annoyance, I kept my voice soft out of consideration for his sensitivity to sound. "You could have balance issues."

"What exactly do you think you're going to do about it if I start to fall over? Catch me?" He made a scoffing sound.

"You're not going to get rid of me by being unpleasant. I deal with far worse manbabies than you on a regular basis."

He exhaled a long, harsh breath through his nose, and I got

the sense he was trying to keep his temper in check. When he spoke again, his voice was brittle. "Look, I appreciate all your help, but there's no reason for you to waste your time sitting around my house for the next twenty-four hours. I'm not going to do anything but try to get some sleep, and you'll be right next door if I need anything. I can manage alone."

"Absolutely not." I crossed my arms. "That's not what your doctor said."

"What if I promise to check in with you regularly by text? I'll text you every hour if that's what you want." He was starting to look desperate.

I could imagine how unpleasant my presence must be for him, especially right now when he was in pain and off-kilter from his concussion, but he was just going to have to put his pride aside for the sake of his health.

"Carter said you need someone *with you*. Even if I was inclined to ignore his advice, what would your family think if I left you on your own after promising to look after you? They'd never forgive me. More importantly, I'd never forgive myself."

Ryan dragged a frustrated hand through his hair. "Maggie, for fuck's sake. I just want to be alone."

"Someone once told me that when people claim they want to be alone is when they need company the most."

He scowled and cast his eyes to the heavens.

"I'm sorry," I said. "I truly am. I know I'm the last person you want to see right now, but unless you want me to call Wyatt and ask him to come take my place, I'm afraid you're stuck with me."

Ryan stared at me for a long time. Long enough that I thought he was going to take me up on my offer to call Wyatt. Instead, after a deep sigh, he muttered, "Fine," and trudged off toward his house.

I caught up to him as he was unlocking his front door. He went inside, leaving it open for me to follow.

As I'd suspected, the layout of Ryan's house was similar to mine, though his hadn't been updated as recently, nor was it decorated for the purpose of looking good in online photos. Instead, it was furnished for comfort and practicality, with a mix of sturdy solid-wood furniture and a cushy-looking black leather couch and recliner.

Everything that met my eye was clean and scrupulously neat. Spartanly so. No clutter besmirched any visible surface. Despite the fact that he'd had no expectation of company, not a single dirty dish or stack of forgotten mail sat out to offend the senses. No wonder Ryan had been appalled by my messy house.

"You *are* Marie Kondo," I said as he dropped his keys in a ceramic bowl that looked like it had been painted by his niece.

He turned his back on me to toe off his shoes, offering not a word or even a glance in response.

"You've got a lot of books," I observed, wandering over to peruse a low bookshelf. "I didn't know you were such a reader."

It was an odd collection of titles, largely consisting of inspirational self-help books ranging from the agnostic to the deeply spiritual. Books by Brené Brown, Mitch Albom, and Deepak Chopra sat alongside Paulo Coelho, Hermann Hesse, Henry David Thoreau, and selections of religious thought from Christianity, Judaism, Buddhism, and Hinduism.

The silent treatment from Ryan continued. Ignoring my existence was apparently his new strategy for putting up with me.

As I watched him bend over to place his shoes under the bench by the door, I noted the aching slowness of his movements. All they'd given him in the hospital for his post-traumatic headache was acetaminophen. Unfortunately, it was the strongest pain medication he was allowed, and he wouldn't be due another dose for hours yet.

"Your head hurts, doesn't it?"

"A little," he admitted, which I took to mean it hurt a lot. "The car ride didn't do it any favors."

"Can I get you anything?"

His eyes lifted to mine finally, his expression pained. "I'm supposed to ask you that."

"I'm not a guest right now. I'm here to look after you. I wish you'd let me."

He dipped his head and took a breath. "There's nothing I need right now, but I'll let you know if that changes."

I nodded, appreciating what a big concession that was for him. "Okay."

"I'm gonna lie down for a while." He started to turn away then hesitated, looking uncertain. "You can make yourself at home. If you want to sleep, I guess—"

"I'll be fine out here," I said. The couch looked perfectly comfortable, and there were plenty of books to read. "Don't worry about me."

I STARTED awake sometime in the middle of the night to find Ryan looming over me. "What's wrong?"

"Go back to sleep," he whispered, setting the book I'd fallen asleep reading on the coffee table. "I didn't mean to wake you."

There was a blanket covering me that hadn't been there when I'd dozed off on the couch earlier. I sat up and rubbed my eyes. "Is everything okay?"

"Everything's fine."

"Did you get any sleep?" I asked as I scooted over to make room for him on the couch.

"Not really." He dropped down next to me and slumped back against the cushions with a tired sigh.

"Your head's still hurting." I could see it in his careful movements and the stark lines of tension in his face.

Ryan swiveled his head toward me, letting the bleak look in his eyes confirm my observation. "Sorry I woke you up. I was afraid you might be cold."

"Here." I draped half of the blanket over his lap. It had been getting chilly at night lately, but wasn't yet cold enough to switch on the heater.

He pulled the blanket up over his arms and tipped his head back against the couch, letting his eyes drift closed.

A glance at my phone told me it was almost three in the morning. Time for Ryan's next dose of acetaminophen. "If you tell me where you keep your Tylenol, I'll get it for you."

"Behind the mirror in my bathroom," he answered without opening his eyes.

I slipped off the couch and found my way to his bedroom. The door was wide-open and the lights all off. As I picked my way through the dark room to the bathroom, my stomach tightened at the heady, familiar scent of Ryan that permeated the air. Swallowing thickly at the memories it triggered, I switched on the light in the bathroom.

It was just as clean as the rest of the house, with the towels neatly folded and the small vanity counter empty except for a few toiletries. I found the Tylenol in the medicine cabinet and heroically resisted the temptation to snoop through the rest of its contents.

On my way out, I paused in the bathroom doorway, letting my gaze roam around the dim bedroom I'd never been invited into when we'd been dating. Like the rest of the house, it was tidy and spare, the unmade bedsheets the only sign of disorder.

Flicking off the light again, I went to the kitchen and filled a glass of water.

"Here, take these," I said softly as I rejoined Ryan on the

couch. When he'd downed the pills and all the water, I took the glass from him and set it on the coffee table. "Can I get you something else? Are you hungry?"

His head had already tipped back against the couch, and it moved slowly from side to side. "No, thank you."

I found his subdued politeness more worrying than his recalcitrance earlier. If he wasn't even feeling well enough to resist my help, he must really be in pain. My fingers itched to reach for his hand, and I curled them into a ball. "Is there anything I can do to help? Anything at all that might make you feel better?"

He shifted to lie down on his side, surprising me by laying his head in my lap. "Talk to me," he said, tugging the blanket over him.

"Talk to you?"

His eyes had closed again. "I can't sleep, can't read, can't watch TV. Can't do anything but lie around thinking about how much my head hurts."

I tucked the blanket around him. "Poor Freckles."

The way his mouth twitched at the nickname emboldened me to stroke my fingers through his hair. He let out a soft sigh and rested his hand on my knee. "That feels good. You can keep doing that."

As I slid my fingertips through his soft curls and over his scalp, I felt him relax a little. "I could read to you."

"If you want," he murmured.

My eyes lit on the book I'd been reading earlier, *The Subtle Art of Not Giving a F*ck*. In order to reach it, I'd have to displace Ryan's head from my lap, which I wasn't eager to do. "What's with all the self-help books, anyway?"

"Just trying to gain some perspective."

"Did it work?"

"Hard to say." He opened one eye, squinting at the book I'd

chosen from his bookshelf. "The point of reading them is to open your mind to new ways of thinking that challenge your fallback mindset, not feed into your confirmation bias."

"Is that right?" I said, biting back a smile. "Any particular books you think I should read to challenge my mindset?"

He snorted softly. "No way in hell am I falling into that trap."

I rubbed the muscles at the base of his skull. "Does that make your headache feel better or worse?"

"Better. Definitely better."

"Good." I fell quiet for a moment as I concentrated on massaging Ryan's neck. Until I remembered he'd asked me to talk to him. "I enjoyed meeting the rest of your family tonight, even if it wasn't under the best circumstances. You're lucky to have so many people in your life who care about you."

At the hospital earlier, it had occurred to me that if I got into an accident, the waiting room would be empty. I didn't have any close family anymore. My best friend and emergency contact was my ex-sister-in-law in Connecticut. The rest of my friends were scattered across the country. None of them would be able to leave their jobs and families and fly here just to come to the hospital. I wouldn't have anyone to drive me home, much less stay with me. It was a depressing thought.

Ryan squeezed my knee as though he'd guessed what I was thinking. If he had, he was kind enough to not say anything.

"Tanner's the one who owns a bookstore?" I said, trying to keep the conversation going.

He grunted in the affirmative as I worked on a knot in the back of his neck. "He just signed the papers two weeks ago."

"He used to work at King's Creamery, didn't he?"

"Yeah. He quit a couple of months ago."

"I thought his name sounded familiar." I'd seen it on some of the older head counts and wondered why he wasn't there anymore.

"He was never happy at that place. He's a lot better off now doing his own thing."

I scratched my fingernails through Ryan's hair. "A bookstore...that's a risky investment these days. Any small business is, in a town this size, but brick-and-mortar bookstores are a particular challenge."

"He's got a solid business plan," he said with an edge of defensiveness in his voice.

"I'm sure he does. I wasn't trying to imply otherwise."

Ryan pushed himself upright and glared at me. "It's a labor of love for him and an investment in the town. You have to be willing to take risks in order to build something special."

"You're absolutely right." I slid my fingers between his in apology. "Some risks are worth taking."

He kept hold of my hand as he leaned back against the couch and frowned at the floor. "I put up some of the money for the bookstore. I'm a silent partner."

That explained his defensiveness. "You wanted to invest in the town and your brother's happiness."

He toyed with my fingers as he stared off into the distance. "Tanner needed this, and he's going to be damn good at it too. Our mom would have wanted me to help him."

I'd never known anyone with such a big heart. Ryan had so much goodness in him, it shined onto everyone he met. The way he was always taking care of the people around him made me wish I had someone like him in my life. Someone who was willing to stick around for keeps. "You know how I said you're lucky to have your family? They're even luckier to have you."

His expression softened as his eyes found mine, seeing far too much as always. "Having people in your life, caring about them and letting them care about you, it's a choice. You could have that too if you let yourself."

Ryan's well-intentioned words hit me like a bucket of cold

water. Hadn't he just turned me down when I'd offered to do exactly that? I'd been willing to take a risk on him, but he hadn't felt the same.

I clenched my jaw and slipped my hand out of his. "It hasn't worked out so well for me when I've tried it."

He cringed, guilt written all over his face. "Maggie...I..."

Jumping to my feet, I snatched his glass off the table. "I'll get you more water," I said and fled to the kitchen like a coward.

As I stood at the sink trying to calm my jumping pulse, I heard Ryan come up behind me. Even though we weren't touching, I could feel him there, feel the nearness of him like a heat lamp shining on my skin.

I held my breath as he took the glass from my hand and set it on the counter. When his hands settled on my hips, I screwed my eyes closed to try and block out the memories of the last time we'd stood like this.

"Maggie." His voice was a tortured rasp, the longing in it so palpable it shuddered through me.

I spun around and backed up against the counter.

"I fucked up," he said. "I was wrong."

I licked my dry lips as he held my gaze. "About what?"

"About how I feel about you."

Oh god. I can't breathe.

I didn't know whether to run or throw myself into his arms. My brain wanted to do one thing and my body wanted to do the other.

Slowly, giving me time to pull away, Ryan lifted his hand to my face. I sucked in a sharp breath as his fingertips stroked over my cheek, unleashing a shower of tingles that crackled down my spine.

"What are you doing?" My voice had been reduced to a thready whisper.

He dipped his head and brushed the tip of his nose against

mine. "I can't stand it anymore, having you here and not touching you the way I want to."

"Is this the concussion talking?" I threw the words up between us like a shield in a desperate attempt to save us both.

Instead of backing down, he lifted his head and gazed at me with clear, solemn eyes. "This is me needing you."

"I can't just turn off my feelings, Ryan. Not with you." I was still trying to avert this disaster, even as every atom in my body strained toward him. The physical pull between us was unrelenting.

"Neither can I."

I closed my eyes as my heart tried to beat its way out of my chest. It was what I'd wanted to hear, wasn't it? But did he mean it? Even if he did, should we be doing this? Maybe this *was* the concussion talking. Recklessness and lack of impulse control were symptoms of traumatic brain injury.

"Maggie, look at me."

It was the same voice Ryan had used when he'd seduced me. I didn't have it in me to resist.

He took my hand and held it against his chest. His heart thumped against my fingers, quick and steady. "I've been lying to myself. The feelings I was afraid of? They've been here all along. I can't keep pretending you don't mean anything to me when you've already worked your way into my heart."

I let out a shaky breath. "If we do this, it'll be messy."

"Yeah it will," he said with a slow nod. "I don't give a fuck. Do you?"

"No." The answer slipped out before I'd consciously made up my mind. But I meant it. My willpower had fought a valiant battle, but it'd never really stood a chance. This was what I wanted. "Some risks are worth taking."

The smile that broke over Ryan's face was so sweet it blew up my heart like a helium balloon. "Will you please let me kiss you?"

Instead of granting permission, I pressed my mouth to his, taking what I wanted. I was done holding back. Done denying myself.

The moment our lips met, I melted against him, fisting my hands in his shirt to close the space between us. A groaning sigh shuddered through his chest, and he hauled me up against him with a desperation that matched my own.

His tongue plunged into my mouth, claiming me as his. Tiny whimpers spilled out of me as I strained against him, aching for more contact. I couldn't get enough of him. The taste of him, the feel of his body, the sound of his needy, gasping breaths—it was all as intoxicating as any drug.

He broke off the kiss and dropped his forehead heavily onto my shoulder, breathing hard and shaking. "Fuck," he groaned. "You're just so...fuck."

I wasn't so far gone with desire that I could miss the strain of agony in his voice or the tension radiating through him. Cradling his head in my hands, I touched my lips to his cheek. "You're in pain."

His arms wound around me, and he pressed his face into the crook of my neck. "I want you so bad. If it wasn't for this damn concussion, I'd take you to my bed right now and give you anything you asked for."

"Anything?" I breathed, sliding my hands through his hair.

His answering growl resonated with promise. "Anything."

God, I wanted that so badly. My whole body quivered at the thought of it. But Ryan's needs took precedence over mine right now. "We'll have to save that for later."

"I hate that I can't have you. If there was any way at all..."

"I know," I murmured, shushing him.

He hugged me tighter. "Will you do something for me in the meantime?"

"What's that?"

"Will you sleep beside me? I just want to close my eyes and hold you."

Oh. *Oh.* My heart. This man was surely going to be the death of me.

"Of course I will."

I took Ryan's hand and led him to his bedroom, turning off lights along the way. The streetlight in front of the house leaked in around the edges of the blinds, faintly illuminating the unmade bed.

"Do you have a T-shirt I can borrow?" The jeans and button-down I'd changed into after work were more comfortable than my professional wardrobe but less than ideal for sleeping.

Ryan moved to his dresser and opened a drawer. By the time he turned around with a T-shirt in his hands, I was already shimmying my jeans down my legs. He stood stock-still as he watched me take off my shirt. When I slipped out of my bra, he swallowed loud enough for me to hear it.

Naked except for a pair of underwear, I walked toward him and took the T-shirt out of his hands. "Thanks."

"You're killing me, sweetness." His voice was hoarse, and I could see his shoulders trembling with the effort of holding himself still.

"You can't expect me to sleep in a bra and jeans." Smiling, I pulled his T-shirt on, then made my way to the bed and slipped between the covers. "Come get in bed, Freckles."

He dragged his T-shirt off with a grunt and crawled into bed, curling his body around mine and pillowing his head on my breasts. "Am I too heavy like this?"

"Not in the slightest." Trying to soothe away some of his pain, I stroked my fingers through his hair.

His shoulders sagged with a contented sigh as he nestled closer. "I missed you."

"I missed you too." The implications of that provoked a flicker of apprehension, but I refused to let it affect me. I'd made my choice, and I was exactly where I wanted to be. We could deal with the future later.

"I'm sorry I was such an asshole before."

"Shhh. Go to sleep."

Gradually, the rise and fall of his chest slowed and his muscles slackened against me.

I could love you if you let me, I thought as I lay in the dark, holding Ryan while he finally slept.

27

RYAN

The glow of daylight through my eyelids gentled me back to consciousness. My arms tightened around something warm and soft that smelled like heaven, and I smiled as I realized I was spooned around Maggie.

Humming in contentment, I cuddled her closer and nuzzled the skin between her shoulder blades. She let out a sleepy moan as she shifted, rubbing her ass against my morning wood.

That woke me up real damn fast. As the blood in my veins heated, I slid my hands under her shirt and up her rib cage to her breasts.

"Good morning to you too," she mumbled, stretching her arms overhead. "Does this mean you're feeling better?"

"Much." My headache had receded to a dull background throb. Even better, moving my head no longer seemed to cause a sickening wave of pain.

Oh yeah, I could work with this.

I skimmed one of my hands down Maggie's stomach and over the sensitive skin of her hip, relishing the way she arched against me in response.

"Are you hungry?" she asked, yawning.

"Ravenous." My hand skated down her inner thigh to draw her legs apart. "Eating is an excellent idea."

When my fingers ventured inside the band of her underwear, she caught them with hers. "I meant for food. You haven't eaten in hours."

I growled in frustration as I flexed my captured fingers. "Do you mind? I'm trying to debauch you."

"As much as I appreciate it, that kind of activity is not approved by your doctor."

"I'm pretty sure I can go down on you without hurting my brain, sweetness." I dragged her hand down inside her underwear with mine, finding her as wet and eager as I'd suspected.

Her breath hitched, and for a second I thought I'd won. But then she pulled my hand away and rolled over to face me. "Pretty sure isn't good enough. Carter said it's important to really take it easy the first forty-eight hours."

"Babe, come on..."

A smile curved her lips as she pressed a too-quick kiss to my mouth. I caught her by the waist when she tried to pull back, but she shook her head and tapped a finger against my lips. "I have to pee anyway."

Knowing when I'd been beaten, I let her get up. But I watched that beautiful ass of hers every step of the way to the bathroom. After she'd closed the door, I rolled onto my back and laid my forearm across my eyes as I took stock of myself.

I felt a hell of a lot better than last night, but I definitely wasn't one hundred percent. Besides the lingering headache, I could tell I was a little off. Edgy. Drained. Slow-thinking. But also strangely exhilarated. My whole body hummed with energy, from the top of my aching head to the tips of my fingers and toes. Everything felt lighter and easier, like a crushing weight had been lifted off my chest.

I had Maggie back and no regrets about it whatsoever.

Maybe the concussion had lowered my emotional defenses last night, but it hadn't driven me to do anything I hadn't wanted to do. It had only forced me to face the truth.

This thing between me and Maggie had gone way beyond sexual attraction. There were no lines I could draw or boundaries I could enforce that would keep me from losing my heart. She already owned it. Maybe she always had.

I'd never felt this kind of desperate, aching *need* for anyone before. Maggie hadn't just gotten under my skin, she'd filled an empty space inside me like no one else ever had. That wasn't something I could shake off or ignore.

My whole goddamn life I'd been searching for a partner. Someone I could picture myself settling down with for the long haul. Someone who felt like coming home. But I'd struck out time and again. Every relationship fell flat. There was always something missing. I'd dated dozens of women over the years—women I'd liked and cared for and been attracted to—but I'd never *needed* a single one of them.

After a while, I started to think the missing element was inside me. There had to be something wrong with me that made me incapable of falling in love.

When I learned about my dad's ALS, I decided it was a mercy the universe had arranged for me to be alone. If I had to get sick, at least I wouldn't have to watch the woman I loved lose me piece by piece. It was the one silver lining to the existential storm cloud hanging over me. I clung to it for comfort, but I also took it as a sign that I was fated to get sick like my dad. Didn't matter that it wasn't a rational belief. It had worked its way into my head and dug its claws in deep.

So how fucking cruel was it that Maggie had come along *now* and made me feel all the things I'd convinced myself I'd never feel? Turned out I wasn't broken after all. I just hadn't found the right person to unlock my heart. The universe had ripped my silver lining away and thrown the perfect woman into my path after I'd made my peace with being alone. What a bastard trick to play, dangling the thing I wanted most in front of me when I couldn't have it.

Well, fuck it.

As long as Maggie was here, I was going to wring every bit of joy I could out of the limited time we had before she left. I could squeeze a lot of living into the next four months. Why shouldn't we enjoy the hell out of each other until then? Didn't I deserve a small taste of happiness, even if I couldn't hold on to it?

It was okay to let myself have this, because Maggie would be gone long before anything could get bad. When her contract ended in February, she'd move on to her next job and forget about me. She might find it hard to go, but she'd never choose me over her career. She'd have to leave me behind, and that would keep her safe.

At least that way she'd be far from here after we ended it, instead of right next door constantly reminding me of what I'd lost. The physical separation would make it easier for both of us. Even if she said she wanted to try to keep things going long-distance, it wouldn't last. We'd start to drift apart as soon as she got busy with her next job, and she'd get used to living her life without me again. It wouldn't hurt her as much that way since she'd be the one who left.

Until that time came, I was all in on the here and now. Fuck the future. Dwelling on it wouldn't change anything. For the next four months, I was only thinking about the present.

When I heard the bathroom door open, I dragged my arm off my eyes to savor the sight of Maggie walking toward me in my old Highland Games T-shirt with her soft, round breasts swaying and her nipples showing through the fabric. "You're beautiful, you know that?"

She leaned over the bed to kiss me. "Your head still hurts, doesn't it? Tell me the truth."

I smoothed my hands over her hips, keeping her close. "Only a little. It's a lot better."

"I'm glad. How about some breakfast?" When I waggled my eyebrows suggestively, her laugh flooded my chest with warmth. "How about I *cook* you some breakfast? You need to keep up your energy, not deplete it."

"Fine," I said, knowing she was right. With all the things I wanted to do with her, I'd need to be at my best. No way was I settling for half measures anymore.

WHEN CARTER HAD LISTED ALL the things I couldn't do during the first forty-eight hours of my recuperation, I'd wondered how the hell I was supposed to pass the time without reading or looking at screens. Stare at the ceiling? It wasn't as if I'd be able to sleep. It had sounded like torture.

But with Maggie here it was more like heaven. We mostly stayed in bed snuggling and talking and napping on and off. I tried to get frisky a few times, but she wasn't having any of it. Stubborn damn woman. Since I was still a little foggy and tired, I didn't put up too much of a fight. She was right about me needing to take it easy, even if I hated to admit it.

People had been blowing up my phone with concerned texts since Friday night, but since I wasn't allowed to read them I let Maggie take charge of responding for me. When well-wishers started showing up at the house, she put a note over the doorbell asking people to knock softly so as not to disturb the concussion patient.

Adriana stopped by with a mountain of food from her mom's restaurant, Wyatt brought over a get-well cake from

Andie's aunt, the B shift crew dropped off some cookies and a card signed by everyone in the department, and the Highland Games club sent me a bouquet of flowers that got me all choked up because my emotions were still running amok, dammit.

By the time Monday morning came around, I'd made it out of the initial forty-eight-hour recovery period and was feeling well enough that I convinced Maggie to go back to work. But we continued to see as much as we could of each other throughout the week. She came over after she got home from work every evening to help me eat all the food people had brought, and spent the night sleeping next to me in my bed.

On Thursday, Tanner drove me to my GP for a follow-up, and I got the official okay to drive, engage in moderate exercise, and report back to work for light duty. *Halle-damn-lujah.* I was feeling pretty stir-crazy by then, not to mention horny as fuck.

When Maggie let herself in that night, I met her at the door and bent her backward in a deep, searing kiss. I must have kissed her hundreds of times this week, but the instant our lips met it was like a shot of electricity straight to my nervous system. All that pent-up desire surged hot through my veins as I devoured her sweet mouth like candy.

"Hi," she said, breathless and smiling, when we finally came up for air. "You're feeling perky tonight."

"I went to the doctor for my follow-up today."

The smile faded from her face, replaced by a tiny line between her brows. "You didn't tell me that was today. I could have driven you."

"I didn't want you to be distracted worrying." I pressed my lips to her forehead to kiss her frown away. "Tanner drove me."

"What did the doctor say?"

I drew back with an uncontainable grin. "She said I'm doing great. Well enough to go back to work."

Maggie's eyes lit up like sapphires as she pulled me in for a celebratory kiss. "Congratulations! That's the best news ever."

"I'm also approved for driving, screen use, and moderate aerobic exercise." I waggled my eyebrows. "You know what that means?"

A knowing smile played over her lips. "What does that mean?"

"Sex."

I'd barely gotten the word out before she grabbed me by the front of my shirt and towed me into the bedroom. "Take off your clothes," she ordered, pushing me toward the bed.

Biting back a grin, I reached behind my head to drag my shirt off. "Bossy, bossy."

"Now your pants." The heat sparking in her eyes made my abs tighten with anticipation. "Hurry up."

"Feeling impatient, are we?" I was playing at being cocky, but my fingers shook as I fumbled with the button on my jeans. I'd waited so long for this. We both had.

Maggie watched my movements with rapt focus as I shoved my pants and underwear down and kicked them aside. I'd never been naked in front of her before, and my skin flushed hot as her gaze took a slow, meticulous journey over my body, absorbing every inch of me.

"Your turn," I said, starting toward her when I couldn't bear it anymore.

"No." She caught me by my forearms. "Now it's *your* turn."

My pulse jumped at the smoky promise in her voice, and I let her ease me back onto the bed. She knelt between my thighs and leaned over me, sliding her palms down my stomach like I was a prize she intended to savor.

Pleasure rippled through me as she pressed her lips to my skin and trailed hot kisses over my chest, mapping my torso with her mouth. I slid my hands into her hair to loosen it from its ponytail and shivered at the silky tickle of it on my skin as it fell in a curtain around her head. Lying back again, I closed my eyes and let sensation sweep away my fractured thoughts, losing myself in the paradise of Maggie's warm lips, hot breaths, and tender, exploring hands.

As she slowly traveled lower, my dick throbbed in time with the heavy, insistent drumming of my heart. I grabbed fistfuls of the comforter as my abs twitched under her teasing lips. She was taking her sweet time, taunting me to drive me out of my mind with desire, and it was all I could do to hold still and let her have her way.

When she finally wrapped her hand around me, I nearly skyrocketed off the bed.

"Oh fuck," I groaned as she squeezed hard enough to make lights dance under my eyelids.

"I like you like this. At my mercy." Her fingernails dug into my thighs, shooting a frisson of pleasure-pain up my spine. "I can feel you trembling."

I opened my eyes to find her watching me while she stroked me slowly. The loving, enraptured look on her face drove a rush of breath from my lungs. A feeling too immense and powerful to contain swelled inside me. I'd never needed anyone as much as I needed her.

"Maggie—" I broke off with a choking sound as her tongue flicked out to give the tip of my cock an exploratory lick.

Her eyes gleamed as she smiled, clearly intent on torturing me the way I'd tortured her. Another teasing lick followed. And another. The woman was going to break me, and I couldn't fucking wait.

"You taste as good as I knew you would," she said and dragged her tongue up my dick like a goddamn popsicle. My hips bucked when she hit the sensitive spot on the underside of the head, and she dug her tongue into it, applying pinpoint pressure that had me shaking beneath her.

"Please," I whispered, fighting the urge to flip her onto her back and bury myself inside her. "Maggie…"

An animal-like sound tore out of me when she sucked me deep. *Fuck. Yes.* It was all I could do not to thrust myself down her throat as her hot, wet mouth enveloped me. My fingers curled into her hair helplessly as she turned me into a panting, shuddering mess, every pull and stroke of her tongue unraveling me a little more.

"Oh shit," I hissed as I felt the edge of the cliff rushing toward me. "I can't… I need…" I just barely managed to drag her off before it was too late. "I want to feel you come around me."

"That can be arranged," she said and surged toward my mouth.

I kissed her between heaving breaths as I pawed at her clothes with clumsy hands. "These need to go."

Sitting back on the bed, she stripped off her sweater and wriggled out of her leggings. Fully naked now, she crawled up my body, straddling my thighs as she covered my mouth with hers again.

Feverish and half mad with need, I gripped her hips and dragged her against my aching cock. *Too rough. Too goddamn rough.* I'd leave bruises on her if I didn't take it easy. Summoning the fraying tendrils of my control, I loosened my fingers and stroked the satin skin I'd manhandled.

"You can be rough," Maggie whispered in my ear as she rocked against me. "I like it."

My eyes rolled back in my head as a groan reverberated through me. I almost came right there, she was so damn perfect. But then she said something that yanked me right out of my delirium.

"Do you have a condom?"

Fuck. It had been so long since I'd needed one, I wasn't sure where they were or if they'd expired. I should have stopped at the drugstore while I was out with Tanner, but I hadn't fucking thought of it.

At my hesitation, Maggie pushed herself upright and propped her hands on my chest. "I'm okay going without if you are. I've got an IUD and I've been tested since the last time I had sex. I assume you have too."

"I have," I said, sliding my hands up her sides. Now that she'd raised the possibility, I wanted to have her bare more than I'd ever wanted anything. "Are you sure you're okay with it?"

"I trust you." The sure, steady look in Maggie's eyes stripped me to the bone.

Swallowing thickly, I cupped her cheek and drew her down for a kiss. "I trust you too."

Our tongues slid together as the kiss grew more heated. I loved kissing her, the give and take as we both battled for dominance. I could have kissed her for hours—and had over the last few days. But with her naked body rubbing against mine, I was greedy for a lot more than kissing.

I reached between us and stroked my knuckles over her swollen folds. She shivered, canting her hips, and pushed herself upright.

Her eyes locked with mine as she took me in hand and rubbed me over her entrance. All around but never inside. Teasing me again. *Fucking woman.* The effort to hold still had my muscles quivering, but I could tell Maggie was having a hard time too. Her eyes had fallen half closed, and she was trembling almost as much as I was.

With an impatient shiver, she finally guided me into her. Her head lolled back as she slowly sank down, shuddering when she'd taken my full length. "Holy hell, you're big."

"You good?" I croaked, nearly rendered incapable of speech

by the feel of her all around me. I wasn't sure how long I'd be able to hold on. I'd intended to take my time and do this right, but I could already tell I wasn't going to be capable of much subtlety or finesse. Just looking up at Maggie was practically enough to push me over.

She was the most stunning woman I'd ever known. Her sunshine hair hung around her face as her soft lips parted in an expression of hazy bliss like she was drunk on my dick. A pink flush tinged her skin from her cheeks to her full, round breasts and down to her lush, fleshy thighs. I wished I could take a snapshot of her like this, so I'd have a keepsake of this moment.

"Good doesn't do justice to how you feel," she said and rolled her hips.

Holy shit.

I let out a low, raw growl and ran my hands up her thighs to grab her backside. But Maggie had other ideas. Capturing my hands, she pushed them into the pillow above my head, interlacing our fingers as she leaned her weight on them.

"Oh, fuck, that's good," I rasped when she rocked against me. Each slow thrust of her hips drove me deeper inside her, wringing gasps and moans from both of us. Utterly transfixed, I watched the emotions play out over her expression as she ground against my pubic bone, taking her pleasure from me.

"Come on, baby." Bracing my feet on the bed, I thrust my hips to increase the friction, and she cried out as the new angle hit a sweet spot inside her. "That's it. Let me feel you come around me."

Her cries grew louder as she rocked faster, chasing relief. She threw her head back, and I gasped when she clenched around me. Her cries died down to whimpers as her orgasm pulsed through her, squeezing me tight. Once the waves had ebbed, I grabbed her hips, slamming her down on me as I rutted against her mindlessly, again and again, until I was coming hard and shouting her name as I shattered to pieces.

Maggie collapsed onto my chest and nestled into my neck. Overcome with tenderness, I cradled her in my arms while we both struggled to catch our breath.

"Tell me it's not always like this for you."

I held her tighter as I stroked her hair. "Like what?"

"Tell me you feel as overwhelmed as I do." Her hand curled into a fist on my chest. "I need to know I'm not the only one who's never felt anything like that before."

Part of me wanted to deny it, to put some distance between me and her. But I couldn't do it. I couldn't answer her vulnerability with a lie.

"You're not the only one," I whispered, uncurling her fingers and threading them with mine. "It's never been anything like this before."

"For me either."

We lay there in silence as the weighty implications of that settled over us.

Eventually, Maggie lifted her head and rested her chin on my chest. Sorrow hovered around her eyes as they looked into mine. "If there was ever a man who could make me want to stay—"

"Don't finish that sentence." I hugged her to me and pressed my face into her hair. "I don't want you giving anything up for me. I wouldn't let you if you tried. Okay?"

She released a shaky breath. "Okay."

Relief swept through me at her easy assent. As much as I longed to make her mine, I couldn't allow that to happen. We weren't meant to last. This time we had together was stolen. When it was over, Maggie needed to leave me behind. I had to make sure she did, even if that meant pushing her away.

It was going to wreck me, I could already tell. I'd never let myself need anyone like this before. I wasn't sure what would be left of me without her.

But I could comfort myself knowing she'd be okay. She'd get to enjoy the rest of her life after she left here. That was what mattered. It was the only thing that mattered.

28

MAGGIE

Sunrise found me wide-awake, lying next to a sound-asleep Ryan. I should have been sleeping as hard as him after last night. We'd stayed up into the early hours, coming together over and over, taking each other in every way we could. And yet here I was, awake long before my alarm and unable to get back to sleep.

What we'd done felt like more than just sex. A *lot* more. It felt like we'd turned a corner, for better or worse. The intense connection, the intimacy, the trust—it all had swirled together into this intense, overpowering emotion I didn't know how to name.

Yes, you do.

It had been a long time since I'd been in love, but not so long that I couldn't still recognize the symptoms. I knew exactly what this terrifying, thrilling, slightly queasy feeling was.

You love Ryan.

The back of my throat burned at the realization. I wasn't supposed to fall for him this hard when there was no hope of any real future for us. Not without one of us uprooting our whole life, which wasn't an option. He'd already told me he wouldn't let me do it for him, and I couldn't let him do it for me.

So where did that leave us?

I rolled onto my side, tucking my hands under my pillow as I stared at Ryan's sleeping face. My chest tightened with the certainty I was going to hurt him when I left. I was going to hurt both of us.

And yet I couldn't seem to regret it. Butterflies careened in my stomach just thinking about the things we'd shared last night. He was the sexiest man I'd ever known, but also the most caring. The same touch that set me on fire could make me feel safe and cherished. And then there was the fervent, needy way he'd clung to me, as if I was his sanctuary.

How could I regret any of that? Our time together might be limited, and we might be setting ourselves up for heartbreak, but I had to believe it was worth it. Hearts were resilient muscles. They'd mend in time. Better to have loved and lost, right? If Tennyson was to be believed, anyway.

My phone's alarm went off on the nightstand behind me, and I rolled over to shut it off. When I rolled back, Ryan's eyes were open.

His mouth tugged into a heart-melting smile. "Hi."

I smiled back as I touched my fingers to his beautiful dimples. "Sorry about my alarm."

"Come here." He pulled me up against him, and our legs tangled together as he placed an impossibly gentle kiss on my lips. "Sorry about the stubble burn."

"I'm not complaining. Feel free to give me as much stubble burn as you like."

His smile took on a mischievous twist. "Is that so?"

I laughed as he rolled me onto my back, crushing me into the mattress as he nuzzled my neck with his prickly face. I wrapped my legs around his waist and we both stilled when his hard, pulsing cock came into contact with my over-sensitive sex.

Ryan let out a long breath and shook his head. "You have to get ready for work."

"I do," I agreed sadly. "I have a meeting this morning."

He kissed me and rolled off. "I've got to pee anyway."

"Good luck peeing with that morning wood," I called after him as I leaned over the edge of the bed, looking for my clothes.

My sweater and leggings were easy to find, but my underwear was nowhere in sight. Dropping onto my hands and knees, I flipped up the bed skirt and peered underneath. *Ha!* There it was. Right next to a stack of books.

Odd. Why keep books under the bed? Unless it was porn. The spines were all facing away from me, so it was hard to say. Had I just stumbled upon Ryan's secret erotica stash?

My curiosity aroused, I stretched my arm out to grab a book off the nearest stack and dragged it out from under the bed.

How To Be Sick by Toni Bernhard.

Definitely not porn. But why was it hidden under the bed? For that matter, why did he own it at all? An uneasy feeling settled in my stomach as I stared at the cover.

Ignoring the voice of my conscience that said I shouldn't be snooping, I reached under the bed and dragged out the whole stack of books. As I flipped through the titles, the uneasy feeling grew into a yawning pit in my stomach.

Dying: A Memoir. The Bright Hour: A Memoir of Living and Dying. Until I Say Good-bye: My Year Of Living With Joy. Through the Lens of Love: Facing Terminal Illness.

Every single book was about terminal illness and dying.

"Do you want me to make some eggs before you go?" Ryan said as he emerged from the bathroom, tugging up a pair of shorts. He stopped when he saw me sitting on the floor with the books from under his bed, and his mouth snapped shut with an audible click.

"Why do you have so many books about dying?" I asked, afraid to find out the answer.

"Why are you looking under my bed?" he countered in a low, tight voice.

"My underwear got kicked under there. Now you answer *my* question."

His face looked like it had been carved from stone. "I didn't realize I needed to justify my reading habits."

"This isn't pleasure reading, Ryan."

Instead of answering, he turned and walked out of the room.

I hastily pulled on my clothes and went after him. I found him in the kitchen, rinsing out the coffeepot. "Ryan."

"You want eggs or not?" he asked, not looking at me.

"I don't have time to eat." Stepping up behind him, I wound my arms around his waist. He held himself still, but I could feel his muscles vibrating with tension. "I want you to talk to me."

He unwound my arms and walked over to the pantry. When he spoke, his voice was hard and flat. "There's nothing to talk about. They're just books."

"I might believe that if you weren't acting like I'd uncovered some deep, dark secret you've been keeping hidden."

Ryan's hand stilled on the coffee canister, and I saw him take a breath before he stalked past me on his way back to the coffeemaker. "Maybe I'm just pissed at having my privacy violated."

"I've practically been living in your house for most of the last week. I wasn't aware there were off-limits areas."

He slammed the metal coffee canister down hard enough to make me jump. "The fact that they were out of sight under my bed should have been a clue!"

My stomach lurched at the intensity of his anger. His shoulders were shaking with it as he stood with his back to me. I had to swallow twice before I found my voice. "I'm sorry for snooping. It was wrong. You have every right to be pissed about that."

"Thanks for your permission." Sarcasm iced every word.

"You can be mad at me if you want, but you can't expect me to forget about it now that I've seen those books."

His knuckles whitened as he gripped the counter. "Don't you need to go to work?"

I did. I really did, but I couldn't leave yet. Not until I knew he was okay.

"Ryan, you're scaring me." The wobble I couldn't keep out of my voice finally got him to turn around.

He folded his arms across his chest. "There's nothing for you to worry about." His defensive posture and pinched expression begged to differ.

"It doesn't seem that way from where I'm standing."

"You're going to have to trust me."

Well, he had me there, didn't he? I'd told him last night that I trusted him. If I couldn't let this go like he wanted, wouldn't that make me a liar?

I still trusted that he'd never do anything intentionally to hurt me. But something was obviously wrong, and the man had a documented history of downplaying his own pain and refusing to let people help him. So no, I didn't necessarily trust him to act in his own best interest.

We stared at each other across the kitchen, waiting for one of us to break first.

"It's because of my dad," Ryan said, fixing his shuttered gaze on the floor. "He got sick a few years ago."

"Your real father?"

A stiff jerk of his chin was his only answer.

I closed the distance between us and fitted myself against him.

He uncrossed his arms and wound them around me. It wasn't exactly the vigorous hug I would have liked, but it was better than nothing. "We were never close," he said in a tight voice. "But I guess I was trying to understand what he was going through."

"I'm so sorry."

The muscles in Ryan's back went rigid. "I don't want to talk about it. I mean it, Maggie. Don't ask me about him."

It couldn't possibly be healthy for him to keep something so clearly painful bottled up like this, but I wasn't willing to upset him even more by pushing the issue. "Okay. If that's what you want."

"You're gonna be late," he said quietly. A dismissal. He wanted me to go.

I stubbornly hugged him tighter, unwilling to leave with hard feelings between us. "I'm sorry I looked at the books under your bed. I shouldn't have pried."

"Apology accepted."

I lifted my face to his, but his expression gave away nothing. "Are we okay?"

He squeezed my shoulders and mustered a smile. "Of course we are."

It felt like a lie.

"Are *you* okay?" I asked.

"I'm fine," he said. "Really."

That too had the feel of a lie.

"I promise." He took my face in his hands and pressed a soft kiss to my lips. "Go to work. Everything's fine."

I didn't believe that for a second. But whatever was going on with Ryan wasn't something that could be fixed right at this moment. Maybe it would be best to give him some space for now. Once he'd had time to cool off, he might be more willing to open up to me. I hoped so.

"Okay." I curled my hand around the back of his head and kissed him again. "I'll see you tonight?"

He nodded. "Have a good day."

Reluctantly, I let go of Ryan and left to get ready for work.

MY MEETING that morning was with Nate and several members of his leadership team. I was close to completing the first phase of my engagement, but I had some additional questions about the sales department's ongoing projects that I needed to get answered.

As I sat in the conference room, listening to a senior district manager tell a rambling story about an incentive program he'd set up for his sales reps, I couldn't stop thinking about Ryan and those books stashed under his bed. The way he'd acted when I discovered them didn't sit right with me.

Why keep the books hidden away like he was ashamed of them? Why did he find it so upsetting to talk about his father? And why did he have *so* many books about illness and dying if he and his father had been estranged? None of it made sense to me.

The more I thought about Ryan's reaction, the more convinced I was that he was keeping something important from me, and the more worried I became.

"Does that answer your question?"

I returned my attention to the present and the district manager sitting across from me. "Yes, thank you," I said, since he'd actually answered my question five minutes ago before he'd launched into his tangential anecdote.

"Anything else?" Nate asked in a clipped voice. He'd been even more terse and defensive than usual this morning. Though I couldn't exactly blame him for feeling like I'd put him and his department under the gun when that was precisely what I was doing. Sales had the worst cost revenue ratio of all the departments in the company, which made them the most obvious targets for cuts. Nate was no fool, so he must have read the writing on the wall.

"No, that covers it," I answered, keeping my expression pleasant. "Thank you all for your time."

While everyone filed out of the conference room, I typed out another text to Ryan. I'd texted him several times since I'd arrived at the office, but he hadn't responded, which wasn't helping to put my mind at rest.

When I stood to gather up my things, I noticed Nate lingering by the door alone.

"Can you spare a minute?" he asked.

I forced a smile and braced myself for an unpleasant conversation. "Of course."

My wariness increased as Nate turned to close the conference room door. But when he faced me again, he appeared uneasy rather than confrontational. Hesitant, almost—something that looked out of place on Nate, who seemed to do everything with the brisk purpose of a man in a perpetual hurry. The way he shifted his weight from one Gucci loafer to the other was as out of character for him as it would be for me.

"I hope you don't mind," he said, "but I wanted to ask how Ryan's doing."

The question took me so off guard I didn't know how to react for a second. Nate had never voluntarily brought up my relationship with Ryan before—or any personal subject, for that matter. Not once. Even at the hospital, we'd only exchanged minimal civilities in the waiting room.

I wished I knew how to answer. Yesterday, I would have happily told him Ryan was doing great. But after this morning, I wasn't so certain that was true. Maybe I'd have a better idea if Ryan would *text me back*.

"His headache finally cleared up on Wednesday, and he's been feeling back to his old self since then," was what I decided to tell Nate.

"That's good." Watching the relief roll across his face was like watching a suit of steel armor crack open to reveal a real live human being with actual emotions inside. I marveled at it, wondering who this man before me was and how Nate kept him so tightly locked down the rest of the time.

And then he went and surprised me even more.

"I did some reading up on concussions," he said. "Sometimes the symptoms can be severely impairing and last for weeks or even months."

Maybe I shouldn't be so astonished by Nate's concern for Ryan. He'd been one of the first to arrive at the hospital, after all, even if he hadn't said much once he was there. But the thought of Nate sitting around googling concussion outcomes made my heart lurch against my breastbone.

"He's really lucky it wasn't more serious," I said, reaching up to press my hand against the twinge in my chest. "Tanner took him to his follow-up doctor's appointment yesterday, and Ryan got the all clear to go back to work on light duty."

"Thanks for letting me know." Nate's expression verged on warm. It wasn't quite a smile, but the light behind his eyes put it on the smile spectrum. He was remarkably attractive when he wasn't frowning or scowling. His sharp jaw, firm chin, and bold nose lost their harshness, letting his handsome features shine through.

"You're welcome," I said, offering him a genuine smile as I readjusted my previous impressions of him.

"Will you tell Ryan..." More uncomfortable shifting ensued,

like a person exposed in ways he wasn't adapted to. "Tell him I'm glad he's doing better."

"I'd be happy to." I bent to gather my things, doing him the kindness of averting my eyes from his discomfiture. "You should call Ryan and tell him yourself. Now that he's able to use his phone again, I'm sure he'd love to hear from you."

"I will," Nate said with a touch of dryness. "But I wanted to get the straight story on how he's doing, and I thought I'd be more likely to get it from you than him."

"That's probably true," I agreed, feeling my smile ebb as I thought about the way I'd left things with Ryan this morning.

I wanted to ask Nate about Ryan's father, but talked myself out of it. It would only anger Ryan further to learn I'd been asking about him behind his back when he'd told me to leave it alone. I couldn't justify another betrayal of his trust. If I wanted answers to my questions, they'd have to come from Ryan himself.

"Was there something else?" I asked when Nate continued to stand in front of the conference room door without saying anything or moving to leave.

His chin tipped up as his armor snapped back into place, returning his expression to its customary hardness. "You've targeted my organization for cuts, haven't you?"

Right, so the friendly part of our chat was over. Oh well, it had been nice while it lasted.

"I'm not targeting anything," I said, drawing my own armor around me. "The financials do that for me."

"You know what I mean."

"I don't have to tell you that the sales organization's budget has increased consistently over the last five years without showing a corresponding increase in generated revenue."

"No, you don't." His jaw locked up as if I'd jabbed a painful bruise. "I'm just wondering how bad it's going to be."

"Nothing's been decided yet."

Sharp hazel eyes identical to Josie's bored into me. "But you have a pretty good idea, don't you?"

I did, but I couldn't share it with him, which he had to know. "I'm still in the information-gathering stage. I won't be presenting my final recommendations to the CEO for another month."

"Ryan said you were trying to save as many jobs as you could."

I blinked, unable to hide my surprise. I hadn't realized Ryan and Nate had ever discussed me or my work. "He told you that?"

"Is it true?"

"Yes, but—"

"Is there anything at all I can do to protect my people?" A hint of desperation leaked out through tiny fissures in his armor. "If there is, tell me and I'll do it, whatever it is."

Compassion softened my voice as I leveled with him to the extent I was allowed. "The sales organization is top-heavy and bloated. Some head count will have to be eliminated in the restructuring. There's no getting around that."

"What if I gave up my salary and bonus?"

"It's a noble sacrifice, Nate but—"

"I know it's not a solution to the overall problem, but it could at least save a few jobs."

He looked so brittle and beside himself, for a moment I thought he might be about to have breakdown, with me as the awful cause.

"You're right," I said as gently as I could. "It's not a solution to the problem."

His bleak nod tore at my heartstrings, making me want to offer some kind of comfort—reach out to touch his too-tense arm or even give him a hug—though I doubted he'd take kindly to any such gesture. Which left me with nothing but empty words to give him.

"It's an admirable offer, Nate. And I promise to keep it in mind. I really am doing everything I can to minimize layoffs."

I watched him roll his shoulders as he pushed the part of him that felt things back down deep inside.

"Thanks," he said with as much emotion as you'd use with a stranger who'd held a door for you. "I appreciate it."

My stomach churned with helplessness as he strode out of the conference room. Nate had taken a risk by baring so much of himself, and I hated to think of him walking away with the conviction it had been for nothing. He'd put his trust in me, and I didn't want to let him down.

On my way back to my office, I typed another text to Ryan, who still hadn't responded to me. *I just had the most surprising conversation with Nate.*

I'd hoped it might pique his interest enough to inspire a reply, but he remained disconcertingly silent over the next two hours.

By lunchtime, when I still hadn't heard a word from Ryan, I decided I'd waited long enough. I fired off a few quick emails, postponed the one meeting on my calendar that afternoon, and left the office for the day.

Ryan's silence had me feeling slightly frantic. He'd given me a spare key to his house that I'd used to let myself in every night this week after work, and I used it again now without a second thought.

As I pushed the front door open, Ryan jolted upright on the couch. All the lights were off and the blinds closed, plunging the room into dimness.

He blinked at me in surprise. "What are you doing here? Why aren't you at work?"

"I left early." I closed the door behind me, frowning as I noticed the bottle of whiskey sitting on the coffee table.

"Why?"

"I was worried about you. Have you been drinking?"

"No." He swung his feet to the floor and leaned forward as he scrubbed his hands over his face. "I've just been thinking about it."

"You're not supposed to drink alcohol after a concussion."

"I know that," he snapped. Pushing himself to his feet, he snatched the bottle off the table and stalked to the liquor cart in the dining room to put it back with the others. "That's why I didn't do it."

The fact that Ryan had been lying in the dark thinking about drinking only made me more concerned about him. "You didn't answer any of my texts."

"I didn't see them. I had my phone off." He disappeared into the kitchen as if we weren't in the middle of a conversation.

"Why'd you turn your phone off?" I asked, following him. "Did your headache come back?"

He grunted as he yanked the fridge open. "No, my headache didn't come back."

I looked around the kitchen as Ryan twisted open a Gatorade and chugged half of it down. Everything was exactly as it had been this morning. The dishwasher still stood open and empty, ready for dirty dishes, but there didn't seem to be any. "Have you eaten today?"

"I'm fine," he muttered, not meeting my eye.

"Yes, I can see that. Clearly you're doing great."

He slanted a resentful look at me. "I don't need a fucking babysitter anymore."

"How about a friend?"

"Is that what you are?" He flung the words at me with a harshness meant to wound.

It set me back on my heels. I had to fight to keep my voice steady. "Yes. Of course I'm your friend, Ryan."

"Only temporarily. You'll be gone soon, remember?"

I had no idea where all this bitterness had come from. Was he so good at concealing it that it'd been there all along and I hadn't noticed? Or had something set it off? Was all this about the books I'd found under his bed or had something else happened? "Phones exist, in case you've forgotten. I'm not going to disappear off the face of the earth."

He made a caustic scoffing sound. "Sure you will."

"I wouldn't do that." Every inch of my body ached to reach out for him and try to close this horrible distance between us. But I was afraid he'd reject my touch, and I didn't think I could take it if he did.

"You should." The look he fixed on me was so empty and cold it chilled the blood in my veins. "Do me a favor, okay? When you go, don't look back. Just forget about me."

Having delivered this advice, he walked out of the kitchen.

I drew in a deep, unsteady breath, taking a moment to pull myself together before I trailed him into the living room. I found him hunched forward on the couch with his face propped in his hands.

"I could never do that," I said, trying to keep the hurt out of my voice. "Even if I wanted to."

Ryan didn't move. "It'll be better for you if you do."

"How could you think that? What is going on with you?" My throat burned as I sank down on the couch next to him. "Ryan, please talk to me."

His head twisted from side to side. "I can't."

"Yes, you can. What brought all this on? Is this about those books under your bed?"

Not a word.

"Why do you have so many books about dying? And why are you keeping them hidden?"

His only response was a flinch when I said the word *dying*.

"You're scaring the shit out of me right now." Anxiety clawed at my insides. I had to touch him, if only to reassure myself. Tentatively, I laid a hand on his back. At least he didn't shake it off. That was something. "Please don't shut me out like this, Ryan. Tell me what's going on."

"I didn't plan on you," he mumbled at the floor.

"What does that mean?"

He slouched back against the couch and stared up at the ceiling. "I had this whole plan worked out. There were rules in place to keep everyone safe."

"What rules? What do you mean safe?"

"I'd made my peace with it—or I thought I had. And then you came along and blew it all to hell. No more peace." He wasn't making any sense, but he seemed to need to get something off his chest, so I let him keep going without interrupting. "I fucked it all up," he muttered, talking to himself as much as me. "I let myself need you. And it hurts so fucking much because I can't have you. I wish I'd never met you."

"Ryan," I choked his name out, fumbling to clutch his hand as anguish burned through my chest. Just this morning I'd worried about hurting him when I eventually left, but imagining it and seeing him in pain firsthand couldn't compare.

Finally, his head swung my way. But the desolation in his eyes didn't offer any comfort. "I'm glad you're leaving. It'll keep you safe."

There was that word again. *Safe*. It sent a chill through me. "Safe from what?"

"From me. Because I'm cursed."

"What do you mean you're cursed?"

His jaw bunched as he looked away.

"Ryan?"

"My father died a few months ago."

That would have been shortly before I arrived in town. And Ryan had never said a word or given any hint he was grieving. I squeezed his hand. "I had no idea."

"I hadn't seen him in decades. He was a selfish son of a bitch and I hated him." Anger twisted his expression as he stared across the room.

"I'm so sorry he was like that. You deserved so much better."

"I didn't tell anyone when he died. They would have tried to comfort me by offering condolences and platitudes I didn't want to hear. I couldn't stand to have everyone telling me how sorry they were when I wasn't sorry he was dead." Ryan looked like a man cracked in half. Like he was bleeding out from an invisible wound. He swallowed thickly and let his gaze fall on our intertwined hands. "All I feel when I think about him is resentment. It's not fair that he outlived my mom. She was a good person and he was a piece of shit. Why did she have to die of cancer at forty but that asshole got to live all the way to seventy even though he had ALS?"

A queasy lurch tilted my insides. "Your father had ALS?"

Ryan's eyes were as dull as I'd ever seen them. When he spoke, his voice was matter-of-fact, as if he'd run out of emotions. "He had the kind that's hereditary. Autosomal dominant. Do you know what that means?"

"No." It'd been too long since I'd taken any biology courses. But I could already tell it was bad.

"It means there's a fifty percent chance I was born with the same gene mutation that caused my dad's ALS."

Shock iced my veins as I struggled to remember everything I knew about ALS. It was fatal. Incurable. It caused muscular atrophy and the gradual loss of basic functions like walking and talking and eventually breathing.

Ryan watched me, stone-faced, allowing time for me to grapple with his last statement before he continued. "Onset of symptoms usually occurs between the ages of forty and seventy-five, so it could happen to me any day now. The average life expectancy after diagnosis is two to five years."

My whole body felt numb. I searched for something to say, but nothing felt adequate. I was too shaken to speak. Too scared. Too grief-stricken.

Ryan's flat voice broke the oppressive silence. "That's what I didn't want you to know. And now that you do, I'd like you to leave."

He got up and walked out of the room, leaving me rooted to the couch, still in shock.

A second later, his bedroom door slammed shut with a finality that shattered my heart into pieces.

29

RYAN

I wasn't surprised when I heard Maggie open my bedroom door a few minutes later. Frustrated and disappointed, yes. But not surprised. I knew she'd keep pushing. It was too much to ask just to be left alone, goddammit.

"You're still here," I gritted out. I couldn't see her because I was lying on my side with my back to the door. But since I didn't want to see her, I didn't bother to move.

"Of course I'm still here."

"I was hoping you wouldn't be." I hated myself as I said it, knowing how hurtful the words were. But I couldn't stop myself, not with this panic stirring in my gut. I was barely holding it together and just wanted to be alone in a quiet, dark room. I needed her gone.

"Too bad," Maggie said, impervious to my poison barbs. "I'm not going anywhere."

I felt the walls closing in around me and lashed out as fear dug its claws deeper into my chest. "I don't want any of your fucking pity, okay? You don't need to stick around out of guilt."

Even my raised voice couldn't make Maggie back down. Instead, her temper flared to match mine. "I'm here because

I care about you, you jackass! I cared about you before I found out about this, and I still care about you now. So you'll just have to get over yourself, because you're not getting rid of me. The harder you try to push me away, the harder I'll resist. I thought you would have figured that out by now."

A thick silence fell after her outburst, broken only by the sound of her harsh, exasperated breaths. I squeezed my eyes shut when I heard her start to walk around to my side of the bed. Her footsteps stopped when she was standing right in front of me.

"Are we going to talk about it?" she asked in a softer voice.

"No." I wasn't going to open my eyes and look at her. I wouldn't do it.

But when she sat on the edge of the bed, my eyes snapped open of their own accord. She was so beautiful and brave and strong it tore me to shreds. I hated her seeing me so weak and broken. She'd want to fix me, but there was no fixing what was wrong with me. I'd only disappoint her.

I'm sorry. I'm so sorry. I can't be what you deserve.

She stroked her hand down my arm with a touch so tender it made my eyes burn. "I know you don't want to, but we need to talk about it. *You* need to. It's obviously been eating you up inside."

Still I said nothing, even though I knew she'd already won. There was no fighting her off. My defenses weren't tough enough.

"Ryan—"

"I've never told anyone else," I said, blinking back the tears threatening to spill.

Her hand stilled on my arm. "No one? Not even your family?"

"George knows, but only because he was keeping tabs on my

dad. He's the one who broke the news to me. I made him promise not to tell anyone."

"Why?"

I couldn't keep the bitter accusation out of my voice. "So they wouldn't look at me the way you're looking at me right now."

Her lips pursed. "Yes, it's the worst thing in the world to have people concerned about your well-being. How dare I."

"You don't understand what it's like."

"No, I don't. I couldn't possibly. So help me understand." Her fingers tightened on my arm, giving it a gentle shake. "Tell me what you're feeling so I know how to help you."

"There's no helping me, Maggie." Her face blurred before me, and I squeezed my eyes shut again. "Don't you understand? That's why you need to get away now, while you still can. Before it gets bad."

She lay down on the bed and wrapped her arms around me. "What if I don't want to get away from you? Did you ever consider that when you were making your noble plans for us?"

My throat thickened. "Dammit, Maggie."

"I know." She kissed the top of my head as her hands smoothed up and down my back. "I'm a real pain in the ass. Which is why you can keep lying there passively like a great big lump if you want, but I'm going to keep hugging you until you hug me back. I've got all night and infinite patience."

Against my will, the seed of a smile twitched my lips. "You know I can easily shake you off, right?

"Go ahead and try it if that's what you really want."

It wasn't. How could it be when the only place I'd felt happy in years was in her arms? With a defeated sigh, I curled myself around her, clinging to her waist.

"That's what I thought," she murmured as she gathered me to her chest.

We held on to each other for a long, quiet moment. Now that

my secret had been dragged into the open, everything felt heavier and more fragile between us. I didn't know how to walk through this new landscape the truth had created. I wanted to protect Maggie and keep her safe, but how could I do that when I was the one most likely to do her damage?

"How long have you known?" she asked eventually.

"Three years." It felt like yesterday. Time had been rushing by too quickly ever since George showed me that letter from my dad. I wished like hell he hadn't. I wished he'd shredded the damn thing instead, and I'd never found out.

"And all that time you've been carrying this around by yourself?"

I shrugged. Why should I burden anyone else with it? It was bad enough that I had to know. If everyone knew, they'd never let me forget, not even for a minute. Even if they didn't say anything, I'd see it in their eyes every time they looked at me, and it'd follow me around everywhere I went. At least this way I could push it to the back of my mind and try to pretend it wasn't there for a while.

"Is this why you quit dating?" Maggie asked, combing her fingers through my hair.

"I don't want to put anyone else through what might be coming."

She fell quiet again as she massaged the knots of tension in the back of my neck. "Isn't there some kind of test they can do that will tell you if you inherited the gene or not?"

The sour taste of acid rose in the back of my throat. "Yes."

"Have you had the test done?"

"No."

"Why not?

I slid my hand up the back of her blouse, seeking comfort from the warm touch of her skin against my palm. "I don't think

I could stand to find out for sure that I have it. I'd rather not know at all."

Maybe that made me a coward, but I'd tried to talk myself into taking that damn test a hundred times over the last three years. I just couldn't do it. I wasn't strong enough to live with the truth.

Maggie gave me a sympathetic squeeze. "But what if you don't have it? All this fear might be for nothing."

My stomach twisted at the hope I heard in her voice. She was clinging to it like a life preserver, telling herself the worst wouldn't come true. I'd gone through a phase like that myself at first. But it hadn't lasted. After a while the fear had burned away all of my hope.

"But what if I do?" I said. "I can't take the chance. Once I know, my life will feel like it's over."

"So you'd rather live with an unknown hanging over you?"

"We're all living with the unknown. At least I'm living."

"Are you?" she asked. "What kind of a life is it if you won't let yourself be loved because you're keeping this terrible secret from everyone who cares about you?"

"Ignorance is better than knowing for sure the worst is about to happen. Trust me." I didn't want to look death in the face with the certain knowledge it was coming for me sooner rather than later. One day I might have to, but if I could put that day off a little longer then I damn well would.

"Okay," she said. "I can't claim to know what it feels like. You're the only one who can make that choice."

"You're not going to tell me to take the test?" It was what I'd feared from the moment she found out. I'd been bracing myself for a fight over it, assuming she'd pressure me to get tested.

She pressed her face into the top of my head. "I don't have the right to make a decision like that for you."

I breathed out in relief and hugged her tighter. "I need you not to tell anyone about this, okay?" When she didn't say anything, I drew my head back to look her in the eye. "You can't tell anyone, Maggie. Promise me you won't."

She bit her lip, reluctant to agree. "Only on one condition."

"What?" I asked warily.

"You promise to talk to me about it."

I relaxed, burrowing back into her. "We already talked about it."

"That's not enough. This thing is too much for you to bear alone. You have to open up and let someone in. Even more importantly, you have to be willing to ask for help when it gets to be too hard. It's up to you who you want to talk to. It can be a therapist, it can be someone in your family, or it can be me. Take your pick."

I grunted. "Since you already know, I guess I pick you."

To tell the truth, it didn't feel as bad as I feared it would now that she knew. Confessing had left me emotionally wrung out and raw as a nerve, but also a little lighter. With Maggie lending me her strength, the weight I'd been carrying around my neck didn't feel quite as heavy. The fear that the world might be about to end still colored the edges of my mind, but the shadows weren't as dark anymore, and the future felt a little easier to face.

She cupped my face to draw my eyes to hers. "You have to promise you'll talk to me whenever you're having a hard time. No more stuffing your emotions down and suffering in silence. If you can keep that promise, I'll keep your secret. But the moment I sense any resistance, I'll go straight to Josie and tell her everything."

"That's blackmail," I grumbled. Of course she'd go to Josie, who'd probably organize a whole goddamn intervention followed by a "Sorry You Might Be Dying" party.

"Yes, it is." Maggie smiled as she gazed at me with eyes so

bright and loving I could lose myself in them. "Don't think I won't go through with it either."

"Oh, I know you will."

She pressed a kiss to my forehead. "It's okay to lean on other people sometimes. The world won't end if you admit that you need help."

I grunted at the rebuke in her tone. "That's awfully rich, coming from you."

"Who do you think taught me that, Freckles?

Well, damn. She had me there.

"Ryan?"

The hitch in her voice had me going still. "Yes?"

"I'm scared."

I swallowed hard and squeezed her as tight as I dared. "Me too."

Maggie curled herself around me and tucked my head under her chin. Our legs tangled as we wriggled to get closer, fitting our bodies together like puzzle pieces. She felt so good, so *soothing*, up against me. I couldn't even remember what I'd been running from anymore. Why had I been so scared? How could I have thought it would feel worse to tell her when what I actually felt was this stupendous tidal wave of relief?

I let out a long, shaky breath. "I guess maybe I'm a little bit fucked-up over this shit."

"I know, baby. It's okay." She stroked a gentle hand through my hair. "It feels better to admit it to someone, doesn't it?"

"Maybe a little." I clung to her like a night-light glowing in the dark, a bulwark between me and the emptiness I'd been feeling for so long. "I hate it when you're right."

"No you don't."

"No," I agreed, wishing I could freeze time in a bottle and stay inside this moment with her forever. "I don't."

Something that hadn't changed between us was the timer

counting down the days until Maggie left. When our time was up, I'd still have to let go of her, and she'd still have to let go of me.

As much as I wanted to hold on to her forever, it wouldn't be right to keep her here. Her life was out there waiting for her. No way in hell was I letting her give anything up for me.

30

MAGGIE

"Is there any meat besides turkey?" I leaned around Ryan for a better look at the extravagant buffet dinner laid out on the kitchen island of his childhood home.

"It's *Thanksgiving*," he said, staring at me like I'd asked if there was going to be a human sacrifice after dinner.

"I know that," I said as I added an extra scoop of macaroni and cheese to my plate, "but I don't like turkey."

Ryan had brought me as his plus-one to the King family Thanksgiving dinner at his stepfather's house. We'd been spending as much time with each other as possible the last few weeks, meshing our lives together more and more as we settled into a comfortable routine.

It had surprised me how quickly things had begun to feel normal again after Ryan had confided his terrible secret to me. Who would have thought something so devastating could become an accepted part of your reality in only a few weeks? The human brain was a miracle of resilience, the way it could adapt to a new definition of normal so thoroughly that it forgot what the before times had felt like.

It wasn't like the great big awful scary thing threatening

Ryan's future had gone away or gotten any less awful or scary in the last few weeks. I still thought about it a million times a day, like a splinter I couldn't stop poking. I'd simply gotten accustomed to living with the knowledge, as if it had always been there.

Sharing his secret had brought us closer together, to an extent that might be terrifying if I let myself think about it too much. I didn't want to question what we were doing or wonder what would happen when my contract ended in February. Not at the risk of spoiling what we had right now.

Ryan's return to shift work meant I spent one out of every three nights sleeping alone, which shouldn't have been a hardship but felt like one. We always spent the other two nights together, either at his place or mine, and apparently my brain had decided that falling asleep next to Ryan was part of the new normal as well. Sleeping without him just felt wrong.

Sometimes when he was on shift, I'd lie in bed trying to remember what my old life had been like. The one without Ryan in it, where I'd slept alone every night and moved from job to job and city to city without making friends or feeling connected to anything around me.

Had I actually *liked* living that way? It was hard to believe now. My brain had rewritten the code for normal, and my old normal felt as alien as a distant, inhospitable planet.

How was I supposed to go back to that now that I knew what I'd be missing? Primarily, I'd be missing Ryan. But also this town I'd grown unaccountably fond of, along with some of the people who lived here. Like Ryan's friends and family, who were beginning to feel like my friends too.

Every time I thought about leaving, I started to get a pain in my stomach. So I tried not to think about it. The future might be a big, uncertain question mark, but life in the here and now with Ryan was pretty much perfect.

"How can you not like turkey?" he asked as he mounded enough mashed potatoes on his plate to feed a small army. "Everyone likes turkey."

"Vegetarians don't." I reached up to run my fingers through his hair under the pretext of smoothing it down. I didn't think I'd ever been with a man I wanted to touch as much as I wanted to touch Ryan. Whenever we were out in public together, I had trouble keeping my hands off him.

A fond smile quirked his lips. "Okay, everyone but vegetarians likes turkey."

"I don't really like turkey either," Riley volunteered as she leaned across the island to grab a dinner roll. "It tastes like napkins."

"Thank you!" I gifted her with a smile before directing a smirk at Ryan. "See?"

"That kid doesn't like anything," Ryan said, giving Riley a wink. "All she eats is bread and pasta."

"Sounds like she's got great taste to me."

"I don't understand you." Ryan shook his head as he drowned his heaping plate with gravy. The man put away more calories in a day than anyone I'd ever known. But as he and his Highland Games friends were fond of saying, *it takes weight to move weight*. "What do you eat at Thanksgiving if you don't like turkey?"

"The other half dozen traditional Thanksgiving dishes? It's not like there's any shortage of non-turkey food on the table. But my sister-in-law always has a honey-baked ham in addition to a turkey."

He gave me a look of mock horror. "Ham on Thanksgiving? Sacrilege. Everyone knows ham is for Easter."

"My mom makes lomo de cerdo every Thanksgiving," Manny's wife, Adriana, said at my elbow. "With pozole, arroz, and ensalada de manzana."

Her mother owned a local Tex-Mex restaurant, and I'd eaten enough of her food to have no doubt that whatever her family ate at Thanksgiving was excellent. Certainly much better than the reheated catered food we were getting at George King's house, no matter how expensive it might be.

"It's a world gone mad," Ryan grumbled. "Ham and pork loin at Thanksgiving. Next you'll be telling me you don't like pumpkin pie."

I tilted my head. "Wellllll…"

He held a warning finger against my lips. "Don't you dare say it."

Fighting a smile, I kissed his finger before tugging it away from my mouth. "Pumpkin is an inferior pie."

"It's like I don't even know who you are right now." He shook his head in disbelief as he leaned in for a kiss.

The warm, earthy scent of his skin made my pulse jump as always. He looked especially handsome today dressed up for the holiday meal. I couldn't wait to get him back home later and peel them off him.

As if he could read my mind, Ryan's mouth curved in a smile that was one hundred percent pure sex. He reached up to touch a strand of my hair, which I'd worn loose because I knew how much he liked it. "You look beautiful," he said, his voice going husky. "I like that dress on you a lot."

"Hey, lovebirds, move it along!" Manny called from behind us. "You're holding up the line."

Tossing a smug look at Manny, Ryan pressed his hand to my back and guided me into the dining room. George King had… interesting taste. Every room seemed to feature a variety of dead animal parts, and the dining room was no exception. The chairs were upholstered with hairy cowhide while a dramatic antler chandelier that looked like a leftover prop from *Hannibal* dangled above a weathered wood table that impressively seated fourteen people.

I was relieved by the lack of place cards, which left me free to sit next to Ryan. Bottles of wine were passed up and down the table while the rest of the family filtered in with their plates. George and Heather were the last to enter the dining room, once everyone else had been seated—minus Riley, who had volunteered to babysit Manny's children during the meal.

The way the friendly chatter broke off at George's entrance, you'd think the headmaster had just walked in on a classroom of misbehaving students. A portentous silence replaced the formerly relaxed atmosphere as George and his wife, Heather, took their seats at opposite ends of the absurdly long table. I braced myself for some sort of solemn pre-dinner Thanksgiving tradition, but after offering a grace so perfunctory I blinked and nearly missed it, George gruffly instructed his assembled guests to "dig in."

As soon as the family patriarch picked up his fork, everyone else followed suit and directed their attention to eating. The mood remained subdued, however, as if George's presence had sucked all the fun out of the room.

"I do believe this is the biggest table we've ever set at Thanksgiving," Heather observed, attempting to jump-start the conversation. She was a fit, attractive bleached blonde who was notably younger than her husband, as one would expect of a wealthy CEO's third wife. "It's the first time all you older kids have been paired off at a holiday. How about that?"

"*Most* of them, anyway," George said as he aimed a withering look at Nate, the only one of his offspring besides the two youngest who'd shown up without a plus-one today. "As usual, Nate's lagging behind the pack."

Nate's shoulders stiffened and he pressed his lips together, enduring his father's censure in silence.

I'd seen the two of them interact at work enough to pick up on the strain in their relationship. But outside the professional environs of the office, the lack of warmth in George's manner to his children was far more conspicuous. He spoke to them across the family dinner table in the same brusque manner he used on his underlings at work.

Heather soldiered on as uncomfortable looks were exchanged around the table. "It's just so nice to see everyone all coupled up. And it's about time too. We haven't had a wedding in the family since Manny's, and that was ages ago."

"I was starting to think none of the rest of you would ever get married," George said as he sawed at a slab of turkey on his plate. "I don't know why you all seem to find it so difficult. It's absurd that I have so many grown children and so few grandchildren."

An uneasy silence followed this remark. Until Wyatt broke into a mischievous grin. "Bet you didn't think Tanner would be the one to take the plunge next, did you, Dad?"

George flicked only the barest of glances in Wyatt's direction before focusing his cheerless gaze on Josie. "Actually, I had Tanner pegged as the second most likely after Josephine. I'd hoped she and Carter would have moved things along by now, but they seem determined to prove me wrong."

Carter busied himself downing a mouthful of wine while Josie smiled tightly at her father. "I told you not to hold your breath on that, Dad."

I shifted uncomfortably in my seat and glanced over at Ryan, but he had his attention firmly glued to his plate. As did most of the other people around the table.

"You're not getting any younger, you know," George said as he stabbed a piece of turkey with his fork. "At your age you don't have that many years left to start a family. You can't afford to keep dragging your feet."

Josie's expression iced over. "Thanks, Dad. That's real touching. Your concern for my decaying reproductive potential is duly noted."

She'd never been shy about challenging her father at work either, while I'd found Nate much more inclined to toe the line. But George also seemed to take Josie's back talk in stride, as if he approved of her backbone. Whereas I'd seen him take Nate's head off more than once for daring to offer a mildly contradictory opinion.

An awkward silence descended, broken only by the clanking of silver flatware on china. Heather once more took it upon herself to end it. "Tanner, I hope you and Lucy don't plan to make us wait too long for those grandbabies," she said, bestowing a smile on the newly engaged couple. "Bella and Jorge could sure use some cousins."

"They've actually got eight cousins on Adriana's side already," Manny said as he slathered butter on his roll. "They're fine."

"I'm with Heather on this," Wyatt said. "Why wait for the wedding? I think Tanner and Lucy should start popping out kids as soon as possible." He leaned around Andie to grin at Tanner, who answered him with a scowl.

Wyatt appeared to be the only one at the table having a good time. I got the sense he was the agent of chaos in the family who enjoyed stirring up the simmering undercurrents of tension around him. I suspected it was a defense mechanism he'd developed to deflect attention from his own insecurities. If this was what family dinners had been like growing up, I could understand why.

Andie flicked Wyatt on the ear. "Stop being an ass."

"Yeah," Lucy said and flicked his other ear.

Wyatt pouted, rubbing his ears, and Andie stuck her tongue out at him.

Adriana attempted to steer the conversation into safer waters. "Isabella's so excited to be a flower girl, she won't stop talking about it. I keep telling her the wedding isn't for a year, but kids her age have no conception of time."

"I can't wait to see what kind of mischief that little imp gets into during the ceremony," Ryan said with a smile. "It's going to be a hoot."

"What I'm wondering is who'll be the next to get engaged after us?" Tanner leaned around Andie to shoot a pointed look at Wyatt.

The chaos agent shrugged innocently. "I don't know. I guess we'll have to see."

"I'm starting a pool," Cody said. "Pick the couple and the month they announce their engagement. Ten dollars a pop to get in on the action."

"Who's the favorite?" Manny asked, looking interested, and I saw Adriana nudge him under the table.

Cody thought about it. "Josie and Carter have been together the longest."

Carter took another drink while Josie pretended to ignore the conversation by dissecting a slice of turkey with the focus of a brain surgeon.

"I think Wyatt could be a dark horse and surprise us all," Manny said.

Andie snorted, and Wyatt gave her a sidelong look before turning to Ryan and lobbing his next chaos bomb in our direction. "What about Big Red over there? The way he and his new girlfriend have been making eyes at each other, I wouldn't count him out of the race."

Ryan stiffened beside me but covered it by wiping his mouth with his napkin. "You should probably keep me out of it," he said mildly. "Unless you like losing your money."

One of Wyatt's eyebrows ticked up like he'd been hoping for

more of a reaction. I reminded myself there was no way he could have known what a painful subject he'd just rubbed in Ryan's face. If he had, he never would have done it. But that didn't stop me from cutting him a glare baleful enough to wipe the smile off his face.

"I'm in for ten bucks on Josie," Nate announced, slicing a smirk at his sister, who shot a murderous look back at him.

While the debate raged on and the King siblings continued to poke each other's exposed nerves in the way only siblings could, I reached under the table and laid my hand on Ryan's thigh.

He gave me a tight smile as he curled his fingers around mine. My whole body warmed at his touch, and I smiled back, wishing I could drag him away from here and lavish him with affection. His expression softened, and he released my hand to drape his arm on my chair, stroking his fingers over the nape of my neck.

"Maggie," George said, commanding my attention.

I kept my smile in place as I looked toward the head of the table. "Yes, George?"

"Any chance of moving up your presentation next month? I'd rather not wait until the twentieth."

The presentation he was asking about was the road map for improving the company's efficiency and financial health that I'd been hired to deliver. I was scheduled to present my recommendations to him next month for his approval. If it passed muster, I'd spend the final two months of my engagement here helping to set things in motion and assisting the executive team with implementation.

"Come on, Dad," Josie interjected. "Don't make Maggie talk about work on Thanksgiving."

"I don't mind," I said, still smiling pleasantly. "I'm a consultant, so if you want me to talk about work on a holiday, I'm happy to bill you my hourly rate." Being in business for myself meant I wasn't beholden to George in the same way as his other employees. If he wanted to exercise his authority over me, he'd have to pay for the privilege.

George's lips puckered and pulled to one side. "It can probably wait until tomorrow."

"I'll look at my calendar and get back to you first thing," I promised. "I'm sure we can work something out."

If George wanted his presentation early, I wasn't inclined to disappoint him, even if it left me racing against the clock. Keeping the CEO satisfied was what I got paid the big consulting bucks for.

Unfortunately, his mention of my upcoming presentation only reminded me of the limit on my time here in Crowder. I was more than halfway through my six-month contract. The way time had been flying by, it would be over before I knew it.

I should be actively looking for my next engagement, so I'd have something lined up when this one ended. There were some leads I'd intended to investigate further and people I'd been meaning to reach out to, but I'd been putting it off. I couldn't seem to make myself take substantive steps toward moving on.

Just the other day, I'd gotten an email from a former client asking if I was available to come back for another engagement. Instead of requesting a meeting to talk about it, I'd put him off with a vague answer about my schedule being in limbo and a promise to touch base after the new year.

My schedule wasn't in limbo. After February, my calendar was wide-open. If I didn't do something soon, I'd be out of work.

No matter how many times I reminded myself of that fact, I didn't feel any more motivated to commit myself to another job that would take me away from here.

Ryan's fingers squeezed the back of my neck. "You okay?" he asked quietly, sensing my shift in mood.

Gazing into his eyes made it easy to find my smile again as I nodded. "Just fine."

When dinner was finally over and the table had been cleared, Ryan dragged me outside to the patio, away from everyone else. "Sorry about dinner," he said, pulling me into a hug.

I burrowed into his solid warmth to escape the chill of the late November evening. The outside air smelled like woodsmoke. The weather had finally gotten cold enough to justify the lighting of fireplaces, although the temperature had yet to get anywhere near freezing. Maybe by Christmas. "Are they always like that?"

Ryan's hands rubbed my arms to chase away the goose bumps I shouldn't be having when it was only fifty degrees. Three months in Texas and I was already getting soft. "More or less. They tend to bring out the worst in each other. Or maybe it's just stress that does that."

"By stress you mean George, I assume. He's not exactly warm and cuddly, is he?"

"I would have warned you, but I thought you'd have figured it out already from working with him."

"It's one thing for him to pit his children against each other in a business environment. It's something else to see him disparage their personal choices over the family dinner table in front of guests."

Ryan sighed against my temple. "He's not an easy man to be around."

I pulled back enough to lift my face to his. "You don't seem to have any problem with it."

His mouth twisted as he played with the ends of my hair. "As you may have noticed, he goes easier on those of us who aren't related to him by blood. It's only his own kids he rakes over the coals. I think he actually believes he's being a good father. I get the sense that's the way his own father was with him."

"That's sad."

"It is sad." Ryan's eyes focused on mine and his brows drew together. "What was that presentation he was asking you about?"

"*The* presentation. The big one he hired me for."

"Oh." His eyes widened in understanding. "The one you have to make the hard decisions for."

"The very one." I had less than a month to come up with a creative solution to King's Creamery's problems—either that or decide how many layoffs it would take to keep the company solvent.

"I know you can't talk about it..."

"I really can't."

Ryan nodded, accepting that, and brushed his lips against my cheek. His hands tightened on my waist as he dipped his head to kiss the underside of my jaw. The touch of his tongue had me flushing hot despite the cold air. My eyelids fluttered as I sank my hands into his hair, not caring that I was mussing it up.

Leaving a soft bite on my throat, he kissed his way up to my ear, the puff of his breath making my knees feel weak. "I'll have to see if I can help take away some of that stress later."

"What do you have in mind?" I whispered, shivering with anticipation.

He pulled back, his lust-filled eyes moving over my face. "It's more fun when I surprise you, don't you think?"

Yes. God, yes. "How soon can we leave?"

Chuckling softly, he rested his forehead against mine. "Another hour, maybe. Think you can wait that long?"

"I don't know." My fingers curled around his enormous biceps. "I might not make it."

"I'm afraid you'll have to." His lips found mine in a swift, greedy, drugging kiss that was over way too soon. Before it could get too good, he pulled away with a pained groan and cupped my cheek. "But once I get you home…" The rough edge of his thumb dragged across my bottom lip. "You're *mine*."

Yes, I was.

More than I was ready to admit to him or myself.

31

MAGGIE

I didn't get nervous often, but a trickle of cold sweat worked its way down my back as I stood at one end of the conference room facing George King and Terry Goodrich. Neither of them had said a single word as I went through my big presentation, carefully explaining my plan to increase the company's profitability.

Terry had chuckled at several points, however, which didn't strike me as a good omen.

It was a bold plan. Some might call it drastic.

Or completely crazy, even.

But I had the data and case studies to back up every one of my recommendations. I'd spent the last three weeks putting everything I had into this plan, and I knew it would work, even if it seemed a little out there.

But would George King go for it? That was the big question.

Hell if I could tell. The man had the poker face of a cement wall. He was giving me nothing.

As for Terry, other than his worrying chuckles, he'd stayed silent, wisely waiting for the man in charge to weigh in.

Finally, after what felt like an eon, George leaned back in his chair and scratched his jaw. "So let me get this straight. You're proposing to save us money by *raising* employee salaries?"

I nodded, projecting confidence. "The data show your last three company-wide pay raises have resulted in a corresponding increase in profits, but you haven't significantly increased wages since 2007. Therefore I'm proposing a company-wide minimum wage of fifty thousand dollars to be phased in over the next three years."

George frowned. "Without major layoffs?"

"I've recommended a five-percent reduction of head count primarily aimed at reducing redundancy in the upper and middle management ranks where I've found the most inefficiency."

"And you want to put a cap on executive salaries?" George said as if he couldn't quite believe he'd heard me right. "Including *mine*?"

Terry let out another one of his chuckles, which I steadfastly ignored. "You make almost three hundred times the salary of the typical full-time worker in your company. Over the last fifteen years, your pay has increased four hundred percent while during the same period employee wages have remained essentially stagnant. The rest of your C-suite averages twenty times as much as a typical worker. A company-wide cap limiting salaries to no more than seven times the lowest paid employee would still allow you and your senior leadership team to earn a comfortable $350,000 a year in addition to your generous bonus packages."

It was Nate who'd given me the idea when he'd offered to give up his salary to save jobs in his department. I'd started running the numbers and realized how much of a difference it could make if all the high-paid executives offered a similar sacrifice. I'd refrained from crediting Nate for the suggestion, however, in case George didn't like being asked to give up millions of dollars of his annual personal income. It wouldn't be doing Nate a kindness to throw him under the bus with me. If George approved my plan, *then* I'd give Nate the credit he was due.

"Ballsy," George said.

Terry chuckled again. "Told you."

I'd liked Terry before today, but right now I was seriously considering throwing my favorite Jimmy Choos at him.

Taking a silent, steadying breath, I forged onward. "As I demonstrated in my slides, the thing that's costing you the most money right now is worker turnover. That loss of employee knowledge and wasted investment in training is seriously impacting your bottom line. Your own market research shows the demand for your products is there, but you don't have the workforce to produce and deliver it. Raising wages will significantly improve employee retention *and* productivity, resulting in increased production at higher profit margins without having to add more head count. By investing in your employees instead of your executives, you'll stop leaking money and start making it again at rates you haven't seen since you began implementing cost-cutting measures during the Great Recession."

"Huh," George said.

I didn't know what to make of that *huh*. Was he impressed? Angry? Considering it? About to fly into a rage and fire me? I didn't have the slightest clue, and I considered myself good at reading people.

There was a chance I might be done here. As in "escorted out of the building by security" done. If I'd pissed him off enough, I didn't doubt George King would do it. They'd still have to pay out my contract, but I wouldn't have a job or a reason to stay in Crowder anymore.

At the thought, another bead of sweat trickled down between my shoulder blades and soaked into my bra band.

"That's not even taking into consideration the positive publicity a move like this will generate," I added. "You'll be hailed as a modern-day Robin Hood helping the working class by stealing from himself, which lines up perfectly with the company's progressive branding. You can expect sales to increase from the boost in brand visibility, and you won't have trouble hiring anymore because people will be clamoring to work here."

"I've heard enough," George said. My stomach clenched when he flicked his hand in a dismissive gesture. But then he looked at Terry and jerked his head toward the door. "You can go now."

Terry pushed himself to his feet with a grunt and clapped George's shoulder on his way out. "Good luck."

The conference room closed behind Terry with an ominous *thunk*, leaving me alone with George and no idea what he was thinking.

"Siddown," he said, nodding at a nearby chair. "You're too goddamn tall. Hurts my neck."

I lowered myself into the chair he'd indicated and folded my hands in my lap.

He leaned forward and rested his forearms on the table, considering me in silence for a long moment. "That salary cap idea of yours is going to go over like a bag of steaming hot dogshit with my top executives."

"You're right," I agreed, not trying to sugarcoat it. "They're going to be unhappy. But out of more than two thousand full-time employees, only thirty-five will be impacted by the salary cap. That's a lot fewer unhappy employees than you've got right now."

His mouth twisted. "Yeah, but they're the ones with the most access to me, which means I'll have to listen to their bitching."

I elected not to respond to his point. If his personal discomfort was going to be a deciding factor, my whole plan was dead in the water. I'd gambled on the fact that George King was tough enough to deal with a little inconvenience for the sake of his company's long-term health, and mean enough not to give a fuck about anyone's bitching.

"Let me ask you something," he said. "How are we supposed to attract and retain top talent in the executive ranks if we can't compete with the kind of salaries they could command at other companies?"

"One advantage of being a family-run private company is access to a pool of promising executive talent who are motivated by more than a paycheck."

The corner of his mouth twitched. "I've got a lot of relatives, but not enough to fill my entire C-suite."

"No," I said. "That's where the judicious use of bonus plans and other non-salary compensation can make your offers more competitive. But I wouldn't overestimate the price tag of competence. Executives who make seven figures are rarely that much better at their jobs than executives who make six figures. And the opportunity to join a thriving, well-run company can be its own incentive."

George leaned back in his chair again. "I hope you're right, because I'm about to test that theory."

The slow smile that spread across his face reminded me unsettlingly of Wyatt. I had a feeling I was about to have a chaos bomb lobbed in my direction.

32

MAGGIE

Ryan was in my kitchen when I got home that night. Cooking dinner, by the look and smell of it. He turned away from the pot he was stirring on the stove and gave me a smile that made my chest feel like it was bursting with sunbeams. "Hey, sweetness."

I dropped my bag on the table and walked into his waiting arms, letting them catch me in a tight hold. There was nothing in the world like hugging this man. Being surrounded by him made me feel safe and accepted in a way I hadn't experienced… maybe ever before in my life. Coming home had never felt so good before.

Home. That was what this sense of peace and rightness was. That was what Ryan had come to mean to me. This temporary rental house in this town I never expected to hold so dear felt more like home than the Long Island City condo I'd owned for ten years. And it was because Ryan was here waiting for me.

"Everything okay?" he asked, rubbing his hands in comforting circles on my back.

"Yes," I said as I nestled deeper into his chest. "What smells so good? Besides you, I mean."

His laugh rumbled through me. "I'm making chili and cornbread for dinner."

"Sounds heavenly." *This is what I want. It's where I belong.* I was more certain of that than ever.

"Well? Don't keep me in suspense." He tipped my chin up to search my face. "How'd the presentation go?"

"Good," I said, feeling a flutter of trepidation at the conversation we were about to have. As far as I was concerned, it was excellent news, but I wasn't certain how Ryan was going to react. "George approved every one of my recommendations. He wants to start moving forward with everything right away."

"Hell yeah!" Ryan lifted me off the ground in a rib-crushing squeeze, grinning as he covered my face in kisses. "Congrats, babe. I knew you'd knock it out of the park."

"I wasn't nearly as confident as you," I said when he set me down and I could use my lungs again. "I went pretty far out on a limb with some of my proposals, and I wasn't sure how George would react. It could have backfired on me big time."

"But it didn't. Because you're a hardcore badass and George knows it. That's why he brought you in."

"There was a moment today when I was convinced he was about to fire me."

Ryan's hand squeezed the back of my neck as he brushed his lips against mine. "I'm really glad he didn't."

I hope you mean that.

"So when do I get to find out what your daring plan to save the company is?" he asked, smiling down at me. "I know it's got to stay all hush-hush until they're ready to announce their next moves, but how long do I have to wait?"

"Oh, well…" I glanced at the pot on the stove. "Do you need to do anything more with the food?"

"Not until the cornbread comes out in fifteen minutes. The chili's just simmering until we're ready to eat."

"Good. Come sit down for a minute." I towed him into the living room and over to the couch.

Ryan frowned as he sank down next to me. "What's up? Is there bad news?"

"No, it's not bad news, just...unexpected. But it's good. At least I think it is."

His brows went up. "Well don't make me guess."

I looked up into his face, hoping he'd be as happy about this as I was. "George offered to extend my contract. I'm staying here."

Ryan went still. "For how long?"

"Another six months."

"Wow," he said. "That's...great."

"Is it? You sure about that?" The hesitation in his voice wasn't filling me with confidence.

"Of course it is." His hand cupped my cheek as he kissed me. "More time with you is a good thing."

"I'm glad you think so because..." I gathered a deep breath. "He wants me to take a permanent position with the company after that."

Ryan reeled back like I'd sucker punched him. "What position?"

"I'm not allowed to say yet."

"You're not taking it though." The muscles in his jaw were rock-hard.

I opened my mouth, then closed it again, compressing my lips together. I'd suspected he might react...badly. But it still hurt to hear it. It felt like a rejection of *me*, even though I knew it wasn't about that. This was all about Ryan and his compulsive need to protect everyone, even at his own expense. He thought he was doing this for me.

His eyes went wide at my silence. "Jesus Christ, you're not actually considering it, are you? You don't want to stay here."

"I do, actually. I've been thinking about it a lot, and staying here is exactly what I want to do."

"What about your consulting business? You can't give that up."

"For this job I could. It's less money, but it has other advantages that make up for that. More stability and security, for starters. I wouldn't have to travel all the time and jump from one company to the next. Sticking around for once to build something meaningful and permanent sounds pretty appealing to me right now." I wasn't just talking about the job, and I could tell from the panicked look in Ryan's eyes that he knew it.

He shot off the couch and paced across the room, dragging an agitated hand through his hair. "Maggie. *Fuck*. You can't do this." The despair in his voice cut across my heart. "You can't stay here for me."

"I'm not staying for you. I'm staying for me. Because I've realized it's what I want." I offered a wry smile, trying for lightness. "Turns out I actually like this stupid town despite the godawful heat in the summer."

He didn't find my change of heart as amusing as I did. "I won't let you do this."

My eyebrows lifted. If he wanted to make this a battle of wills, he was about to find out how stubborn I could be when I make up my mind. "The thing is, you don't actually get a say in this. It's my life and my career. If I want to stay, I'll stay."

"I don't want you here, dammit!"

The force of his anger prickled over my skin, but I knew him too well to be intimidated, even if it stung. I stood and calmly walked toward him. "I don't believe you. You're just afraid to let yourself be happy."

"If you stay, I won't have anything to do with you." His voice was cold like his eyes. "I mean it. You'll be on your own. I won't let you see me."

Foolish man. Did he really think a softy like him could out-ice the ice queen? He didn't stand a chance.

"You can try to stop me." I folded my arms across my chest. "Good luck with that."

"Don't do this." He was pleading now, his words tinged with desperation. "I'll never forgive myself if you stay with me."

"That's too bad because I'll never forgive myself if I leave you. Either way, one of us is going to feel guilty. At least my way we get to be together, whereas your way we're both alone and miserable."

"Maggie, please."

"It's too late to talk me out of it. I already accepted the role."

"You can tell them you changed your mind."

"I'm not going to change my mind, Ryan. I'm staying." I drew a breath and said the words I'd been holding inside for weeks. "Because I love you."

He flinched and closed his eyes. "Don't say that."

"Too late. I already said it."

Red rimmed his eyes when they opened again. "You don't mean that," he said, still pleading.

"You know I do."

When I moved closer, he edged backward until he met the wall. "I won't let you love me."

"You can't stop me." I slipped my hands around the back of his neck, stroking the soft, warm skin below his hair. "Even if you cut me out of your life and refuse to see me, it won't matter. I'll still love you." Tipping my head up, I pressed my lips to his cheek as his body trembled against mine. "No matter what you do. No matter what happens. In sickness and in health..." He drew in a sharp breath, and I cradled his jaw as I kissed his other cheek. "I'll keep on loving you with every breath in my body, whether you want me to or not."

With a choked sound, he dropped his head to my shoulder and slid his arms around me.

"I love you," I said, holding him close as I smoothed my hands over his back. "You're mine now. I'm not letting you go."

"Maggie." He swallowed heavily and clutched me harder. "I'm scared."

"I know," I whispered, holding him as tight as I could. "I'm scared too. But it's going to be okay because we've got each other now." Whatever lay ahead, our lives would be better together than apart. I believed that with every cell in my body.

A great, shuddering sigh racked Ryan's frame. He lifted his head, and his tear-filled eyes found mine. "I didn't mean it when I said I didn't want you here. I'm sorry I said that."

"I know, Freckles." Smiling, I leaned up to kiss a tear from his cheek. "I didn't believe you for a second."

He turned his head to find my lips, kissing me like he needed to ground himself, like he was suffocating and I was air. "I love you."

My breath caught as the words wrapped themselves around my heart and squeezed. Deep down in my gut I'd believed that he loved me, but I hadn't thought I'd hear him say it. Not yet. Not when he'd been so damned determined to push me out of his life.

Ryan's fingers slid into my hair as he pressed frantic kisses to my jaw, my eyes, my forehead. "I tried so hard not to, but I couldn't help loving you. The first time I looked into your eyes, it knocked me off my feet and I've been falling ever since."

I exhaled a sob as happiness bubbled through my veins. His lips touched mine in a soft, soothing caress that flooded my eyes with tears despite my best efforts to blink them back. I wasn't a crier, dammit. This man had ruined me, exactly like I'd known he would. He'd shined his light on me and burned a hole through the dam holding back my emotions. He'd made me laugh. Made me happy. Made me weak and vulnerable. Doted on me. Protected me. Claimed me. *Loved* me.

Shining eyes the warmest color of gray I'd ever seen searched my face. The uncertainty and fear in them made my throat close.

I reached up to touch his brow, trailing my fingertips over the furrows to smooth them out. "Ryan..."

He kissed me, hard and searing, as if he was branding me. His tongue pushed past my lips to stroke deep inside my mouth as he yanked me against him. I pressed back, my hands grasping at him as our mouths moved together in a feverish slide.

"Fuck," he rasped, spinning us around. His hand cushioned my head as my back hit the wall with a bone-jarring thump. "I need you, Maggie." A hard thigh pressed between my legs as his weight pinned me. "Need you so bad."

"I'm yours," I gasped into his mouth, rubbing against him to ease the ache between my legs. "Take me."

He shoved my skirt up and grabbed my underwear in a fist. The thin lace stretched, then ripped, and he cast it away. With fumbling hands, he shoved his sweatpants and boxer briefs down before he attacked my mouth again with a growl, kissing me like he had no choice, like he couldn't help himself.

Our bodies locked together, his cock pulsing between us as we devoured each other with lips, teeth, and tongues. Rough hands gripped my thighs, lifting me off the floor and positioning my legs around him.

The thick head of his cock notched against me, and I let out an impatient whimper as my insides tightened, aching for relief. Ryan thrust his hips, shoving himself all the way in. My head lolled back with a gasping moan as that delicious girth stretched me wide and filled me all the way up, joining us together.

He pressed his face into my hair, his muscles quivering as he slowly slid halfway out before driving deep again with a grunt. Again and again he slammed into me, each thrust jolting through me with a shower of pleasure. I clung to him, my breathless cries begging him to take me harder. He gave me what I wanted, my desperation feeding his.

Every merciless snap of his hips built toward a crescendo so intense it became unbearable. Finally, the pressure inside me hit the breaking point, and a tidal wave of relief surged through me, shaking me apart and turning my muscles to jelly.

Ryan's grip on me tightened, his movements growing strained and jerky as my orgasm pulsed around his cock. I held him as he came with a deep shudder that reverberated through both of us. He hugged me close and buried his face in my neck, his shallow, heaving breaths hot on my skin as I pushed a hand through his damp hair.

"I need you," he whispered, lifting his head to nuzzle my cheek. "So much."

"I'm yours," I whispered back, kissing him as we held each other up. "I'm not leaving you."

———

LATER, after Ryan had saved the burning cornbread from the oven and turned off the chili, we lay on his bed facing each other with our legs tangled together.

I trailed a finger over the hourglass tattoo on his biceps and across the meaty curve of his shoulder, appreciating the sumptuous geometry of his body. "Just so you know," I said, "I didn't mean to fall in love with you either. But I was a total goner the first time I saw you with your shirt off."

A smile curved his lips, bringing out his beautiful dimples. "I get that a lot."

"I'll bet you do," I said and tweaked his nipple.

Growling in protest, he hooked a hand around my head and pulled me toward him. His teeth sank into my bottom lip before he soothed it with a tender, lingering kiss.

"I've never been in love before," he said as he laid his head back down on the pillow.

I smiled, reveling in the sound of the word *love* coming from his lips. "How does it feel so far?"

"Scary as fuck. But also like the best thing that's ever happened to me."

"Worth it?"

A tiny line appeared between his brows. "Only time will tell."

My smile faded as a heaviness settled in my chest. "Are you glad I'm staying?" I asked, needing reassurance. "Be honest."

He threaded his fingers with mine, his expression regretful. "I know you want me to be, but I can't honestly say I am. I'm sorry, sweetness. I want better for you."

I nodded, knowing I should have expected as much. Ryan was almost as stubborn as me. He wasn't going to let go of all his self-sacrificing tendencies at once.

"Hey." He pushed a stray lock of hair off my cheek with gentle fingers. "I'm really fucking happy you're not leaving though."

The love in his eyes pulled a smile back to my face. "I guess I'll take it."

He reached for me, flipping me onto my side as he arranged my back against his chest. I closed my eyes with a contented sigh at the feel of his solid warmth curled around me.

"I want to know more about this permanent position George offered you."

Tension stole back into my shoulders. "Are you going to try to talk me out of it?"

"No, I'm done with that." He nuzzled a kiss against the back of my neck. "Promise."

"Good." I stroked my fingers over the arm he'd wrapped around my waist. "If I tell you, you have to promise not to tell anyone. I mean *no one*—not even Manny. It has to stay a secret until they make the announcement."

"My lips are sealed."

"Chief operating officer."

Ryan propped his head on his arm so he could look at me. "George offered to make you COO?"

I nodded. "Nobody knows this yet, but Terry Goodrich is retiring next year."

"Huh." Ryan rolled onto his back and stared up at the ceiling.

"What?" I sat all the way up, pulling my legs underneath me. "What's wrong?"

His head swiveled toward me with a frown. "Do you have the offer in writing?"

"Yes."

"And it seems legit? You're sure he's not blowing smoke up your ass?"

"Yes. There's a substantial penalty if he reneges. You think he'll renege?"

His jaw bunched as he looked back up at the ceiling. "I don't know. Maybe."

"Hey, look at me." I laid my hand on Ryan's stomach, and his eyes locked on mine. "Even if this job falls through, I'm still not leaving. I've got plenty of savings, and I can afford to be picky about the kind of consulting work I take. I don't have to travel all the time. I can do more remote work so I only travel occasionally. Okay?" I curled my fingers in his shirt. "I'm not going anywhere."

He reached for my hand and brought it to his lips before

tugging me down onto him. I fitted myself against his side, and he pressed a kiss to my head when I rested it on his chest.

"I gotta be honest," he said as his fingers stroked down my arm. "Everything else aside, I don't love the idea of you working for George on a permanent basis. It's one thing for you to be there as a consultant, but once he's got you under his power, he'll manipulate you like he does everyone else who works for him."

"He can try."

"You can't trust him, Maggie."

"It's business. I never trust anyone."

Ryan's answering hum vibrated through his chest under my cheek. "If he offered you COO over his own kids, it's because he thinks he can use you for leverage somehow."

I propped my head up on my hand. "You think one of them should be COO instead of me, don't you?"

I'd been worrying about it ever since George offered me the job. I didn't have any clue how Josie and Manny were going to feel about this, but Nate was definitely going to be upset. They might all decide I was their enemy, and I hated the thought of it.

Ryan shook his head and touched my cheek. "That's not for me to say. I don't know enough about it."

I covered his hand with mine and kissed his palm. "But you're afraid George is going to use me to hurt them somehow?"

"Could be." His thumb stroked over the crest of my cheek. "Or it could be something else entirely. All I know is he's going to use you for something, and he won't give a damn how you or anyone else feels about it."

I laid my head back down and laced our fingers together on his chest as I tried to guess what George's plan was. "I know everyone's been waiting for him to name his successor and step back as CEO."

"They've been waiting for years. Don't expect him to give

that power trip up anytime soon. He's having way too much fun making everybody fight over his scraps while he leads them all around by the nose. And now he's tossing you into the mix as his ringer." Ryan's fingers tightened on mine. "I don't like it."

"He'll have to make a decision eventually though. He knows it's in the company's best interest to ensure a smooth transition of leadership." I lifted my head again, meeting Ryan's troubled gaze. "Whoever he picks to take over from him, it's definitely not going to be me though."

"Did he tell you that?"

"No, I'm telling *you* that. I have no interest in ever being CEO. I'm not going to get in Manny or Nate or Josie's way, if that's what you're worried about."

Ryan nodded, only partially appeased. "He'll make them think you are. You can count on that."

"Don't underestimate them. They're smart enough to draw their own conclusions. I'm not going to let him use me as a weapon against them. I promise you that. I won't knowingly do anything to hurt them."

"It's not the knowingly part I'm worried about. It's all the moving pieces you don't know about that are liable to bite you in the ass."

"George King is a savvy businessman, but I happen to be pretty savvy myself."

"I know you are. But I'm going to worry about you anyway. George can be a mean old son of a bitch sometimes." Ryan cupped my cheek, smiling faintly as he dragged his thumb along my lower lip. "And you can act as tough as you like, but you're really just a softhearted marshmallow on the inside."

My lips curved as I leaned in to press them to his. "I'm *your* softhearted marshmallow."

"Damn straight, you are." His hand hooked my head when I started to pull back, dragging me in for a longer, deeper kiss.

"I love you," I said, skimming my nose along his jaw.

"I love you too." His arms tightened around me, wrapping me up in a tight hold. "That's why I don't want to drag you down with me."

I raised my head, letting him see my exasperation. "You're not dragging me anywhere. I *chose* you, and then I pretty much bullied you into keeping me around."

A soft laugh huffed out of him. "You definitely don't like to take no for an answer."

"I wish I could make you understand how much better my life is with you in it."

"For now, maybe." Ryan's lips compressed as his eyes flicked away to stare off into the metaphorical distance. "I don't want to put you through what's coming."

My hand cradled his jaw and drew his eyes back to me, refusing to let him hide his pain away. "We don't know for sure anything's coming."

"But if it is..."

"Then we'll face it together. As a team. Whatever life throws at us, the good and the bad. Okay?"

He exhaled a deep breath and pressed his lips against my forehead. "Yeah. Okay."

I rolled onto my back and pulled him on top of me. He came willingly, propping himself on his elbows as he settled between my thighs with an appreciative hum.

A warm wave of love swelled inside me as I gazed up into Ryan's beautiful, solemn face. I skimmed my fingertips over the freshly healed scar at his hairline before pushing them into his soft hair. "I was just wandering until I found you. I didn't even know how empty my life was until you showed me what happiness felt like."

A soft smile warmed his eyes as he brushed his lips over

mine. "I've been looking my whole life for you, Margaret. What took you so damn long?"

My heart reached for him as I curled my fingers in his hair, keeping him close. "I was lost," I said. "But I'm here now."

33

RYAN

The Douglas fir Maggie and I had picked out at the Christmas tree lot twinkled in the corner of the living room, splashing multicolored spots of light across the ceiling and floor. I'd never put a tree up in my house before, not once in the fifteen years I'd lived here. I always hung lights and a wreath on the outside, but there'd never seemed to be any point in decorating the inside when it was just me here by myself.

I sipped my beer as I stared at the tree, kicked back on the couch with my bare feet propped on the coffee table. The lights were pretty, but my mind was miles away, still thinking about the conversation I'd had earlier today. And the one I needed to have tonight.

"Here," Maggie said, plopping next to me on the couch with a glass of eggnog. "I brought you a cookie."

Turning my head, I smiled into her beautiful blue eyes. "Thanks, sweetness."

She tasted her eggnog and scrunched her nose. "I think I put too much whiskey in this."

"No such thing," I said and bit a wing off the angel sugar

cookie she'd handed me. "These are good. Where'd they come from?"

"George's assistant, Connie."

"That was nice of her."

"She likes me," Maggie said as she took another sip of eggnog. "Always befriend the assistants. They're far more useful than any of the male executives."

"What'd you get her for Christmas?" I asked, offering Maggie some of my cookie.

"A spa gift certificate." She leaned in with her lips parted, and I lifted the sugar cookie to her mouth.

A rush of heat coiled through me as her teeth sank into the tender pastry and her lips grazed my finger. Her lids lowered and she let out a soft moan, lashes fluttering at the sweet taste melting in her mouth.

Holy hell.

When her tongue flicked out to lick a crumb from the corner of her mouth, I seriously thought about pushing her back on the couch and making her moan like that again and again.

Grunting, I dragged my eyes away and shoved the rest of the cookie in my mouth so I wouldn't be tempted to kiss Maggie. I couldn't let myself get distracted right now.

"Gotta hand it to Connie, she makes one hell of a sugar cookie," Maggie said, sitting back again.

I nodded and took a drag of my beer, trying to work myself up to say what I needed to say.

"You okay? You've seemed distracted all night."

"Yeah." I leaned forward to put my beer bottle on the coffee table before turning to face her with what I hoped was a reassuring smile. "I just need to talk to you about something."

She followed my lead and set her eggnog down. Her concerned eyes searched my face as she reached for my hand and twined our fingers together. "What is it?"

Squeezing her fingers, I leaned in and pressed a quick kiss to her lips. "Everything's okay. It's not bad."

"All right." Her expression softened, but traces of worry remained.

"I had a telephone appointment with a genetic counselor today."

Surprise widened her eyes. "You did?"

"I'm going to see my doctor next week, and I'm taking the test to find out if I got the ALS gene from my dad."

"What changed your mind?"

"You did."

Being with Maggie had healed something in me. She'd made me stronger. Strong enough to face the future instead of hiding from it. There were so many things I couldn't wait to do with her —travel, find a bigger house for the two of us to share, get married if she'd have me. I wanted to start making plans for our life together. But to do that I needed to know the truth about my odds so we could make practical, realistic decisions.

It was time to step out into the light and let it wash me clean.

"Ryan." The tenderness in her eyes wrapped itself around me, confirming I'd made the right choice. "You don't have to do that for me."

"Yes, I do. It's one thing for me to live in the dark by myself, but I can't make you live that way too."

She shook her head. "I can live with whatever you can."

"Maggie, you don't understand. You've done something I thought was impossible. You've made me feel hopeful for the first time since I found out about this ALS thing. I don't want to live in the dark anymore."

It was like my life had ended the night George broke the news about my dad's ALS. The person I used to be died that night in that leather wingback chair, staring up at that stupid rack of mule deer antlers. That letter from my dad might as well have been a bullet. It killed my misguided belief in my own invincibility and shattered my sense of control over my life. It destroyed the part of me that wasn't afraid of fear, the part that refused to lie down, the part that had been optimistic enough to want things for myself.

But now Maggie had brought me back to life. She'd made me want things again, made me willing to take a risk on the future, made me brave enough to stand up to my fears.

"I'm doing this for me," I told her, and damned if it didn't feel good to be able to say that and mean it. "But it's because of you that I finally can. Now that you're in my life to stay, I need to know what our future's likely to look like."

"Ryan," she whispered and pulled me into her arms. "None of us knows what's waiting for us down the road. Life throws curveballs all the time. Knowing your odds doesn't change the fact that they're still just odds and anything could happen."

"I know," I said, nestling into the crook of her neck. "But I'm done hiding from the truth. I want my eyes wide-open when I walk into the future with you."

"I'm so proud of you." She kissed the side of my head. "How long will it take to get the results?"

"Two to three weeks." Fear prickled over my skin at the thought of knowing the answer, but it was a ripple on the surface of a tiny pond compared to the waterspout of paralyzing dread it used to be.

As if she could sense my apprehension, Maggie hugged me even tighter. "Whatever you find out, I'll be here for you. Nothing's going to stop me from holding on to you and enjoying the hell out of every second we have together."

Gratitude thickened my throat, and I captured her mouth in a slow, tender kiss, luxuriating in the sweet taste of her and the warmth that spread through me like honey. When we parted, I rested my forehead against hers. "Thank you."

"For what?" Her fingers stroked my jaw. "Kissing you? I'm happy to do that as much as you like."

Laughing, I nuzzled her cheek. "For caring. For showing me what I'd been denying myself. For not taking no for an answer."

The universe hadn't been taunting me by throwing Maggie into my path. She wasn't a cruel trick. She was an angel sent to save me. A lifeline to tow me back to the land of the living. She was a gift I planned on enjoying to the fullest, for as long as I was allowed.

34

RYAN

Panting from my jog across the parking lot, I pushed through the doors of the King's Creamery corporate headquarters and skidded to a stop on the polished stone floor of the lobby.

I hadn't set foot inside this building since I was a kid. It'd been so long, I'd forgotten how fucking big the place was. I didn't have any idea where Maggie's office might be. And had they always had that security desk blocking access to the elevators? In my rush to get here, it hadn't occurred to me I might need a damn appointment to see my girlfriend.

"Hi, Ryan!"

I turned at the sound of my name and broke into a relieved smile when I saw Tanner's fiancée, Lucy Dillard, standing at the coffee cart.

I strode toward her. "Lucy! Thank god!"

"Oh!" she squeaked as I bent down and hugged her. "Okay. Hi." She was a tiny thing, not much more than five feet, so my big frame swamped her little one. "It's nice to see you too?"

I released her, and she drew a breath as she took a bewildered step backward. That was when I noticed the plastic-wrapped muffin in her hand. The one I'd just flattened in my enthusiasm. *Shit.* "Sorry about your muffin. I'll buy you a new one."

"That's okay," she said, her lips tilting in a smile. "I'll just pretend it's a blueberry pancake."

"You sure?"

"Don't worry about it." A line formed between her brows as she gave me a searching look. "Is everything all right? You're not here looking for me, are you?"

"No, I'm here to see Maggie."

"Oh, good." She relaxed with a bubble of laughter. "Not that I'm not happy to see you, but you seemed a little frantic. Are you sure everything's okay?"

I nodded, trying to school my agitation. "I was just passing by and wanted to surprise her, but I don't know how to get to her office."

Yeah, I probably should have let Maggie know I was coming. But I didn't want to give her the news over the phone, and she'd have gotten all worried if I didn't offer a reason I wanted to stop by.

"That's no problem," Lucy said. "I can get you up there."

"That'd be great. I'd really appreciate it."

"I just need to wait for my coffee, if that's okay. It should be ready any second."

"No hurry at all," I lied. "Totally fine."

I bottled up my impatience while we waited for the barista to finish making Lucy's latte, which only took a minute but felt more like an hour. Once Lucy finally had her coffee, she took me over to the reception desk and signed me in as her guest. The security guard issued me a visitor's pass, and Lucy buzzed me through the turnstile with her badge. While we rode up the elevator, she gave me directions to Maggie's office on the eighth floor.

"You sure you don't want me to walk you there?" Lucy asked when the elevator stopped at her floor.

"No, I can manage on my own," I said, giving her a quick and careful hug without spilling her coffee or further molesting her muffin. "Thanks for your help."

"Anytime." She waved as she stepped off the elevator. "Take care!"

I tapped my foot as the elevator slowly crept up to my stop. When the doors slid open, I rocketed through them and set off for Maggie's office at a brisk clip, ignoring the curious stares I got as I swerved around slow-moving office workers.

Lucy's directions led me there easily enough, but when I peeked through the glass wall of Maggie's office, there were a couple of people in there with her. Shit. Now what?

I should have thought this through better, dammit.

As I stood in the hallway, trying to decide what to do, Maggie noticed me standing there and started in surprise. Her brow creased with worry as she got to her feet.

"Excuse me for a moment," I heard her say as she moved around the desk.

I met her at the open door to her office with a sheepish expression. "Sorry. I didn't mean to interrupt you."

"Is something wrong?" she asked, keeping her voice low. "Why didn't you tell me you were coming by?"

"It's nothing," I said, regretting my impulsiveness. "We can talk when you get home. Go back to your meeting." I turned to go, but she caught my wrist.

"Ryan?" Her anxious gaze darted over my face. "Stay. We can talk now."

I opened my mouth to tell her it was fine and she didn't need to interrupt her work, but she was already walking back into her office and asking the two men waiting there if they'd mind finishing the conversation another time. They politely scurried off, quick as could be, and Maggie waved me inside.

It was a nice office. Not nice like the fancy fake offices you saw on TV, but nice for the company. It was spacious, with a big picture window and blinds that could be closed for privacy, as opposed to all the dinky closet-sized offices with no windows and no blinds that I'd passed on my way here.

"You didn't need to do that," I said guiltily. "It can wait."

"Ryan." Maggie gave me a quelling look as she shut the office door. Moving on to the miniblinds, she twisted them all closed. Once we'd been shielded from prying eyes, she came over to stand in front of me. "Talk."

"The doctor called with my test results."

"Okay." She gathered a breath and reached for my hands, clutching them tightly in hers. "Tell me."

"I don't have the gene," I said as my heart thumped wildly against my ribs. "I'm in the clear." I'd been working hard to play it cool, but now that I'd shared the news with her it finally felt real. My smile broke free as a flood of happiness burst through my chest.

Maggie let out an inarticulate screech of joy and threw herself into my arms. I caught her, laughing, and spun her around as she showered me with exuberant kisses.

"Is it really true?" she said, clasping my face in her hands. Her cheeks were flushed with color and her eyes shiny with tears. "I'm not dreaming, right?"

"Not dreaming," I said, grinning like a fool. "It's for real."

She let out another exuberant shriek and lunged at me. I spun her around some more while we kissed each other stupid, going at it with a messy, wanton enthusiasm that was most definitely Not Safe For Work.

Which of course was the moment I heard the door open and

someone say, "What in creation is going on in here? This is a place of business."

Tearing my mouth away from Maggie's, I set her back on the floor and turned to find Josie smirking at us from the doorway. "Shit," I breathed, wiping my mouth. "You just about scared the pants off me, Josie."

She slipped inside and shut the door behind her. "That's funny, 'cause it looked to me like you were about to lose your pants another way, Ryan."

"Ha ha," I said as Maggie pressed her face against my shoulder to muffle her snickering.

Josie's smirk tugged wider. "I could hear you two halfway down the hall. What's all the ruckus about?"

"What ruckus?" I asked, playing innocent.

"Yeah, could you describe the ruckus?" Maggie piped up, then broke down laughing again as I grinned at her.

Josie shook her head. "Y'all are hiii-larious. Now tell me what the heck's going on. Did something happen?" She looked from one of us to the other, and her eyes went wide. "Oh my god, are you getting married?" she whisper-screeched, marching over to seize Maggie's left hand.

"No," Maggie wheezed, still laughing. "Nothing like that."

"Oh." Josie's lips pursed as she released Maggie's hand. "Too bad."

"Not yet, at least," I said, giving Maggie a long look.

She stopped laughing straightaway and stared back at me, her eyebrows slowly lifting.

I shrugged, letting my smile go crooked.

"Wait, are you getting married or not?" Josie asked, watching us.

As Maggie and I both turned to face her, I realized I didn't have a ready explanation for our celebrating. Not without admitting I'd been hiding a life-altering secret from my family, which I wasn't looking to do at this precise moment.

Fortunately, Maggie was a lot quicker on her feet than me. "I'm staying in Crowder," she told Josie, as smooth as anything. "Your father's extended my contract here another six months."

That was my smart cookie. The news about her being made COO was still top secret, but the extension to her contract made for a nice cover in the meantime.

"Yeah, I already heard," Josie said. "It's great and all, but it's not exactly ruckus worthy." She folded her arms, surveying us with skepticism. "Are you sure you're not engaged? You'd tell me if you were, right?"

"I've decided to move to Crowder permanently." Maggie slipped her arm around my waist, her lush lips curving in a smile as she reached up to wipe her lipstick off my face. "I'm going to make this my home base and shift my consulting business to more remote work so I don't have to travel as much."

"Hey, that is great news!" Josie said, sounding delighted. "Now you two won't have to do the long-distance thing."

"That's right," I said as I used the pad of my thumb to rub away a smudge of lipstick at the corner of Maggie's mouth. "I get to keep her right here where I want her."

"And hey, that means you're free to get married whenever you want," Josie pointed out helpfully.

Maggie gave her a head shake. "You're as bad as your father."

Josie affected an expression of deepest offense. "How dare you. I just want the people I like to be happy, and you two seem really happy when you're together. That's all."

"If I were you, I wouldn't count us out in that engagement pool," I said and arched my eyebrows at Maggie.

A curt rap sounded on the door of her office. Josie pulled it open and stepped back to admit Nate.

"Is everything okay?" he asked as Josie closed the door behind him. "One of the guys in legal told me he saw Ryan come in here and then he heard crying."

"Everything's fine," I assured him.

"This company is as full of gossips as the rest of the town," Maggie said with a laugh.

"You better believe it." Josie gave Nate a taunting slap on the back. "Guess what? Maggie's going to be moving here permanently."

He went stock-still as his gaze cut to Maggie. "Permanently?"

The way he was looking at her triggered my protective instincts, and I placed my hand on her shoulder. He was bound to lose his shit when he found out she was getting COO over him, and I worried he was going to make Maggie the focus of his resentment. Family gatherings were about to get even more tense and unpleasant.

Maggie squeezed my hip and smiled at Nate, unfazed by his demeanor. "I've decided to run my consulting business out of Crowder after my contract here ends."

"Isn't that great?" Josie said, giving Nate another slap on the back. "She's sticking around long-term."

"Yes," Nate said, not quite relaxing. "That is great news."

"You might want to rethink your bet in Cody's pool," Josie said. "I have a feeling Maggie might be joining the family."

Nate smiled tightly as his gaze darted to me. "Congratulations."

"Josie's just trying to stir up trouble," Maggie said with a tempering smile. "No one's talking about getting engaged."

Yet. But I was sure as shit thinking about it. Making Maggie my wife was one of the things at the top of my to-do list.

For once, thinking about the future didn't bring a chill of foreboding. I was living in a whole new world suddenly. Everything felt different. Or maybe it was just me that was different.

This morning I'd gotten out of bed believing I had a death sentence hanging over me. But now the future was wide-open and bright with possibility. The rest of my life was something to look forward to with excitement instead of dread.

Unable to contain my giddiness, I pulled Maggie against me and cupped her cheek to bring her lips to mine. I didn't fucking care that we were in her office, or that Josie and Nate were standing right there watching, I just needed to kiss her again.

She tasted like honey on my tongue, like heaven on earth, like forever.

"What was that for?" Maggie asked, her luminous blue eyes searching mine.

"Because I'm happy. And because I like kissing you. If you don't mind, I'm going to keep doing it for the rest of our lives."

"See?" Josie elbowed Nate. "Someone's coming around the outside to lead the pack."

"Hmm," Nate said.

"Not to be rude or anything," I said, "but my girlfriend and I need to have a one-on-one, so I'd appreciate it if you two would kindly fuck off."

"And we're gone," Josie chirped, making a beeline for the door with Nate right behind her. "Congrats, you two!"

"Yeah, congrats," he muttered with his characteristic enthusiasm.

The door slammed, leaving me and Maggie alone again.

"Hi," I said, grinning down at her.

"Hi." Happiness bubbled and fizzed between us as she wound her arms around my neck.

I hauled her closer so all her lovely, soft parts pressed against my hard parts. "What's your calendar look like for the foreseeable future? Because I just came into some unexpected free time, and I was hoping you could slot me in for the rest of your life."

"You're in luck," she said, her eyes shining with the same bright, fierce devotion burning inside me. "I happen to have an opening for happily ever after."

EPILOGUE

RYAN

"I hate my birthday," I grumbled as I unfastened my seat belt.

"Yes, you've mentioned that once or twice in the past few hours." Maggie gave me an indulgent smile before getting out of the car.

Scowling, I pushed the passenger door open and met up with her behind her SUV. "I don't like being the focus of so much attention."

"Really?" She reached up to smooth my hair back into place where I'd messed it up by dragging my hand through it. "I never would have guessed that about you."

When she turned to go, I caught her arm and pulled her back.

"I *really* hate surprise parties, Maggie."

She shrugged. "I tried to talk them out of it, but I was outvoted." Throwing me a fortieth birthday had been a group effort instigated by my siblings. Primarily to torture me, I had no doubt. "Just be grateful I warned you about it ahead of time so you could gird your loins."

I tugged her against me and slid my hands up her sides as I

nuzzled her ear. "What if we just went home and you girded my loins for me?"

She turned her head to give me a slow, savoring kiss. Right when I started to think I might get my way, she pulled back and patted my cheek. "Nice try, but no. All your friends and family are waiting inside to scare the shit out of you, so I'm going to need you to look appropriately surprised when they all jump out and scream happy birthday."

I scowled again. "Explain to me how that's not supposed to be traumatic? What kind of lunatic actually enjoys that?"

"Buck up, Freckles. At least there'll be cake and plenty of beer." Maggie seized my hand and tugged me toward the brewpub. "Now wipe that grumpy look off your face. If you can pretend you're happy to be here for the next three hours, I'll give you a reward when we get home."

"What kind of reward?" I asked, intrigued.

She shot a sly look over her shoulder as she towed me through the parking lot. "There's one more birthday present I'm saving for later."

"Is it anal? Please say it's anal."

Her shoulders lifted with a shrug. "You'll have to be a good boy if you want to find out."

Suddenly, tonight was looking up.

"HAPPY BIRTHDAY!"

I tried not to wince as fifty of my closest friends and family screamed at the top of their lungs. Honestly, what kind of sadist had come up with this idea for birthday parties?

Maggie reached around and goosed me from behind, startling a laugh out of me as everyone closed around us to offer hugs and birthday wishes.

We were in a private party room at the Pumpjack, a local craft brewery and beer hall housed in a century-old building that had formerly been a hay and grain warehouse. The beer was good and there was plenty of it. The food was even better, but it was hard to eat much of it with so many people to greet. I had to settle for snatching the occasional appetizer bite off the trays of passing waiters as Maggie and I worked our way through the room mingling with everyone who'd showed up.

Despite my grinchy opposition to celebrating my birthday, I wasn't having the worst time after all. Under duress, I might even admit it was nice to have all the important people in my life together in one place.

"Here," Manny said, exchanging my empty beer glass for a full one.

"This is why you're my favorite brother," I said, clinking my glass against his.

"He's my favorite daddy too," Isabella declared from her perch on my shoulders. She'd been sitting up there for the last fifteen minutes and didn't seem inclined to get down anytime soon, which was fine with me. I could carry her all night if she wanted.

"Yeah, but who's your favorite uncle?" I asked, squeezing her little fingers.

"You are!" she shouted and gave my hair a tug.

"That's what I like to hear."

"But also Uncle Wyatt," she added after some more thought.

I let out a groan as Manny snickered. "I can't even win on my birthday. You know, kid, I don't see Uncle Wyatt carrying you around on his shoulders all night."

"That's because he's too weak," Isabella said, and Manny nearly snorted beer out of his nose. "He's not big and strong like you are."

"Damn right," I said. "You be sure and tell that to Uncle Wyatt the next time you talk to him, okay?"

It occurred to me I hadn't seen much of Wyatt tonight. I'd only talked to him for a minute when I'd first arrived. I glanced around to see where he'd gotten to, but was distracted by Maggie's appearance at my side with a plate of food.

"Here, eat this," she said, holding a boneless chicken wing up to my face.

I opened up and let her put it in my mouth. "You're the best girlfriend ever."

"Congratulations, Ms. Chief Operating Officer," said Adriana, coming over to join us after checking on Jorge, who was in the able charge of Riley. "We're so pleased you're staying at the company."

"Thank you. I'm really glad to hear you say that." Maggie's gaze met mine as Adriana hugged her, and I flashed an *I told you so* grin.

The company had just announced Terry Goodrich's upcoming retirement and Maggie's appointment to replace him as COO. Publicly, she'd been as cool as iced lemonade, but privately she'd been stressed as fuck. Not that she needed to be, since the news had been met with overwhelming enthusiasm.

It helped that George had given Maggie a lot of the credit for the slate of new policies the company had begun implementing at the beginning of the year. Unsurprisingly, the increased minimum wage and executive salary cap had been wildly popular with everyone except a tiny group of higher-ups who'd had their paychecks slashed. Maggie had been hailed as the town hero. I was surprised they hadn't thrown her a ticker-tape parade down Main Street or erected a statue of her in the town square. She was so popular right now, she could probably run for mayor and win in a landslide.

Despite that, she was still fretting about my family's reaction to the news. Maggie had a thick skin when it came to most people's opinions of her, but it upset her to think that she might be the cause of tension between me and my family.

"She's worried we all resent her now," Josie interjected as she joined our group. Carter was working at the hospital tonight, so she was on her own.

"Hi, Aunt Jojo!" Isabella yelled, leaning over my head to wave. "Look how tall I am!"

"Hi, baby girl." Josie blew her air kisses. "You look like a giant up there."

Adriana smacked Manny in the chest. "Haven't you told Maggie you're happy for her?"

"I did!" he protested. "I swear."

"It's true," Maggie said as she fed me another chicken wing. "Manny was first in line to congratulate me."

"He works too many hours as it is," Adriana said, slipping an arm around her husband. "The last thing he wants is a job that'll keep him at work even longer. Trust me."

I'd already tried to tell Maggie as much. As soon as they made the announcement, I'd called Manny myself to clear the air in case he had any hard feelings about my girlfriend being named COO. His sentiments had matched Adriana's. He'd assured me he was happy right where he was, managing plant operations, and had zero desire to leave that behind and spend his days running interference for George. Needless to say, I was relieved as hell.

"What about you?" I nodded at Josie, who I hadn't spoken to since the announcement the other day. "Were you hoping George would offer it to you?"

"Who said he didn't?"

"Did he?" Manny asked.

"No," she admitted. "But if he had, I'd have turned him down flat. I moved back here so I could slow down and have a life.

Plus, I'd rather give myself a root canal than sign up to be Dad's second-in-command. No offense," she added to Maggie with an overbright smile. "Enjoy the job! Good luck!"

Maggie laughed. "Thanks, I'll need it."

"You'll be just fine," I said, smiling at Maggie. "You can handle George."

"I can't think of a nicer barracuda for the job, and I mean that from the bottom of my heart." Josie saluted Maggie with her glass.

"Hear, hear," Manny and Adriana said, following suit.

"There's only one other person I know who coveted that job," Josie said, sipping her beer.

"How is Nate taking it?" I asked. Neither he nor George had shown up yet, and I was a bit concerned about the two of them coming face-to-face. Especially with Maggie here to rub salt in Nate's wounds.

Josie exchanged a troubled look with Manny. "Not great," she said quietly. "I'm a little worried about him, actually."

"Did he say if he was planning to come tonight?" Manny asked.

Josie shook her head. "He hasn't been answering my texts or calls."

"Mommy, I have to potty!" Isabella announced urgently, bouncing on my shoulders.

"Hey, let's get you down, then," I said, thrusting my beer at Maggie in alarm.

"Hold it in, baby," Adriana urged while Manny hurried to take Isabella from me.

As Adriana escorted her daughter to the restroom, I swiped a hand across my forehead. "Whew. That was close."

"Is it even a real birthday party if you don't get peed on?" Josie said with a grin.

"If you'll excuse me, all this talk of pee has me needing to go now." I squeezed Maggie's arm and brushed a kiss to her cheek before setting off for the restroom.

When I came back out, I spotted George, who'd just arrived and was talking to Heather. I headed over to greet him and accepted his handshake and gruff happy birthday wishes.

"Can we talk privately for a minute?" I asked with an apologetic glance at Heather.

George nodded his assent, and I led him to a quiet corner of the room where we wouldn't be overheard.

"What's up?" he asked, shoving his hands deep in his pockets.

I stared down at my shoes and cleared my throat. George and I weren't in the habit of doing much talking, and this wasn't an easy subject for me to open up about, even now. "I wanted to let you know that I had a genetic test done, and I didn't inherit the ALS gene from my dad. I'm not at risk of getting sick like he did."

I'd been meaning to tell him for a while. I figured I owed him an update so he wouldn't have to wonder and worry about me. But there hadn't been many opportunities to get him alone.

George was silent for a moment, his discomfort with emotional subjects palpable in the rigid set of his shoulders. Our avoidant tendencies were one of the few things the two of us had in common. "I always wondered if you'd decided to take the test."

As I stared at the man who was the closest thing to a father I'd ever had, the gulf between us felt insurmountably wide. I wondered if it would have been any different if my mother had lived. Probably not.

"You could have asked me," I said.

"You didn't seem like you wanted to talk about it, so I let it be."

"I guess I didn't," I admitted, rolling my shoulders. "I just now got around to taking the test."

His ice-blue eyes zeroed in on me. "What made you do it finally, after all this time?"

I looked across the room at Maggie, who was still talking to Josie and Manny. "I suppose I've got something to live for now."

"I'm glad, son. I wish you every happiness."

"Thank you," I said around the thickness in my throat. "For everything. You've always been there for me even when you didn't have to be."

"You're family," he said, shrugging as if it was nothing. "That's what we do." And then he walked off to rejoin his wife.

My gaze drifted to Maggie again and found her watching me. She gave me a searching look which I answered with a smile to let her know everything was okay. As I started to head back to her, I spotted Wyatt sitting at a table with Tanner, both of them looking oddly subdued, and detoured to join them.

"Y'all know it's a party, right?" I clapped them both on the shoulder as I slid into the empty chair between them. "What are you two doing sitting over here like a couple of wallflowers at a middle school dance?"

"Says the guy with a pathological aversion to birthday parties," Tanner said dryly.

"Maybe I'm changing my tune on that."

"Get a load of you," Wyatt drawled. "The second you fall in love you go soft as a loaf of Wonder bread."

"Nothing wrong with that," I said, stretching my legs out with a grin.

"No there isn't." Tanner's mouth pulled into a smile as he sipped his beer.

Wyatt leaned back in his chair, eying me as he crossed his arms. "So when are you and Maggie getting engaged?"

"I don't know," I said, eying him right back. "When are you and Andie getting engaged?"

Tanner coughed, and Wyatt shot him a scowl.

"What?" My gaze jumped back and forth between them. "Someone want to fill me in?"

"I'm out of the running in the engagement pool," Wyatt muttered into his beer.

I raised an eyebrow. "What does that mean?"

His shoulders twitched with a sullen shrug. "Andie doesn't want to marry me."

Tanner sent him a reproachful look. "That's not what she said, dumbass."

"What'd she say?" I leaned forward, resting my folded arms on the table as I looked at Wyatt. "Did you propose to her and get turned down?"

"Not exactly." He glanced around, and I followed his gaze to the other side of the room where Andie was deep in conversation with Lucy. "I was all set to do it though. I had the ring and everything."

"You bought a ring?" I whistled, impressed the kid had taken the initiative. Based on his past history, I'd assumed Andie would be the one pushing Wyatt to the altar. "That's serious, all right."

He set his jaw and tipped his chin up. "I've never been more serious about anything in life."

"So what happened?"

When he didn't say anything, Tanner spoke for him. "Josh asked Wyatt to be his best man."

"He and Mia are getting hitched finally?" Josh Lockhart had been Wyatt's best friend since they were kids and also happened to be Andie's brother, so it was no surprise he'd asked Wyatt to be his best man. "Good for them."

Wyatt nodded as his fingers tapped a restless rhythm on the

table. "Andie and I were talking about the fact that I was gonna be both Tanner and Josh's best man, and I said I'd have to have two best men at our wedding so I didn't have to choose between them." He paused for a beat. "Then she told me she didn't want a wedding."

"She said she didn't want a wedding?" I said. "Or she didn't want to get married?"

He let out a dejected sigh. "Both."

"Yet," Tanner interjected. "She doesn't want to get married *yet*."

"'Anytime soon' was what she said."

"Did she say why?" I asked.

"She says she doesn't care about weddings and doesn't see the point of spending all that money on a stupid dress and a big party that's only going to bring a bunch of unnecessary stress into our lives."

I cut a glance at Tanner, who was in the middle of trying to give Lucy her dream wedding on a limited budget because she was raring to get married as soon as possible. His mouth pulled into a wry smile as he shrugged at me.

"Andie says she's happy to keep things just the way they are for now," Wyatt continued. "So now I've got this useless fucking ring she doesn't want."

"For now," Tanner pointed out. "Not forever."

"Yeah, but I'm ready for forever now."

My heart went out to the kid. Wyatt hadn't put himself out there often in his life, and it was hard to see him get shot down when he finally did. "Look, I know it's disappointing, but you shouldn't take it personally."

He stared at me like I was speaking in tongues. "She doesn't want to marry me. How am I supposed to not take that personally?"

Tanner frowned at him. "She still wants to be with you, Wyatt. That matters a hell of a lot more than a wedding."

"Easy for you to say when your girl proposed to you."

"Tanner's right," I said. "You can be happily committed to each other without getting married. Andie loves your scrawny ass enough to invite you to move into her house with her. That says more than wearing a ring on her finger."

"I guess," Wyatt mumbled.

I shifted in my seat. "Maggie doesn't want to get married either."

Both my brothers turned to stare at me with identical shocked expressions.

"Did you propose already?" Wyatt asked.

I shook my head. "But we talked about it, and she said she wanted to hold off." I hadn't planned on telling anyone that, but maybe I was getting better at this opening up to people thing.

Tanner pushed his beer toward me. "Hold off for how long?"

I took a drink and wiped my mouth. "She said at least a year or more, until she's settled into her new position. She doesn't want people thinking she married her way into the job."

"I guess I can understand that," Tanner said. "Not that marrying your ass would get her very far."

"That's what I said." I leaned back in my chair and looked across the room at Maggie. "The thing is, she was married once before when she was younger, and it wasn't a great experience for her. I think she's afraid getting married will jinx things. It's not because she doesn't love me. She's just scared. And that's okay. I can wait for as long as she needs me to, even if it's forever." It wasn't a lot to ask, considering how much she'd been willing to give up for me.

"Wow," Wyatt said. "I'm sorry, man."

"You don't have to be sorry." I locked eyes with him to make sure he was hearing me. "That's what I'm trying to tell you. Don't throw away something amazing because you can't have something else you want. Be grateful for what you've got."

"How are you so good at that?" Wyatt said, shaking his head.

"What?"

"Sounding all wise and shit."

I laughed and reached out to ruffle his hair. "Maybe because I'm older and I've had more time to fuck things up and learn from my mistakes."

Tanner snorted. "As if you've ever made any mistakes."

"Trust me, I've made plenty. I just didn't tell you about them because I like to maintain my flawless mystique."

"So does this mean I shouldn't hold out hope for you and Maggie starting a family soon?" Wyatt asked.

"Fraid that's not on the table," I said. "Sorry."

Maggie had already told me straight out that she didn't want to have kids. It wasn't something she'd ever wanted, but she especially didn't want it at her age or this point in her career. I could tell she'd been worried I'd take it hard, but I was okay with it. I didn't need a wedding or kids or a dog or a white picket fence or anything besides Maggie. As long as I had her, I had all that I needed to be happy. Which was exactly what I told her.

"I'm just going to have to enjoy the hell out of being an uncle." I smiled at the two of them as I helped myself to Tanner's beer again. "No pressure or anything."

Wyatt shook his head. "Andie doesn't want kids either."

"Y'all are young," I said. "She might change her mind. Or she might not, and you need to respect that."

Wyatt nodded and looked at Tanner. "It's all on you now, brother."

"Nope." Tanner shook his head. "After the shit Lucy's had to deal with her whole life, another helpless person to take care of is the last thing she needs right now. Maybe one day, but it's not going to be anytime soon."

"Well, hell," Wyatt said. "Not to sound like Dad or anything, but I was looking forward to getting some more rugrats in this family. And I have a feeling Manny and Adriana might be done. I guess that means it's all down to Josie."

"What's down to me?" Josie said, appearing out of nowhere like a goddamn ninja with Maggie right behind her.

"All the credit for this party," I said before Wyatt could put his foot in it any further. "Great job, by the way. Thanks for putting it together." I stood and pulled Maggie into my arms. "Hey, gorgeous."

"Nate just got here," she said after I kissed her.

Wonderful. Nate, George, and Maggie all in the same room. *This should be fun.*

"How's he seem?" I asked, turning my head to look for him.

"He brought a woman," Josie said, looking dumbfounded. "I think she's his *date*."

"No shit?" Wyatt got to his feet to look. "Nate the Chaste is consorting with an actual female human?"

Sure enough, Nate had his arm around a pretty blonde woman. If that wasn't bizarre enough, instead of wearing one of his omnipresent suits that meant he'd come straight from work, he was dressed in a Henley and jeans. It was like looking at an alternate universe version of Nate who had a life outside the office. *Weird.*

"Wait. I know her," Wyatt said.

Now Tanner was on his feet too. "Ew, really?"

"Not in the biblical sense," Wyatt said, punching Tanner in the arm. "That's Sunshine Summerlin."

"Sorry, is that a person's real name?" Josie asked.

"Yeah. Her mom's Mary Alice Summerlin who owns—"

"The garden center," I finished for him. "Sunny works the counter." I'd bought some mulch and petunias from her just last week. Only she never looked like this whenever I saw her at

Summerlin's Feed & Garden. Usually she wore overalls and muck boots with a bandana over her braided hair. Tonight she was all dressed up in a ruffled green dress with her blonde hair hanging in long, loose waves. I hardly even recognized her.

And she was here with Nate, of all people.

Nate, who hadn't brought a woman to a family function ever in his life. Hell, as far as I knew, he hadn't been on a single date since he'd finished his MBA and thrown himself headfirst into the family business.

"She's pretty," Maggie said.

"She's real nice too." I tugged Maggie closer, letting my fingers steal down over the curve of her backside for a surreptitious squeeze that brought a smile to her lips.

"So what the hell's she doing with *Nate*?" Wyatt asked, scratching his head.

Lucy and Andie came scurrying over, both of them breathless and agape.

"Did y'all see Nate has a girl with him?" Lucy said as she joined Tanner at his side.

His perpetually serious expression softened into a smile as he took her left hand in his to gaze at the engagement ring on her finger. "Yeah, we were just talking about it."

"Isn't that Sunny from the nursery?" Andie said, fitting herself against Wyatt.

He draped his arm around her shoulders. "Yeah. Wild, huh?"

She reached up to touch his jaw, drawing his eyes to her. "You know I adore you, right?"

I watched all his tension melt away as a lovestruck smile lit his face. "Yeah, I do. How'd I ever get so lucky?"

When she tipped her head up to kiss him, I politely averted my eyes. Those two were going to be just fine. You could tell from the way they looked at each other that they were both in it for the long haul. All that other stuff would work itself out.

In my head, I still tended to think of Tanner and Wyatt the way they were when our mom died, just a couple of scared, lonely boys who needed me to look out for them. It caught me off guard sometimes to realize they were strong, accomplished men now, more than capable of making their way in the world.

A lump formed in my throat as I thought about Mom and how she'd feel if she could see her three sons as we were now, all grown up and making lives for ourselves with the women we loved at our sides.

"You okay?" Maggie whispered, leaning in to nuzzle my cheek.

I nodded, squeezing her hip as I stole a quick kiss.

"Did anyone know Nate and Sunny Summerlin were dating?" Lucy asked.

"I didn't even know Nate remembered what girls were," Josie said with a shrug.

I turned my attention back to Nate, who'd led Sunny over to George and Heather. George smiled, putting on the charm as he shook Sunny's hand. But as soon as her attention turned to Heather, his smile faded again.

Nate put a stiff arm around Sunny's shoulders and said something to George. It looked like he and his father might be exchanging harsh words. But then Heather let out an ear-piercing squeal and pulled Nate and Sunny into an awkward three-way hug while George looked on stone-faced.

"What do you suppose that's about?" Wyatt asked.

"No idea," Josie said, frowning.

I leaned over and whispered in Maggie's ear. "Is it pegging?"

She drew back to give me a quizzical look. "What?"

"My present." I leaned in again. "Did you get me a strap-on for my birthday?"

"You'll find out when we get home." Her poker face gave

away nothing. "You wouldn't want me to ruin the surprise, would you?"

I made a frustrated noise and opened my mouth to explain that yes, I would very much like her to ruin the surprise and also nothing could ruin the sight of her wearing a strap-on, but Tanner interrupted before I could say any of that.

"They're coming over here."

I looked up and saw Nate and Sunny making their way toward us. They stopped on the opposite side of the table, and Nate's gaze slid past everyone else to land on me.

"Happy birthday," he said with a taut smile. "Sorry we're late."

"I'm just happy you made it," I told him with sincerity. Nate and I had never been all that tight, but I didn't want hard feelings between us because of George's bullshit games. "I'm always glad to see you."

His smile slipped a little, but before anyone could say anything else, Josie spoke up.

"Aren't you going to introduce us to your friend?"

Nate clamped Sunny's hand in a death grip and cleared his throat. "Everyone, this is Sunshine Summerlin," he said. "My fiancée."

---

*Nate, Sunny, and the rest of the Kings will be back in **Mint to Be**, book four in the King Family series.*

*In the meantime, take a Kilt Trip with the members of the Crowder Highland Games Club, starting with friends-to-lovers roommates Gareth and Casey in **Kilt to Order**.*

ABOUT THE AUTHOR

SUSANNAH NIX is a RITA® Award-winning and *USA Today* bestselling author of rom-coms and contemporary romances who lives in Texas with her husband. On the rare occasions she's not writing, she can be found reading, knitting, lifting weights, drinking wine, or obsessively watching *Ted Lasso* on repeat to stave off existential angst.

To learn more about Susannah Nix, visit:

susannahnix.com

Or follow her on social media:

- facebook.com/SusannahNix
- twitter.com/Susannah_Nix
- instagram.com/susannahnixauthor
- bookbub.com/profile/susannah-nix
- goodreads.com/susannah_nix